Ha

Love and marriage don't necessarily go together. Or at least the relationship doesn't always start out that way!

The contract of matrimony is more business than personal with the couples in these two stories. Yet as our temporary wives and necessary husbands spend time with each other, the honeymoon soon becomes very real as they discover they want their marriage of convenience to become a marriage of love—forever!

So put aside your traditional perceptions of white dresses, overflowing bouquets and quaint steepled churches and enjoy the journey as our heroes and heroines go from wedded *business* to wedded *bliss* on a roller-coaster ride to their happy beginning.

If you enjoy these two classic stories, be sure to check out more books featuring marriages of convenience from the Harlequin Romance line.

New York Times bestselling author **Donna Alward** has the best job in the world: a combination of stay-at-home mother and romance novelist. In 2001 she penned her first novel, and found herself hooked on writing romance. In 2006 she sold her first manuscript, and now writes heartwarming stories from her home in Nova Scotia, Canada. Donna loves to hear from readers; you can contact her through her website at donnaalward.com or through her publisher.

Look for more books by Donna Alward in Harlequin series.

New York Times Bestselling Author

Donna Alward
and
Liz Fielding

A DEAL AT
THE ALTAR

HARLEQUIN® MARRIAGE OF CONVENIENCE

Recycling programs
for this product may
not exist in your area.

ISBN-13: 978-0-373-60113-4

A Deal at the Altar

Copyright © 2015 by Harlequin Books S.A.

The publisher acknowledges the copyright holders
of the individual works as follows:

Hired by the Cowboy
Copyright © 2007 by Donna Alward

SOS: Convenient Husband Required
Copyright © 2010 by Liz Fielding

Printed in U.S.A.

www.Harlequin.com

CONTENTS

HIRED BY THE COWBOY
Donna Alward

For Subcare—keep the faith. It does happen!
And with special thanks to Michelle Styles
and Trish Wylie for their unwavering
support and guidance.

CHAPTER ONE

"Miss? Wake up. Can you hear me?"

The deep voice came first, then Alex's vision gradually started to clear.

"Oh, thank God. Are you all right?"

Alex's eyes followed the sound of the voice as she looked up, dazed. Trying hard to focus, she found herself staring into the most beautiful set of brown eyes she'd ever seen. They were stunning, dark brown with golden flecks throughout, large and thickly lashed.

Men shouldn't have eyes that pretty, she thought irrationally, realizing with a jolt that she was captured in the arms of the eyes' owner.

"Oh, goodness!"

The eyes crinkled at the corners at her exclamation, and she felt his hands on her arm and behind her back, helping her to rise.

"Slowly, now. You fainted."

Really? I hadn't noticed. I was too busy being unconscious. She bit back the sarcastic retort when she saw the genuine concern in his eyes. He even made sure she was standing firmly on her feet before releasing her—and then stayed close, as if he didn't quite trust her to remain steady.

He would have fainted too, in her condition and with

this heat…and the lack of air-conditioning in the convenience store hadn't helped much either.

"I'm so sorry," she blustered, brushing off her pants and avoiding his eyes. It had only taken a moment, but she could even now see him completely in her mind. Not just the eyes, but thick, luscious black hair, just long enough to sink your fingers into and slightly ragged at the edges. Crisply etched lips and a large frame in a grey suit.

Someone who looked like him was so far removed from her world it was laughable, and she avoided his eyes from simple embarrassment. She stared instead at his shoes…shiny, brown leather ones, without a smudge of dirt or a blemish. A businessman's shoes.

"No need to be sorry. Are you sure you're all right?"

She bent to retrieve her bag and purse. The first time she'd bent to pick up her dropped crackers everything had spun and then turned black. This time she gripped the bench for support, just in case. To her dismay she realized that she'd spilled her apple juice, and it was running down a crack in the sidewalk. She folded the top over on the paper bag, picked up the juice bottle and looked around for a recycling receptacle.

"I'm fine," she said, finally looking him in the face. Her heart skipped a beat at the worry she saw there. It had been a long time since anyone had been concerned over her. He was a complete stranger, yet his worry was clear in the wrinkle between his brows. Gratitude washed over her for his gallantry. "I haven't even thanked you for catching me."

"You turned white as a sheet."

She chanced a quick look around. Any passers-by who had seen her little episode were gone, and now people went about their business, not paying any attention to them whatsoever. Another face in the crowd. That was all she was. Yet this man...Mr. *GQ...had seen her distress and come to her assistance.*

"I'm fine. Thanks for your help. I'm just going to sit a moment." She coolly dismissed him; his duty was discharged.

Solicitously he stepped back to let her by, but once she'd sat, surprised her by seating himself as well. "Do you need a doctor?"

Alex laughed. Oh, she did. But a doctor couldn't cure what was wrong with her. "No."

The answer was definitive. By the way his shoulders straightened she knew he'd got the message loud and clear. Briefly she felt guilty for being blunt, so she offered a paltry, "But thanks again, Mr...?"

"Madsen. Connor Madsen." He held out his hand, undeterred, inviting her to introduce herself.

She took his hand in hers. It was warm and solid and a little rough. Not a banker's hands, as she'd thought. Working hands. Solid hands.

"Alex."

"Just Alex?"

His eyes were boring into her, and she stared straight ahead at the office building across the street.

"Yes. Just Alex."

It wouldn't do to encourage him. In the early June heat her T-shirt clung to her, the hems on the sleeves heavy on her arms and the fabric pulling uncomfortably across her breasts. And what had possessed her to wear jeans today, of all things? Apparently such a heatwave this early in summer wasn't that uncommon, but for her the temperature only compounded the light-headedness and nausea.

Necessity had forced her wardrobe choice, plain and simple. Her shorts weren't comfortable any more, and at least in her jeans she could breathe. As silence fell, thick and awkward between them, the world threatened to tilt again. The feeling slowly passed as she took slow, deep breaths. "For the love of Mike…" she mumbled.

He laughed, a full-throated masculine sound that sent strange waves through her stomach. "So, just Alex? Intriguing name. Your parents want a boy or something?"

"Probably." She couldn't believe he was still here. After all, beyond the first fuzzy moment that she'd succumbed to his arms, she hadn't encouraged him at all. His attempt at polite conversation had done nothing but awaken an all-too familiar sadness, the heavy weight of regret every time she thought of her parents. "My full name is Alexis MacKenzie Grayson."

"That's quite a name for a small thing like you." His eyes were warm on her and he twisted, angling himself toward her and bending a knee.

"Alex for Graham Bell and MacKenzie for the prime minister, you know? You planning on using it for the paramedics later? In case I faint again?"

He chuckled and shook his head. "You look much better, thank goodness. But you spilled your juice. Can I get you something else cool to drink?" His eyes wandered to the convenience store behind them.

Her stomach rolled at the thought of a sugary sweet, slushy drink. Every teenager in a ten-block radius had been buying them today. The very idea of them had Alex's tummy performing a slow, sickening lurch. She pressed her lips together.

"Or are you hungry? There's a hot dog cart down the street."

She stood, desperately trying to get some fresh air while exorcising the thought of greasy hot dogs from her mind. But she rose too quickly, her blood pressure dipped, and she saw grey and black shapes behind her eyes once again.

His arms were there to steady her, but she dropped her paper bag to the ground, the contents falling out as they hit the concrete.

His fingers were firm on her wrist as he helped her sit back down. "Put your head between your legs," he demanded quietly, and for some reason she obeyed.

Alex avoided his eyes as she sat up moments later. "Sorry about that," she mumbled, completely mortified at the awkward silence that fell between them like a ton weight. This had to be an all-time low. Blacking out not once, but twice, in front of her own personal Knight in Shining Armor. And wasn't he annoying, this Mr. Perfect Chivalry, sitting there calm as you please?

She expected him to mumble his apologies and hurry away. Instead he knelt and began picking up what she'd dumped on the ground in her haste.

Oh, God. Her humiliation was complete as he paused, his hand on the plastic bottle of pre-natal vitamins. His eyes darted up, caught hers. In them she saw sudden understanding. Now, of course, it all made sense. At least it made sense to him. *She was still trying to assimilate everything.*

"Congratulations."

Her smile was weak. He couldn't know. Couldn't know how her life had been turned completely upside down with a three-minute test only a few short weeks ago.

"Thank you."

He watched her carefully as he sat again on the bench. "You don't sound happy. Unplanned?"

She should end this conversation right here and now. He was, after all, a complete stranger.

"That's none of your business."

He had no cause to know her personal troubles. It was her problem. And she'd solve it. Somehow.

"I beg your pardon. I was only trying to help."

She grabbed the vitamins and shoved them into her purse. "I didn't ask for your help."

The pause was so long her scalp tingled under his scrutiny.

"No, you didn't. But I offer it anyway."

And who else was going to step up and give her a hand? She was alone, nearly destitute, and pregnant. She had no one waiting for her at home. *Home, she thought sardonically. Now, there was an idea. She hadn't had a real home in a long time...too long. Five years, to be exact. Five years was a long time to be at loose ends.*

At present she was sleeping on the floor of a friend of a friend. Her back protested every morning, but it was the best she could do for now. She'd find a way, though, she thought with a small smile. She always did, and had done since being left alone and without a penny to her name at eighteen.

Connor was a friendly face, and also the first person who actually seemed to care. Perhaps that was why she made the conscious choice to answer his question.

"Yes, this baby is unplanned. Very."

"And the father?"

She looked out over the bustling street. "Not in the picture."

He studied her for a few moments before replying, "So you're alone?"

"Utterly and completely." Despair trickled through in her voice and she shored herself up. No sense dwelling on what couldn't be changed. Her voice was again strong and sure as she continued, "But I'll manage. I always do."

Connor leaned forward, resting his elbows on his knees. "Surely your family will help you?"

"I have no family," she replied flatly, discouraging any further discussion of *that topic. She had no one.* Loneliness crept in, cold and heavy. *Not one soul. Anyone she'd truly cared about in the world was gone.* Sometimes she almost forgot, but now, faced with a pregnancy and no prospects, she'd never felt more isolated.

After a long silence, he spoke again. "Are you feeling better? Would you like some tea or something?" He smiled at her, friendly, and her heart gave a little foreign twist at this complete stranger's obvious caring and generosity.

"You needn't feel obligated. I'm fine now."

"Humor me. You're still a bit pale, and it would make *me* feel better."

It was a lifeline to hold on to. It wasn't like her life was a revolving door of social invitations. "Tea might be nice, I guess."

She looped her purse over her shoulder. "So where are we off to, Connor Madsen?"

"There's a little place around the next corner."

She chuckled a little. "You use that line often?"

"I don't believe I've ever used it before, as a matter of fact." He adjusted his long stride to her much shorter one.

"I wouldn't recommend using it again," she remarked dryly.

"You're coming with me, aren't you?" Connor shrugged out of his suit coat and draped it over an arm. "To be truthful, I don't spend much time in the city, picking up women. Or for any other reason, for that matter."

He was wearing a white dress shirt that fit snugly over wide shoulders, then tapered, tucked into slim-waisted trousers. Alex hadn't believed men that good-looking actually existed, and here she was going for tea with one. One who had already seen her faint. She shook her head with amazement.

"So, if you're not from the city, where *are* you from?" *Small talk. Small talk was safe and not too revealing. She could handle niceties.*

"I run a ranch about two hours northwest of here."

"Ah." Well, she certainly wouldn't have to worry about seeing him again after today. She'd be able to look back on it as a bizarre, fantastical dream. A Knight in Shining Chaps, it would seem.

She giggled, then clamped her mouth shut at his raised eyebrow. "Is this the place?" she asked, changing the subject.

"It is." He held the door—more good manners, it seemed—seated her at a table and went to get drinks.

The coffee shop was trendy, and didn't seem to suit either of them. She pictured him more as a local diner type, drinking black coffee from a thick white mug while some middle-aged waitress named Sheila read the specials of the day. Despite his formal appearance today, she got the impression that he wasn't totally comfortable in a suit.

In moments he returned with two steaming mugs…

one of peppermint tea and one with straight black coffee. The café didn't suit her much either. She usually bought coffee from a vending machine, or drank it thick and black from behind the bar—not that she'd been drinking much lately. Still, she was touched and surprised that he'd thought to get her something herbal in deference to her pregnancy.

"Thanks for the peppermint. It was thoughtful of you."

"I'll admit I asked the girl behind the counter for something uncaffeinated. And the peppermint might be, um, soothing."

He handed her something wrapped in waxed paper. "I got you a cookie, just in case your blood sugar was low."

Alex wondered how he knew so much about the biology of pregnancy as she unwrapped the long, dry *biscotti* and tried a nibble. It seemed safe. A sip of the peppermint tea confirmed it. "Thanks. I think we're good."

His shoulders relaxed. "I'm glad. I'd hate to have a repeat of earlier."

She laughed a bit. "You'll have to find another method for your next damsel in distress."

Connor sipped his coffee, sucking in his lips as the hot liquid burned. "You seemed to need it. Plus, my grandmother would flay me alive if I didn't help a lady in need."

"I thought chivalry was dead?"

"Not quite." His smile was thin. "And this way I can procrastinate."

"I beg your pardon?" She put down her mug and stared at him.

"I have a meeting this afternoon. I'd rather spend the

afternoon shovelling— Well, you get the idea. I'm simply not looking forward to it."

"Why?"

He avoided her prying eyes and stared out the window. "It's a long story." He turned back. "What about you? What are your plans for you and the baby?"

She took another long drink of tea to settle the anxiety brewing in her belly. "Our plans are pretty open. I'm working for now. Trying to figure out what to do next. It's temporary."

"You're not from here. I can tell by your accent."

"No. Ottawa."

He smiled. "I thought I sensed a little Ontario," he teased. "But there are so many easterners here now that for all I knew you could have lived here for years."

"Three weeks, two days and twenty-two hours," she replied. "I'm working at the Pig's Whistle pub for now." She needed to find something else, away from the second-hand smoke. But her tips were good, and she'd have a hard time finding a boss as accommodating as Pete had been.

He didn't have to answer for her to know what he was thinking. It was a dead-end job, and hardly one she could support herself *and* a baby on. She knew right away she'd said too much.

His brow furrowed a little, and she somehow felt she'd failed a test. Which was ridiculous. He didn't even know her, and they wouldn't meet again, so his opinion shouldn't matter at all. She was working on coming up with a solution. Just because she hadn't come up with one yet, it didn't mean she wouldn't. Heck, she'd been finding her way out of scrapes for years. This one was going to take a little more ingenuity, that was all.

It was time to end this whole meet-and-greet thing. She pushed away her tea. "Listen, thanks for helping this afternoon, and for the tea. But I should get going."

She stood to leave and he rose, reaching into his pocket.

"Here," he offered, holding out a card. "If you need anything, call me."

"Why would I do that?"

His face flattened and he stepped back at her sharp tone. "I'd like to be of help if I can. I'm at Windover Ranch, just north of Sundre."

She had no idea where Sundre was, and had no plan to discover the wonders of Windover Ranch, so she figured there'd be no harm in responding to his solicitude by being polite. She tucked the small white card into her jeans pocket.

"Thanks for the offer. It was nice meeting you, Connor."

She held out her hand, and he took it firmly.

Her eyes darted up to his and locked.

Another time, another place. She lost herself momentarily in their chocolaty depths. Perhaps in different circumstances she might have wanted to get to know him better. It was just her luck that she'd fainted in front of the first hot guy she'd seen in a good long time.

And it was the height of irony to meet someone like him when she was obviously unavailable. She was pretty sure that being pregnant with another man's child was probably number one on a guy's "not in this lifetime" list.

"Goodbye," she whispered, pulling her hand away from his grasp.

Her steps were hurried as she exited the shop, but she couldn't escape the gentle and understanding look he'd given her as she'd said goodbye.

CHAPTER TWO

"HAVE YOU SEEN today's paper?" Connor stopped his agitated pacing and faced his grandmother.

Johanna Madsen looked coolly over the rims of her glasses, her shrewd eyes assessing. Not a single white hair was out of place, curled back from her temples stylishly and stopping at her collar.

"Yes, dear, of course I have."

Connor started pacing the elegant sitting room again, feeling fenced in among the classic furniture and expensive knickknacks. His head was ready to implode. How could she sit there so implacably, a study in calm? This was big. It was huge. It was probably the end of Windover.

"We almost lost the farm after the last scare. This'll put the final nail in the coffin, Grandmother."

"My, you are upset," Johanna replied with a tiny smile. "You never call me Grandmother unless you're piqued at me."

"Whatever." Connor stopped pacing and faced the elderly woman squarely. "I want to know what you're willing to do to help me save our heritage."

She laughed, a raspy, rusty sound that made Connor's lips twitch even as he waited for her answer.

"Our *heritage*? You've been thinking about this all day, I can tell."

On the contrary. For a few hours that afternoon he'd forgotten about his current troubles, focusing on another's issues. A slight girl with jet-black hair and astonishing blue eyes. With a baby on the way. Where was she now? He hoped she was still all right. When her face had paled and she'd wavered, he'd simply acted, while no one around had batted an eyelash.

And even at her worst she'd still maintained a sense of humor. He admired that. It didn't take a genius to figure out she was in a bad way. For the father to simply disappear like that…Connor frowned. He had no compassion for cowards. A real man stood up and did what needed to be done.

And so, apparently, did Alex. Because the only sense he'd got from her today was that of strength and stubbornness, not hopelessness and self-pity.

And why, considering the current pickle he found himself in, was he thinking about her when he should be focusing on convincing Gram to release his trust fund?

"Connor?"

"Yes, Gram," he answered sharply, turning back to the woman who looked so much like his father. Right now her expressive eyes were troubled, and the mouth that always looked like it held a secret joke was a thin line.

"Look," he relented, "you know as well as I do why I'm here. There's already a ban imposed on beef exports. It's the same scenario as before, only this time it'll be harder to convince the world our beef is safe. Meanwhile I have a herd, a growing herd, that I can't slaughter but that still has to be fed and cared for."

"And you want the cash?"

"My birthday is less than a year away. Surely you can release it a little early?"

Her blue hawk-like eyes bored into his as she folded her hands in her lap. Hands that had once been rough and workworn but now held a small smattering of delightful rings. "No, my grandson, I can't do that. Your parents' will clearly states that those monies be held in trust for you until your thirtieth."

Connor cursed fluently; Johanna merely raised an elegant eyebrow. He glared at her, and she stared him down.

Damn it. She was strong—too strong. She'd lived her life, worked the ranch herself, knew what tough meant. She'd chosen comfort, a condo with a mountain view for her retirement. But she'd lost none of that prairie woman's steel.

"Gram. I can't do it. Not without the resources."

"You are your father's son. You can."

"He never had to deal with this." He said it and knew without a doubt he was right. The last scare had nearly bankrupted them, and they'd kept going by the skin of their teeth. But now...there was nothing in reserve. The only way to keep Windover running was with cold, hard cash. And it was clear now she wasn't going to give him any. His heart sank. He'd fail after all.

Like hell I will. His lips thinned with frustration and determination.

"Legally I can't release the money, Connor. You know I would if I could."

Her eyes softened just a little, and he saw the deepening wrinkles there.

"I don't want to see Windover go under either," she continued. "It means as much to me as it does to you. You know that."

He did know it. She'd spent all her married life there, had delivered his father, seen grandchildren grow and thrive.

"I'm just trying to find a way, and everywhere I turn there seems to be a roadblock." Exasperated, he ran his fingers through his hair.

"There is one other provision, remember?" she remarked blandly.

She couldn't be serious.

"The one other way for me to claim that trust fund is to get married. Gram, I'm not even seeing anyone! What do you want me to do? Post an ad at the general store? Perhaps I could find a mail order bride on the Internet!"

She shrugged, undaunted by his sarcasm. "Mail order brides have worked in the past, as you well know." She rose from her chair and stood, her five-foot-ten frame slim and imperious, but mischief sparkled in her eyes. "I suggest you get busy, my boy."

"Busy? Doing what?"

She laughed again, throwing him a flirtatious wink. "Why, courting, of course!"

COURTING. *HMMPH.* Connor snorted as he accelerated through the exit ramp onto Highway Two. The idea was as preposterous as the old-fashioned word. Courting. As if he had time to romance a woman, entice her to marry him and have the ceremony before the banks called in their loans. Besides, who did he know that was single?

He came from a community where everyone had known each other from diapers. Most of the town women he knew were married, or on their way to the altar. There was no one he could think of that he would consider marrying. And if it got out that he was looking for a stand-in wife he'd be laughed out of town. And what woman would settle for that anyway? What woman should have to?

Nope. He'd simply have to come up with a different solution.

There would be government money—aid for farmers affected. At least he wouldn't have to cull—for now. But the aid cheque wouldn't be enough to cover the growing mountain of expenses while on-the-hoof prices cratered.

He could sell the southwest parcel.

Just the thought of parting with that spectacular piece of land caused physical pain to slice through his gut. His father would never have split up the farm, and Connor knew he couldn't either. Even in the lean years, during the Depression, when farmers had left their land behind to look for work, the Madsens had stayed and made it through. It was what they did.

He missed the sound of his dad's voice, and his strength. Oh, what he wouldn't give for that wisdom now, to sit at the kitchen table working through it. Together—Connor, Jim, and Dad—they would have come up with a plan. Only now it was up to him.

He turned up the radio to drown out the thunder that was exploding around him. It had been stuffy, sweltering today. The rain would cool things down, and hopefully there wouldn't be any hail. He was going to need all the feed crops he could get. When you couldn't sell beef, you still had to feed it.

Connor sighed, wrestling with his tie with one hand while steering the truck with the other. He'd put on the suit to meet with the bankers—and, yes, he admitted it, to impress his grandmother. It hadn't worked, in either case.

Which brought him right back to courting.

Marriage was for a lifetime. Or at least he intended it to be. And as such it wasn't something he glibly approached. It would be a huge mistake to find someone suitable and marry her in haste. He wanted to be in love with his bride. He wanted it to be someone he cherished and honored and wanted to build a family with. And he didn't want to be pushed. He wanted it to be in his own good time, and when the time was right.

There had to be a way. A way he could bring the ranch back from the brink. His parents had been smart when they'd set up the trust the way they had. There was more than enough money in the trust account to keep things afloat while he restructured, figured out where to go next. If he were careful. But how to get his hands on it…?

"I suggest you get busy, my boy."

His grandmother's words rang in his ears as he headed north. What he needed was a practical solution. Something black and white and easy—something that made sense. What he needed to do was stop worrying and take action.

He envied the optimism that Alex had shown today… *"I'll manage. I always do."* Even in her dire straits she seemed capable, even though he knew she was pregnant and alone and without her own place to call home. She had an intrinsic faith that things would work out in the end.

The idea hit him fast and hard, and he almost steered the truck into the ditch as lightning forked in the sky ahead of him.

Alex. He needed a wife. She needed a place to call home for a while, and resources. They could help each other. He hadn't been mistaken in the connection they'd made today as she'd held out her hand and he'd taken her smaller one in his. They could become friends, he was sure. He could do her a favor and she could help him save the family spread.

He remembered how they'd parted. He'd given her a business card.

"Why would I do that?" she'd asked, and he'd known she was too independent to rely on a stranger for help.

But perhaps if she knew he needed her help as much as she needed his…

He changed lanes, steered the truck over the grass median, and gunned it out on the highway in the opposite direction, heading back to town. His heart pounded with anticipation and apprehension.

How did you propose marriage to someone you'd met only hours before?

THE PHONE RANG as Alex came out of the bathroom, clad in flannel pajama bottoms and a T-shirt. She answered it, expecting it to be someone for one of her temporary roommates. Instead it was the pub—asking her to cover a shift. Peggy had up and quit with no notice.

She looked out the window at the rain streaming down the pane. The walk would be hell, even if it was only a few blocks. But it was extra money…and the tips were always better in the evenings.

With a sigh she agreed, and changed into a pair of jeans and her work T-shirt: snug white, with a picture of a whistling pig on the front. She gathered her hair into a careless ponytail, the black ends touching the top of her spine. For a moment she paused, watching as lightning forked across the sky. If she didn't need the money…

But she did. So she grabbed her umbrella from behind the door and made the trek to the pub in the downpour.

It was dim and smoky inside, and for a minute she contemplated the effects of second-hand smoke on herself and her baby. But this was the only job she had, and she couldn't afford to quit while she looked for something else. She had to eat. She had to think of how she was going to feed herself and care for an infant. Tying a black apron around her waist, she grabbed an empty tray and started cleaning up empties and taking orders.

IT WAS ONLY nine when he came in.

The door thumped open the same as it did a hundred times a night, but for some reason she turned towards it. When Connor stepped in, shaking the water from his coat and instantly scanning the room, her pulse jumped. It was too coincidental. He had come looking for her.

When his eyes met hers across the hazy room she knew she was right. He smiled, a lazy, melting smile, and she braced herself. Men who smiled like that were deadly. And the last thing she needed was a distraction as lethal as Connor Madsen.

He made his way through the crush of people to her side. "Hi," he said loudly, over the pulse of country music and boisterous laughter. "Can we talk?"

"Hey, Alex! Table ten needs another round! We don't pay you to stand around all night!"

Alex nodded at Pete, the bartender and owner. Pete came across as all gruff, but she knew he had a heart of gold and a protective streak a mile long. It was one of the reasons she'd stayed as long as she had. As long as Pete was watching, she wouldn't have to worry.

Alex looked up at Connor with consternation twisting her face. "I can't talk right now, I'm working."

"It's important."

"So's my job." She turned away, heading to the bar to pick up the round of beers.

His hand was firm on her arm. "If you care about your baby's future, you'll listen."

That got her attention.

She stared up at him with eyes narrowed, curious despite herself. "Fine, then. But not now. Another time, when I'm not carting beers around."

"What time are you through?"

"One."

"In the morning?"

She laughed then, at his dismayed expression. "Yes, I have four more hours of being on my feet."

He followed her to the bar. Pete asked a question with his eyes, but she gave a slight shake of her head: *No, he wasn't bothering her.*

"I'll come back and walk you home. I really do need to talk to you."

She sighed. "Fine. But for now you're costing me my tips, in case you didn't notice. I need to get back to work. I won't make much money with you standing glowering over me."

She shouldered past him, pasting a smile on her face as she apologized to the patrons at table ten for the delay. When she turned back, he was gone.

At one a.m. they ushered out the last customer and Alex locked the door. Pete eyed her over the bar as he started counting out the float for morning. "Go home," he said, "and I'll finish this. That's the second double you've pulled this week. You look like hell."

"Gee, thanks, Pete." She didn't know whether to be relieved or nervous. If she left now, Connor might be outside waiting. If she didn't, he'd probably get tired of waiting around. On one hand she wanted to see him, see what was so important. On the other she knew it probably wasn't best. She didn't need any extra complications right now—her life was already full of too many.

She grabbed her umbrella from behind the bar and saluted him. "Tomorrow at four?"

"G'night, darlin'," he answered. "I'll lock up behind you."

When she stepped out into the darkness Connor was waiting, standing next to a bench beneath a streetlight. His tie from earlier was gone, and he looked sexily rumpled in the dim light. She swallowed, thankful that she'd spent enough time alone to have some street smarts. And to follow her instincts. Right now her instincts were telling her she wasn't in mortal danger. But the way her body was reacting to seeing him again told her loud and clear that she was in danger of another kind.

She should turn around and go back inside. She reached for the handle, only to hear the lock click into place.

She could handle this. She could.

"My mother used to warn me about strange men and dark streets late at night."

He turned, and in his arms was a bouquet of lemon-colored roses. "Then I guess it's a good thing we have a streetlight and we've already met. I can't do anything about the hour, though."

He held out the roses and she was too stupefied to do anything besides take them, the clear cellophane wrapping crackling in her hands. Where had he found roses after nine p.m.?

And, a better question, why? What was so important he needed to butter her up with flowers first?

Warning bells screamed through her head. Whatever he wanted was something big. She'd only received flowers once before in her life. It had been roses then, too, pink ones. And the gist of the card had been *Thanks for the memories.*

"Thank you," she said clearly. "But I don't quite understand what is so important you think you need to impress me with roses. Even if they are quite stunning," she admitted, sniffing the yellow blossoms.

She laughed a little to herself, remembered reading somewhere that yellow roses signified unrequited love. She needed *that* like she needed a hole in her head.

"You'd better get to the point," she suggested. "The novelty of these will probably wear off pretty fast."

"I have a proposition for you."

She began walking, and he fell into step beside her.

"What sort of proposition?"

"I want you to marry me."

Her feet simply stopped working, and she halted, frozen to the sidewalk. He *what? What sort of cruel joke was this? Poor, pregnant Alex. Surely he didn't think she was that desperate! He could take his pity and—*

Her head lifted until she looked down her nose at him. "I couldn't have just heard you correctly."

He grabbed her forearms, turning her to face him, his hand catching on the umbrella dangling from her wrist. "I want you to marry me." He huffed out a laugh of surprise. "That wasn't how I planned to say it, but there you go."

He wanted her to marry him. Her eyes narrowed suspiciously. What on earth? She realized he was completely in earnest. He was proposing to her in the middle of the street at one-twenty-two in the morning.

"I met you less than twelve hours ago. You're insane. Good night, Connor."

She turned to walk away, and made it a few steps.

"Wait."

The desperation in his voice caught at her and she stopped. "Wait for what? You can't be serious about this."

"I am. And I'll explain it if you'll only listen."

His suit was rather rumpled, and his hair looked as if he'd spent the better part of the evening running his hands through it. Against her better judgment she capitulated. He'd helped her this afternoon, and she felt obligated to him. "You have five minutes."

"Let's keep walking."

Shoulder to shoulder they headed down the street. It was considerably cool after the violence of the earlier shower, and Alex shivered in the damp air. Gallantly he removed his suit coat and draped it over her shoulders. If nothing else, all his actions said he was a gentleman.

"I went to see my grandmother today. I have a trust fund, but I can't access it until I'm thirty."

"So old? I thought most of those were age of consent, or twenty-one or whatever?"

"My parents set it up that way. Anyway, I'm twenty-nine. But I need the cash now."

"I don't see what that has to do with me." She kept walking, her eyes straight ahead. If she looked into his, all dark and earnest, she knew she'd be taken in. She'd been in danger of it earlier today.

She knew what it was to be fooled by a pair of beautiful peepers. And now she knew better than to do it again.

"This'll make sense, if you actually let me explain," he answered. "There is a provision. I can have the money if I'm married."

"I see." She didn't, really, but it was getting slightly less muddled.

"I think Mom and Dad set it up that way so I'd be old enough not to squander it, but that if I got married it would help me and my bride."

"Good logic."

"You're not going to make this easy, are you?"

She felt his eyes on her but refused to meet his gaze. "I don't know you, Connor. But I agreed to listen, so I will."

"Look," he said, with a hand on her arm, stopping her. "If I don't get some cash soon I'm going to lose our ranch. That ranch has been in our family for over a hundred years."

"Why are you in such trouble?" The last thing she needed was a man who didn't know how to manage his own affairs. Lord knew she'd screwed up enough on her own. But at least they'd been *her* mistakes to make and fix. What surprised her most was that she was already intrigued, instead of flatly telling him to take a hike. She couldn't escape the gentle way he'd helped her this afternoon. How he'd bought her peppermint tea and actually seemed to care about what happened to her.

"There's been an outbreak of cattle disease. It took everything I had to get us through the last crisis. But now…another case, up north. It's going to cripple the whole industry. Yet, I've got a herd to sustain. A lot of farms will go under because of this. I refuse to let Wind-over be one of them."

She'd read the news, and knew the situation was as serious as he said. This wasn't mismanagement. This was a situation completely out of his control.

"You need some way to support yourself and the baby. What I'm talking about here is a mutually benefi-cial arrangement. You marry me, I get my trust fund, and Windover survives the crisis. After the baby is born, and you're back on your feet, you can do what you choose, and I'll make sure there's money in your bank account every month."

"A paper marriage, then?"

He sighed and looked down into her eyes. Yep, she'd been right. A woman could lose herself in those choco-late eyes and find herself agreeing to all kinds of mad-ness.

"Yes. It won't be a traditional marriage. Look, it's not like this is what I wanted for myself. Believe me, I've exhausted every possible angle trying to find a way to keep things going. I'm looking at this practically. I get what I need and you get some help. We are both in pre-dicaments here and are in the position of being able to help each other. Nothing more."

"Marriage isn't supposed to be a business arrange-ment."

That took him by surprise, she could tell. It proba-bly did seem strange, coming from a woman who was practically homeless, single and pregnant. He might be shocked to discover how she truly felt about love and marriage. Not that she'd ever breathe a word of that to him. No way.

"I know. It's supposed to be love and commitment

forever. And I do want that someday." His cheekbones softened as he looked away. "A wife who loves me as I love her, and children of our own. A partner to share the ups and downs with. Honor and strength, and knowing you're stronger together than apart."

A devastatingly sexy man with traditional values. Could he possibly know how rare that was?

"I'd be a means to an end," she confirmed, the words coming out strangled. She shook off his hand and started walking again.

"That sounds cold," he said gently. "We would be helping each other. I want that happy ending…and I'm assuming you do too. Someday in the future. We'd be doing what we need to do *now* to survive. I'm hoping we would become friends."

Friends. Now, that sounded dangerous. Her footsteps made squishing noises in the film of water on the concrete. What he was suggesting was outrageous. Preposterous. Humiliating.

"I think you're crazy." She stopped outside a pale yellow house. "Thanks for the walk home."

"Alex, please. Don't say no yet, OK? Just think about it. I know it's not romantic. But leave all that behind and look at the facts, OK? You'd have some security for yourself and the baby, and a comfortable place to live for the rest of your pregnancy. Your needs will be looked after, I promise."

She shrugged out of his coat and handed it back.

"Don't you have a girlfriend you can propose to?"

"No." The answer was flat and final. "Take until Monday to consider it. I'll be back in town then. If you take the time to think about it, you'll see that you'd be helping me immensely. The least I can do is repay the favor."

It was too practical, too perfect, and too convenient. Perfect plans always ended up getting blown to smithereens and leaving her standing alone after the dust had settled. If her life had taught her anything, it had taught her that.

"Don't get your hopes up." Without looking back, she went inside and shut the door.

CHAPTER THREE

ALEX WAS ZIPPING UP her backpack when a car door slammed.

She couldn't see the vehicle, but a quiver along her spine told her it was him before she even peered out through the peephole. Sure enough, he was skirting around the front of a huge pickup truck. She pressed a hand to her heart, trying to calm the thumping there. He was early. She had planned on him meeting up with her at the pub later. But it was barely ten, and he had obviously remembered where she was staying.

She opened the door before he had time to knock. Connor's boots halted abruptly, and they stared at each other. She didn't know what to say, and as the silence stretched out she grew more and more uncomfortable. She chewed on her bottom lip, while he stood so still she could barely make out the slight rise and fall of his chest as he breathed. It was like he was waiting to see what she'd say before he decided what to do. Offering her hand to him seemed silly, a kiss on the cheek presumptuous. She stuffed her hands into her pockets instead.

He was looking very different than he had on Friday. In a very good way. Long, muscled legs filled out faded jeans, and he wore a plain black T-shirt that accentuated the broadness of his torso. Her eyes darted upward; his hair, shaggy at the ends, was as tousled as ever. His forearms, brown from the sun, were lightly sprinkled with hair, tapering to strong wrists. They disappeared into his jeans pockets when he caught her staring at him.

"Good morning." He smiled, but his eyes were focused on her lips, which she was still biting nervously.

"You're very prompt." The words came out more sharply than she'd intended, but the fact of the matter was she was more affected by his appearance than she cared to admit.

His jaw ticked ever so slightly in response to her tone. "I've got to be back by lunchtime."

Wow, wasn't this romantic? She rested her weight back on a hip. *Gee, honey, don't mean to rush you, but could you answer my proposal so I can get back to the cows?* He didn't say it, but that was how it made her feel. Suddenly she doubted her decision. Things were happening too fast. A week ago she'd just been trying to pay her share of the rent. Today she was actually contemplating moving out to a farm in the middle of nowhere in a bogus marriage to a man she didn't even know. This was so surreal.

"I don't mean to rush you." He tried an encouraging smile instead.

"You think by turning on the charm I'm going to follow along meekly?" Her eyes shot fire at him. "You need to do more than flash your pearly whites to convince me."

He stepped back, properly chastised. "I beg your pardon," he responded stiffly.

She couldn't help it. The whole situation was ludicrous. Her lips curved up slightly in response and she let her eyes twinkle at him. "I would think so."

She knew the moment he got that she was teasing.

His eyes warmed, glowing back at her, and a reluctant smile tugged at his lips.

"It doesn't matter. I'm ready." She pulled the backpack out from behind the door and stepped out on to the porch.

"You mean you'll do it?" His jaw dropped.

She kept her smile in place. She was glad he hadn't been sure of her; that made what came next a little easier.

"Well, not exactly."

"I don't understand. Either you're coming or not." He leaned his right arm against the porch pillar, pulling the shirt taut against his ribs.

Alex licked her lips, unsure of how to begin. "I'm not sure marriage is such a good idea. We hardly know each other." She braved a look into his eyes. "For all I know you're some wacko, looking for an easy target."

His gaze was steady on hers. He didn't laugh, didn't smile, but took her comment seriously. "And do you really think that?"

"No," she admitted. "But this is pretty unorthodox, you have to admit."

"A business dealing, no more. I help you, you help me."

He made it seem easy, when it wasn't—not at all. This was her future and her baby's that she was tampering with. Alex, who hadn't relied on anyone in years, was suddenly considering becoming dependent on a relative stranger for her security and well-being. There was nothing simple about that. The one thing that kept her even considering it was the lack of choices she seemed to have lately.

She stepped back, putting a few extra inches of distance between them. "What I mean is, this is all happening so fast."

"I know that. Which is why I had an idea this weekend. How about a trial period first? You come up to Windover, stay a while, before you make your decision. If you decide it won't work, I'll bring you back here."

When the strain evaporated from her face like magic, he knew he'd done the right thing.

"I think that is a very sensible approach," she responded. Her eyes cleared of worry and she treated him to another one of her genuine smiles.

"I certainly don't want to chain you to the place if you're going to be miserable for the next…how many months? I thought this might be a way to test the waters."

"Four months," she replied thinly. Chained to the place? The place wasn't worrying her half as much as being chained to *him*. And it would likely be more than four months. Once the baby came she'd need some time to recover; to figure out what to do next.

Suddenly her eyes narrowed. "How long a trial period?" She knew he was operating on a timeline, and a short one, and she didn't want to feel pressed to make this decision in the first forty-eight hours, or some silly thing.

"I don't know. No longer than a week."

Her breath came out in a rush, but her words came out cautiously. "OK. A week I can do."

"In that case, let's get going."

She lifted her backpack as he spoke, surprised when his hands took the weight from her. Her shoulder tingled where his fingers touched.

She'd forgotten his penchant for chivalry, which was surprising, since he was constantly polite. It was hard to get used to that in a man. Simply not what she'd been used to.

"Thank you."

"Where's the rest?"

She looked at her toes. "That *is* the rest."

"This is all you've got?" He halted by the door of the truck, his fingers on the handle. "No suitcase?"

"This is it," she said firmly. She would not, could not, get into a discussion of why her life was packed into a solitary bag. Someday she'd settle, find something permanent. Then she'd make the home for herself that she longed for.

Wordlessly he opened the door, helped her in, and put the pack behind her seat. Nerves bubbled up in her stomach. What on earth was she doing? This was crazy. Insane. She knew next to nothing about him.

He got up into the cab beside her and started the engine as she fastened her seatbelt. At least she'd had the foresight to do a bit of checking on him of her own. Saturday she'd hit the library and the computers there, looking up information on the man and his ranch.

Surprisingly, there'd been several hits to her query, and she had read with fascination articles regarding Connor and, more interestingly, his family. His father had been prominent in the beef industry, and under his hand the farm had flourished. The Madsen ranch had been around for over a hundred years. Now she understood why Connor was determined to make it through this crisis.

One hit had turned up a recent "spotlight" on Connor—he had done an interview on innovative breeding. His picture had come up beside the print, and she'd stared at it. He sure didn't look like some creep, despite the oddness of his proposal. He was twenty-nine, sexy as the day was long, and apparently smart and well respected. Her eyes darted to the imposing figure beside her, concentrating on the road.

She wished she'd found something more personal—a vital statistics sort of thing. Where was his family now? He'd only mentioned his grandmother. What were his interests, his quirks?

The only way she could find out that information was to talk to the man himself. She wasn't at all sure she could marry him, even if it were only a legality. She'd be stuck with him for the next several months. There was her baby to consider. She had to do what was right by her child.

Her hand drifted to her tummy as a current country hit came on the radio and Connor exited on to the highway. It was too early for her to feel the baby's movement, but already her shape was changing and her waist was thickening. It was her child in there. She hadn't planned on having children for years yet, and certainly not alone. But she was attached to this life growing inside her, knew that no matter what, she wanted to be a good mother. How could she do that if she couldn't even afford a place for them to live?

Alex stared out the window at the city passing by in a blur. A trial run was her best option right now. At least it left her a way to get out.

THE LANE WAS long and straight, unpaved, leading to an ordinary two-story house in white siding with blue shutters.

Alex stared at it, not sure what to think. She looked out both windows…there weren't even any neighbors.

No, wait. There. On that distant knoll to the southeast there was a speck that might have been a house. The land surrounding them was green and brown, spattered sparsely with trees. Basically empty. Isolated.

Beyond the house were outbuildings of various sizes. Alex, city girl, had no idea what they were used for beyond the basic "looking after cattle" umbrella. Another pickup sat in front of a white barn. To the side were tractors. Not the small, hayride sort of tractor she had been used to growing up in southern Ontario. But gargantuan monsters painted green and yellow. The kind she'd need a stepladder to get into.

Connor pulled up in front of the house and shut off the engine. "Here we are," he said into the breach of silence.

"It's huge," she answered, opening the door and hopping down. "The sky…it seems endless."

"Until you look over there." He grinned at her, came to stand beside her and pointed west. Her eyes followed his finger and she gasped.

She had focused so hard on the house that she'd completely missed the view. It spread before her now, long and gray, a jagged expanse of Rocky Mountains that took her breath away. They were a long way away, yet close enough that she saw the varied shades, dark in the dips and bowls, lighter at the peaks, tipped with snow even in early June.

"That's stunning." Stunning didn't cover it. Something in the mountains simply called to her, touched her deeply. Made her feel alive and strong.

"They keep me from feeling lonely," Connor murmured, and she realized how close he was to her ear. There was something in his tone that touched her. All this space…and he lived here alone. Something about him in that moment made her realize that he had a gap in his life, an emptiness he wanted to fill.

She wondered what had put it there, but was in no position to ask. And she wasn't entirely sure she wanted to know the answer either. She sure didn't want him to delve into *her* past, so she said nothing.

"Why don't you show me the inside?" She changed the subject, pulling her eyes from the scenery and adopting a more practical air.

He grabbed her bag from the truck and led the way inside. She took off her sneakers, placing them beside his boots on the mat in the entry, and followed him past a living room and a stairway to a large, homey kitchen.

"You hungry? We should have some lunch." He put her bag on an old wooden rocker and turned to face her. His jaw seemed taut with tension, and she realized that he was finding this as odd and uncomfortable as she was. Now, here, in his house, it became ever more clear that they were practically strangers.

"I could use a sandwich or something."

He took meat and cheese out of the fridge, condiments, and grabbed a loaf of bread from a wooden breadbox on the countertop. "I don't know what you like," he offered apologetically. "So we can fix our own, I guess." Silence fell, and to break it Connor began stacking meat and slices of cheese on his bread. He reached for a bottle of mustard, looked up, and saw an odd expression on Alex's face.

"Are you OK?" His hand halted, poised above his sandwich.

"It's the mustard. I'll be fine." She swallowed visibly.

He stared at her, his mouth gaping open with some sort of fresh horror, and a drop of bright yellow landed on his corned beef. He looked down, his expression horrified at the offending blot, wondering if it was enough to make her ill. God, he hoped not!

Connor heard her snort and looked up, confused. Her hand was over her mouth and she was trying futilely not to laugh. Before he knew it, he was laughing too.

"Oh, the look on your face," she gasped. "Pregnancy does make cowards out of men!"

Putting the mustard bottle down on the cupboard, he chuckled while she caught her breath. "Do you feel as awkward as I do?" he asked.

"Incredibly."

The laugh had done much to dissolve the polite tension that had risen between them. "I don't want you to feel out of place here. I want you to feel at home."

"I want that too."

"You'll find I'm easy to please, Alex." He smiled easily as he said it, but her cheeks colored. When he realized she'd taken what he'd said a little too literally, his smile faltered as they stared into each other's eyes. He became aware of the way her breasts rose and fell beneath her T-shirt. She was still breathless from laughing.

"I don't need much," she murmured. "A place to sleep and some good food. I want to try to help out in any way I can. I'm not used to being idle."

"Farm work isn't for you."

Her mouth thinned. "I'm not going to break, Connor. Women have been having babies for thousands of years."

"I realize that." His eyes didn't relent. "But you're not doing heavy farm work. There's a garden behind the house if you like the outdoors. I don't want you to be bored, Alex, but I don't expect you to be some indentured servant either. Honestly, if I didn't have to cook at the end of the day it would be a gift from heaven."

Choices. Time that was her own, to do as she wished—making dinner or tending the tiny plants of the garden in the fresh air and sunshine. The freedom to clean, do laundry, on her own time.

Perhaps that sounded mundane and tedious, but to Alex it seemed wonderful. Growing up, she'd always envied her school chums whose moms had baked cookies for class parties, or who had invited her over for home-cooked meals. Not to be unfair, her parents had been great, but their lifestyle hadn't exactly been traditional. It would be almost perfect. If only…

If only it weren't such a sham.

Still, if he were willing to go through with it, the least she could do was carry her own weight.

"I'll be honest, I haven't had much experience in the whole domestic arena…" she waved a hand "…but I'm a fast learner." She went to the counter and began making her own sandwich of turkey and cheese. She took one look at the tomatoes and passed on to the nice, friendly lettuce, eschewed mayo and went for the pepper.

"All right, then. I'm going to take this with me." He gestured with the thick sandwich in his hand. "I wish I could stay and help you get settled. But I've got a couple of calves that need tending, and if the hands didn't have any luck this morning I'm going to have to call the vet. Will you be OK?"

He looked so apologetic that she couldn't be mad. After all, the whole reason she was here was because this place meant everything to him. She couldn't expect him to forget that and play host for the afternoon.

"I'll be fine. I can explore on my own. Go." She

smiled and shooed him with a hand. "If you stayed in you'd just worry about it, wouldn't you?"

He looked relieved that she'd let him off the hook. "Yes, I would. I'm glad you understand. I want you to know..." His feet shifted a little as he admitted, "I'm happy you decided to try this out. I'm going to make sure you don't regret it, Alex."

She got the sinking feeling that she *was* going to regret it, deeply. Because when he was kind, when he was considerate, she knew she couldn't stay immune.

She followed him back to the door, watched as he shoved his feet in his boots, pulling up the heel with one hand.

"Your room is at the top of the stairs. Turn right and it's the first door. There's a white spread on the bed."

"I'm a big girl. I'll manage."

"I'll be back in around six."

At this point she started to laugh. "Connor. Seriously. Go do what you have to do."

He offered her a grateful parting smile, but then he was gone and the house was empty and quiet without him.

Alex went back to the kitchen and finished her sandwich, washing it down with a glass of milk. The morning sickness was starting to pass now and, still hungry, she snooped through the pantry and found a bag of oatmeal cookies. She grabbed two, then put her backpack over her shoulder and went to explore.

At the top of the stairs she turned right, but she was immediately faced with two doors. Did he mean the first one at the end or the first one right in front of her? She chose the latter and, turning the knob, stepped into what had to be Connor's room.

The spread wasn't white, it was brown with geometric shapes dashed across it in tan and sienna. He'd made it that morning, but there was a spot on the edge, just about in the middle, that looked like perhaps he'd sat there while getting dressed. The air held a slight odor of leather and men's toiletries, mingled with the fresh scent of fabric softener. She put down her bag and went over to the chest of drawers. On the top was a bowl, containing some errant screws and pins and what looked like a screwdriver bit, probably removed from his pants before they went in the laundry. Beside the dish was a framed picture. In it she saw Connor, much younger, perhaps twenty or so, standing beside a boy with the same dark hair and mischievous eyes. They each had a hand on a shorter woman standing in front of them. The woman was slight, with black hair, and she was laughing. In her hands she held a gold trophy. Off to the right stood their father, tall and strong, his hand on the halter of a large black cow.

So he did have a family. A brother and two parents. And from the smiles they appeared happy. But where were they now?

She'd trespassed long enough. If Connor had wanted her to know about his family he would have told her. And he might tell her yet—once they knew each other better. But she wouldn't pry. It was his business, his secret to reveal or to keep. She respected that—after all, she had skeletons of her own. She backed away from the dresser and picked up her bag on the way out the door.

The next room was undoubtedly the one he'd meant. It was large, with a double dresser and mirror and a sturdy pine bed. The coverlet was white and lacy, lady's bedding, and Alex wondered if it was a spare room or if it had belonged to his parents. She put her bag on a chair beside the nightstand. After the floors she'd slept on, the dingy rooms with nothing pretty to redeem them, this was too much. Too pretty, too feminine. Too perfect. She didn't want to mar that pristine white duvet with whatever might be on the bottom of her bag. She took her clothes out and put them in the dresser. All she had only filled two drawers. A plastic bag held toiletries— soap, shampoo, toothbrush, deodorant. Those she took to the bathroom at the end of the hall and placed them on a wire rack that had one empty shelf. Other than that her bag only contained a journal and a pen and a picture. The picture she left in the bag, stowing the pack in the otherwise empty closet. The journal she tucked into the nightstand drawer, out of sight.

Going back downstairs, she decided then and there that if she were going to pull her weight at all she'd better get cracking. After all, it wasn't fair if for the next six months her only contribution to this arrangement was signing on the dotted line and leaving Connor to do all the work. He was willing to support her, not only now but after the baby was born, if only she'd marry him first. It definitely made her feel guilty, knowing she got the easy part of the deal. The least she could do was make sure he had a good hot meal at the end of the day and a clean house to come home to. If he wouldn't let her do any of the manual labor, she could at least look after things in the house.

Except she'd never done anything like it in her life. And now the fate of herself and her baby depended on her success.

CHAPTER FOUR

THE TOP OF the fridge held nothing but extra bread and some frozen vegetables. *He's got to have meat around here somewhere,* she thought, and searched high and low until she came across a huge Deepfreeze in the basement.

She took out a package that said *"cross rib steak"* and remembered going to her grandmother's house when she had been a small child. Her grandmother had made this dish... Swiss steak...and it had been fork-tender, surrounded by onions and gravy, all layered on mashed potatoes. Surely there was a recipe book somewhere that would tell her how to make it?

She searched the kitchen for such a book, and came up with a small binder. The cover had a crudely drawn picture of an apple on it and the words *Mom's Recipes* in black marker. Inside were pages of handwritten recipes, in no particular order. Maple Chicken was next to Dad's Chocolate Cake. Bread and Butter Pickles next to Come and Get 'Em Cookies. She sighed as the microwave dinged out a message that the meat was thawed. This *was* going to take forever.

She finally found a recipe that said "Smothered Meat" and thought it sounded about right. Retrieving a roasting pan from a low cupboard, she put in the meat and then added water, onions and bay leaves that she found above the stove in a motley assortment of spices. She turned on the oven and slid the roaster in…step one complete.

She could do this. She could. Just because she'd never learned to cook, it didn't mean she couldn't, she told herself. All you had to do was follow instructions. It couldn't be that hard.

Potatoes didn't take that long, so maybe she'd really live on the edge and attempt something for dessert. Jazzed up with motivation, she grabbed the red binder again and flipped through the pages, looking for one that sounded good. These were his mom's recipes, probably the ones she made most often. She stopped at a page that looked like it had been handled often. Caramel Pudding. She read the recipe. Easy enough. Flour, egg, butter, milk, leavening, salt…brown sugar, boiling water. How hard could it be?

An hour later she slid the pan into the oven beside the meat and sighed. The instructions had sounded deceptively simple. However, they didn't seem to translate into her hands. She looked at the countertops. They were strewn with flour and sticky batter and dirty dishes. The first order of business had to be cleaning up this disaster zone before she went any further.

She was halfway through the dishes when she remembered the meat needed tending, the sauce thickening.

The mess doubled. Again.

The next time she looked at the clock it said four-fifty-five. She was exhausted, and with a whole new appreciation of women who willingly did this every blessed day of their lives. She was certain now that she'd had the easy job—waitressing, instead of being in the kitchen!

It took her twenty minutes and two Bandaids to peel the potatoes, and she grumbled that she was really going to have to caution Connor on having his knives too sharp.

She found a glass casserole and emptied a bag of frozen corn into it, put it in the microwave and let her rip just as Connor was coming in the door.

"Hey," he called from the front door. "How was your afternoon?"

I'd rather have been chased by the hounds of hell, she thought grumpily, but pasted on a smile and said, "Fine."

He came into the kitchen and sniffed. "Do I smell caramel pudding?"

She smiled for real, the curve of her lips fading as she saw how weary and defeated he looked. "I found your mom's old recipes."

He came over to the stove, lifted the lid on the potatoes bubbling away. "It's good to come in and not have to worry about supper. Thank you, Alex."

Don't thank me yet, she thought, none too sure of success. The pudding seemed oddly flat, and she hadn't checked the steak yet. At least the potatoes seemed to be holding their own.

"Your afternoon didn't go well?" she surmised quietly.

When he sank into a chair and ran his hand through his hair, she knew she'd guessed right.

"We lost one. The other's touch and go."

"I'm sorry," she offered, her stomach suddenly churning with nervousness. He was expecting a great home-cooked meal after a rotten afternoon. He couldn't know she'd never made anything that wasn't out of a can or ready with one touch of a microwave button. She took the roaster out of the oven, and as the corn finished she drained the potatoes.

"Don't be sorry. It happens. But you know, no matter how much you think you get used to it, you never do."

She filled his plate with potatoes and a generous scoop of corn, then a large slice of steak from the roaster. The gravy was thinner than she'd expected, and seemed suspiciously lumpy, but she hoped for the best and ladled it over the top of his potatoes.

She fixed her own plate and sat down across from him. "I hope the other one makes it," she offered as he picked up his fork. Only to pause with it still stuck between his lips.

"Is something wrong?"

Connor looked up at her hopeful eyes and made himself swallow. The corn was still cold in the middle. "No, no," he reassured her, cutting into the steak. She looked so vulnerable, so eager to please, that he didn't have the heart to tell her.

The meat was cooked and tender, but the gravy... something was off. It was too pale and runny. He bravely took a scoop of potatoes and gravy and found a ball of flour rolling on his tongue. He smiled up at her, but he could tell she knew by the crestfallen way her lips turned down and her cheeks fell.

"It's horrible. Disgusting. You can't eat this."

"Sure I can. It's definitely edible."

Alex tried a bite with the gravy and made a face. "*Eeeew.* What did I do wrong?" She took a mouthful of corn and hurriedly spit it into her napkin. "And the corn is still frozen! Oh, I can't do anything right!" she cried. "You put in a horrible afternoon and then come in to this!"

"You *can* do things right," Connor said gently. He got up from his chair and took her plate. He put it in the microwave and heated it up more. "It's not your fault that I had a tough day. And you worked hard to try to make me a nice dinner. That was a sweet thing to do, Alex."

"Don't patronize me. I don't want to be sweet. I want to be helpful!" she burst out in frustration. "I've been on my own for five years and I've been outdone by a bag of frozen vegetables!"

He gave her back her plate, then heated his own. "The corn just needed more time."

"But I followed the directions on the bag!" She stared morosely at the offending kernels, now piping hot. Cooking was the only thing he'd asked of her, and the meal was a disaster. It wasn't a good way to start a trial period for marriage.

Connor couldn't help but laugh. "It takes a bit longer when you cook a whole bag at a time." The casserole was filled with enough of the vegetable for at least three more meals.

"And the gravy is revolting. But I followed the directions to the letter!"

"Where's the gravy browning?"

"Browning?"

He had to turn his face away to hide a smile. That was why it was pale. She hadn't used any browning. If he knew Mom's recipe, it probably said to thicken the juices with flour and water. And the lumps… If she didn't know how to make gravy, she wouldn't know how to make it without clumps of flour in it either.

"Connor?"

"I'll show you how to make gravy. It takes practice."

Alex pushed her plate away. Other than the corn, the tasteless, flour-pitted gravy had ruined everything. How on earth could she carry her own weight when he had to teach her how to cook? Never had she felt so defeated.

She scooped the odd-looking pudding into two bowls. "Do you put ice cream on it?"

"I'm out, but milk's just as good. Sit down. I'll get it."

He poured a little milk on the pudding and served it. He took a bite, sucked in his cheeks, and pushed the bowl away.

"I'm sorry, Alex."

Tears sprang into her eyes. She had never felt such a complete failure. Well, if this wasn't a whole new discovery. Alex, who always seemed to manage, to find a way, was completely hopeless in the kitchen. The one thing she could contribute in this whole arrangement and she was a culinary idiot.

"What did you use to make it rise?"

"Arsenic." At his horrified expression, she shook her head. "Baking powder, like the recipe said," she insisted.

He went to the cupboard and took out a small orange box. "You mean this?"

"Yes."

He started laughing. "This is baking soda, not powder."

"There's a difference?"

"Oh, yes. If you taste your dessert it'll be sharp, and a bit bitter."

She did, made a face, and struggled to swallow the solitary bite.

"I'm a complete failure. And of no use to you, obviously. I'm sorry, Connor, for wasting your time and mine." She pushed out her chair, haughty as a queen, and made for the stairs.

"Hey," he interrupted, lunging after her and grabbing her arm. "One disastrous meal does not a deal-breaker make."

"Why not? You sure can't eat my cooking for the next six months. You'll starve, if I don't kill you with food poisoning first."

"Have you ever cooked before?"

"No."

"Then why on earth did you think you'd suddenly be perfect at it?"

"I didn't think it would be so hard," she murmured, leaning against the banister of the stairs. Tears threatened again. "Oh, these stupid hormones!" she said, frustration finally bubbling over. "I hate crying! I *never* cry!"

Thankfully he ignored the tears and remained pragmatic about the whole issue. "I know how to cook because my mom taught both my brother and me. I'm no great chef by any means, but I can show you the basics."

Alex took several breaths in and out, calming herself. She was the only one throwing a fit here. Connor was being particularly good-humored about the whole thing. Because of it, she decided to give him a little insight into her past.

"My mom never cooked much. We were sort of the take-out and convenience food house on the block," Alex admitted, not sure why he was being nice about it. "But I can do stuff out of cans and frozen entrees really well."

Connor laughed, and Alex smiled up at him. His eyes were warm, framed by those shaggy dark locks. He wasn't mad. Not even a little. Even though she'd wasted that food and made a horrible mess of everything. Connor Madsen had a generous spirit, she realized, despite the unorthodox relationship they seemed to have started. He was certainly nicer than she deserved.

"You need this money badly, don't you?" she asked him.

He nodded slowly, his eyes swallowing her up in their dark, honest depths. Their bodies stood close together, and for a moment she wondered how it would feel to put her arms around his waist and simply rest against his strength.

"Bad enough to put up with terrible cooking and hormonal mood swings?"

A ghost of a smile tipped the corners of his lips. "Yes."

She wondered how long he'd lived here alone, and why. Why hadn't he married yet? He certainly wasn't lacking in the looks department. In fact, she was constantly having to remind herself to be practical—which was hard, considering she was already fighting attraction. She mentally added things up: his stellar manners, his consideration, his understanding and lack of a quick temper. He was the kind of man she thought she could trust, and more than anything that counted for a lot. Even knowing him a short few days, she sensed his integrity and strength. He would keep to any bargain they made.

"I'll probably regret this."

His hand lifted to cup her chin gently. "I sincerely hope not." Her eyes strayed to his lips, serious now, but shaped so that she couldn't help but think of kissing him.

"It's not forever, Alex. But you need to decide if you can trust me. You need to take that leap of faith."

"After a few days? No one in their right mind would make such a decision," she breathed, feeling the tug between them again.

"My great-great-grandparents met on a Wednesday and got married the next day. But you need to decide for yourself."

He started to pull away. She stopped him with her fingers gripping into his arm. "Wait."

He waited patiently, steadily.

"Trusting comes hard. Surely you can understand that? I can't afford to screw this up, Connor. I need to know what I'm doing is right for my child."

He put his hands on her shoulders, dipping his head to place a soft kiss on her forehead. "You wouldn't have told me that if you didn't already trust me," he whispered against her skin. "And you know it. It's OK to be frightened."

He was right, and it scared the daylights out of her.

"Marry me, Alex." The calm force of his voice almost made it a command.

She closed her eyes and jumped.

"All right. For better or worse, the trial period's over. I'll marry you, Connor Madsen."

CHAPTER FIVE

THE RADIO WAS playing softly in the kitchen when he entered, and the table was set for two, but Alex was nowhere to be found. On the counter was a crockpot. He lifted the lid and the appetizing smell of chili wafted out. His stomach rumbled in appreciation. She had told the truth when she'd said she was a fast learner. It didn't look like they'd have a repeat of last night.

"Alex?"

"Out here."

He followed the voice to the deck that faced west. She was standing at the railing, facing the dim outline of the mountains, squinting against the sun.

He stared at Alex. The deepening sunlight framed her figure, outlining her curves, and he was shocked to feel desire streaking through him like a current. Where in the world had that come from? Of course she was attractive—he wasn't blind—but he hadn't factored that into the plan. He frowned slightly. It had been a long time since a woman had had that effect on him. He'd been focused on Windover, and working things out, and hadn't taken the time to pursue a relationship. And he honestly hadn't considered how much having an extra person around would change things. He'd looked forward to being alone with Alex all day, perhaps too much. He had thought of how her eyes snapped and flashed as she angered, how hard she was on herself for the smallest error. How independent she was. But they'd made a bargain. And he had to keep personal distance.

"Are you all right?" Her voice was sweet and a bit shaky.

"I'm fine." He shoved his hands in his pockets, keeping back. "Dinner smells great."

She turned back to the view. "I found the recipe on the kidney bean can. I told you I could make things out of a can."

He smiled. "Mmm, progress."

"You haven't tasted it yet," she remarked wryly, and he took a place beside her at the rail, making sure their elbows didn't touch. He could still smell her, though, light, citrusy, and his nerves clawed at his stomach.

"Can we eat later? Let's take a walk. You haven't even seen anything of the ranch yet, and you're going to be here for at least the next several months."

They hadn't really had a chance to talk much about themselves, only about the deal they were making. They could be friends, and maybe, just maybe, he'd forget about how pretty she was in the late-day sun.

"Is it OK to leave the chili on?" Her eyes looked up at him, worried.

"That's why it's called a slow cooker," he teased. "Your meal will still be here when we get back."

They walked out past the lane and to the edge of a field, side by side but careful not to touch. A grove of trees and a fence separated the field from another meadow. Cows bawled in the warm sun as they grazed, their jet-black hides shining in the early-evening light, and Connor took a deep, restorative breath.

"It's part of you." Her voice interrupted their silence.

He exhaled slowly, surprised she understood so intrinsically. "Yes. It always has been."

"I can tell. It's in the way you look at the land. I've never had anything like that. I envy you."

Connor recognized the low note of sadness in her words and responded. "What was your childhood like, Alex?"

She stared straight ahead while he gazed at her profile. She was beautiful in such a simple, natural way, and she tried to be strong. But there was something in the wistful turn of her lips that made him sense the pain beneath the surface, and he longed to make it better. It had always been his thing, trying to fix whatever went wrong. But he knew better than most that there were some things you just couldn't fix—and he'd thought he'd left that protective streak behind.

The smell of fresh-cut hay filled the air around them, familiar and comforting, as she began.

"My parents were historians. We had a house in Ottawa. But we were gone so much…it was more like a base of operations. We traveled a lot."

She glanced up at him, her smile contrite as magpies chattered in the poplars.

"You said you were alone. Where are they now?"

She stopped, bit down on her lip, and squared her shoulders. "Dead. When I was eighteen they were going on a work trip to Churchill. They were taking a bush plane in…it's so remote…but the plane never made it."

So she was utterly alone. Alone like him.

"I'm so sorry, Alex."

She started walking again. "My parents were smart people, but they thought they were indestructible. They had little insurance. By the time I was done paying estate taxes, my lawyer, and their outstanding bills, there was hardly anything left. The bank took the house and I got an apartment, worked as a waitress."

She let out a long breath; that was all she was comfortable revealing at this point. They really didn't know each other well enough for her to reveal the nitty-gritty details. The loneliness. The longing for a normal childhood.

"That's my life in a nutshell. What about you, Connor? Did you ever want to do anything besides farm?"

He had. As a teenager he'd wanted nothing more than to be a farm vet, and he'd planned out his future like a roadmap. He'd work from Windover, and he and Jim would run the ranch together after Dad retired. And his family had supported that dream. He had taken his science degree and been about to enter vet school when he'd given it up to take sole control of the ranch operations.

"I was going to be a vet."

Their feet made whispering sounds through the tall grass. "So what happened?"

"I was home from university that summer. Dad had a load of cattle headed for the States, and Mom and Jim decided to go along."

His voice flattened, sucking out the emotion, making it sound like a news report rather than a life-altering personal event.

"They were a little south of Lethbridge when the wind must have caught the trailer. Someone said it looked like a weird downdraft, but we never knew for sure. Anyway, they went off the road. All three of them were killed."

His throat bobbed, suddenly tight and painful, and he was unable to go on. But he remembered that day as vividly as if it were yesterday.

He'd driven down himself. Half the cattle were injured, two were dead, and three had to be put down.
He still saw the stains of red on the highway, smelled
the death there. The cattle could be replaced, but in a
single, devastating moment he'd lost his whole family.
By the time he'd arrived they'd already been taken to
the morgue. In a split second he *was* Windover. Everything was suddenly empty, like a colorless void. It
wasn't right, working without Jim's jokes by his side,
or his dad's warm wisdom, or his mother's nurturing
support. They were just...gone. He'd never understood
why he'd been the one left behind. Always wondered if
he could have somehow prevented it if only he'd gone
along. Instead, he'd taken the day and had gone to Syl-
van Lake with friends.

His feet had stopped moving, and he was ashamed to
discover tears in his eyes. Alex said nothing, just twined
her fingers with his and squeezed. He cleared the ball
in his throat roughly.

She understood. Their upbringings were diametri-
cally opposite, yet a single moment in each of their lives
had devastated them completely. He sighed. She'd been
hurt as badly as he had. And he wouldn't risk being the
one to do it to her again. All he'd need would be more
guilt.

They turned back, the house visible, rising alone
against the sky in the distance.

"I didn't realize we'd come so far," Alex remarked,
and for a few minutes they pondered the significance
of that statement.

Connor changed the subject, away from them and
to the much safer topic of the background of the ranch.
"This place...I've never considered leaving. Even my

great-great grandfather stuck it out through a horrible winter. That's how Windover got its name, you know."

She left her fingers within his, a link between them on the path. "How?"

"He put up a rough cabin that first year. There was just the two of them, and the story goes that they were almost ready to pack it in when a Chinook blew in, melted most of the snow, and brought instant spring in the middle of March. He called it the wind over the mountains, and when they bought their first livestock it became Windover Farm and later Windover Ranch."

He had roots that went so deep. How could he ever understand someone who'd been rootless most of her life? She was glad now she hadn't revealed more than she had. They'd led completely different lives.

"Do you think we can go through with this?" she asked, angling a sideways glance at his profile.

"The wedding, you mean?" Connor nodded. "I think we are both realists. Despite the obvious differences in our situations, our personalities seem to match. Considering the predicament we find ourselves in, it seems like a workable solution. Practical. I know you have your doubts—anyone would—but if you'll let me show you that you can trust me…"

"Show me?"

The air cooled around them as the sun dipped further behind the mountains. "If at any time in the next few weeks you want out, I'll take you back to Calgary myself. Take this time, Alex, to find out who I am. To be sure I'll keep my word."

"But what happens in the end?" She swallowed. After two days she was already envying him his home, the one she'd always longed for and he'd always had. On one hand she told herself not to get attached to the kind of life she could have here at Windover, because it wasn't permanent. The other part of her told her to enjoy it, absorb all that she could and save it as a beautiful memory.

"I don't have all the answers. But, knowing what we know, surely we can part as friends in the end?"

"Do you think it'll be that easy? Going back to being alone?"

"Do you?"

The house grew closer with each slow step.

The thought of living alone now seemed dull and pointless, even after such a short time. It was a joy to know that someone was coming home at the end of the day. It gave the time she spent a point, a meaning. She'd have her baby when it was over, but who would Connor have?

"Who knows? We've both been alone for a long time. Maybe we'll drive each other crazy and you'll be glad to be rid of me." She tried a cocky smile, but faltered at the look in his eyes as they stopped at the edge of the dirt road.

He turned to face her, his warm gaze delving into hers, drawing her in and making her thoughts drift away on the evening breeze. His hand lifted to her cheek. "I think there's a very good chance you're going to drive me crazy," he murmured, his thumb stroking her cheek tenderly.

She stepped back in alarm, her face burning from the intimate touch and the clear meaning of his words. She left his hand hanging in thin air. A truck approached and spun past them, stirring up loose gravel and clouds of dust.

When the air cleared they said nothing, but crossed the road and made their way up the lane.

SHE WOKE AT dawn and checked her watch. It was barely five. Squinting, she glared at the window that was letting in all the lemony fresh sunshine. Last night she'd been so distracted she'd forgotten to pull the blinds. Her cheek still remembered the weight of his hand, caressing the soft skin there. Her drive him crazy? Not if he drove her nuts first. He was giving her the opportunity to back out. And she should. She was far too taken with him already. He was too strong, yet kind and understanding.

And he looked far too good in a pair of faded jeans. Add in that messy, slightly ragged hair, and any woman would be a goner. She should run, very quickly, in the opposite direction.

But the truth of the matter was this was by far the best way for her to provide for her child. She couldn't go back to where she'd been staying, as the tenant had decided to move in with her boyfriend when Alex left. She'd quit her job at a moment's notice. And now was no time to start from scratch.

She stared at the window. The flimsy white curtains didn't do much to keep out daylight, even when the sun was rising on the other side of the house. Tonight she'd make sure the blind was down. She sure didn't want to wake at five every day.

Footsteps passed outside her door, quiet, stocking-footed. A floorboard creaked beneath the weight. Connor was up already? She pushed the covers back and stepped out onto the hardwood floor. She'd missed his rising yesterday. She might as well get up now that she was awake, start learning what he liked for breakfast—

and how he cooked it. If she weren't going to be allowed to help *outside,* she meant to do her best inside.

She went downstairs dressed still in her pajamas—cotton shorts and a tank top. When she reached the kitchen, Connor already had a skillet on the burner and was half buried in the refrigerator, pulling out ingredients. He was dressed in what she now realized must be his customary uniform—faded jeans and a plain T-shirt. Her mouth grew dry as he dug deeper, the seat of his jeans filling out. She was in serious trouble here.

The touch of his hand on her face last night had prompted strange dreams. In them he'd stroked her cheek and kissed her. And it hadn't been a brotherly kiss either. In her slumbers he'd taken her mouth wholly, completely. His lips had been soft, deliberate, and devastating. His hands had glided over her skin. Tender. Possessive.

He straightened, turned with eggs in his hands, and jumped.

She wanted to disappear through the floor. Belatedly, she realized her fingers were touching her lips... and that her nipples were puckered up almost painfully. All from the sight of his bottom in some worn denim.

"I didn't expect you up for hours yet."

Blushing, she turned away, searching the cupboard for dishes. *Hormones,* she tried, quite unsuccessfully, to convince herself. It had to be the excess hormones in her system making her feel so...carnal.

"I forgot to pull the blind last night," she said to the plates. "You always up this early?"

He put a carton of eggs on the counter and nodded. "Ranching isn't exactly a nine-to-five business. You hungry?"

She was ravenous…and she couldn't blame *that* on her pregnancy. She'd found it incredibly difficult to eat after their walk, despite the fact that the chili had actually turned out fine.

"Normally I don't eat until later, but after last night…"

The words hung between them, not only a reminder of their walk but of the strange feeling of intimacy that had followed their personal revelations. She needed to keep things casual. She'd walked away from his touch last night; he had no idea she'd started fantasizing about him. She didn't want things to become more uncomfortable between them.

"What are you making?" She asked it quickly, to dispel the sudden feeling that he was remembering too.

"Scrambled eggs, sliced ham, and toast."

"Will you show me?" She stepped forward, feeling a little silly that at twenty-three she didn't even know how to scramble eggs. She wanted desperately to contribute, but having Connor have to show her everything… he could probably do it much faster himself than taking the time to instruct her. Setting her jaw, she vowed to pay close attention and learn—quickly.

"Sure." He cracked eggs into a bowl and handed her a whisk while he put butter in the pan. "Here. Beat the daylights out of those for a minute."

Her lips curved up without warning. She was really starting to like his sense of humor. He was relaxed and joking, which meant he wasn't letting what had happened affect their relationship. Perhaps being married, even for such a brief time, could be enjoyable. Their personalities meshed. And, yes, the ranch was isolated, but Alex was used to being alone and didn't find it too solitary. For the first time in a long time she felt a little hope that things would turn out all right after all. If only she could learn her share. If only they could maintain their boundaries.

As she was whisking he explained about adding salt and pepper and she paid close attention to quantities. He let the butter melt in the skillet, and then poured in the eggs.

"Once they start to set a little, then you keep pushing them around," he explained, and handed her the spatula.

She stuck it in the pan but splashed a little egg batter over the side. "Like this," he explained, and moved in behind her, covering her hand with his own on the spatula.

Alex's breath caught. Connor had showered last night and now, at the start of day, the scent of his soap was mingled with the smell of man in the morning. His body was warm and firm, close behind her, and the intimacy of the moment curled through her. OK, maybe this marriage wouldn't be as enjoyable as she thought. Not if she had to spend the next several months hiding the fact that he made her pulse race every time he was close. Last night's tender caress was only the tip of the iceberg.

His voice was oddly thick as he pulled away. "You're getting it now," he mumbled, and moved to put slices of bread in the toaster.

She pushed the eggs to one side and managed to fry the ham slices without incident. Silently they sat at the table to eat, while the light around them grew brighter.

"I called my grandmother last night."

She nearly choked on her toast. "You did?"

"I explained I was getting married." His smile was grim. "I think she'll probably come up here today to check you out."

She hadn't counted on grandmothers. And his had to

know that this wasn't a regular marriage. This had been a real, functioning family, she was sure. And that meant that his grandmother would likely be outraged at the fact that he was marrying a relative stranger for money.

"Why did you do that? I didn't sign up for irate grandmothers!" Her voice rose in panic. Not only was she a stranger, but an inept one. She didn't know much about being domestic and less about farming. Surely his grandmother would find her completely unsuitable? Alex wasn't ready for that type of criticism to be heaped on her head. After the ridiculous sexual thoughts she'd had about him lately, she couldn't seem to keep up with all the emotions he inspired in her. Last night had been sympathy, tenderness. Then carnality, embarrassment. And right now she was seeing the red cape of anger. If this was going to be a rollercoaster, she wanted off.

Connor didn't see the huge problem in telling his grandmother anything at all. After all, Gram had told him to get courting. Perhaps she hadn't meant quite this quickly, but Johanna Madsen was a practical woman. She'd figure out the truth very quickly. She was the one who had put him in this position, so she could say nothing about how he handled it.

Thankfully, he knew that Gram wasn't too hung up on conventionalities. But, more than that, Gram was the only family he had left. His honor, his family loyalty, demanded he be honest and upfront about it.

"She's all I have, Alex." He studied the ornery set of Alex's chin and smiled at her stubbornness. In the light of early morning she was beautiful, without artifice. All that was amplified when her eyes snapped with anger and her cheeks flushed. Perhaps it was the pregnancy, but her skin had a luminescence—and he'd caught sight of lots of it when she'd arrived in her pjs.

Yet she wasn't soft. There was a strength, a resolution about her that he admired. Alex Grayson was no pushover…and Gram would respect that if nothing else.

"Gram's pretty gruff, but she loves me and understands what's going on. Not only that, but if we're going to move ahead with this then it only makes sense that you meet my family right away. The most important thing to remember is she hates deception. She's way too smart for that, and will see through you like anything."

Alex put down her fork, her lips contorted grimly. "So you automatically think I'll lie to her? Thanks a lot."

"Of course not. That's not what I meant!"

"It sounded pretty clear to me." She gave up all pretence of eating. "Do you want me to tell her exactly why I'm here? Because I got knocked up by a low-life, have no prospects, and latched on to you for your money?"

"That's not exactly how I'd put it, no. Besides, I asked you."

"Like that'll matter. Does she even know I'm pregnant?"

"No." Surprising Gram with a fiancée last night had been enough, Connor thought. They'd get to the baby in time. After the wedding would be time enough to tell Gram that there would be a third Madsen in the household before long.

He swallowed roughly. Only the baby wouldn't be a Madsen. How could he have forgotten that?

"She's naturally going to think I'm a gold-digger. Thanks a lot, Connor."

She took her plate to the sink, nausea suddenly battling with her anger. At this rate she wouldn't have to worry about baby weight gain. She was always in such a tumult that she never seemed to finish a meal!

Bracing one hand on the counter, she closed her eyes, willing away the sickness. When she spoke, her words were soft and accusing.

"Isn't not telling her a form of deception?"

"I'm going to tell her, of course," he countered. "It's not exactly something we can keep hidden. I thought I'd give her a little time to get used to the marriage idea first."

"Coward," she mumbled.

"I beg your pardon?"

Alex scraped her plate into the garbage. "I can't believe you're afraid of your granny," she accused.

"I'm not a coward for not hitting her with all the details at once," he defended. "I did nothing wrong by letting my grandmother know we're getting married."

He frowned as he looked at her lips, thinned into a condemning line. Great. If she were this upset about meeting his grandmother, she was going to go ballistic when he told her the rest of the news.

"Unfortunately, I have an association meeting in Red Deer this morning. I'll be gone most of the day. Remember what I told you and you'll be fine. Just be yourself, Alex, and be honest, and I'm sure she'll love you." It was paltry pacification and it failed miserably.

"So you're lighting the fire and leaving me to put it out? Last night you said for me to trust you. Then you pull something like this. You didn't even *consult* me. Did you seriously think I'd be OK with this?"

"I honestly didn't think it'd be this big of a deal. I'm still not completely sure why it is."

"Oh, it's a big deal. *Huge*. Today I get to be judged. Alone."

For a moment he considered skipping the meeting. He hadn't considered how upset she might be over it, and in hindsight he probably should have talked to her first before calling Gram. But he'd been disconcerted after their talk last night, and he hadn't considered all the ramifications. And he'd learned something new—something that surprised him. Going toe-to-toe with Alex was invigorating. When they argued they left all pretence and awkwardness behind. They were *honest*. It was liberating.

Alex sighed, a mixture of frustration and resignation. "I'd better get started tidying this place up, then."

He took his empty plate to the sink. She was furious. It was in the way her eyes refused to even glance in his direction, in the icy set of her cheek. It shouldn't matter, but it did. Despite how *alive* she looked when she was wound up, he didn't like being at outs with her.

"I'm sorry, Alex. I certainly didn't intend to upset you. With any luck I'll be back by lunch, and she won't be here yet. Or I can make a few phone calls. Maybe I can reschedule the meeting, and then we can face her together."

She turned, raised her chin defiantly.

"I can handle your grandmother," she retorted. "It's the fact that I have to that I don't like."

"Point taken."

"If you want me to stay, don't let it happen again."

He couldn't help but smile a bit at her steel. She might be down but she would never admit to being out. The more they talked, the more he realized how resilient she was. He wondered what she'd left out about her life last night during their walk. "Agreed."

He stepped closer to her and laid a hand on her cheek. A few tendrils curled around her face and whispered against the rough skin of his hand. Her hair... He'd resisted the temptation thus far to sink his hands into that rich carpet of darkness. But this morning it was out of her customary ponytail and rippled down her back. There wasn't a man in this hemisphere who could resist hair like that.

"I'm sorry I didn't think this through better." He made the apology clear. "But, Alex?" At the questioning look in her eyes he smiled. "You're amazing. I don't think I've ever seen a woman more determined than you. You'll be great."

He pressed a kiss of reassurance to her forehead as he left for his chores. He'd lied. He'd met one woman more determined...and Alex was going to meet her too, very soon.

CHAPTER SIX

THE EGGS AND HAM, what she'd managed to eat of them, stayed down. Alex showered, dressed in clean jeans and T-shirt, and wished she had something nicer to wear. Grandmothers were not on her top ten list of things she wanted to do today. Alex knew that if she didn't pass muster, chances were the wedding would never take place.

She fussed with the hem of her shirt. Well, there was nothing she could do about her dearth of a wardrobe. Instead she went to work, tidying the house, dusting and vacuuming, and making sure the appliances gleamed. She took pleasure in looking in at the rooms, tidy and shining. It felt…already…like a home.

She frowned. Two days. Two days and she was thinking of this as home. She had to be careful and remember that this was temporary. If she got too invested, then she was only setting herself up for heartache when it became time to leave. And leave she must. They would go their separate ways, and she would find a new place for herself and the baby she'd be bringing up alone.

But first she had to deal with Connor's grandmother. The fact that she had to made her blood boil. Of all the nerve. Connor had sat there, calm as you please, and just *announced* that he'd told his grandmother about their plans. Now he was off "working", and she was left to deal with the fallout alone. How typically male!

She'd get lots of mileage out of this one. He owed her big time for dropping this on her and leaving.

She was heading upstairs when a horrible thought took hold. What if the revered lady arrived expecting to spend the night? Was Alex already in the room she would expect to occupy? Would his grandmother be expecting her to be sharing Connor's bed?

The thought of sleeping next to Connor all night made her stomach roll over. It was bad enough the tricks her mind was playing on her; she wasn't sure how she could handle lying close to his body through the night, listening to his steady breath, feeling his warmth. She had no business feeling this elemental attraction to him, not when their relationship was temporary and she was pregnant. And who knew what would happen while they were sleeping? She was apt to wake up draped over him, and how embarrassing would that be? As if Connor would be attracted to her—poor, plain Alex, pregnant with another man's child. Briefly she remembered how gently he'd touched her last night, and her stomach twisted again. Maybe it was possible that he was attracted, she supposed, but someone had to keep a clear head around here!

She could switch her things to the other spare room. It wouldn't take but a moment, and then Mrs. Madsen could have the white room. She was just taking the steps with fresh linens in her hands when the doorbell rang. Her heart sank. She'd run out of time.

She put the linens on a chair and opened the door with a heavy and panicked heart.

"You must be Alexis. I'm Johanna Madsen, Connor's grandmother."

Of course you are. Alex held the thought inside and tried to keep her mouth from dropping open. The woman was tall and imperious, dressed in a stylish black pant-suit with a real silk scarf twined about her neck.

But she was looking at Alex in a friendly, grand-motherly sort of way, not with the glare of suspicion and dislike that Alex had completely expected.

"Please, come in," Alex said automatically, then felt ridiculous. Johanna belonged here so much more than she did!

Alex stepped aside and Johanna came in, pulling a suitcase behind her. Alex's heart sank. Johanna *was planning on staying.*

"Connor's gone to a meeting," she said haltingly, hating the uncertainty in her voice.

Johanna's brow crinkled in the middle. "All this fuss—all these meetings he has to attend when there's hay to be cut. It looks like a good crop. He'll need it."

"He will?"

Johanna smiled at Alex indulgently, making Alex feel like a simple child. "When you can't sell beef, you've got to feed the ones you've got." She put a friendly hand on Alex's shoulder. "Let's have tea."

Alex was helpless to do anything but follow Johanna into the kitchen. The woman had been in the house less than five minutes and already she was in charge. Alex wasn't sure whether to be offended or strangely relieved as she paused in the doorway to the kitchen, unsure of what to do.

Johanna placed the kettle on the burner, and then knelt down with her head in the cupboard, searching for teabags. A rancher's wife, born and bred. It made Alex feel even more like an impostor.

"So, when are you due, Alexis?"

Alex's mouth *did* drop open then, and she stood paralyzed. Johanna took the kettle off the burner and poured, unhesitating in her movements. The woman was making tea like she'd just asked about the weather. Connor had distinctly said he hadn't told his grandmother about the baby. How on earth could she know? The shirt Alex was wearing covered most of her belly, and she was barely beginning to show. She should have been prepared for the question, but she wasn't, and she floundered horribly.

"Mrs. Madsen..."

"Oh, dear. None of that, I hope." Johanna turned with a carton of milk in her hands. "You can call me Gram, like Connor does, or Johanna—whichever suits you best."

Alex paused. She was on shaky footing. The woman before her was shrewd, and exuded an aura of power and competence that Alex found intimidating. Yet at the same time she seemed very down to earth and without artifice. Alex couldn't read her at all, and her discomfort grew as the woman raised a questioning eyebrow at her continued silence. Somehow she had to try to gain control of the conversation, yet without seeming adversarial. She'd already argued with Connor this morning; she wasn't sure she could stand to go three rounds with his grandmother.

"Mrs. Madsen." She used the formal name as a shield. "I'm sorry. Your question took me by surprise," she finally got out.

"You *are* pregnant, aren't you?" Johanna turned her

back to Alex, putting the cream and sugar on a tray with the teapot.

Alex dropped her eyes and her shoulders tensed. Never in her life had she felt more deceitful, more un-deserving. Johanna had guessed about the baby—and that was sure to create problems. The best way to deal with it was head-on.

"Yes, I am. Fourteen weeks."

"And Connor says you met on Friday?" Johanna turned back, bringing the pot to the table.

Oh, didn't that sound lovely? Alex flushed. *By the way, I'm marrying your grandson. I've known him for less than a week.* She might as well march right upstairs and repack her bag. She knew how it looked, no matter what the reality was. In a cool voice she replied, "Yes. I fainted downtown and he came to my rescue."

To her surprise, a tender smile spread across Johanna's face. "Oh, my. That sounds just like Lars."

"Lars?" Alex was intrigued by the radiant look that transformed Johanna's face, making her look twenty years younger.

"My husband—Connor's grandfather."

Johanna brought the tray to the pine table while Alex hesitantly perched on a chair. They sat across the table from each other while Johanna poured the tea. Alex was wary, but found herself curious about Connor's grand-father, and what kind of man held the power to put that particular soft look on Johanna's face.

Alex wanted to believe this woman was on a friendly mission. But until she could be sure she had to be very, very careful.

"Lars was the noblest man I ever knew." Johanna chuckled a bit, on a lovely little note of remembrance.

"When we met I was fifteen. I had a bicycle, you see. I'd fallen off and scraped my knee quite badly. Lars saw me by the side of the road." She smiled warmly at the memory. "His father... Connor's great-grandfather... had bought a truck for the farm the week before. Lars put my bike in the back and drove me home. He was twenty-three and, oh my, so handsome. It's where Connor gets his looks, you know." She stared at Alex knowingly over the rim of her cup.

Alex shifted in her chair. How was she to respond to that? Of course Connor was handsome. Devastatingly so. But to agree would be admitting to an attraction she didn't want, and to ignore the comment...she didn't want to be insulting, either. It would make her look like she was only after his money. She couldn't win.

"Connor is handsome. You'd be blind to miss it," she stated matter-of-factly, revealing essentially nothing.

"It's the Madsen men." Johanna nodded sagely. "There's a picture of Lars's grandparents around somewhere, on their wedding day. He was a looker too." Johanna rose and retrieved the bag of cookies from the pantry, handing one to Alex. "It was Lars's grandfather who settled this place, you know. The government was offering homesteads. He traveled all the way from Norway to start a life here. And the farm has never left the family.

"Which is where you come in." Johanna pushed her mug aside. "I know that this isn't a regular marriage. My question is, why are you willing to marry a man you hardly know? And how much of his money do you expect to get out of the deal?"

"I beg your pardon?" Alex put down her mug, confused at the sudden turn of the conversation. First she was friendly, and now she was putting the screws on her? Alex was finding it hard to keep her balance. She understood now that it had all been a part of Johanna's strategy. Lull her into a friendly conversation and then hit her with the big guns. Alex burned inwardly with indignation. She wasn't a bad person. This whole situation wasn't as cold as it sounded.

"What's in this for you, Alexis? Because being a rancher's wife isn't the easy way out, let me assure you."

Johanna's eyes were sharp, her lips a thin, unreadable line. Alex had never seen a woman so completely put together: not a hair out of place, not a wrinkle in her clothing, even though she'd been nearly two hours in her car. Alex tucked a stray piece of hair behind her ear and tried to shake away the feeling of a chastised child. She hadn't done anything wrong or deceitful. She'd made the mistake of falling for the wrong guy once, and now she was dealing with the aftermath in the only way she knew how. She didn't deserve to be judged.

Alex dropped her cookie to the table. "I don't have any plans of being a rancher's wife. And I resent the implication that somehow I'm *extorting* money out of your grandson. I'm doing this for one reason and one only. Security for me and my baby."

For a few months she could pretend she lived in this secure, traditional world. A husband and a house, and no stress about where the next meal was coming from. It was a sham, all of it, but she had a desperate need to belong somewhere, even for such a short time. But how could she explain that to this woman? Their family tree went back several generations, right here on this farm. She would never understand how displaced and alone Alex had been for most of her life.

"When Connor met me I was alone, working as a waitress, with no real home and a baby on the way." She looked squarely into his grandmother's eyes, and gambled that Connor had outlined their agreement already.

"This all took place because he wants to save Windover, plain and simple. Connor marries me so that he can access his trust fund. After the baby is born we'll go our separate ways, and he'll help support us until I can get my feet under myself again."

She didn't use the word "divorce", even though it was the proper term. Somehow it seemed cold and hateful, even in a platonic marriage such as this. She did not look away from Johanna's serious expression. Alex didn't want to anger Johanna, but neither would she be a doormat, nor accused of being a gold-digger.

"And, to be clear, Connor approached me, not the other way around. I didn't go looking for a sugar daddy, if that's what you're implying."

"I think I already knew that." Johanna's eyes showed nothing of what she was feeling. "But I had to hear it anyway. You are doing this for your baby. What about the child's father?"

Alex winced. Ryan had been charming—too charming. Alex had fallen for him quickly, absorbing the affection and attention into her love-starved soul. But deep down she'd known he wasn't the keeper type. When she'd announced she was pregnant he had hit the door so fast she'd felt the draft. In another situation she would have said *good riddance to bad rubbish.* But this time was different. She was alone again, but with an innocent, precious baby to consider. One she was determined would have a stable, secure life.

"The biological father has no interest in parenthood, I'm afraid. He left me, and the baby I'm carrying."

Johanna rose and took her cup to the sink. Turning back, she said softly, "What do *you* ultimately want, Alexis?"

A home. Again the answer came unbidden, and it wasn't one she cared to share. This was only a temporary home and she had to remember that. What Connor had proposed would make it possible for her to build her own home, a safe, welcoming place for her child. A child who would always feel wanted and loved and a first priority. All the things her parents had tried to provide but somehow she'd missed.

"I want a good life for my baby. I want to make a home for us. I just want a place for my baby to feel loved and safe."

Johanna walked over to the table and placed a hand on Alex's shoulder. "That's a damned good answer."

Alex couldn't keep up with the changes from friend to foe to friend again, and somehow knew she was failing this test miserably.

Johanna's hand was warm on her shoulder, and Alex hadn't known how much she'd missed simple human contact. Something about Johanna's hand, firm and sure, sent feelings rushing up in Alex, and she struggled to hold them rippling beneath the surface. She couldn't remember the last time she'd even been hugged. The older woman could never understand what a simple touch could do...

"Thank you," she whispered, sweeping a few crumbs into her palm to try to escape the moment.

"How long has it been?"

Alex straightened. "Since what?"

"Oh, my dear, it's obvious," Johanna murmured, nothing but kindness softening her face. "Since someone loved you."

The tears came so quickly, so completely unexpectedly, that Alex was powerless to stop them. Johanna came forward and tucked Alex into her embrace, and she cried into the older woman's shoulder. Cried for the second time that week, when it had been years since she'd shed tears. Not once in the time she'd been alone had anyone acknowledged that she hadn't been loved. Had anyone cared that she might be lonely and afraid. But she was. She was terrified of failing. Of not being enough for her child. She was frightened, quite simply, of the unknown future.

Her breath came in halting gasps, and she desperately tried to even them out as she tasted the salt of her own tears. She had to get herself together.

Connor stepped through the front door, halting abruptly at the sight of his grandmother holding a sobbing Alex in her arms. His throat constricted at the picture they made. So much for maintaining distance. Because the sight of his fiancée and his grandmother together did something to his heart he knew he'd never get back.

CONNOR STEERED THE tractor to the edge of the field and left it. Tomorrow he'd be back to continue on. Now he'd drive back to the house in the truck.

The noon meal had been tense. He'd rushed the meeting, anxious to get back early so he might arrive before Gram. But he'd been too late. When he'd entered, Alex had turned to the small bathroom off the kitchen, embarrassed, to wash her tear-streaked face and regain control. When she'd returned she had pasted on a smile and apologized that she didn't have his lunch ready. He hadn't cared less about lunch. What he'd really wanted to know was what his grandmother had done to provoke such an emotional response. He remembered Alex protesting before that she hated crying. But she'd been in the middle of a full-blown jag when he'd come in.

It was obvious his grandmother approved of Alex, no matter how unorthodox their situation.

Connor started up the pickup and shoved it into gear, a line appearing between his brows. Seeing them together that way…it had been *right* somehow.

"She's already had enough hurt in her life, that girl," Gram had warned under her breath, while Alex had been in the next room, repairing the damage to her face.

He had no plans of hurting Alex further at all. In fact, the more he saw of her, the more he knew he had to protect her. They had made a deal that benefited them both, but ultimately they were from two very different worlds. Now it was up to him to uphold his end.

He would be her friend, but there was no room for anything more. Not if he were to be fair.

As he'd left the house, Gram had said something else. "Be very careful, dear," she'd said, a hand on his arm. "I've never seen a creature more hungry for love and affection than that child."

Pulling up into the yard, he noticed Gram's car was gone. Perhaps she'd gone back to Calgary and her own apartment? Connor's stomach fluttered nervously at the thought of being alone with Alex. "Stupid fool," he chided himself as he hesitated at his own front door. If they were to be friends only, there should be nothing to be nervous about.

Alex was coming through the living room with a basket of laundry in her arms as he entered. Both stopped in surprise.

"Gram went home?"

Alex laughed, putting down the basket. "Hardly. She's put her bag in the third bedroom and dug in for the duration."

"Oh." Connor's voice registered disappointment and he put on an optimistic smile. "She'll be a great help to you."

"Oh, yes," Alex replied, a happy smile on her face. "I was terribly worried about meeting her. And we did have a few uncomfortable moments. But once she knew about the baby..."

"She knows?" He stepped forward, surprise lighting his face. All Gram had said at lunch was not to hurt Alex; she'd mentioned nothing about knowing about the pregnancy. Now here was Alex, carefree and happy. He hadn't seen that particular look on her face before, but he recognized it now. It was devoid of strain and worry. She looked like a woman who'd been given a free pass. Connor hadn't thought it possible, but it made her even more beautiful.

"Yes," she chirped. "I must have answered her questions satisfactorily. She's already making wedding plans."

Connor's head spun. The words *don't hurt her* and *hungry for love* echoed through his brain. He'd expected stiff resistance once she knew about the baby. Instead Gram had moved in?

"Is it too soon?"

"What?" he came out of his stupor and shook his head. "Oh. No, of course not, I'm surprised, that's all."

"I was too. We had a big talk this afternoon, though, Connor. Your grandmother is an amazing woman. She said she understood I didn't know much about cooking, and when I told her I'd never gardened she said I could use a helping hand. That she'd missed it, living in her condo the way she does."

"She did?"

"Uh-huh. And she said she'd help plan the wedding too."

This was getting out of hand. Weddings and gardens and babies… Connor's very logical, sensible plan was suddenly spiraling out of control. And all under the hawk-like eye of his grandmother. He agreed that she was wonderful. He also knew she was shrewd. This was her way of keeping a finger in the pie. He knew it and resented it. But he couldn't send Johanna back to Calgary. Alex was already looking forward to the help. And he was so busy with the ranch he didn't have time to spend with her except in the evenings. It wasn't fair for him to expect her to while away her days all alone. If having Johanna here made her happy, he'd keep quiet. And he'd keep his eyes wide open. Helping was one thing. Meddling, however well intentioned, was another.

Besides, the less time he spent with Alex the better. Because sooner or later he'd see her looking at him like she was right now, and he'd be stupid, and kiss her like he wanted to, and complicate *everything*.

He changed the subject.

"She gave you your first lesson in cooking, I take it?" He looked past her shoulder to the pots bubbling on the stove.

"Yes. But she said she was going into town to have supper with a friend and not to wait up."

"Probably Millie's," he surmised, naming Gram's oldest and closest friend. And if she revealed what was going on at Windover Ranch, news of his impending marriage would be common knowledge by coffee time tomorrow.

He discovered he didn't mind as much as he'd thought he would. For a moment he stared at Alex, picturing her in a long white dress, her mass of dark hair falling over her shoulders, and he couldn't breathe. Alex lifted the basket again, momentarily placing her palm on the slight bubble of her belly, and his heart contracted painfully.

Connor was as hungry for love as Alex… But he could not, would not, seek it from her. She was leaving, and the one thing he knew he could never do was abandon Windover.

CHAPTER SEVEN

"MIKE'S ON HIS way over. He's going to run things for me today. I've gotta go into Red Deer after lunch."

Connor made the announcement as cheerfully as he could, successfully hiding his dark feeling of despair. It was nice of his friend Mike to lend a hand, but Connor was fighting a losing battle and he knew it. The source of the outbreak was still being investigated. If anything tied it to his herd he'd have to cull the whole lot. Windover would be finished. And no amount of money would save it, trust fund or not.

He picked at his pancakes, not actually eating much. If Windover was finished, he should release Alex from their agreement. Yet he wasn't ready to let go. He wasn't giving up on Windover yet, and he wasn't going to give up on her either. Sure, he could release her, but then what would she do? He'd made her a promise. And he'd deliver on it no matter what.

"We need to go shopping." Johanna interrupted the silence.

Alex and Connor looked up from their breakfast to stare at Johanna.

"I got groceries yesterday," Alex explained, her eyes darting between Johanna and Connor with confusion.

"Not that kind of shopping. Clothes shopping. You

need a wedding dress, and you're already squeezing into your jeans."

Alex flushed. "I can manage," she said, spinning a piece of pancake in the syrup on her plate.

Connor nodded. "Gram's right. I'm sorry, Alex, I should have seen to it before now. But things have been…"

"Busy. It's fine."

He looked at her, dressed in the same jeans and T-shirt he was growing used to seeing. She'd asked for nothing, nothing at all. She had to have some new things. That was all there was to it. When he'd made this proposition, looking after her welfare had become his duty, and he simply should have seen before now how threadbare her wardrobe was.

He looked outside at the rain falling. One of the reasons he'd decided to meet with John, Cal and Rick was that the rainy day meant no haying. He'd called them early, asking them to meet. They were ranchers, like him, who had everything to lose. And they hadn't hesitated when he'd suggested getting together.

"Why don't we go this afternoon? I can drop you off on my way, pick you up on the way back."

Alex put down her fork. "I don't want to inconvenience you, Connor."

"It's no inconvenience. In fact, I insist." He forced a grin. "Come on, I didn't think you'd fight me on a shopping trip!"

Johanna interjected. "A bride needs a suitable dress, and maternity clothes will soon be a must. We're going to need a whole day, dear."

Connor met his grandmother's gaze, relieved. He'd been thinking that Alex had no wedding dress. She had no more than what she'd brought in that single bag. Yet he hadn't known how to go about saying it without hurting Alex's feelings. Coming from Johanna, it seemed less critical than he'd imagined.

"We can go this morning."

"Really, you two, this isn't necessary…" Alex interjected, pushing her plate away.

"Nonsense. Connor, there's no reason why you can't join us for the morning, have lunch, and drop us off after at the formal wear store to shop for dresses." She winked at him. "We *will* spare you the wedding dress shopping."

A morning shopping wasn't normally what he'd call fun, but when he looked at Alex he saw reluctance mingled with a tiny bit of anticipation. When was the last time someone had treated her to a shopping spree? When was the last time he'd taken a day off?

"I'm game if you are, Alex."

Alex had never had anyone treat her to a day of shopping, and the sheer novelty of it was exciting. Yet she hesitated to agree. She didn't have any money of her own, and felt like enough of a freeloader already, without Connor and Johanna paying for an entirely new wardrobe.

"I'm sure Connor would like to see you in something other than jeans and T-shirts," Johanna went on, aiming a pointed glare in Connor's direction.

Alex met Connor's eyes. There was nothing in the warm depths that criticized her appearance. In fact they crinkled at the corners a bit, giving her a strange sense of reassurance. She couldn't read what he was thinking, but his face was relaxed and amiable as he responded, "You deserve it."

She certainly didn't feel like she deserved it, and she

was so used to looking after herself that she wasn't comfortable with someone else footing the bill. She certainly didn't want Connor to feel as if she were taking advantage of his generosity, or his grandmother's either, for that matter.

"It's settled, then." Johanna resumed eating, bringing Alex's misgivings to a screeching halt. "We can take my car, Connor. It'll be much easier than the truck."

Alex got the sneaky feeling she was being railroaded, but knew it would be fruitless to argue. Besides, if she didn't get some new clothes soon she'd be running around with her pants unbuttoned. Practicality warred with guilt, and practicality won.

"I'll get ready," she answered faintly, still not convinced it was a good idea.

THE FIRST PLACE they hit was a shopping mall, arriving just as the stores were pushing back their metal and glass doors.

"You need maternity clothes," Johanna insisted, and led a reluctant Alex inside by the hand. The first customers of the day, they got the saleslady's undivided attention.

"Only the basics," Alex insisted, looking at Connor. He hung back, and she wondered why in the world he'd agreed to come along. Surely he didn't consider this "fun"? As Johanna fluttered around, she wondered what exactly Connor *did* think constituted fun. She didn't even know that much about him, yet here she was planning their wedding and shopping for clothes. Clothes *he* was going to pay for.

She didn't want to be accused of taking more than she needed. She looked around at the racks of clothing, amazed at how stylish and cute they were. She picked up a black crepe top, with ties to the back and tiny pink flowers dotted over it. In a very few short months her tummy would be rounded and full. She touched the warm area where right now her baby lay. Motherhood. Somehow, shopping for maternity wear drove home the fact that she was going to be a mother more than anything else had—even the crazy deal with Connor. Someday in the near future she was going to have a tiny bundle to love, to nurture, to care for.

"Are you OK?" Connor touched Alex's shoulder.

Alex half turned, letting out a breathless laugh. "It just hit me. I'm going to be a mother."

Connor smiled. "You started to turn pale." He scanned the racks, and shook his head at the sight of his grandmother chatting animatedly with the clerk. "So—excited, or scared to death?"

She couldn't help it, she laughed, suddenly very glad he'd come along. "A little of both?"

She had an ally in Connor, although she had no idea why she deserved it. Johanna held up a hand, waggling it in the air and rattling hangers.

"I think I'm being summoned." She aimed a wry smile at him, gratified to see his own mirror hers.

"I predict you'll be a while, from that gleam in her eye. I've seen it before. I'll go find us some coffee."

"That sounds good," she answered, unable to draw her eyes away from his. It was silly to be here, gazing into each other's eyes, but somehow they'd locked and clung until her heart grew heavy in her chest.

His eyes shifted to over her shoulder.

"Here. Try these on. I thought you'd be happier with casual." Johanna interrupted the moment and Connor quietly left. In some strange way she felt better when he was by her side, but she certainly didn't expect him to hang around a maternity shop and comment on fit and style.

Alex was led away, then ensconced in a changing room, handing clothes in and out as she tried on several outfits. In the end she agreed to two pairs of jeans, two pairs of summer shorts, several casual cotton shirts, a sweet pajama set in white with lace trim, and a good outfit for special occasions—a black skirt with a ruffled hem, paired with a scooped-neck floral top.

"It's too much." She put a hand over the top of Johanna's left as the older woman signed the credit card slip.

"Nonsense. Alex, you need these things. It's a pleasure to provide them for you. I always only ever had a son and grandsons to buy for, and boys are too practical. It's a treat for me just to be able to buy something pink and feminine. Indulge me."

Alex took two of the bags in her hands. "And I thank you. But…I'm used to providing for myself."

"You're working hard to learn up at Windover. You are trying to be what Connor needs right now. That's payment enough for me. I know Connor agrees."

She was what Connor needed? A screw-up in the kitchen? A stranger who knew nothing about ranching? As far as she was concerned, she'd been on the receiving end of all the benefit and hadn't given much in return. Now Johanna was treating her like a real granddaughter. The girl longing for a home was irresistibly attracted to that, while the practical woman inside knew that it would only hurt more in the end when she had to leave.

Johanna took the remainder of the bags, nudging her out the door. "Come on. You need shoes."

Connor had been waiting outside and now handed her a paper cup, the tab folded back already and the letters "dec" printed roughly on the top. He'd thought to get her decaf, she realized as Johanna herded them on to the shoe store. His consideration was a constant surprise.

Feeling somewhat helpless, she watched as Connor waited patiently on a bench outside the store while she bought casual shoes, a pair of black patent slingbacks for dressy, and white satin slippers for the wedding.

By lunchtime, their arms were laden with bags. In addition to the footwear and maternity clothes, she'd purchased new socks and underwear at the department store. She'd also taken some of her own money, what little there was of it, and bought Connor a pair of new T-shirts. The one he'd had on first thing this morning was worn around the collar. She couldn't think of anything else appropriate to buy, but she was determined not to go home with nothing for him. She hadn't ever bought a man clothing before, and without knowing sizes was a fish out of water. Socks were too impersonal, and underwear...far too intimate. But T-shirts she could manage without too much trouble. Besides, it would be a treat to see his wide chest in them, the way the sleeves outlined the dip in his triceps...

"I'm famished. Let's have lunch." Johanna led Alex down the hall to the restaurant housed on the corner.

Alex waited while Connor requested a table, then put a hand on his arm when Johanna excused herself to go to the ladies' room. "Lunch is on me. Please."

She'd accepted enough today. She didn't have much, but she had enough of her own money left after the T-shirts that she could at least buy lunch.

"You don't have to do that." He took a seat in the booth opposite her.

"But I want to. I'm not used to...to charity." Guilt and shame trickled through her simply from saying the word.

"You're not charity. I'm getting something out of this deal too, remember?" He reached over and put his hand on top of hers. "You're helping me, Alex. Right now it's safe to say you're all the hope I've got."

His thumb was tracing circles over the side of her hand and she didn't think he was even aware he was doing it. Let alone realizing what the simple touch was doing to her insides.

She swallowed. "Then indulge me. You've done so much for me already. Let me buy you lunch."

He hesitated a moment, but relented. "Deal. But I'll warn you. Watching you shop works up my appetite."

Alex laughed as a waitress brought tall glasses of iced water. "Now that the sickness seems to be getting better, I could eat all the time."

His thumb kept circling. "You know, Alex, I can't believe I didn't think of this before now. It's not right that you have to come to me for every penny. There are things you're going to need—for yourself, for the house, getting ready for the baby. I'll make sure I get you a checkbook and a debit card. I'm sorry I didn't look after it before."

He was going to trust her with his bank account? Alex tried not to gape and instead grabbed her water and sipped, hiding her shocked face.

His thumb stopped and he squeezed her hand. "Did I say something wrong?"

"No, no, not at all," she stammered, then cleared her

throat as it seemed to suddenly become hoarse. "I'm just surprised, that's all."

"Is there a reason I shouldn't trust you?"

"No!" She finally lifted her eyes and saw he was watching her steadily. Like he already knew the answer. "Of course not. It's just…"

How could she explain what such a practical, simple act meant to her? That he trusted her to such an extent that she could use his money without asking? That it was one more thing binding her to him and giving her this uncanny sense of normalcy in an otherwise unorthodox arrangement?

"It makes sense, that's all. I've taken you away from your income…I agreed to provide for you. That doesn't mean you don't get some say in the matter."

"It's more than I expected. You and your grandmother—you've been far too generous with me. She paid for *everything* this morning. I'm not used to that."

Connor took a sip of his water, pulling his hand away from hers. "Don't you feel one bit of guilt. Gram is having a ball. She hasn't done this since…well, in many years. But she and Mom used to do it all the time."

"They were close?" Alex prodded gently.

Connor nodded. "Yes, they were. Gram always said, 'Melissa, you're my best daughter.' I think she always wanted a little girl of her own, but there was only Dad. She and Mom were peas in a pod. I think she was a little disappointed that one of us wasn't a girl and she didn't get a granddaughter to spoil."

She smiled at the fond tone of remembrance in his voice. It was good he remembered the good times. She wished she could, but somehow all she seemed to feel was regret and a sense of being cheated out of something.

"Mom and Gram used to take little trips like this all the time...sometimes even for something as silly as buying school supplies for Jim and me. But they always had fun. Dad always said it was an excuse for them to get away from the farm for a day and treat themselves."

"So that's why you came today?"

He looked up and saw Johanna approaching. "I thought you could both use a little of that."

She couldn't believe she hadn't considered it before. When Connor had lost his parents, Johanna had lost a son, daughter-in-law, and grandson. That pain had to be with her still.

"Have we ordered yet?"

"Just waiting for you." Connor scooched over and made room for Johanna to sit.

"Whew. I worked up an appetite this morning. Haven't had this much fun since—"

When she broke off, Alex looked up at Connor and was happy he'd told her what he had.

"Connor was just telling me about his mother. And how you used to sneak off for day trips like this."

"Oh, we did. We always came back with more than we went for, but we had a ball. You're a lot like her, you know."

"I am?" Alex put down her menu and her eyebrows lifted with surprise. "I wouldn't think so."

Johanna laughed, the rusty sound that always made Alex smile. "Oh, yes. The dark hair, pretty eyes. But more than that, you're strong. Stubborn, too, I can tell. And you have a big heart, Alex. I saw that right off. Don't you think so, Connor?"

Alex dropped her eyes, both at the unexpected praise and the blatant attempt at matchmaking. Did Connor see that in her too? How could he, when she couldn't see it in herself?

He covered the awkward moment with a laugh. "I certainly agree with the stubborn thing," he joked, then related the tale of her first cooked meal, and how determined she was to conquer the kitchen. "If supper last night was any indication, your stubborn streak will serve you well. The ham was delicious."

Alex accepted the compliment graciously, but wondered, as the server took their orders, if he did think she was much like his mother and if that was a good or a bad thing. His long leg bumped hers beneath the table and her stomach twisted. How were they supposed to come through this unscathed and unchanged? She was already feeling like a real part of this family, being included and welcomed...and the wedding hadn't even happened yet.

Johanna changed the subject, asking about wedding details, and they got so occupied with the topic that Alex quite forgot her misgivings until later.

After lunch they left the mall, and after a few quick turns Connor parked in front of a small strip-mall, gave them his return time, and Alex found herself entering a formal wear store. Mannequins dressed in white gowns stood in one window, one with a tuxedoed man on her arm. Inside were two solid rooms of formal wear. She took off her shoes, gripped her purse nervously, and followed Johanna into the reception area.

"May I help you?" A young woman, dressed in the latest fashion, looked up from the appointment book behind her desk.

"Yes. Johanna Madsen, and this is Alexis Grayson. We're shopping for a wedding dress today."

"Congratulations!" The woman smiled. "Come right in."

Alex was silent as Jennifer, as it stated on her name tag, and Johanna hashed over what sort of style would suit her. Never in her life had she shopped in such a place! All around her were dresses in white and cream satin, some adorned with lace, others with intricate beading and crystals.

A bride.

But not a bride. An impostor. This wasn't a real marriage, and to pretend it was, was sacrilege. She didn't deserve a fancy white dress with all the trimmings.

She pulled on Johanna's arm. Johanna sent Jennifer an apologetic look.

"Excuse us a moment."

"I can't do this." Alex looked at Johanna evenly. "It isn't right. We both know this isn't a real marriage. It feels wrong to put on this big show when we both know that in a few months it'll be over. Let's just go somewhere else and pick out a nice dress and it'll do. Please. This is all…too much."

Johanna must have taken pity on her, because she acquiesced. "All right. But, Alex, people are going to wonder if you show up at your wedding in an everyday dress. You should at least have a proper dress. Connor's friends…his neighbors…will expect it."

She was engaged in a losing battle and she knew it. Not only that, but there was a small part of her that wanted to do him proud, to show up on their wedding day looking the way a bride should look. To see that gleam of appreciation in his eyes, even if it wasn't for real.

"Oh, all right. But nothing over the top."

Johanna found the sales clerk again, and before Alex could say *Here comes the bride* she found herself again in a changing room, three separate dresses hanging before her.

The first two didn't seem quite right, but the third time was the charm. Alex emerged from the change area smiling. "I like this one."

Standing before the full-length mirror, she fell in love with it.

Strapless, the satin bodice was short, gathered in an empire style just beneath her breasts, with a thin stripe of satin ribbon marking the seam and the top of the bustline above. Beneath, it flowed gracefully to the floor, a filmy overskirt of organza adding romance to the look. It was simple and stunning. She pressed a hand to her belly. Even if she started to show more in the next few weeks, the empire waist and overskirt would camouflage things perfectly.

"I'm going to get your shoes," Johanna murmured, her voice tinged with emotion. "It's beautiful, Alex," she added, before disappearing to the car to retrieve their earlier purchase.

The slippers slid on, and Alex knew that this was the one. "I love it."

She checked the price tag and almost choked.

"I can't let you do this," she protested to Johanna, but it was to no avail.

"You can and you will," the old lady returned decisively. "I promise you, you will not regret it, Alexis."

Jennifer spoke up. "It doesn't need a bit of altering. Amazing, really. We can have one ordered in for you within eight weeks."

"This wedding is happening a week from Saturday," Johanna said coolly, while Alex was still stupefied by the eight-week ordering time. "Go get changed," she ordered Alex. "I'll look after everything."

Thirty minutes later they were in the car, heading west, the trunk loaded with maternity clothes and the back seat holding one very new, very extravagant dress, and one very nervous bride-to-be.

CONNOR WAS A smart man. And he knew better than to ask what in the world was in the garment bag that Alex had carried from the car and into the house. Alex was looking relaxed and happy, and even seemed a little excited as she scooted up the stairs with her wedding finery, presumably so that he wouldn't see. It was endearing, really, despite the odd situation they'd put themselves in.

And for some reason Alex and Gram seemed to get on like a house on fire. Mealtimes were fun now, with easy banter and the two of them ganging up on him about wedding details. Honestly, he didn't care. All he wanted was a small, nice ceremony. Something intimate and simple. The details he was more than happy to leave to the women.

Summer days were long, and it was a good thing, because he was so busy it kept him from thinking too much. Besides haying and the feed crops and looking after livestock, there were many more phone calls and e-mails lately, all dealing with the crisis. The U.S. borders were closed indefinitely to all Canadian beef—and other markets were following suit. Something, *something* had to happen soon. With every bill paid, the balance in the bank account got lower and lower. After his meeting he was no further ahead. Everything was at a standstill. Everyone was waiting for the verdict on the source of the disease. Everyone he knew was praying that their herd wouldn't have to be slaughtered. And all the while the money he did receive domestically was a drop in the bucket compared to what he needed.

The one time he relaxed was in the evenings, coming in to Alex's and Gram's company. Their happy chatter and laughter lightened his load more than he wanted to admit.

Two days after the shopping trip, he escaped to the den to work on the computer. Grace Lundquist had been by with the account book, and it didn't look good. He sighed, rubbing his temples as he rested his elbows on the desk. He wished he could put it aside and maybe watch some television with Alex and Gram. Resolutely he set his jaw. There had to be a way to work the numbers. He went over the columns again, wondering where he could save and what absolutely needed to be spent.

"Long day?"

Alex's voice interrupted him, and he couldn't help the warmth that spread through him with just a few words from her lips. "The longest."

"Can I come in?"

He swiveled in his chair, turned to see her hesitating in the doorway, her form backlit by the light from the kitchen. "Of course you can."

She offered a small smile, stepped lightly inside. "I forgot to give you something the other day. It's not much, but…"

She held out the bag containing the shirts. "I thought you could use a new supply."

He took the bag from her hands, peering inside.

"T-shirts." He looked up, a smile smoothing the lines of worry from his face. "You didn't have to do that."

She sighed. "I couldn't spend the whole day shopping and not bring something home for you. I only wish I could have...well, never mind."

"They're great. I appreciate the thought as much as the gift, Alex." It had been many years since anyone had thought to give him a present "just because."

Her eyes slid to the computer screen and the open books on the desk. "It's bad, isn't it, Connor? I can tell by the stress written all over your face."

He didn't even attempt to hide it as wrinkles marred his brow. "It's bad. The whole industry is crumpling around us."

"Will we make it? Won't your trust fund money help?"

His throat grew so dry it hurt. She had said "we", not "you". He wasn't sure if it helped knowing she was in it with him or not.

His ancestors had started with nothing and made this place work. His great-grandfather had persevered throughout the Depression when other farmers had abandoned their land, looking for work. It damn near killed him to admit, "I don't know. It'll help for a while, but I don't know."

She nodded, but he saw the flicker of uncertainty on her face. "Alex, no matter what happens with Windover, I made you a promise. I said I would help provide for you and your baby, and I will."

"You always keep your promises, don't you? Don't worry about the baby and me. We're all in this together." She came even closer, close enough that he had to lift his chin to look in her eyes, see the faint flush on her cheeks.

She smiled down at him, her face soft with understanding. "If it'll help, we can just have a Justice of the Peace here for the wedding. I don't need all the trappings that Johanna seems determined to have."

There was no way he was going to deprive her of a nice wedding. Not after all she was willing to go through to make this whole plan work. "It's not that much when you look at the big picture," he conceded. "A small, intimate affair is no problem. And secretly..." he smiled up at her "...I think Gram is having a marvelous time."

She leaned back against the desk, resting her hips there. He saw the pouch forming at her waist and wondered at the tiny life growing inside her. When he looked up and met her eyes again, she was smiling. It was a smile of contentment, of happiness, of peace.

"He's growing."

"I noticed." He realized she had called the baby "he" and wondered if she had some maternal instinct that told her it was a boy.

"Each day I feel stronger. Each day," she said softly, "I know I'm happy I'm going to be a mother. That's not something I expected. That's something I can thank you for."

"Me?" How in the world was he possibly responsible for that?

"I had no idea what I was going to do when I found out I was pregnant. When Ryan left me I...well, I certainly knew I was on my own. But you...being here... it's given me something. I don't know if it's Windover, or the open space, or the kindness you and your grandmother have shown me..." She shrugged. "But I'm not afraid now. I don't feel alone. Thank you for that."

Instead of making him feel better, he felt the weight

of increased responsibility. For several years now his whole life had been responsibility—running Windover single-handedly, finding a way to keep it. Now he was responsible for this slip of a girl, one who'd been hurt as much as he, and her unborn child.

"You look so tired," she whispered, and her finger moved of its own accord, tracing along the edge of his face, tucking some errant hair over his ear. "Why do you put so much on yourself?"

"Because there's no one else," he replied, his voice weary and worn.

She tilted up his chin. "Not anymore. Let me help you, Connor, like you help me."

He reached down and touched her hand, gripping her fingers and pulling her down until she sat on his lap, while the chair leaned back with a resonant creak. Her hands fell instinctively over his shoulders, and wordlessly he looped his hands around her hips, holding her close.

She was warm, comforting, solid. Someone he could lean on and not fall. Her heart beat steadily against his shoulder and he pulled her closer. "Just this," he whispered and, somehow knowing exactly what he needed, she lifted her knees until she was snuggled in his arms.

And they sat that way in the twilight, until the sun disappeared behind the mountains and the moon rose over the prairie.

CHAPTER EIGHT

CONNOR STOOD IN the centre of the dressing room at a formal wear shop in Red Deer, rolling his eyes as the salesman fluttered around, checking seams and hems. This had been his grandmother's idea. He had thought he'd wear one of the two suits hanging in his closet. But, no, Gram had insisted he buy a new one. At least she wasn't asking him to rent a tuxedo. The plain black suit was well cut and of fine material. The shirt he wore was snowy white and stiff, contrasting with the light blue silk tie. It was more than he was used to, but he had to admit it looked nice.

He had considered resisting, but then he'd thought of Alex and her wedding dress in the plastic garment bag in her closet. He remembered how she'd sat on his lap, saying nothing, just being there for him, and he knew he would do it for her. For Connor, the week before the wedding had passed in a blur. Between working, the stress of dealing with the industry crisis, and wedding plans, he'd hardly had a moment to call his own. He should have been preoccupied with thoughts of the ranch, but instead all he'd been able to think about was marrying Alex.

He'd asked her for a paper marriage. Certainly he couldn't show her that his feelings were changing. Thankfully, he hadn't had any moments to share with

Alex this week. After their intimate scene the other night, it was far better to keep some distance between them. Especially since it was the very last thing he wanted. But what would happen after Gram left, and the two of them were left alone at Windover? He couldn't avoid her forever. And being near her...did something to him so unexpected and astonishing that he wanted to run *from* it as much as he wanted to run *Z* it.

He removed his jacket and handed it back to the salesman. He'd have to be very careful. They hadn't discussed any sort of time frame, yet he knew that when the baby was born and she was on her feet she'd want to be on her own, to start her own life—one that didn't include him. That was the arrangement they'd made, and he'd honor it.

He'd passed by the baby keepsakes in the jewelry store yesterday, wanting to buy a gift for her child yet knowing it would be a mistake. In the end he'd walked away from the silver money banks and cups. It was not his place to do such a thing, and no matter how his heart longed to, he knew it was impossible.

He had to guard his heart. Because she could have it all too easily.

WHEN HE STEPPED into the house, his errand finished and the garment bag in his hand, everything was quiet and still. "Alex?" His voice echoed through. Knitting his brows, he hung his suit over a doorknob and went in search of her.

He found them, together, in the garden in the mid-afternoon sun, their heads shaded from the sun. Gram wore her wide-brimmed straw hat, and Alex had taken one of his battered ball caps from the hook and pulled her dark ponytail through the back.

For a while he indulged himself and watched. They were laughing and chatting, Gram's knees resting on a green foam pad and Alex, more flexible, squatting beside a row of peas, pulling out weeds and depositing them in a metal bucket. Gram said something under her breath, and Alex's lilting laughter floated across the air to him. He smiled in response to the happy sound.

When he'd brought her here, she hadn't known a pea plant from a dandelion.

Alex reached for a weed, a little too far, lost her balance, and landed on her rump in the dirt.

Johanna lifted her head, tilted back her hat, and laughed heartily. He couldn't help but join in, and Alex swiveled her head to the sound.

He was chuckling, and she turned a brilliant shade of red that had nothing to do with hours in the sun.

"Sitting down on the job, Alex?" His long legs stepped over the rows of vegetables until he stood before her, offering his hand. "Gram won't give you a break? She always was a slave driver."

Alex took his hand. It was warm and rough, and her face flamed more at the touch. Since that night in the study she'd been careful to keep her hands to herself. And perhaps it was silly to get worked up over a little bit of contact. But each time he touched her it was easier to imagine things weren't as platonic as they seemed. She withdrew her fingers slowly, savoring the touch. It was all she would allow herself. It wouldn't do for her to get fanciful ideas only to have it ruin the tentative friendship they'd forged. Friends were hard to come by, and she'd had precious few over the years.

"Perhaps some lemonade's in order." Johanna's voice intruded. "I'll go in and whip some up."

Alex pulled her hand from Connor's and tried to smile at Johanna. "Let me help you."

"Alex, wait." Connor's voice stopped her. "Gram, we'll meet you inside in a minute." He turned back to Alex. "There's something I want to show you first."

He took her hand and led her around the side of the house towards the east lawn, where the ceremony was to be held. She followed, brushing her free hand against her leg to try and rid it of the garden dirt. "I hope the weather holds for Saturday," she tried cheerfully, knowing she sounded overly chatty but unable to stop the nervous quiver in her voice. "If it rains, I suppose we'll have to move everything inside."

"That would be a shame," he rejoined smoothly, and her feet stopped abruptly at the sight that greeted her.

"You...did you...make this yourself?"

She stared at a pristine white arch, perfectly curved and accented with fine half-inch lattice. She'd thought the only canopy they'd have on Saturday would be the fluttering leaves on the poplar tree, but this would add a special touch.

"I did."

"When did you find the time?" She pulled her hand from his, all eyes for the fine craftsmanship. Her fingers ran down the side, imagining it twined with ivy and a few roses here and there. "Oh, it's beautiful, Connor. Simply beautiful."

She turned back to him, gratified to see him smiling widely at her.

"You really like it? I wasn't sure it would fit in with your plans. This wedding stuff is a little out of my league. My brain shuts off when I hear the words 'floral arrangements' and 'table linens'."

"Fit in? It's perfect. Is this why you were spending all your evenings in the barn? I thought you were working with the livestock."

He raised his hands. "Guilty as charged."

She circled it, smoothing it with her hand, making it almost a caress. "I've always wanted one, but I figured the cost to rent one was too much, so I never even mentioned it."

Her voice trailed away. "I'll shut up now," she whispered, blushing while he stuck his hands in his pockets and laughed.

"You're welcome. I'm glad you like it."

"I do. It's perfect." *Like you,* she thought suddenly. He was nearly perfect. The perfect gentleman, solicitous and caring, generous and understanding. Hardworking and modest, and willing to accept her and her unborn child without judgement.

He stared at his feet suddenly. "I know Saturday isn't a regular wedding day, but…"

"I know what you meant by the thought, Connor." She smiled, a little ray of shy intimacy. "It's a romantic notion for a rancher, you know. And I appreciate it more than I can say."

Against her better judgement she went to stand before him and laid a hand on his forearm. "It's not wrong to have wishes, to pretend that this is something that it isn't. If we just went through with it, no fuss, no muss, it'd be cold…I'm glad you're not that type of person. It means a lot, knowing you want it to be special in some way. Even if it's not the real way." Even as she said it she felt wishes of her own start to rise up, and she pushed them down, struggling to remain practical.

His hand slid out of his pocket, folding her palm in his as his dark eyes plumbed her lighter blue ones. For a long moment he seemed to search for words, finding none.

Alex squeezed his hand, longing to stand on tiptoe and reassure him with a kiss, knowing she could not. The moment dragged on until she could hardly bear it.

"Gram probably has that lemonade ready," he murmured roughly. "We should go in." He touched a finger to her nose. "You're getting a sunburn, and I'm sure you don't want to walk down the aisle with a red nose."

She put a testing hand up to her face. "You're right. Let's go in."

He led the way, and all the while Alex felt like she was getting in far deeper than was prudent.

"I got my suit today," he said, taking a seat at the table and stretching out his legs. "Another thing you can check off your list."

"That's good. Because you've got two days before the wedding and everything is pretty much done." Johanna put a pitcher of pale yellow liquid in the middle of the table while Alex took out three glasses.

"Johanna's taken care of everything," she said, placing a tumbler before him. "Things are all set for Saturday. I could never have done it alone."

Doing it alone probably would have consisted of a Justice of the Peace in the living room, but watching Alex blossom under his grandmother's attention had been rewarding. She was more open, smiled more. There was a warmth that had been missing before, that now radiated from her. Gram had been right. Alex *had* been hungry for love. The way she was appreciative of everything, how she seemed to understand the meaning behind the smallest gesture, made him realize she took nothing for granted. It saddened him that her life had been difficult, yet it was singularly the strongest thing that drew him to her.

She certainly did not deserve to be hurt again, and he'd make sure that their relationship stayed in a place where they could always be friends. If his wedding promises meant nothing else, they would mean that.

In forty-eight hours, she'd be Mrs. Alexis Madsen. The minister would pronounce them husband and wife and he'd kiss her and they'd cut the cake and...

And he'd kiss her.

Dear Lord, he hadn't thought of that. His hand swiped over his mouth. Kissing Alex, in front of witnesses. If holding her hand caused her to blush, what would a kiss do? Would she sense his hesitation, or wonder at his motives? Could he satisfy himself with one kiss?

Connor pushed his chair away hastily, rising and putting his glass in the sink. "Thanks for the lemonade. I've gotta go."

Alex stared after Connor with wide eyes, hearing the screen door slap into the frame with a bang.

"What got into him?"

Johanna laughed, eyes twinkling. "I think he's realized he's getting married in two days."

Alex's eyes stared at the door as if she could see him on the other side of it, hurrying to the barn. "Two days," she whispered, desperate to quiet her churning nerves at the thought. In two days they would stand before his family and friends and make promises they didn't intend to keep.

Alex swallowed the lump in her throat, watching him cross the yard with long strides. Before that happened Alex knew they had to talk. Because there were promises, real ones, that needed to be made before they proceeded with this sham of a marriage.

THE PORTABLE ARCH was in place beneath the huge old poplar, and the white folding chairs, numbering only twenty-four, were in small, precise rows. Several feet away, over by the deck, was a dance floor, large and roughly constructed of plywood by an obliging neighbor. Leaned up against the deck were four long, foldable tables that tomorrow would be adorned with white tablecloths, all borrowed from the church. Inside the house, small cakes and sweets were in boxes in the freezer. Millie, Johanna's longtime friend, was providing the wedding feast. On one hand Alex was touched by the willingness of the Madsens' friends to help, yet on the other it only increased the pressure she felt, knowing she would be Mrs. Connor Madsen in name only.

Alex surveyed the backyard, her hands twisting nervously. She wasn't entirely sure Connor was going to go through with it. Ever since yesterday afternoon he'd made darn sure he'd kept his distance, only appearing when absolutely necessary. If he were having second thoughts, she wished he'd come and say so, put her out of her misery. One minute she was nervous as sin about the ceremony, and the next she was petrified she'd have to send the guests home due to lack of a groom.

Today he'd escaped early to the fields, only coming in for meals. The minister had arrived at five sharp, and Connor had rushed in from the barn to hastily go over the details of the ceremony tomorrow. But he'd been distracted, fidgeting like he wanted to be anywhere else. And who could blame him? She wasn't the world's greatest catch, now, was she? Granted, she'd improved, thanks to Johanna's help. She was learning about gardening and her cooking was getting better. She was for the first time putting down some roots, just like the fragile green plants sprouting in the garden.

Roots that were going to make it even harder to leave when the time came. But the fact remained she was pregnant with another man's baby. And even if she wanted to help Connor financially, her earning potential was severely limited. She'd never gone to school beyond twelfth grade. She knew in her head that this was only for a few months, but her heart was constantly disagreeing with her, picturing much, much more.

A real marriage. A real husband and a real home and a real family.

She laughed to herself. Well, if that wasn't putting the cart before the horse. This whole situation was so unorthodox she could do nothing more than shake her head at her turbulent feelings and hope for the best.

"You're looking glum."

Johanna's voice intruded behind her and she jumped, startled. "Sorry."

"Second thoughts?"

She turned to the older lady, seeing understanding on her face. "It's just…so close, you know?"

"You'll do fine. You've got backbone. You know what's right."

"But is this right?" she implored Johanna with her hands outstretched. "Is this fair to Connor? A temporary wife carrying someone else's baby? I got so wrapped up in the fun of planning tomorrow that I forgot what it's supposed to be about…and what it's really about."

Johanna's eyes softened, a glimmer of a smile tipping the corners of her mouth. "Oh, my dear," she murmured, putting a hand on Alex's hair. "Don't sell yourself short."

Alex swallowed. "But Connor…"

"Is upstairs in the shower, and hungry to boot. I'm off to Millie's to look after some last-minute arrangements."

So she and Connor would have time alone after all. Alex didn't know whether to be grateful or petrified.

When Connor came downstairs, Alex had fixed him a plate. He was clean-shaven, his hair brushed back and glistening with water from his shower. She recognized the fresh smell of his deodorant and the slightly spicy scent of his shampoo, and her stomach clenched.

"I'll get your chicken off the grill," she explained, hurrying outside to the barbeque to retrieve his chicken breast. He sat down quietly as she placed the plate before him, heaped with mixed greens, chicken, and macaroni salad.

"Gram made this before she left?" he asked, putting some of the salad in his mouth.

"No, I did."

His eyes met hers, and she sensed warmth in them for the first time in the past forty-eight hours.

"It tastes like hers. Exactly."

Alex smiled. "Well, I did tell you I was a good student."

"Aren't you eating?" He gestured to the place across from him with his fork.

"I ate earlier."

"I see."

Alex made herself busy around the kitchen while Connor finished his meal, and then, clearing his plate, she took a breath. She had to be a grownup and do this. And do it now before she lost her nerve.

"I think we should talk."

He stilled, wary, and Alex's nerves twisted and turned

as everything she'd planned to say went rushing out of her head completely.

"Talk about what?"

She put his dishes in the dishwasher, keeping her back towards him. *Coward,* she grumbled to herself. She had to do this. She was an adult. Difficult conversations had to be faced.

"About us. About what's going to happen tomorrow."

"I see."

She turned, facing him, but his expression was flat and completely closed off, and she wasn't sure how to proceed. "Please, Connor. I can't pretend that tomorrow is what it will look like."

"I can't either."

His words left her feeling strangely empty. She shouldn't want him to mean his vows, but somehow she did. It was wrong, and misguided, but she would admit only to herself that she had feelings for Connor. Deep feelings. Feelings he surely didn't reciprocate, so she'd do the right thing here.

"Our vows tomorrow...they're the forever kind." She sat in the chair next to him, resting her hands in her lap, the backs pressed together between her knees. "We both know that forever isn't what this is about." *No matter what my traitorous heart is saying right at this moment.* "But I think we should make promises. To each other, tonight, about what we can expect over the next several months."

"You mean temporary vows?"

"Yes," she breathed with relief, glad he understood what she was getting at.

He sighed, and she resisted the urge to reach up and tuck that errant piece of hair behind his ear, the one that always seemed determined to curl. His eyes searched her face, and she knew that she would never be able to resist him when he looked at her that way.

"This means a lot to you, doesn't it?"

She nodded. "Tomorrow…we'll just be making empty promises. I'm not comfortable with that. Because there are things I want to promise you. Truly."

Trembling, she reached out and took his workworn hand in hers. "I promise you, Connor, that for the time we're married I will do all I can to make your life easier, not harder. I'll try my best to look after the beautiful home you've entrusted me with, and—" she smiled faintly "—I'll try not to poison you with my bad cooking. I'll be a friend to you, and a comfort, if you'll let me. I'll help you in any way I can. You've only to ask. Those are the promises I can make to you."

Oh, his eyes. So warm, with compassion and understanding and with an edge of something she didn't quite comprehend. He covered her hand with his own and squeezed. "I have promises to make to you, too," he said softly. "Look at me, Alex," he commanded, when she dropped her eyes.

She met his gaze and was caught, unable to look away.

"I promise, Alex, to provide for you, and the baby you're carrying, for as long as you need. I promise to share my home with you, so that it's your home too, because you've been without one for so long. I promise that I won't be the one to hurt you, not when you've been hurt already. I will be *your* friend and *your* comfort, if you'll let me." His voice dropped, an intimate whisper as he repeated her own words back to her. "I'll help you in any way I can. You've only to ask. Those are the promises I can make to you."

Her eyes filled, shining with unshed tears at his words. He meant them. She knew it. And for her they were more romantic than any flowery vows from a book could ever be. Somehow this handsome man—still so much a stranger—knew exactly what she needed and was willing to give it to her, wholeheartedly, unreservedly.

In that shining moment she knew another truth that would make tomorrow even harder.

She was falling in love with Connor Madsen.

"Alex? Are you OK?"

Her eyes had closed against the brief shaft of bittersweet pain that pierced her as she realized the one man she couldn't have was the one she was falling head over heels in love with. Swallowing, she pushed back her chair and broke their hand clasp. "I'm fine. I'm just tired," she explained, avoiding the skeptical look that raised his eyebrows with doubt. "I think I'll get ready for bed. There's a lot to do tomorrow."

She avoided looking at him, knowing her abrupt change of mood had to be confusing.

"Mike's looking after the chores tomorrow. There's no need for either of us to get up at daybreak," he offered. "You should sleep in. Get your beauty rest."

"Thanks. For…for everything. Good night, Connor."

She fled before he saw the tears that glistened on her cheeks.

CHAPTER NINE

THE WEDDING DAY dawned clear, with a light blue sky sparsely dotted with fluffy white clouds. Alex woke at six. She'd retired early the night before but, instead of taking advantage, she knew she had to get up and help Johanna get things ready before she dressed in her gown.

Quietly she slipped from her room and down the hall to the bathroom. She wanted to avoid Connor at all costs this morning. It had nothing to do with it being bad luck to see the bride, but more about keeping a level head. It would be all too easy to let the romance of the day sweep her away. What she needed to do was make sure everything was in readiness for the guests. Make it seem real. She ran hot water and washed her face and brushed her teeth before tiptoeing back to her room to get dressed.

Connor heard her shuffling about. He'd been awake since four, but had stayed beneath the sheets, thinking. It had nothing to do with habit and everything to do with getting married today. Getting married to Alex.

He remembered the promises she'd made him. She tried hard, he could see that. She wanted to make things right for him, and for the life of him he couldn't figure out why. What made him so special? He was nothing more than a rancher trying to keep afloat.

Her eyes had held a suspicious sheen last night, and he'd thought for a moment or two that she was going to cry. But not Alex. He saw now she was strong, practical. The kind of woman who would face whatever needed facing without histrionics and tissues. The more he knew her, the more he respected her. And the more he found himself daydreaming about her prairie sky-blue eyes and the dark waterfall of her hair.

He swung out of bed, hurriedly pulling on a pair of faded jeans. There was something he needed to take care of—something that had kept him awake in the pale, sun-washed hours of dawn.

He heard her footsteps echo softly to the bathroom down the hall, and he slipped into her room to wait.

When she came back, his heart stopped at the sight she made. She halted her footsteps in surprise, seeing him sitting on the rumpled coverlet of the bed. In no more than a second he saw her tousled hair falling over her shoulders, the pristine white pajama set, which accented the fullness of her breasts and the growing bump at her midsection, and which ended mid-thigh, revealing shapely legs and pretty, dainty feet. The sight of her, fresh from her still-warm bed, made his heart stop.

"G...Good morning," she stuttered in surprise.

At her appearance, he rose, wiping his palms against the thighs of his jeans nervously. "I heard you get up. I hope that's OK?"

"Why wouldn't it be?"

"You're the one standing in the doorway like you're afraid to come in any further."

She *was* afraid. Thoughts of Connor had dominated her dreams, and he had been the first thing she'd thought of upon waking. For him to be here, now, in the quiet morning hours, seemed so...intimate.

She abruptly realized that she was standing in white

maternity pajamas which fell a bit shy of modest. Heat flooded her cheeks and down her neck.

He was waiting, and she went the rest of the way in. He took a few steps so that they were scant inches apart.

"What are you doing here?" she whispered, keeping her voice low.

He stepped even closer, so close she had to tilt her neck to look into his face, feeling the heat of his body radiating through the thin cotton she wore.

"Today is the big day," he whispered huskily.

Her head dropped so he couldn't see how flustered she became at the thought. "Everything is ready."

His hand found hers, and he squeezed her fingers. "Except for one thing."

Her eyes darted to his in confusion. This was feeling distinctly like romance, and after having him haunt her dreams she had little defence against him. As she gazed into his face his eyes darkened with something she didn't understand. But when he held her hand that way, and looked deeply into her eyes, her brain simply turned off and she started to babble.

"I can't see how anything is missing. We've seen to the cake, the flowers, the minister—"

"Alex."

She stopped talking and only stared, letting intimacy surround them in the silence. A jolt flashed through her entire body every time he said her name in *that* way, and in admitting it called herself ten times the fool. This wasn't part of the plan at all. She was far more comfortable dealing with Connor when he was being practical and realistic. The memory of saying their promises to each other last night echoed through her brain. It had been a turning point, she realized. For both of them.

They'd spoken from their hearts—and she couldn't speak for Connor, but voicing her intentions had made one thing crystal clear to Alex. She loved him. But this was a marriage of convenience only, and her girlish fancies were only serving as a terrible distraction. She had to remember why they were doing this. She had to remember that they needed to stay only friends if she were to come out of this with her heart intact.

"I'm a bit nervous, that's all." Her eyes fell on the closet, where even now her wedding dress hung, white perfection. She felt unworthy of it. Unworthy of him. It was meant to be a symbol of purity, but there was nothing pure about Alexis Grayson. Impoverished, uneducated, pregnant Alex.

In a few short hours she'd be wearing it, carrying a bouquet of roses and gardenia. It seemed like a wild, crazy dream.

"Me too."

His admission, instead of relaxing her, made her fingers curl with tension. Good God, one of them being jittery was bad enough. She'd been counting on him to keep a level head through all of this. She reminded herself yet again why she was doing it. Security was something she'd always craved, and now she knew she was going to be responsible for another life. She owed it to her child. This was all he'd asked of her. It wasn't much; it was too much.

Her hand drifted to her stomach and rested against the small mound there. His eyes softened as he placed his own hand, strong and warm, on top of hers.

"He's growing."

She swallowed and somehow managed to get out, "Every day."

She closed her eyes at the warmth of his hand seeping through her pajamas and into her core. In the time she'd been here he'd never touched her in such a way, or expressed an intimate interest in the life growing within her. The bubble of her belly was firm and taut, and when she opened her eyes his were shining down at her. He understood, she realized. In that moment, with his hand warm on the life she carried, for the first time she wished in her heart that this baby was his. He would be a wonderful father.

He cleared his throat as he removed his hand. "Are you wondering why I'm here?"

Without his touch her skin cooled, leaving her empty. She couldn't get used to that feeling, then. She'd miss it far too much when it was gone.

"Is there something we forgot?"

The hand that had touched her stomach slid up and cupped her neck gently, drawing her forward as her heart thundered. What was he doing? In all their days here together the closest they'd been was that night in his office, and that had been comfort. This didn't feel like comfort. It felt like…passion. Her body trembled beneath his hand. She wasn't prepared for passion. She wasn't prepared for what that might mean. This had to be about maintaining a friendly relationship so no one got hurt at the end. Why was he pulling her close, his gaze fixed on her lips?

"In a few short hours," he murmured, "we'll share our first kiss as husband and wife." His other hand lifted to slide under the hair at her neck. "I don't want our very first kiss to be in front of our guests. Private is much better, don't you think?"

"You… I… Oh, dear."

"I'd like to get it out of the way now," he said, and bent his head.

Her breath slid out, shaky and scared. "Connor," she started to protest weakly, "I don't…" If he kissed her now, she'd be lost completely.

He erased whatever should have come out next by placing his lips gently on hers.

His lips were warm and soft, and she let go of all her fears and misgivings and kissed him back. Greedily she tasted him, her heart leaping as his lips opened and invited her in. Still he was soft, patient, and devastating, as his mouth slid from hers and dropped fleeting kisses on her cheeks, her eyes, the tip of her ear. Oh, goodness, this was no "you may kiss the bride" kiss. This was a "give me five minutes and I'll have you in bed" kiss, and her knees turned to jelly at the thought of the still-warm bed only a few feet behind them. He caught her weight in his arms. Only when she heard herself moan did his mouth return to hers, consuming, leaving her full, then emptying her completely. Heaven. Heaven had to be being kissed by Connor Madsen.

Her arms lifted and wound around his neck, and she pressed herself closer to him, feeling the buffer of the baby between them. She'd never been the kind of woman to dwell on what could never be, not until the baby and Connor. Being with him, close to the life she'd always wanted and never had…something had changed inside her, stopped her from running from feelings and memories and made her sentimental and wistful. At this moment, with his lips warm and loving on hers, she felt the shadow of the girl she'd been in the woman she'd become, and knew the bittersweet pain of wanting what could never be. They had said they would be friends, and it had worked well until today. But from this day forward they would be married, in name only. And with shattering tenderness she tried to wordlessly show him that she would give him everything, if he'd only take it.

Breathing heavily, he pulled away, putting his hands firmly on Alex's shoulders. "God, I'm sorry. I didn't intend for that to happen."

Alex stepped away from his touch, the hands that were still burning fire through her skin. Her body was strangely weightless, humming like a plucked string.

"Me either."

Silence fell, heavy with implications. Because neither of them was saying it had been a mistake. Or expressing regret. Or promising it would never happen again.

"I should go help with chores, since I'm already up."

He made it to the door before he turned back. "Alex?"

"Yes?"

She kept her back to him. She didn't dare face him right now, not with what she knew was nothing other than naked longing on her face, and she incapable of hiding it.

"You're going to make a beautiful bride."

He escaped downstairs while she pressed her fingers to her tingling lips.

BY TWO O'CLOCK, Johanna shooed Alex out of the way. "Everything is ready, and Millie's on her way over with the food. Go start getting ready. I've a surprise coming for you in half an hour."

Alex halted halfway to the stairs. "A surprise? But you've done too much already."

"Hush. Go run yourself a bubble bath."

"Yes, boss," Alex grumbled. Everything was ready…

but Alex had never met most of the guests coming today. She wanted everything to be perfect.

If a month ago anyone had told her she'd be soaking in a tub of scented bubbles, preparing for her wedding, she would have had a good laugh. Now she wasn't laughing. Her body was a bundle of nerves. Suddenly this whole marriage thing had changed…since that kiss this morning.

She was sure it had meant more to her than to him. After all, it was easy to get swept away by desire, and she couldn't blame him for that. But as far as deeper feelings…Connor was marrying her to save Windover. She must not forget that. She could feel all she wanted, but she couldn't let herself act on it again. If she did she risked her heart truly being involved, and her heart was already damaged. She'd lost enough. If she could care less, she wouldn't lose as big. Right now she had to think damage control.

Stepping out of the bubbles, she wrapped a thick blue towel around herself and stared in the mirror. Today she was a bride. After tonight she would be Alex Madsen, Connor's wife. Johanna would go home, no longer chaperoning and running interference. And she and Connor would still be sleeping in separate bedrooms.

She dried her hair, letting the natural curl spring free in the silky locks. Her makeup she'd do last, at her dressing table. She slipped from the bathroom into her room.

There was no maid of honor to help her get ready today. Instead she was alone, and strangely she preferred it that way. Away from probing eyes and questions, away from the expected teasing and innuendoes so typical of weddings.

Johanna was downstairs, talking to her friend Millie,

the rattle of dishes and happy chatter syncopating the air. Steps came up the stairs, heavy ones. She waited, wrapped only in her towel. Drawers opened and closed with muffled thuds in Connor's room. Yes, things had changed. Even knowing he was on the other side of the wall, and that she was standing nearly naked in a towel, had her pulse leaping erratically in her throat. Girlish fantasies, she chided herself. *Get a grip, girl.* She frowned into the mirror.

Maybe it was just wedding fever. Weddings did strange things to people.

The shower started and she tried *not* to imagine him standing beneath the hot spray.

Dropping the towel, she dressed in the undergarments she'd bought for today. They weren't expensive, or even very fancy, but ordinary white cotton panties, with a swatch of lace at each hip, and a strapless bra, necessary for her growing breasts. She smiled at her reflection. She'd always wanted bigger breasts—but getting pregnant wasn't exactly how she'd planned on getting them.

Soberly she pulled on pantyhose—the control-top type for this one day, to minimize the bulge at her waist. She took the satin and organza creation from the white bag and stepped into it.

She was struggling with the last three inches of zipper when a knock sounded at the door. "Who is it?" she called. If it were Connor, there was no way she was opening it. The last thing they needed today was bad luck.

"It's Johanna. With your surprise."

Alex opened the door a crack. "OK. You can come in. I need help with my zipper anyway."

Johanna laughed, coming in, another younger, absolutely gorgeous woman with her. "Alex, this is Carmen. She's here to fix your hair and makeup."

Alex beamed, holding out a hand. "Nice to meet you. Especially nice since I'm not very good at either hair or makeup."

Carmen smiled. "Your hair is much like mine. Where's your headpiece?"

Johanna connected the hook and eye clasp at the back of the dress. "It's over there, on the bed." She turned Alex to face her. "That dress is perfect. I'll be back after I've dressed. With one more thing."

When Johanna returned, Alex was getting her lips painted. With one last brush, Carmen stood back. "There. You are perfect."

Alex rose, looked in the mirror, and wanted to cry.

Her eyes were large, and somehow more luminous than she could have imagined, while her skin appeared dewy and flawless. Her lips were etched and painted with a colour very close to her natural pigment, and her hair was pulled back gently from the sides, the remainder curling simply down her back. A small circlet of flowers sat daintily on her head, a thin, filmy veil drifting to her waist.

"I look like a bride." She touched a finger to her cheek that glistened with something like glitter. Oh, she'd tried desperately to avoid feeling like a fairytale princess, to stay grounded and realistic. Now her stomach danced with the thought of walking to Connor's side looking this way. What would he think? A flush crept up her neck. After the demonstration she'd put on this morning, he would certainly think she meant this to be a real wedding.

"A very beautiful one," Johanna whispered, and Alex

spun to see tears in Johanna's eyes. "Connor won't know what to do with himself."

Alex laughed. After this morning, she knew that Connor would know exactly what to do with himself. But she was pleased, more than pleased, with her appearance. "Thank you so much," she said to Carmen, squeezing her hands. "I love it."

"You are welcome." The woman packed up her bag and smiled on her way out the door. "I'll see you next week, Mrs. Madsen."

"Now. Sit for a moment. I have something for you."

"Something else?" Alex perched on the edge of the stool, facing away from the mirror. "Surely not."

"You know the saying. Something old, something new…"

"Something borrowed, something blue."

"That's right." Johanna pulled over a matching stool and sat, careful not to wrinkle her pale blue suit. She opened her clutch purse and took out a small box. "This should cover the 'borrowed' and 'blue' part."

Alex took the box with shaking fingers. Opening the lid, she found a square velvet box. Inside were nestled a sapphire and diamond necklace and earring set.

"They're gorgeous."

"Lars gave them to me on our tenth anniversary. Connor's mother wore them on her wedding day. And now it is your turn."

Alex carefully removed the earrings, took out her own pearl studs which she had planned on wearing, and replaced them with the antique sapphires. "Oh, Johanna." The oval stones were surrounded by tiny winking diamonds. She held up the necklace and Johanna fastened it around her neck.

"This isn't right. You're making this feel like a real wedding. And these are family heirlooms. It isn't right." She raised her hands, preparing to remove the earrings.

Johanna stopped her with a hand. "You need to keep an open mind."

It's not my mind I'm worried about, it's my heart, she thought wistfully, rising and impulsively hugging the woman she had to struggle to keep from calling Gram.

"Well," she choked, getting a little misty, "I have borrowed, blue, and new. I guess three out of four isn't bad."

"You'll have your fourth, don't worry." Johanna paused by the door. "I'll be back; it's almost time. Once Connor is in place I'll come get you."

She returned quickly. "It's time, Alex. Are you ready?"

Alex nodded. "As ready as I'm going to be."

Johanna smiled. "I've brought your bouquet. And I've got the ring. Connor's already asked me twice."

Neither she nor Connor had any attendants; instead Johanna was serving as their witness, carrying the ring and signing the marriage certificate. Alex followed her down the stairs, out the front door, and around the corner of the house. Connor stood with his back to the guests, chatting with the minister. Alex stared at his back. There was no turning back now. For better or worse they were going through with this sham, and her heart was a tangled mess of guilt and the illusion of romance. She would walk down the grassy aisle between the chairs and meet him, agreeing to spend her life with him. Only she, Connor and Johanna knew it was to be an abbreviated union.

Johanna gave a signal, squeezed Alex's hand, and left to take her seat. As soon as she was seated, Alex heard a guitar start a rendition of Pachelbel's "Canon", and somehow, she wasn't sure how, she made her feet move to the music.

Connor turned when the music started, and she paused as their eyes met. His brows lifted briefly in surprise, then a huge smile of approval swept over his face, the heat of it tangible even from several feet away. Faces turned in her direction, but she focused on none other than Connor and his melted-chocolate eyes as her slippers silently crushed the grass beneath her feet.

She stopped when he took three steps out of position and lifted his hand, offering it to her.

She took it.

"You look beautiful," he whispered, making her heart swell. He led her under the arch and before the minister, to begin their life together.

CHAPTER TEN

THE MINISTER'S VOICE intoned clearly. Numb, Alex's fingers shook in Connor's, her lips quivering as tears trembled on her lashes. To anyone looking on, she looked like a proper, emotional bride, gazing lovingly at her husband-to-be. She *felt* that way, though she didn't have a right to. Didn't have the right to pretend this was real. She was vaguely aware of the small sea of faces looking up at them, at the whisper of the breeze through the thin poplar leaves, of the sound of magpies chattering in the line of trees along the north pasture. She was more aware that Connor was holding her gaze steadily, of the way his suit jacket fit over his broad shoulders, of how he'd missed the tiniest spot shaving just beneath his left ear.

The next ten minutes passed in a haze, a series of impressions that left Alex feeling more and less than she'd expected. The feel of Connor's hand holding hers; the sound of the minister's voice offering a prayer; handing her bouquet off to take his fingers in hers.

She'd expected more clarity, more guilt, more shame. Less emotion, less longing, less love. Then why, oh why, did everything seem so *real?* So right—preordained, even? Was it only because she wanted it to be something it was not?

Then it was done. Connor took a gold band, studded

with a half-dozen tiny diamonds, and slipped it on to her finger, sealing their covenant of lies.

"You may kiss the bride."

That line came through her consciousness crystal clear, and she lifted startled eyes to Connor's. They were warm with understanding and the little secret of the kiss they'd already shared in the weak morning sunlight. Sealed with a kiss…

His mouth touched hers, paused, deepened, lingered, until he pulled away just enough that her lips followed ever so briefly. She stared at the fullness of his mouth, smudged with the colour of her lipstick, and her cheeks flamed as clapping erupted.

It was done. In the space of a few minutes and a single kiss she was Mrs. Connor Madsen. She let him take her hand and guide her down the aisle between the seats toward the shaded side of the house.

"ARE YOU OK?"

Connor's voice held more than a trace of concern, and Alex pasted on a smile, holding it there until she was sure it would stay on its own.

"Of course I am."

"You've hardly eaten anything."

There was a very good reason for that. Alex stared down at the sliced beef and potato salad on her plate. Now there was no turning back, and because of it, the gravity of what they were doing had sunk in. The marriage certificate was signed. And even if it hadn't been, she knew she'd made the horrible mistake of giving her heart to a man who didn't want it.

To stop his worrying, she popped a piece of meat

into her mouth and chewed. "There. I promise I'm not going to starve."

"You're supposed to be happy."

Connor leaned closer to her bare shoulder as they sat at one of the white-covered tables. To anyone watching it looked like nothing more than a new husband whispering something intimate to his bride, but to Alex it was a knife to the heart. Her wedding day. It *was* supposed to be happy, joyous, carefree. Instead it was bittersweet. Filled with wishes instead of dreams come true.

"I am happy," she lied, still keeping the forced smile in place. "It's been…a little tiring."

His hand rested warmly on her shoulder. Didn't he realize what he was doing to her with every tender glance, every simple touch?

"It won't be much longer." Connor nodded toward the band warming up on the deck, above the makeshift dance floor. "We can have a few dances and disappear."

Her fork clattered to her plate. Disappear? Like brides and grooms did?

"Sure," she choked out, trying desperately to swallow as she started coughing. She reached for her water glass, staring at the gold band winking on her finger. It didn't look like the typical thing Connor would buy. If he'd asked her, she would have said a plain, cheap gold band would have sufficed. She hadn't bought him one at all, and thought now perhaps she should have. But he'd commented once that he didn't wear rings because they were too much of a danger around the farm equipment. She hadn't persisted because in her own mind it would have tied him to her in a way that wasn't real.

The band played a few riffs, the drummer ran a little solo down his set, and the singer stepped up to the mic.

"Ladies and gentlemen," he said, gesturing with a hand, "Mr. and Mrs. Connor Madsen!"

Amid the clapping, Connor rose and held out his hand. She took it, let him lead her across the lawn to the plywood floor. There he took her into his arms as their guests smiled on.

Alex knew none of them. She'd been introduced after the ceremony, but she was still a stranger in this community where everyone knew everyone else and had for years. It drove home the fact that she didn't belong.

"You look beautiful," Connor murmured in her ear. "In case I haven't told you already."

Oh, his words. They had the power to hurt her now, when she knew he didn't actually mean them. Or perhaps he did mean them, just not the way she wanted him to.

Their feet shuffled to the slow beat of "Amazed", while Connor pulled her closer so that her belly was pressed firmly against him. His suit coat was gone, and the heat of his skin radiated through his white shirt, warming her in the evening cool. He'd loosened his tie, and the warm smell of his aftershave mingled with the scent of the wild roses that grew along the edge of the driveway. Her eyes closed as his fingers tightened around hers, and she rested her head against his shoulder.

I love you, Connor. She spoke the words in her heart, wishing she could say them aloud. How could she not? He was the first person to care about what happened to her in a long time. He was her rock, and she knew deep down she shouldn't rely on him too heavily, seeing as she'd be leaving in a few months. Yet she couldn't help herself. She was tired of being alone. The sigh slipped out before she thought to stop it.

Connor felt the soft breath of her sigh against his neck and swallowed. He wasn't sure how she'd managed it, but what had started out as a fine, sensible, platonic solution wasn't sensible or platonic any longer. He let his fingers slip up her back and under the lush dark curls cascading over her shoulders. Beautiful, and brave—so very brave. She didn't realize it, he bet, but she had that pregnancy glow that grandmothers talked about. A luminescence, a tranquility about her. Had he really thought he could marry her and then let her go? A strictly business arrangement?

Why couldn't there be a way to have both? If the time came and she still wanted out, honor said he'd have to let her go.

But what if he could convince her to stay in the meantime?

The song ended and they pulled apart. Going with instinct, Connor refused to relinquish her hand as she started to step away, instead giving it a tug and pulling her back to his arms. She looked stunned and he smiled, his teeth flashing in the twilight. His eyelids drifted closed and he kissed her.

There'd only been that one kiss under the arch during the ceremony, and he was determined to make this one good. There was clapping and cheering, but Connor blocked it out, urging her to respond, his blood firing recklessly as she finally did, lifting her hand and threading it through his hair as he held her close.

Their mouths parted; Connor gave a last seductive nibble on her lower lip. Her cheeks flamed as red as prairie fire.

"Whoo-eee!" The lead singer made a point of whooping it up. "We'd better have another dance, dontcha think?"

They started another country ballad and other couples joined them on the floor as Connor laughed, his heart lightening a bit. She wasn't immune. That kiss hadn't been faked. Their bodies slid together again, more relaxed.

"Do you like your ring?" he asked in her ear.

Alex looked up at him. "It's beautiful. But I didn't think you were going to buy something this fancy. You didn't need to spend the money…"

On something that was temporary. He heard the end of the sentence as clearly as if she'd spoken it aloud, but he chose to ignore it. "All it cost was a small cleaning bill," he explained, looking down into her eyes. Tiny rhinestones winked within her hair, he marvelled. "This ring belonged to my great-grandmother."

She paled, visibly. "You gave me a family heirloom? Are you crazy?"

He saw her eyes dart to Johanna, who was laughing and chatting with Millie and Reverend and Mrs. Wallace.

"I did. My mother wore it, and as my wife you should too."

"But…but…" She swallowed, then looked him square in the eye. "We both know I'm not really your wife."

"We could ask the minister. I'm pretty sure the certificate is legal."

She laughed in spite of herself. "I'm not sure that's a good idea."

"Don't worry so much."

"Well, if that isn't pot calling kettle," she retorted, leaning back to accuse him with her eyes. "It just doesn't seem right, you know?"

"I wanted you to have it. Right now let's enjoy dancing, OK? I haven't danced with you before, and this should be a night of firsts."

He let his body do the talking then, holding her close and swaying her gently to the music. He looked up; couples glided by them, smiling foolishly at the newlyweds.

The song ended, more beers were popped open at the coolers, and the band started a toe-tapping two-step.

"Come on," he called, tugging her arm, but she resisted.

"I can't."

"What do you mean, you can't?" Everyone and their dog knew how to two-step by the time they hit grade school, didn't they? He tugged her hand again.

"Seriously." Her smile dropped. "I don't know how. And I don't want to embarrass myself." Couples circled the dance floor, turning and stepping, and her eyes widened. "I'll trip everyone up."

He relented, pulling her to the soft grass to the side. "Then you'll have to learn," he answered. "Like this."

He held her in his arms. "You step backward. One, one-two-three, one, one-two-three, so that you keep going in a circle."

She tried it, did it twice, fumbled on the third. "I feel like an idiot."

"You look like an angel," he fired back, putting his hand back on her waist. "One, one-two-three." This time she managed several steps.

"OK. Now in time."

"You mean that wasn't?"

He laughed, full-throated, eyes twinkling. "Honey, that was half-time. We gotta double it up."

And they were off. "Don't look at your feet," he advised. "Relax." They circled around on the grass, her smile growing with each successful step.

"OK. Now we're going to try a turn."

"You're crazy."

"Oops, here we go," he answered, leading her smoothly through the turn. She returned to face him, back in step.

"I did it!"

In her excitement she forgot to one-two-three, her feet stuttering, halting them again. "Darn it."

"It's OK. Here we go again. And this time we'll turn you the other way."

He waited until she was going smoothly, then danced her over to the floor and lifted her up. He nodded to the band to keep going, they joined the circle and two-stepped with the rest.

When it was over, she was breathless and laughing. "That was fun! And I didn't even mess up too much!"

"You hungry now? You didn't eat much at dinner." He placed his hand at her back, feeling the warmth of her skin through the smooth fabric.

"I'm OK. Maybe some water."

They left the group waltzing away and headed to the refreshment table. The first stars were coming out and the air was cooling. Citronella torches lit the perimeter of the celebration area, keeping the mosquitoes at bay and casting a warm flickering glow over the gathering.

"I'm sorry about earlier," she apologized, her hands turning her plastic tumbler around and around.

"I think I understand. It wasn't exactly what it appeared to be, was it?"

"No."

He frowned, unsure of how to proceed. It was too

soon. If he did anything silly or sentimental she'd chalk it up to the mood of the day. And she'd be partially right, he admitted to himself. Weddings did bring out the romance in people. But what he had planned was more long-term…a wooing, he supposed, to use an old-fashioned term, and one he'd derided his grandmother for using only weeks ago.

He only had a few months to accomplish it, and he knew he had to make the most of every opportunity, wedding day or not.

"How's Junior holding up? Are you tired?"

"A little. But everyone's still here…"

"We can make our excuses. It's almost—well, expected."

Again the awkward silence.

"Alex, dear." Johanna slid up behind her and squeezed her shoulder. "I must be going. Millie's offered to drive me since…well…" She held up her glass and ice cubes tinkled. "I'm staying there tonight. Wouldn't be right, me staying here."

Alex averted her eyes, embarrassed. It wasn't like this was going to be a typical wedding night of champagne and passion, now, was it? Her body heated with the very thought of it.

Johanna continued on, unfazed. "You made a picture," she beamed. "And you too, Connor."

"You know, Grandmother, it used to be 'Connor dear' and then 'Alex'." He grinned widely. "But then, look at her," he went on, dropping his eyes to his wife's profile. "Today, *she* should come first."

Alex snorted, making light of his gallantry, yet unable to hide the telltale blush that bloomed on her cheeks.

"Get used to it, dear boy." Johanna winked at Alex

outrageously. "But you should probably throw the bouquet soon, don't you think?"

Alex nodded, not sure whether to be relieved the day was drawing to a close or to resent the fact that she was being told what to do *again*. For the most part she hadn't minded someone else taking the lead, relieving her of some of the responsibilities and decisions, but she'd been on her own long enough that at times it chafed.

Johanna left to notify the band, and Connor retrieved her bouquet from the table. "This is your last official duty of today," he commented. "Then we can disappear if you want."

The band leader called for all the single ladies, then held out his hand to help Alex up the stairs to the deck. She let the roses fly, straight into the hands of a pretty young blond with roses in her cheeks.

Duties done, Connor danced one more dance with his wife, then shepherded her to the front door, lifted her in his arms, and carried her over the threshold.

CHAPTER ELEVEN

"PUT ME DOWN, YOU IDIOT!"

Alex's laughter echoed through the dim foyer as she squirmed in his arms. Goodness, he'd lifted her as though she were as light as a feather, the warmth of his body flooding through her as her arms looped around his neck instinctively. Her heart raced at being in his arms, even if he were only acting silly.

They smiled at each other a long time, until Connor quietly commented, "It's good to hear you laugh."

"I haven't done it much lately. Neither have you."

"Perhaps now we can change that," he remarked, taking a step toward her.

Her heart leapt in her chest as he approached, but he merely passed by her and went to the fridge.

"The music will go on for another hour. Why don't you go change out of your dress? There's something I wanted to do earlier that I forgot."

She was about to refuse when the band began another song, the bass and drums pounding loudly, quelling any argument she might have made for retiring. "Oh, all right," she relented, heading for the stairs.

She struggled with the zipper at the back of her dress for nearly five minutes, but she'd be darned if she'd ask for his help. After that kiss on the dance floor, and the way he'd looked at her all night, the last thing she needed was his help undressing.

She paused, her hands splayed across her burgeoning belly, assessing. Before too long it would be very clear why they'd got married, and everyone would think the baby was Connor's. What, then, would people think when a few months after he or she was born they separated and she left with the child?

And why in the world was she worried about what others would think? It had never mattered before—but then she'd never let herself rely on anyone before either. She'd only had herself to worry about. She was finding that not being alone, even temporarily, was a big adjustment.

Alex pulled on baggy sweatpants and a sweatshirt. She hung up the dress carefully, running her fingers over the bodice wistfully. Oh, what a wedding day. And what a laughable wedding night. Alex in shabby clothes while her new husband made a midnight snack. Not a candle or bottle of champagne in sight. No white silk lingerie or rose petals spread on the bed.

When she returned downstairs the band was still playing and laughter echoed throughout the yard. Connor was placing wine goblets on the table. She followed and sat down.

"You look comfortable."

"I suppose." She helped herself to a strawberry from a small dish he'd placed in the middle of the table and dipped it in yogurt. "What do you think they'd say—" she gestured toward the backyard with her strawberry "—if they could see us now?"

His tie was gone and his shirt unbuttoned. Casually he twisted the top off a bottle of sparkling grape juice.

"Who cares? I didn't do this for them."

"Then who did you do it for?"

Brown eyes clashed with hers in the gray light. The longer he was silent the more she was drawn in, until she almost believed he'd done it for her. But that was silly. She'd told him already that a simple Justice of the Peace would have sufficed.

"For Windover," he said finally, settling back in his chair.

Of course. And she'd done it for the security of her child.

She picked another berry off the platter. "Thank you for everything you've done," she said, more strongly than she felt. She had to be realistic. That kiss during the dance had been merely for show, to avoid unpleasant questions. She understood that now. Nothing in the situation had changed, besides the fact that she had feelings that she couldn't reveal without making everything go pear-shaped. "Let's hope things go smoothly from here on in."

He poured the liquid into the glasses. "I knew you couldn't have champagne, but I wanted us to have a toast. It only seemed right." He recapped the bottle and chuckled. "A twist off top, though. Reminds me of college days."

He was trying to keep things light; the least she could do was go along. "A lovely vintage, I'm sure."

He handed her the glass, standing close by her side. "To the beginning of a great future, for both of us."

She raised her glass with a shaky hand, touching the rim to his before drinking. She should offer something in response, but everything she wanted to say would come out wrong.

She remembered looking up at the sky and seeing the first star appear earlier.

"To dreams coming true."

She closed her eyes and made a brief wish in her heart.

She'd put such childish things behind her long ago, but now, with so much at stake, she dared fate.

"To dreams," he answered, touching her glass in response.

ALEX WOKE LATE, past nine, to dim light and the sound of rain spattering against her window. Connor would have been up ages ago, despite the late hour they'd gone to bed, and she'd fully meant to get up at the usual time and make breakfast. He wouldn't be haying today, she realized.

Now that the wedding was over, she got out the clothes she'd been hiding—maternity jeans and a cute stretchy T-shirt in pale yellow that would grow with her over the coming months. She examined herself in the mirror. More comfortable, yes, but also very clear now that she was expecting. It was a relief and a strain all at once. But she couldn't hide it forever.

At the bottom of the stairs she was surprised to see Connor sitting at the table, drinking coffee.

He looked up as she stepped inside and smiled, a slice of warmth that made her tingly all over as his eyes assessed her new clothing.

"Well, well. I bet that feels better."

"Much."

"No more popping buttons or strained zippers?" He lifted his coffee cup, eyes twinkling above the rim.

"No, but thanks for pointing that out."

She went to the fridge, took out the milk and poured a glass for herself.

"A lot of men find pregnant women extremely attractive."

And would you be one of them? The question popped into her mind but not out of her mouth. Innuendoes had no place now. The most important thing was to keep things friendly and remember the end goal. Security for her baby, prosperity for Windover, and her heart left intact.

"It's probably something about the so-called 'glow'."

"I suppose. But it's more than that." He abandoned playing with his mug for a moment and studied her earnestly. "There's something about a woman, knowing she's carrying life inside her, nurturing it, loving it… It's…" His voice dropped off.

Despite the discomfort she was feeling at the moment, she urged him to continue. "It's what?"

"Sacred."

He rose and put his cup in the dishwasher, avoiding her gaze, and she knew he'd revealed more than he intended. Goodness, he couldn't be fighting attraction too, could he?

Of course not. That was more wishful thinking on her part.

When he turned back his cheeks were more relaxed, eyes friendly. "I didn't mean to be backward in paying a compliment," he explained. "What I meant to say is…I hope you're not self-conscious about it. You look wonderful."

She had been getting over the self-conscious bit— until now, that was, and she turned away before he saw her embarrassment.

"Have you been out to the barns already?" She changed the subject.

"Mike did the chores again, as a wedding present, so I slept in."

Despite her fatigue, sleep had been long in coming, and she wondered if it had for him as well. Had he lain on his side of the wall with wishes of his own? Had he been thinking, as she had, about what she'd always hoped her wedding would be? The real one, not the acting job they'd done yesterday. Although at times it hadn't felt much like acting...

"I've got meetings in Leduc this afternoon. I'm going to shower—unless you want to go first?"

"No, I'll clean up, I think," she replied, waving her hand at the leftover mess from the previous day. Empty trays littered the back counter, and their fruit platter and wine glasses sat partially full from their midnight repast. "Your grandmother will be coming back for her things, too."

It was a reminder that after this morning they'd be living here alone, unchaperoned. It added a degree of intimacy, an *element,* that lived and breathed as tangibly as both of them.

"By the way, the rodeo is next week." He shoved his hands in his pockets. "Don't make any plans, OK? I want to take you to the finals at least. It's a fun time."

She'd never been to a rodeo in her life. Her only experience with it had been changing the channel when the Calgary Stampede coverage came on in the summer. Men in dirty boots and cowboy hats, getting on livestock that *smelled* and getting knocked off. She smiled weakly. "I'm not sure rodeo's my thing."

His smile faded so quickly she knew she'd end up going just out of guilt.

"At least think about it." His voice had cooled considerably. "Everyone from around here goes. It might look funny if you didn't."

She fought the urge to remind him it had only been the previous night that he had said he didn't care what people thought. She certainly didn't want to start an argument only one day after their wedding.

He jogged up the stairs two at a time while she blew out a breath, wondering how they were going to stumble their way through the next six months if already they were tiptoeing around each other, dissecting words.

HE SHUT HIS binder and pushed back his chair now that the meeting was over. His thoughts should have been about the dire news he'd received today...but all he could think about was how he'd bungled things with Alex this morning.

First of all he'd gone on and on about how beautiful pregnant women were, then he'd got shot down about the rodeo. He'd forgotten, quite simply, that she wasn't a rancher's wife. She'd have no interest in rodeo, and the original agreement was only short term, so why would she bother putting herself out? She didn't want to stay here, so why did he want to convince her to stay?

He cared about her. He wasn't made to live alone, without being surrounded by family, and being with Alex felt *right*.

If she didn't want to go to the rodeo, he shouldn't press. As he packed up his briefcase, he realized that maybe she was self-conscious about the state of her pregnancy. Of the questions that would arise from relative strangers. It had probably been insensitive of him to mention it. But if he hadn't... He didn't want it to seem like he didn't want to take her anywhere. To keep her hidden.

"Oh, for Pete's sake," he muttered, scowling. Would he walk on eggshells for the next months, worried about making the wrong move? It had never been hard for him to make the difficult decisions before. He'd always been the strong one.

But the stakes were higher this time, and for the first time in his life he admitted something to himself. Something he'd avoided acknowledging throughout his grief for his family, or during the whole ranch crisis. Something he would never have disclosed to another living soul.

He was scared.

THE EVENING WAS QUIET, with only the fading sounds of the birds echoing through the soft twilight. Connor had disappeared after dinner, taking the ATV and going to the south pasture to check on stock. Now that the kitchen was cleaned up, Alex eschewed television, or even a book, and instead sat rocking gently in the porch swing, listening to the sounds of impending night and watching the moon rise off to her left.

Connor had worried about her feeling isolated out here in the middle of nowhere, but the brittle truth was that she'd felt far more alone in the various cities where she'd lived. She knew now that *people* did not cure loneliness. Only one thing did, and that was belonging.

But for how long?

There was an owl somewhere close by, his call echoing plaintively as she caught sight of low headlights ap-

proaching from the pasture. Soon after the drone of the
ATV engine reached her ears, then muted as it disappeared behind one of the barns. Minutes later Connor
appeared as she rocked the swing with a bare toe, sending it swaying gently back and forth.

"Everything OK?"

"Yeah. What a night."

"I know." She smiled up at him, pointing. "There's
an owl over there somewhere."

Suddenly a sorrowful howl threaded through the silence.

"Do the coyotes bother you?"

The toe kept the swing going. "No. I think they sound
wild and beautiful."

She patted the swing beside her, inviting him to sit.
He did, the swing creaking beneath the increased weight.
Just having him this close warmed the air around her,
raising the hairs on her arms. She stroked her fingers
down her arm, and without a word Connor rose, grabbed
an oversized fleece from the hook inside the door, and
handed it to her.

"Thanks."

He sat again, and they rocked in companionable silence as the night deepened and the coyotes howled
plaintively.

It was a marvel how they could sit and not feel the
need to speak. It was one of the things she most enjoyed
about his company. It was comfortable.

"I've thought about the rodeo. I'd like to go, if you
still want me to."

His body stayed still, but his head turned to the side,
watching her. "You don't have to if you don't want. I
don't want to pressure you."

"It would look odd if I didn't."

"So what? That doesn't matter. And there will likely be questions that you may not want to answer. I don't want to put you in that position."

"Are you saying you don't want me to go?" She met his eyes earnestly. "I can understand that. I mean, it's not like I'm going to be here that long. If you want to keep it low-key…"

He flinched. "That's not what I meant at all. I want you to be comfortable. You're welcome to come or not. It's up to you."

Now the silence was awkward and heavy.

After a few minutes he spoke. "This is the damnedest thing."

"I know." The swing creaked softly as it rocked back and forth. Alex kept her gaze fixed on the white moon as it rose across the prairie.

"Married, but not married. Stumbling around trying to make sure we say the right thing. Perhaps it would be better if we were just honest."

Fat chance. Alex knew she couldn't tell him how she felt. Not with their agreement being what it was. If he thought it was awkward now, what would it be like if she unburdened herself only to hear that he didn't feel the same?

"How honest?"

He laughed a little. "How about, I'd like you to come with me on Saturday, but I understand if you don't want to."

He was way too devastating when he laughed like that, his eyes sparkling darkly.

"I'd like to come. It'll be something new."

"About the questions you might face…"

Alex smiled, so widely he goggled. "What's so funny?"

"Nothing," she breathed, touching her hand to her tummy. "Oh, my."

"Alex?"

"The baby's moving." Her grin was a wide hosanna of joy. "Oh, Connor. I thought the last few days it was gas." She laughed. "But this is definitely it."

Instinctively she reached out and grabbed his hand, placing the wide palm on her hard cotton-covered tummy. "There. No, wait." She adjusted his hand, ignoring the startled expression that widened his eyes and flattened his chin.

He stared at his hand, then looked up to meet her gaze.

"Wait. She's really moving now."

"She?" He cocked his head inquisitively. "You think it's a girl? I thought you thought it was a boy?"

"Why would you think that?"

"That night in the den. You said, 'He's growing'."

"Well, I can't exactly call my child 'it' can I? For some reason I think now that she's a she. Mother's prerogative," she added with a smile. Alex couldn't explain it fully, but lately, as her shape had changed, she had a feeling that it was her little girl in there.

His hand was spreading its warmth, and she loved how it felt, solid and sure. If she had her wish, he would be the father to her baby. She removed his fingers, lifted up her T-shirt a few inches, and put his wide hand back on her bare skin.

The baby responded, sending a butterfly vibration skittering against their flattened hands. Connor's gaze flew up to hers.

"That is the most incredible thing I've ever felt," Connor whispered hoarsely. "What does it feel like inside?"

She shifted her shoulder so she was leaning more against him, the pose both intimate and comfortable. "I don't know. Sort of like a gas bubble rolling around, only bigger. Like..." *Like the butterflies I got when you first kissed me,* she thought.

"Like what?" His breath was warm against her hair.

"Like Christmas."

He smiled. She felt it against her scalp even though she couldn't see his face.

His hand shifted, still beneath the hem of her T-shirt, the tips of his fingers slipping cautiously beneath the waistband of her jeans.

It would take no more than a slight turn and she could fit against him. Kissing him. Feeling his hands on her skin, where she so desperately wanted them. Carnal. There was no other word for the way she felt right now. Pregnant or not.

But she'd die before making the first move.

CHAPTER TWELVE

HIS BODY WAS so close and warm that it was hard to think, and she scrambled to think of a topic to change the subject. She started to panic, until a single thought popped into her brain and she blurted it out. "So, you told me once that you wanted to be a vet before the accident. Why didn't you? What held you back?"

It was a good question, it turned out. The shift was complete, and he drew back a little. The cool night air pricked up goosebumps on her skin and she turned to look up into his face.

"And what would I have done with the farm, the herd?" His eyes evaded hers, staring out into the inky blackness as the moon went beneath a cloud. "The whole plan had been for Dad and Jim to run things while I did the schooling, set up the practice here, then Dad would slowly phase out into retirement and Jim and I would run things together. I couldn't just abandon Windover. I love it here. It fell to me to look after it."

"And you always take your responsibilities seriously."

"That's why they're responsibilities."

Alex heard the sad note in his voice and smiled. "I, for one, am glad of it, because you've saved me from being in quite a pickle."

He adjusted his arm, pulling her more securely into

the curve of his shoulder. "I like having you here—or hadn't you noticed?"

"You were lonely."

His voice came out over top of her hair, quiet against the wistful howl of coyotes on the hunt again.

"Yes, I was."

She hesitated before asking the next question, wanting to know, afraid of prying too deeply.

"Did...did you get to see them? To say goodbye?"

She felt his throat constrict, bob against her head, and she wondered if she'd indeed gone too far by asking such an intimate question. But all he said was a soft, "Yes."

She reached over and squeezed his hand, the one that moments ago had been resting on the soft stretched skin of her tummy. "Then you're lucky. I didn't. They only found—" She stopped, had to swallow against the painful constriction in her throat. This was silly. She hadn't gotten emotional over it for years. But Connor seemed to have the knack of bringing all her emotions shimmering just beneath the surface. She cleared her throat.

"They only found pieces of the plane and some... some body parts. I never had that chance. I wish I had. I wish I could have been prepared."

"Nothing prepares you for having your life ripped away from you," he murmured huskily.

"Suddenly I just resented so much, you know? Don't get me wrong. I've seen some pretty cool things, being the daughter of historians who traveled. But I guess we always want what we don't have. What I wanted was a regular life. A school year where I had perfect attendance. A mom who baked cookies for my lunch or was my Girl Guide leader. I wanted something more... normal."

"Stable and secure?"

"Yes."

"And then you sacrificed your own dreams just to stay afloat?"

"Sounds familiar, doesn't it, Connor?" She smiled against the side of his chest and felt rather than heard his soft chuckle as he silently conceded her point.

"So, Alex Grayson Madsen, what did you *want* to do?"

She perched up on her elbow and aimed an impish grin at him. "You ready?" At his nod, she continued. "I wanted to study to be a chef."

He laughed, the feeling warm and welcome. When her giggles joined his, his heart was lighter than it had been in a long time.

Their laughter faded to smiles, the smiles to soft gazes. Soul-baring didn't come easy to either of them, Connor realized. But they'd taken a step tonight. A step to understanding. A step to trusting. He stared at her full, soft lips, wondered how they would taste if he touched his mouth to hers.

"Alex."

He murmured it, sexy-soft, giving her hand a tug until she rested more closely against his chest. She shuddered as he leaned forward, his hair brushing against hers. The combination smelled like flowers and hay. The baby moved against his hand again as his lips nuzzled her ear-lobe and up along the side, making all the nerve-endings in her neck tighten with anticipation. Instinctively she moved her head against his ear, silently asking for more.

Connor's heart pounded heavily. Never in a million years had he considered that he'd be terrified of touching his own wife, or humbled at feeling a baby kick beneath his hand, especially one not his own.

But he was feeling both awe and need, and he took it slowly, nibbling on her ear, feeling all the electric parts where their bodies touched. She turned her head into his and he brushed light kisses against her jaw. When her weight shifted slightly, he let his hand slide to cradle her ribs intimately.

He sensed her fear and longing, recognizing it because he felt it himself. He couldn't meet her eyes, too afraid that she'd break away if he gave her the chance. With his right arm he pressed gently, until she turned into his body, and then he kissed her like he'd wanted to all day.

Connor was determined to coax her, yet it wasn't necessary as her warm lips met his equally, hungrily. She wanted him, he realized with a start. Without convincing or coercion. His breath came out with a rush and he pulled her up so she lay firmly across his chest, his hand threading through her hair to hold her head in place while his tongue swept into her mouth.

The coyotes howled and his heart sang as she pressed closer to him and his hand slid down over her shoulder, settling just under her arm, with his thumb grazing her full breast. Their cores were pressed together, the firmness of her swollen belly against the taut zipper of his jeans so that she was in no doubt of what was happening to him. Their lips parted and he slid his tongue seductively down the column of her neck.

"I want you," he groaned against her skin, the blood pounding through him furiously. He was sure she could feel a pulse from every inch of his body.

She moaned and arched and he slid up a bit, putting his arms beneath her knees as if to lift her.

"Stop," she breathed raggedly, but his answer was to kiss her again.

She pulled away. "Connor, stop. *Please.*"

He froze, struggling to breathe.

Finally her eyes met his. They were wide, the pupils dark with arousal and tinged with fear.

"I can't…"

"Can't?" He said it softly, but it came out strained. So much at stake, fraught with complications, but all he was thinking about right now was taking her upstairs and loving her thoroughly. He shouldn't feel this attraction, not after this brief amount of time, and not when she was pregnant with another man's baby. Heck, he wasn't even sure if she was still in love with the father or not, and all he could think about was kissing the wounded look off her face.

She pushed herself out of his arms, staring at him now with something akin to panic. He didn't adjust his position. He stayed half reclined on the swing, hiding nothing from her.

"It's too soo…I mean, it's too much," she stammered, her face white in the moonshine.

"You were going to say it's too soon." He blinked slowly, holding her tethered with his eyes. "Which means you want to."

She backed up a few steps and her eyes skittered away. "It's far more complicated than that."

"You're my wife."

Alex's eyes snapped to his, something in her clicking into place at the warm, proprietary tone in his voice. She wanted to believe. But that was the whole problem.

She wanted to believe so much that she wasn't sure she could be objective. She could be only hearing what she wanted to hear. She wanted Connor to want her to stay, but by his own admission he hadn't been in a relationship for a while. It was only natural to get caught up in their situation, wasn't it? But what would happen later? What if he changed his mind, realizing that he didn't want to be married to her anymore?

There was too much at stake to let this progress into something that would only be temporary. And leaving after knowing what it was like to make love to him would be unbearable.

She had to take a step back.

"In name."

His eyes cooled, hot magma to cold ash. "Right."

"Look, it's a hard situation…" She blushed at his snort of sarcasm at her terminology. "We got caught up in the moment, that's all."

"Sure. The moment." He pushed himself up, sitting on the swing now with an unreadable expression masking his face.

"It's simply not sensible, Connor. Surely you can see that? We made an agree—"

"An agreement, yeah-yeah," he broke in impatiently. "I know all about the agreement. I thought it up, remember?"

"You're angry."

He sighed, running his fingers through his hair. It fell raggedly around his face and she wondered how any woman remained immune to him, the way his eyes glowed brown and gold in the moonlight, how he always seemed to have that sexy shadow of stubble by the end of the day…

She shook her head. *Big picture, big picture,* she repeated to herself.

"I'm frustrated. We both know this has gone beyond friendship. Even if you try to deny it, you know it's true."

Her mouth opened and shut like a fish in a bowl. He rose from the swing, and briefly Alex was reminded of a mountain lion, strong, sinuous, stalking its prey. She was helpless as he took slow, deliberate steps until he stood before her, tall, imposing, hard, sexy as sin. Her throat closed over as she tried to swallow. How hard would he press his case? And how strong was she to resist?

His hand, warm and callused, gently cupped the soft skin of her jaw, and her breath came in shallow gasps. She must not, could not, do anything she'd regret.

"Do you know how beautiful you are in the moonlight?" His voice was husky, intimate.

She said nothing, determined to stand her ground, knowing if she spoke she'd say something that would play right into his hands.

"I haven't been able to stop thinking of you since that kiss on our wedding day. But you know that, don't you?"

Dear Lord, he was trying to seduce her, and doing a most fine job of it. Of course she knew, because she'd done nothing but think of him either. She wanted to believe him. The risk-taker in her begged to be freed, to let go and see where it led.

But she was something else now too—a mother. And the baby inside her demanded that she use caution. To be sure. Right now she was sure of two things. She was sure she was in love with him already, and she was sure he wanted her. But beyond that she wasn't sure he loved her, wasn't sure he wanted her to stay here forever. She didn't trust it because she wanted it too much. And taking a risk on love wasn't something she was equipped to do—not anymore.

She calmly reached up, removed his hand, and stepped back.

"I know you want me. But wanting me isn't enough. I have a child to consider. *My baby.* I won't complicate things further than they are already complicated by sleeping with you."

She reached out and placed a hand on his forearm, not wanting him to go away mad.

"Friends, remember? Helping each other. Caring for each other. That's what I need right now. And that's what you need too."

He looked past her shoulder, out toward the mountains that hulked black in the distance. "You're right, of course," he replied, his voice strangely thick. "Caught in the moment."

He turned away, back into the house, leaving her shivering in the night air and more confused than ever.

SOLICITOUS.

That was the word to describe his behavior toward her over the past week. Polite, kind, solicitous. But never intimate. There was nothing to fault in his treatment of her, nothing at all. Yet something was missing. A spark, that hint of something more, that had kept her looking forward to seeing him and dreading it at the same time. She missed it. But it was what she'd asked for.

She zipped up her jeans, pulling her pink maternity top over the waistband. It wasn't exactly what she imagined people wore to the rodeo, but she didn't exactly have an extensive wardrobe. Connor had said jeans were fine, not everyone dressed in cowboy boots and black hats. He'd smiled when he'd said it, but the old teasing was gone.

Had she hurt his feelings so much? It was difficult to imagine. You could only hurt people you cared about, and she wasn't at all sure of him. More than likely it was his male pride she'd wounded. Yes, that was a much more reasonable explanation for his icy, polite manner of late.

"Alex? You ready?"

Connor's voice echoed up the stairs and she looked in the mirror one last time. Her first public appearance as Connor's wife, and now everyone would know she was pregnant.

Everyone would think it was his.

For the first time she realized that today was going to be difficult for him too. He wouldn't admit to the baby being someone else's, so he was going to have to pretend to be a happy expectant father. Or would he? How was he going to react? She wished now that they'd discussed it, but things had been cool and reserved lately, not exactly the best atmosphere for a heart-to-heart.

No matter. Whatever happened today, it was going to take a great deal of acting ability on both their parts.

Downstairs, he was waiting impatiently in the foyer, looking handsomer than she'd ever seen him. Snug jeans fit down his long legs, a white shirt with blue vertical stripes tucked into the waistband, emphasizing the breadth of his chest and shoulders. He wore boots on his feet and held a black hat in his hand.

He was, she discovered, a cowboy at heart.

"I brought you your sweater. The breeze is chilly today."

"Thank you," she murmured, taking it from his outstretched hand. Her eyes lifted of their own accord and met his. For some silly reason she wanted to say *I'm sorry,* although she couldn't have said why. Instead she slid her arms through the sleeves and grabbed the tiny purse she was taking, sliding out the door before him.

The drive to the rodeo grounds was quiet and blessedly short. As Connor found a place to park, she stared at the wedding ring on her finger and broached the subject that had been on her mind the whole drive.

"People are going to notice. Are you OK with that?"

His eyes were glued to the sideview mirror. "I don't have much choice, unless I keep you hidden from now until Christmas."

Ouch. Honesty hurt.

"What I mean is, are you up to answering the questions they're going to ask?"

"Are you?"

"I don't know. I somehow think it'll be easier for me. I'm the pregnant one. The baby is mine. You married me. There'll be some talk about the rushed marriage, but…" She paused as he turned off the ignition and looked over at her. "But you're going to get congratulated on being the father. It might be hard for you to pretend everything is what it seems."

If she only knew.

The truth was, every question was going to be a reminder that the baby *wasn't* his. A slap in the face. And he'd feel it as acutely as he'd felt her rejection last week. Even if her logic had been dead on, it had still hurt. Because he'd fallen for her. And everywhere he turned these days he found reminders that their time together wasn't permanent.

He'd thought that the chemistry between them would have been enough to bridge the gap, for him to work on her, to make her see that he didn't want her to leave. Instead she'd shot him down and left his head spinning.

"I can handle it."

"Then I can too." She attempted a confident smile that fell flat.

He didn't answer, but got out of the truck, came over to her side and helped her down. "Here we go," he said quietly, taking her hand and leading her toward the entrance.

All eyes were on them as they approached the grandstand. Eyes darted instantly to her midsection, and Alex felt like her lips were permanently stretched and superglued into position. Connor held her hand steadily and nodded hello to neighbors and acquaintances.

He leaned over and whispered in her ear. "Do you want to sit down? You might feel less conspicuous."

"Won't that look silly?"

He tugged her hand, pulling her close. "Not when the events are going to start any minute. Try to relax and have fun."

He found them seats midfield and crossed a booted ankle over his knee. The announcer started up, his deep voice carrying over the loudspeakers with an auctioneer-like twang.

It was fun, all of it. Alex found herself leaning on the edge of her seat during the barrel racing, laughing outrageously at the crash-helmeted children "mutton busting", giggling as one after another the woolly sheep rid their backs of their cargo. She gasped at the bareback broncs and snorted with fun at the wild cow milking competition.

During the saddlebroncs, Connor nudged her arm.

"You hungry or thirsty? I thought I might go grab something."

Alex looked around. The stands were jam-packed in the warm June sun, many heads shaded with cowboy hats and hands holding plastic cups of beer or the traditional beef-on-a-bun sandwiches. The scent of the beef did nothing for her and she smiled faintly. "Something cold to drink might be nice."

"Do you want to come with me?"

Her legs were stiff from sitting most of the afternoon, but then she thought of all the neighbors and townspeople, waiting to ask questions, and decided against it. "I think I'll wait here, if it's all the same to you," she answered, trying to smile.

She immediately regretted that choice once he was gone. Alex hadn't quite realized how much she'd relied on the security and protection his presence provided. Now, sitting alone as one by one the riders flew off their horses and into the dusty ring, she felt eyes on her, assessing, calculating. The shape she'd hidden very successfully was now out in the open, and she knew that minds were counting calendars and speculating about the happy event.

Not one person here had heard a whisper of Connor having a relationship, let alone a baby on the way. Now suddenly within a month he was here, married, and with a clearly pregnant wife. She felt every unasked question closing her in until she knew she had to move or scream.

And she'd left Connor to field those questions alone.

She waited several more minutes, feeling like she was in a fishbowl with the water draining fast. As the bull riding began, she left her seat and went to find him.

She caught sight of him from behind at first, standing to one side, a plastic cup in one hand and a bottle of water in the other. His weight was on one hip and she remembered being pressed close to him only a few nights ago, his body hard and sure against hers. He was talking to a young bronc rider who was laughing, his shaggy, copper-colored hair pressed into a sweaty circle from the hat he held in his hand, his jeans sporting one long brown streak of dust.

As she approached from behind the beer tent, she caught the rollicking sound of the man's laugh. "Damn, but that horse was scary. I lasted all of four seconds."

"That's longer than usual, if what the women around here say is true," Connor jabbed, and the man laughed, his teeth even whiter against the dust coating his face.

"Yeah, but what a ride."

She watched Connor take a drink, scuffing his boot in the dirt as he laughed.

Alex stopped. She shouldn't eavesdrop, she knew that. But Connor's voice was rich and low, that same tone that normally sent shivers up her spine.

She retreated behind the beer tent.

She didn't want to hear what answers he provided to the questions that were sure to follow. How many of his neighbors, his associates, had stopped him today and asked about his pregnant wife? He'd been gone over half an hour. How many times had he been expected to show excitement about being a father? How much had he had to pretend that he was in love with his wife? All the while knowing he was lying to their faces?

She couldn't do it anymore.

Her baby deserved more than a mother who lied for money, and that was exactly what it came down to. The longer she stayed, the more lies piled one on top of the other until there was no telling them apart. The beginning and the platonic marriage, then lying to herself that it was all right. Lying to Connor now about her true feelings. Living in constant fear of the truth.

Her stomach lurched painfully; she swallowed back the tears gathering in her throat. It wouldn't do to be caught crying at the rodeo. A bubble of hysterical laughter rose. That sounded exactly like one of the country songs Connor was always playing on the radio. She stepped back, unsure of what to do next.

She couldn't go back to her seat, not alone and not like this. She didn't have keys to the truck, so she couldn't go home. Instead she walked back to the abandoned parking area, toward the pickup under the poplar tree. Her hands shook as she lifted the lever for the tailgate, lowered it down, and hopped up.

Alex slid to the middle of the box, lowered her head to her knees, and tried valiantly not to cry.

She failed.

CHAPTER THIRTEEN

HER SEAT WAS EMPTY.

She must have gotten tired of waiting for him. The bull riding was still ongoing, but had to be finishing soon. She couldn't have gone far...

He wandered around for a good ten minutes before he finally thought to check the truck.

His heart leapt to his throat at the sight of her crouched in the back of the truckbed.

"Alex?"

She lifted her head, tendrils of hair straggling around her cheeks.

She'd been crying. A flash of anger shot through him at whoever had said something to make her cry. He shouldn't have left her alone for so long. Lord only knew what questions she'd been asked. He'd fielded his share, and was left feeling a bit raw as a result.

"What's wrong?"

She straightened, pushed back her hair behind her ears, and wiped her cheeks with her fingers. "Nothing."

"You never cry. You hate crying." He remembered her saying that the night of the ruined meal, and said it with a smile, trying to cajole her out of her tears.

He hopped up on the tailgate and started to approach the back of the truckbed, where she was huddled. He halted when he saw what looked like accusation on her face. Was she mad at *him?*

"Honey?"

"I'm not your honey." She lifted her head, sniffed once, effectively shutting him out. "I'd like to go home now, please. I have a headache."

She was downright frosty, and he took off his hat, squatting down a few feet away from her.

"I'm sorry I left you so long. I got talking and…"

"I know."

The words came out bitingly cold and he froze. "You saw me?"

"I did."

She saw the guilt spread over his face, the way he averted his eyes suddenly and his cheeks flushed. She had to be careful, very careful. She hadn't really heard anything, but by his reaction she knew that he'd been asked those horrible, awkward questions.

The very reason she was upset was the reason that she couldn't tell the truth. It wasn't that he'd left her alone. It was carrying guilt around like a noose around her neck. It was that she knew once and for all that her feelings were unrequited, and it made her more vulnerable than ever before. She should have walked away that first moment he'd had those yellow roses in his hands.

She'd allowed herself to get her hopes up. He'd called her his wife, kissed her, held her. Was she wrong in her interpretation of that? Then, on the other hand, he'd said he was sticking to their original agreement. This had all been a horrible mistake—she knew that now—and somehow she had to fix it. Right after she said her piece.

"What did you hear?" His voice was quiet, and a bit wary, and she bravely met his eyes, giving him the only answer she could.

"You told, didn't you? You told our secret. I thought

it was only going to be you, me and your grandmother. It wasn't for everyone to know."

Connor looked around, then leaned closer, not wanting this conversation to be heard by the general population.

"I didn't say a word, I swear. I wouldn't do that."

"That's hardly the point now, is it?" She sniffed again, eyes clear of any tears now. She knew that she sounded unreasonable but seemed unable to stop. "I realized something today. It's different for you. Not that it should be, mind you, but once word of this gets out I'll judged. I'll be completely humiliated! A pathetic loser! So desperate I'd sell my soul to a complete stranger! You'll be poor Connor, taken in by that money-grubber. Because eventually the truth *will* come out, Connor. And I can't live with that lie any longer. I can't pretend for the world that this is some perfect marriage. Someday you'll let it slip. You won't mean to. But you will."

It didn't occur to her that perhaps she was being a tad melodramatic. Instead she was stripped of her pride, laid bare as the impostor she knew she was. The salt in the wound was that she wasn't as cold and heartless as she appeared. Her feelings ran deep; her wants and desires, longings and fears.

Reduced to this.

"I won't tell, I promise. You can trust me."

"Right."

Connor looked around him; the crowd was milling about now that the afternoon events were completed. Unless they wanted a scene in front of half the town, it would be better altogether if they left now.

"Let's finish this at home, OK? In private. I'm assuming you don't want this to be overheard?"

She ignored the hand he offered her, instead getting to her feet and hopping out of the back of the truck without assistance. He followed her, opening her door and shutting it behind her before jogging around to the driver's side and getting in.

She stared out the window as she spoke to him. "This isn't over, you know. I still have a lot more to say."

"I'm sure you do."

He pulled out of the lot, letting the radio do the talking in the tense silence.

Alex stared straight ahead. She couldn't look at him. If she did she knew she'd lose her nerve. She needed to remain cool and objective right now, the way she should have all along.

The initial agreement had been a platonic marriage for a short term. Money would change hands. Everyone would get what they wanted. Instead she'd come up here in the middle of nowhere, stupidly looking for something that didn't exist. A happy ending. A fool wishing on stars. Now look where that had got her. She would have been lonely, but a hell of a lot happier if she'd stayed where she was.

The fact of the matter was, all Connor needed for the money was a marriage certificate. It didn't hinge on her actually *living* at Windover. Perhaps she should have insisted on that from the beginning. But she'd felt at home at the ranch, and she'd never questioned the decision to remain there until the baby was born. Until now. Why hadn't she thought of this before? She wasn't sure. But she was positive that, knowing her feelings, and knowing they were not returned in kind, she had to leave.

Connor pulled into the driveway and killed the engine. She hopped out, not waiting for him but using her own key to open the front door.

"Alex, wait," he called out from the foyer. She was already at the second step of the stairs.

He put his hand on the banister. "Are you OK?"

"I'm fine," she replied, taking another step.

"You don't sound fine. You don't *act* fine. I think we should talk about this."

"You want to talk? Be careful what you wish for, Connor. Because I'm still really angry."

"You don't hold the franchise on that, by the way." He bit the words back at her, hard verbal pellets. "I'd like to know exactly when I gave you the impression that you couldn't trust me."

She ignored the question, since she didn't have an answer. Instead she spun on the steps and marched back down to the bottom. "You know, we agreed to get married for your trust fund. You agreed to support me and the baby. That scenario doesn't require me to actually *live* here. I'm thinking it's probably best if I find my own place. I'll help out as much as I can if you'll give me some assistance with rent."

His mouth fell open in blatant shock. "Are you joking?"

"Not at all." He crowded her at the bottom of the stairs, close enough that she smelled the aftershave and dust and leather that made up the scent that was distinctly *Connor*. Even now, when she was spitting mad, hurt, and God knew what other emotion in the spectrum, just his smell had the power to bring to the surface all the longing she had for him. She pursed her lips and skirted around him, stalking toward the living room.

"It might be easier all around, rather than pretending that this is something it very clearly isn't."

The words echoed in a very sudden stillness, until his deep voice broke the awkward silence.

"Where would you go?" Already he felt how empty the house would be without her. The thought of her gone, even after so short a time, was like taking a living, breathing house and killing the pulse. In a few short weeks she'd made it a home again.

"It doesn't make sense," he continued. "It's ridiculous... Just take a deep breath and let your hormones settle, will you?"

"Hormones? You're going to blame this on *hormones?*" Her mouth dropped open. She was incensed he'd even insinuate such a thing! "You don't understand anything, do you?"

She turned to run but he caught her by the forearm. "Then you'd better explain it to me. What's really going on?"

Her eyes blazed into his for a long moment. The words *I love you but you don't love me back* raced through her mind, but thankfully stopped at her lips. She took deep breaths, willing him to let go of her arm. When he didn't, it took all the strength she had to answer quietly, deathly calm.

"From where I'm standing, it makes perfect sense. We both knew this plan was over the top to begin with. I'm not handling the strain well. I'm not good at pretending, Connor. I don't like lying. I can't do another six months of this."

If he thought she meant their agreement and *that* deception, well and good. It was better that he didn't know the pretending she meant was pretending not to love him when she did, so very desperately. She'd been humiliated enough. She wouldn't go a step further and make it worse by embarrassing him with flowery statements of unrequited devotion.

Connor withdrew, opened the patio doors and stepped out onto the deck. What was he going to do now? She'd already pulled away from him once; today she was suggesting she leave altogether. How could he explain how he felt now? It was obvious that her withdrawal the other night had been genuine. She didn't want him. He'd come on too strong the other night. He stared across the fields at the mountains, watched a hawk circling above, on the hunt for prairie dogs.

It wouldn't be fair to ask her to stay somewhere where she wasn't happy. But the option was life without her, and he couldn't accept that. Somehow he had to make her see that she could trust him. And trust him with her heart. He had to keep her here to do that.

He'd lost too many of those he'd loved. He wouldn't allow himself to lose another.

"Don't go," he whispered hoarsely, sensing her somewhere behind him. Somehow even the air changed when she was near. He knew he'd been right when she answered.

"I think I have to."

He turned his back on the peaks to the west and shook his head. "I'm sorry. I should have discussed it with you more before we went to the rodeo. I should have made sure you were comfortable with going. I...I hadn't thought out how I was going to answer questions about us. But I swear to you, Alexis, I didn't say anything about our arrangement."

"I felt so...cheap. Like everyone was looking and judging, even without knowing the truth."

Despite any fears, her words sparked something in him he could not ignore. He stepped forward and put his hands on her wrists. "Never. Not you. You are honorable and kind and good."

She pulled her hands away from his. "Someone honorable and good wouldn't have married for money."

"Someone honorable and good wouldn't have convinced a pregnant woman to marry him for a trust fund either."

"But that's why I should go—don't you see? At least if I leave it'll be honest."

He turned away from the earnest look on her face. Honest? Hardly. But the truth would send her running faster than any misapprehensions she was under now.

"I don't want you to go." He said it with his back to her. "That's honest."

"Why? Why does it matter where I live?"

"It just matters, OK?"

She'd looked like a scared jackrabbit the other night after he'd kissed her. If she knew he had real, deep feelings for her she'd panic and bolt. He knew that for sure now.

He kept his back to her as he tried what he could manage of an explanation. "I want you here. I want to know that you and the baby are fine. I enjoy your company, if it comes right down to it. I've rattled around in this old house for so long, having someone else here has spoiled me."

"I'm going eventually anyway. Why does it matter if it's now or in a few months?"

Connor turned and looked at her again. No matter how she protested, he could see her distress by the brightness of her eyes, the way her hand shook as it rested against the soft cotton of her top. She was upset—distraught, even. Now was not the time for her to be making rash decisions.

"You're far too upset right now to make any permanent decisions. I can't let you leave this way, Alex, I'm sorry."

He couldn't decipher the expression on her face. It had flattened with surprise, like she didn't quite know what to make of it.

"You're *forbidding* me?"

"For now, yes." He paused, gentling his voice. "Alex, I'm asking you to stay. To let this arrangement play out."

Oh, dear Lord. What was she going to do now? Her head said *go*. Staying any longer would only make leaving harder in the end. Staying and falling harder for him, knowing he didn't feel the same, would be torture.

She looked into his eyes. She'd never been able to resist his eyes; she should have known better. But in the moment their eyes met it was like she could hear him speaking, although his lips never moved.

Don't leave. Stay with me.

He might not be the biological father to her baby. And they had started out their relationship as strangers. But in her heart she also knew there was something more between them. Whether or not it was love, she couldn't be sure. But she did know there was a heart-to-heart recognition, and more—a need. They filled a need in each other. She gave the only answer she could possibly give.

"All right. I'll stay. For now."

The truce was a tentative one. It was like they both realized how tenuous a relationship they'd forged, one that could be easily damaged, even broken. They walked on eggshells around each other, keeping to the most inane pleasantries. In the following days there were no more intimate rocks on the porch swing, no more kisses in the moonlight or long looks across the breakfast table.

It was, in fact, very much like they'd both envisioned in the beginning. Friendly. Amicable. Completely and absolutely platonic.

Alex alternated between being glad she'd stayed and being angry at herself for not having the fortitude to leave.

Connor was friendly, what she would assume was his normal happy self. He smiled and joked at mealtimes, enquired solicitously how she was feeling, made plans for the ranch when the money came through.

But she missed their intimacy terribly.

She held back too. She took pleasure in keeping the house scrubbed and shined, improved her cooking by sheer force of will, and picked the very first greens from the garden—the first she'd ever grown on her own. But there were no more languid looks from across the room, and when the baby kicked she smiled to herself and ran her hand over her tummy reassuringly. She didn't reach for his hand to feel too, and she missed the warmth of his wide palm on her taut skin.

She didn't ask any more about the crisis with the ranch. Instead they lived each day the same, no peaks, no valleys.

The second Tuesday in July dawned already swelteringly hot. Alex woke with the covers already thrown off. Since it was only six a.m., and the air was already like an oven, she dressed in shorts, a light halter top and her sandals.

Her eyes strayed to the picture on the night table. She'd taken it out of her backpack the night before the wedding and placed it beside her bed. It was the only picture she'd ever saved and bothered to carry with her. In a plain wood frame was a five-by-seven family picture—her, her mother and father, in a studio-type shot. Tucked behind the colour photo in the back of the frame were two newspaper articles. One was a copy of the same picture, and a small story from an Ottawa paper on her parents and one of their adventures. She had been thirteen at the time.

The other article was an extended obituary for her parents after the crash, outlining their achievements.

She'd garnered a whole line in that one. Even with their death, she'd still felt like she'd been less of an achievement than their career.

Alex put her hair up in a ponytail, twisting the tail around and around and anchoring the dark bun with a plain band, keeping her neck free and hopefully cool. When she was done she placed both hands over the place where her child lay. And she vowed that her baby would always know what was important. That nothing mattered more than him or her. For a while she'd indulged in fantasies about how Connor would look, cradling her child in his arms, kissing its tiny fingers one by one. Now she had to adjust those visions to something more realistic... her and motherhood, and making sure her child always felt loved and valued.

Connor was already gone when she went downstairs, so she ate a quick breakfast, washed a load of towels and decided to pick vegetables out of the garden before the heat became unbearable.

When Connor came in at noon he carried the mail.

"Anything good?" Alex finished setting the table and put out a plate of sandwiches and a bowl of fresh greens and tomatoes.

Connor slit open the first envelope. "It's the bank confirmation. My trust fund went through. I officially am in the black." He couldn't hold back the relief in his voice at finally being able to pay the bills. On the other hand, he wasn't sure what this meant for his relationship with Alex.

She'd married him for the security. He couldn't deceive himself on that point. She'd made it abundantly clear in every way possible. A farmer's life was unpredictable, hard, and even lonely. He couldn't expect her to choose this indefinitely. Even if he did want her to. Knowing she was there when he got home, seeing her laugh, cry, argue...all had him feeling more alive than he had in years. She was right. The place would seem empty when it was just him rattling around in it again.

He was too used to losing people he cared about. The last time he hadn't foreseen enough to try to prevent it.

This time he could see trouble coming from a mile away. Connor remembered the feeling he'd had when the baby had moved beneath his hand. Protective. Humbled. Strong. What would it be like to have a son or daughter? To hear it cry and soothe it with a rock in the rocking chair, to see the baby feed at its mother's breast in the pale light of early morning?

He was wishing this was his family, his baby, and he had absolutely no right. He knew that if Alex gave him a chance he'd be a father to her baby, blood or no. If he felt this way after only a few weeks, how would he feel after the baby was born and he had to set her free? There had to be some way he could give her a reason to stay long enough for him to prove to her that he could be what she needed. What she *wanted*.

"That's great," Alex answered weakly. "Sit down and eat. I'll get you some water."

Connor held a ham sandwich with one hand and bit

into it while he sorted through the remainder of enve-
lopes with the other.

"Connor? What is it?"

He had stopped chewing, and the hand holding the
sandwich put it down like it weighed five pounds. He
picked up a brown envelope, staring at the front.

"Connor?"

When he looked at her she saw something new in his
eyes—a real fear. Her stomach tumbled. Whatever was
in that envelope wasn't good.

"Open it," she whispered.

He ran his finger under the seal and pulled out the
papers inside. His tanned face paled; his lips thinned
until they were white around the edges.

Suddenly he started laughing. Not a funny laugh, but
the frightening laugh of a man who'd reached the end of
his rope. Like one who'd finally lost his hold on reality.

"Connor. You're scaring me." Her voice trembled as
she stared at him, her lips falling open as the laughter
halted as quickly as it had begun.

"It's over," he said flatly. His eyes were dull as he
stared up at her. "We're linked, you see. No trust fund
in the world can help me now."

"What are you talking about?" She took a step forward, halting at his look of sheer despair.

His next words broke her heart as surely as they had
broken his spirit.

"I've got to cull the herd. Windover's done."

CHAPTER FOURTEEN

"OH, MY GOD. NO."

Alex sank into her chair, staring blankly at Connor. His face showed no reaction, which scared her most of all. It was like someone had turned off a switch. It had to be shock.

"They've traced the lineage of the affected animal. There's a direct tie to Windover. The herd. My God. The whole herd," he breathed, stricken.

He looked at her with eyes so haunted she knew she'd never forget it as long as she lived.

Windover. The one thing he would do anything for. Any extreme measure...even marrying a pregnant stranger. The one thing linking him to his lost family. The one permanent fixture in his life. His sole responsibility.

Without livestock there *was* no Windover. She didn't have to be a true rancher's wife to know that much.

"So you rebuild," she offered. "You try something else, or replace the herd. You don't give up."

He stared at her. "Don't give up? How the hell would I replace the herd? Do you know how much time and money it takes to build a herd like that?"

She didn't, and the blank look on her face said so.

He snorted. "Do something else." He muttered it almost to himself.

"In the end, it's fate," he continued, his tone bitter and angry. "It doesn't matter how much you do, how hard you try. It doesn't matter."

"Don't say that!" Sitting in her chair, she reached over and gripped his fingers. "At least you know you tried everything. What happened is out of your control!"

"Exactly." He looked at her, and she could have sworn there was something like accusation in his glare. "Everything's out of my control now."

"Don't panic. We'll figure it out somehow."

Alex did something she would never have imagined herself doing. At twelve-thirty in the afternoon, she went to the cupboard, took out the tequila, and poured him a double shot.

For a moment he stared at the amber liquid, but in the end he pushed it away and looked up into her eyes.

She didn't have a clue, did she? All he'd wanted was to show her that he could make this work. That it would be worth it for her to stay.

She thought it was the cows he was upset about. She was wrong. Dead wrong.

It was her. Without the ranch, without the trust fund, without Windover, he had nothing to offer her. Sometime over the last weeks he'd started caring for something other than Windover. Finally, after years of being alone, something, someone, mattered more. He'd started doing it all for *her*. For Alex and her baby. And all he'd done was fail spectacularly.

In that moment he hated her just a bit, for making him love again so much and then making him lose.

"You have no idea what you're talking about, anyway," he accused. "You came here from the city. You don't understand ranch life. You don't understand what all this means to a man like me. You asked me what in our agreement required you to be here. The answer is nothing, Alex. Absolutely nothing. You might as well go back where you came from."

Ignoring the bottle, he stood and headed for the front door.

"Stop."

His footsteps halted at the harsh command, but he didn't turn around.

When nothing came from her, he wondered. Wondered what he'd see when he turned around. Lord, if she were crying he might as well pound himself in the head with a two-by-four. It would hurt less. He'd lashed out at her but wasn't prepared yet to apologize. Everything was too fresh, too raw. His failures. His inability to make things right. Even this baby wasn't his. He was like a big walking advertisement for complete impotence.

"If that's what you want, I'll pack my things."

Her voice came quietly from behind him, and he forced himself to ignore the strange thickness to it. Her emotions were riding close to the surface, and right now he could only deal with his own.

"I've gotta get out of here," he answered, reaching for the doorknob.

"You can't. Please, Connor, I've never seen you like this. In your frame of mind, I'll worry about you driving."

He held the doorknob in his hand. "I'm just going to take the ATV, not the truck," he replied.

"Please don't," she begged. "You're not thinking clearly...you might hurt yourself."

Finally he turned, staring at her with hard eyes, his face a series of angles that spoke pain.

"And would you care, Alexis?"

She gasped, stepping back with her fingers over her mouth. With a searing backward glance he went out, slamming the front door behind him.

Mere seconds later the motor of the quad revved, grinding into gear and fading away as Connor headed north.

Alex went back to the kitchen, her muscles knotted with worry. He was in no condition to drive. He was in such a fragile state right now.

Everything he held dear—his purpose for everything—was being snatched away from him. And she was powerless to stop it.

If only he'd loved her she could have offered comfort, solace. She'd maybe have known what he needed and been able to offer it. But instead he'd taken it out on her, when all she'd wanted was to help.

She poured the tequila down the sink and recapped the bottle. Yes, she was from the city and hadn't had years of ranch experience. And, no, she wasn't that up to snuff with the logistics of it all. But she knew a damn sight more than he thought. She knew what this place meant. She knew he felt like a failure, and she knew he'd regret it forever if he gave up without seeing it through.

She'd offered help. And he'd pushed her away with hurtful words and an impenetrable emotional wall. Never in her life had she felt so superfluous.

If he couldn't see what was standing right in front of him, that was his problem. She wasn't going to stand around begging. She should have packed her things the day of the rodeo. Instead she'd stayed and opened herself up to more hurt.

Now he was out there *somewhere,* driving balls to

the wall on a four-wheeler. She stared at their uneaten lunch, knowing that the time had come for this charade to be over.

She was not his wife, not really. And very clearly she was not what he needed. She grabbed the laundry basket and stepped out to the deck to take her clean clothes off the line before she packed them. He was right. There was nothing to keep her here now.

She pushed back the tendrils of hair that had escaped her bun, breathing deeply. The air had changed somehow. Suddenly the sweltering heat carried a threatening icy chill.

She gazed north, eyeing the clouds curiously. Something was wrong. The clouds were piling layer upon layer and growing darker by the minute. The sun shone on her back, but in front of her the clouds approached, menacing. She saw a flash—lightning. Several seconds later came the low rumble of answering thunder.

Connor must see the weather, she reasoned, figuring him to be back soon. Surely he wouldn't ignore the signs he sensed so easily at other times? She reeled in the line, watching open-mouthed as a gust of icy wind yanked a dishcloth off its pins and sent it tumbling down the farmyard.

She hurriedly took the rest of the clothes down and went back inside. As she put lunch back in the fridge and tidied up the kitchen, the rumble of thunder grew closer, louder. A gust of wind came through the patio doors, flapping the vertical blinds. She jumped at the harsh sound, trying to steady her racing heart.

It took all of ten minutes to pack her things. There were extra clothes this time, a plastic bag of toiletries and her picture to put back among the clothing to protect it. For lack of luggage, she retrieved a cardboard box from the basement and laid her wedding finery carefully within it. Anger and resentment burned within her. Connor had succeeded in doing what everyone else had done before him. He'd made her feel like she wasn't worth it.

Well, maybe she wasn't. But her baby darn well was. Connor would live up to his bargain in that he'd help her get on her feet. After that she'd be alone again… but wiser and stronger. She carried the box downstairs and waited.

After a half-hour of pacing and mumbling to herself, she went back out on the deck, scanning the pasture to the north anxiously. Connor should have been back by now. The clouds were dark, and the odd colour of an angry bruise. She put a hand to her eyes and searched the horizon for any sight of him. Nothing. The sun had disappeared and the first angry drop of rain hit her forehead as she looked up, up.

Lightning forked from the sky, this time the thunder almost on top of it. The storm was getting closer. Alex ran a hand over her belly, trying to comfort herself and her baby. As if it sensed something was amiss, the kicks got stronger and more frequent.

"Shh, little one," she whispered, her eyes never leaving the dirt road through the fields, willing Connor to return any moment. "Daddy'll be back soon."

Once the words were out she knew it was true. Ryan had fathered this baby, but he wasn't Daddy. Connor, with his gentle ways, his quiet strength, was meant to be Daddy to her baby, and somehow she had to make him see that. All her anger flooded away, replaced by concern. Connor was devastated, and that had colored everything he'd said, surely? All the animosity had simply been a reaction. She didn't really feel that way about him—she loved him. And if he thought he would get rid of her that easily…

Her hand stopped circling her belly as her mouth dropped open in horror. It couldn't be…no.

She watched as the swirling clouds changed and a funnel, like the circle of water in the bathtub, pointed down from the clouds, reaching for the earth.

She waited, hoping to see that destructive finger sucked back into the clouds. Instead it reached, reached, until she saw it hit the earth, gathering speed and dust and momentum.

It was close, too close. She cried out as ice-sharp hail bit into her skin and the swirling vortex came closer and closer.

"Oh, my God—oh, my God," she chanted, horrified that Connor was out there. The hail pounded her now, the size of peas from the garden, and she hurried inside.

The wind wailed around the house and she let fear be her guide. All her instincts said to head for the cellar. Alone, in the dark, she huddled beside the Deepfreeze and the wooden shelves, waiting for the storm to be over.

It lasted only ten minutes, but each minute was a lifetime in which she knew without a doubt that she loved Connor with all her heart. Each wail of the wind solidified the knowledge that she was meant to be with him, Windover or not. Each rattle of the windows, each foundation-shaking boom of thunder, told her that nothing in the world was more important than loving him, fighting for him, and bringing up her child with him at her side.

Pride be damned. There'd been enough pride today to fill up ten ranches. Right then and there she made a vow to tell him exactly how she felt.

The wind subsided a bit, the thunder grew more distant, and she crept upstairs to view the aftermath.

Once the funnel had passed by, the rain came in its wake. It was coming down in sheets, cold, driving rain instead of the earlier hail that had preceded the tornado. Numbly she pulled on an old fleece coat of Connor's that hung on the hook by the door. Stepping outside, she covered her mouth in horror at the sight before her.

The house remained untouched, but evidence of the twister was clear.

The poplar, the one under which they'd been married, was gone, it's branches lying scattered and it's trunk shorn completely off, a circle of ragged edges. The outbuildings were in a varying state of disarray. Pieces of roofing were scattered throughout the barnyard; the livestock shelter at the southeast side of the corral was splintered.

Her hair came completely loose from its tether, hanging wildly around her face in the driving rain. She stumbled down the drive, heading north. He'd gone north, she reasoned stupidly, beginning to run. The twister had come from the north.

She forgot the mud splattering over her sandals. Forgot the rain soaking through her clothes and matting her hair. Forgot how dirt smacked up and coated her bare legs.

She only thought of Connor, unprotected, devastated, in such a storm.

"Connor!" she called out as she ran across the road and into the next quarter section.

There was no answer to her call.

She placed a hand instinctively where her baby lay, but kept running. "Connor!"

She ran and ran, but heard no voice, no engine. Her lungs were on fire from running, her abdominals cramping from exertion. "Connor!" she screamed one last time.

She turned in a circle, searching the fields, seeing nothing but matted-down grass and mud.

Nothing.

She stood in the middle of the lane, dropped her head, and finally gave in to the tears she'd been holding in.

Damn him. He'd probably gone and done something completely stupid right at the moment she'd decided to tell him exactly how she felt! The tears came hot and fast even as the rain tapered off, steady and cool. What would she do without him?

Blindly she staggered on, until suddenly she saw a dark green form to the left. Crying, slipping and sliding in the slick black mud, she raced for the quad—only to discover he wasn't there.

He'd left the quad there, with the key in it.

She cradled the soft mound of her stomach beneath his jacket, sinking down and resting her head on the foot peg. In the damp she caught *his* smell rising up from the fleece, and her heart broke. How could he have the nerve to leave her now, just when she was ready to confess everything in her heart?

"I'm sorry," she sobbed, resting her head on the cold metal bar. "I'm sorry..."

"Alex?"

Her head slipped down until she was huddled on the muddy ground, crying uncontrollably. A cow bawled in the distance and she cursed at it, thinking of the injustice that a stupid bovine should live while Connor was out there... After seeing the state of the barn, she knew that no man, unprotected, could survive such a thing.

"Alex?"

"Shut up!" she screamed at the clouds. Now she was hearing things!

"Oh, my God, Alex—what the hell are you doing out here?"

This time there was no mistaking it, and she lifted her head to see Connor running toward the quad.

She tried to speak, she did. But no words would come out. Instead she cried even harder, knowing he was alive. The sobs turned into hysterical, hyperventilating quality wails as she huddled into a ball in the mud.

"Alex, honey—oh, God. Look at you."

She gasped in a huge breath of air, lifted her head, and smacked the cheek hovering close to her own.

"What the hell was that for?" He leaned back, pressing a hand to his red cheek.

She stumbled to her feet. "For scaring me to death, you jerk! For breaking your promise!"

All of her anger faded with the outburst, the adrenaline sapped out of her. She gripped the fingers of her right hand, horrified at what she'd done. "Oh, Connor, I'm so sorry I slapped you!"

She covered her mouth and started sobbing again.

"Hey, I'm all right," he said soothingly, while raindrops dripped from his hair. "What promise?"

She looked up, wide eyes imploring him to understand. "You promised you wouldn't hurt me. The night before the wedding. Our temporary vows, remember? You said you wouldn't be the one to hurt me."

"And I did?"

She looked down at her feet. How could he be so blind? She was covered in mud splatters to her knees. Her jacket was soaked and hanging on her, and her hair drooped around her face. "Of course you did! Look at me! I'm a mess! I came out here looking for you and for what? You have the nerve to stand there looking like that!"

"Looking like what?"

"Like some hero from an action movie, that's what!"

Why couldn't she do what she'd promised herself and tell him?

Because he was living and breathing in front of her, that was why. And it still scared her to death. So she instinctively wrapped herself in some ridiculous armor to protect herself.

"Alex?"

"What?" She glared at him through the driving rain.

"I have the power to hurt you?"

"Why does that matter?" She huddled inside the jacket, which was already soaked.

"It matters to me."

"Why?"

"Because I love you."

It took six giant strides to meet her, but when he did he swept her, mud and all, into his arms and kissed her.

It was Rhett and Scarlett. It was Darcy and Elizabeth, and every romance hero ever written and rolled into one. Rain beat down on their heads as they clung, lips greedy.

"I was so scared," she cried out, pressing kisses to his cheeks, his chin. "I saw the tornado coming and knew you were out here…"

"I tried coming back. I did," he stuttered out. "But it came too fast. I left the quad and took cover in the culvert, but all I thought of was you and the baby…"

"You shouldn't have run out…"

"I should never have said those things…"

They kissed again, a swift meeting of tongues and lips, and the baby kicked between them and they laughed from the sheer joy of it.

"Say it again."

He pulled back, staring into her eyes. "You really want me to?"

"Say it. I need to hear it again to know it's real."

"I love you, Alexis MacKenzie Madsen."

The tears started again. "I love you too, Connor. I just never thought you'd love me back."

He drew her close. "How could I not?"

For a long moment she let herself be wrapped in his arms. Finally she stepped back, shuddering.

"You're freezing. We've got to get you out of this rain."

She didn't argue, but crawled up behind him on the quad and wrapped her arms around his waist. He turned the key…nothing.

"What next?" He cursed at the machine and tried again, but no luck. It wasn't starting. They were going to have to walk.

He helped her off the ATV and bundled her close. "What were you thinking, coming all the way out here in the rain? You're going to get sick."

She stopped him with a tug of her hand. "I was thinking I'd lost you."

Their steps made squishy sounds along the path, the mud caking on their shoes. "I didn't mean it when I said you should go. I was frustrated."

"I know that."

"I was in that culvert, and it was so loud I couldn't have heard my own voice. But I knew that if I made it out I had to tell you I was sorry. That I lied about my feelings."

"You're not sending me away?"

He lifted a hand to her cheek. "Never. I'm tired of pretending, Alex. I think I've loved you since that first moment."

"You're crazy. There's no such thing as love at first sight, you fool."

"I'm not." He squeezed her close. "You opened your eyes and looked into mine and something *happened.*"

"I packed my bags after you left."

His face hardened in alarm as she stopped and faced him, looking up into his eyes.

She stopped his protest with gentle words. "I'd like very much to unpack and start over. The right way."

"Then you meant it? You love me too?" He swallowed hard. She saw the lump bob in his throat and wanted to lean up and kiss it.

"I knew the night before our wedding. When you made your vows to me. I knew I was falling for you and was sure you didn't feel the same. It made marrying you very surreal, Connor Madsen."

"It felt real," he admitted. He took her hand and urged her on, in view of the house now.

"I want to make promises to you—the real ones this time."

"Another wedding?"

"Not so much…but real vows, to you. The things I wanted to say, but didn't. I want to do this right. Things have a way of becoming very clear when you think you've lost someone. Like I thought I'd lost you."

Without another word he turned, gathered her, soaking wet, into his arms, and held on.

Long seconds they clung, each taking strength from the other, while the rain tapered to a drizzle and a weak bit of sunlight snuck out between the clouds behind them.

"This is not how I expected to spend my afternoon," he commented as they resumed walking.

It suddenly occurred to her that he didn't know that the buildings had been hit. "Connor, about the tornado…"

He saw the house, obviously still standing. "How bad?"

"The southeast shelter and the corral fence are gone. So's the poplar, and the barn and other buildings looked like they have a lot of roof damage." She gave it to him all at once, knowing he'd take it easier that way.

"It doesn't matter—since I'm not going to have any livestock to put in them anyway."

Her head fell heavily against his shoulder. She was feeling so sorry for his loss. He'd worked himself into the ground only to have it torn away from him. "I'm sorry about the herd, Connor. I wish there was something I could do."

He stiffened, then let out a breath. "You're doing it."

It wasn't much, but in that moment she was closer to him than she'd ever been. In that moment he was letting himself lean on her, and she knew if he truly meant what he said they'd make a wonderful team.

"We'll make it through," she confirmed. "Somehow we'll figure it out."

He angled his head away so that he saw her face, strong with determination. "You mean you're staying? Even when I've lost everything? I don't think you understand what it means to have to cull the herd. Windover as I know it…as it's been for generations…is done."

She half turned, snuggling into his shoulder and looking up at him. Her jaw set with determination and she wrapped an arm around his waist for good measure.

"What do you mean, done? You've got a huge, fabulous piece of land, a beautiful house, and most of all you've got your biggest asset—you. So you don't have a herd of beef cattle for the moment? You'll figure out something else and we'll go from there."

He shook his head. "I would never have guessed it."

"Guessed what?"

"That you were a rancher's wife."

She grinned then, wide and happy. "Me either. Go figure."

They stepped into the lane that ran to the house. She looked up at the building, so much more than a house. The first home she'd ever really had, the first place she'd belonged since she could remember. Her vegetable garden on the corner, thriving despite her green attempts. There was blue sky behind them now, while the dark clouds continued their journey to the southeast.

Their home. One that had survived other tragedies and was still standing.

"All I've ever wanted was a place to belong, and someone to belong to."

"This house was meant for families, not bachelors bumbling around by themselves." His arms tightened around her. "Stay with me, Alex. Love me. Family me."

"I thought you'd never ask." Alex leaned up, touched her lips to his, while she pressed her body as close to his as their damp clothes would allow.

They reached the door. He swung it open, then shocked her by gathering her, wet coat and all, into his arms and carrying her inside.

He murmured in her ear. "Maybe I wouldn't do this for myself. I probably would have given up and let go, despite the family tradition of hanging on. But for you... for the future...I know I have the strength to rebuild. Because you're with me."

Alex had to swallow the tears that gathered in the back of her throat. "We've needed each other all along," she whispered, curling around him and kissing him again.

EPILOGUE

One Year Later

"GO AHEAD, SAY IT. DA-DA."

Maren Johanna Madsen grinned up with her two teeth and drooled. "Da-da-da-da-da."

"Very definitive. A sign of high intelligence, I'm sure."

Alex leaned over the highchair, kissing the crown of her daughter's dark head. Connor lounged back in his chair while Johanna came from the pantry carrying a gigantic chocolate layer cake.

"Go ahead, Maren, say Grandma," she cajoled, with an affectionate grin.

"Da-da-da-da-da," Maren babbled happily.

Johanna smiled widely, putting the cake on the table and cutting it into slices. "Now, there's a girl who knows where her heart lies, hmm?" She couldn't resist stopping and tickling Maren's belly.

A year had passed since the slaughter decree and the tornado. A lot had changed since then. Connor's friend Mike had stopped running the rodeo circuit and had seriously started breeding quarterhorses by renting a large portion of Windover. Connor had accepted Mike's offer of a partnership in the venture. Maren had been born, and Alex had shown a talent for running an office…so all the records for Circle M Quarterhorses were in her control.

She picked up a sheaf of documents from the counter as Connor leaned back, enjoying cake and coffee. "These came today," she announced. "Although it's merely a formality."

"What is it?"

"Maren's adoption papers."

They'd filed after Maren was born, and Ryan hadn't contested a thing—thankfully. Now their sweet baby girl was officially what she'd always been in his heart—his daughter.

Johanna stopped and put her plate back on the counter as soon as she saw the look on Connor's face. His eyes caught Alex's and held, so full of emotion and love that to stay would have been intruding.

She slipped away, leaving them alone.

The screen door shut quietly while Connor rose, his gaze never straying from the loving eyes of his wife.

"So now she's ours."

"She always was. As much as this one will be."

"What?"

"I'd like a boy this time. But I suppose we'll have to be happy with what we get," she teased.

"One of each would be good," he mused, pulling her close and tucking her head under his chin. "But we can always try again…"

"And again…"

"Until we get it right…"

"Like right now…" He nuzzled her neck and she sighed, only to hear Maren's spoon banging against her tray. Alex craned her head around and smiled at the baby.

"You're really pregnant?"

"I am. Only this time I'm healthy as a horse."

Connor spun around, plucked Maren from her high-chair, banana face and all, and swung them both around. "And this time there's no wild propositions," he decreed. "This time you're both exactly where you belong. With me."

* * * * *

Liz Fielding was born with itchy feet. She made it to Zambia before her twenty-first birthday and, gathering her own special hero and a couple of children on the way, has lived in Botswana, Kenya and Bahrain. Seven of her titles have been nominated for RWA's RITA® Award, and she has won the RITA® Award for Best Traditional Romance in 2001, the Romantic Novelists' Association's Romance Prize in 2005 and the RITA® Award for Best Short Contemporary Romance in 2006. Visit her online at lizfielding.com.

Look for more books by Liz Fielding in Harlequin series.

SOS: CONVENIENT HUSBAND REQUIRED

Liz Fielding

For my patient, long-suffering husband, who unfailingly keeps his sense of humor through all the crises and the rubbish meals when the deadline escapes me, and who makes me believe on those horrible days when the confidence falters. He is my hero.

CHAPTER ONE

MAY COLERIDGE STARED blankly at the man sitting behind the desk, trying to make sense of what he'd told her.

Her grandfather's will had been simplicity itself. Apart from the bequests to local charities, everything had been left to his only living relative. Her.

Inheritance tax would mop up pretty much everything but the house itself. She'd always known that would happen, but Coleridge House was the only home she'd ever known and now, because of a clause in some centuries old will, she was about to lose that too.

'I don't understand,' she said, finally admitting defeat. 'Why didn't you tell me all this when you read Grandpa's will?'

'As you're no doubt aware,' Freddie Jennings explained with maddening pomposity—as if she hadn't known him since he'd been a kid with a runny nose at kindergarten—'my great-uncle took care of your grandfather's legal affairs until he retired. He drew up his last will after the death of your mother—'

'That was nearly thirty years ago,' she protested.

He shrugged. 'Believe me, I'm as shocked as you are.'

'I doubt that. Jennings have been the Coleridge family solicitor for generations,' she said. 'How could you not know about this?'

Freddie shifted uncomfortably in his chair. 'Some of

the Coleridge archives were damaged during the floods a few years ago. It was only when I applied for probate that this particular condition of inheritance surfaced.'

May felt as if she'd stepped into quicksand and the ground that she was standing on, everything that had been certain, was disintegrating beneath her feet. She had been so sure that this was a mistake, that Freddie has got his knickers in a twist over nothing, but it wasn't nothing. It was everything.

Everything she'd known, everything she'd loved was being taken away from her...

'The last time this clause would have been relevant was when your great-grandfather died in 1944,' he continued, as if that mattered. 'Your grandfather would have been told of the condition then.'

'In 1944 my grandfather was a fourteen-year-old boy who'd just lost his father,' she snapped, momentarily losing her composure at his attempt to justify their incompetence. 'And, since he was married by the time he was twenty-three, it wouldn't have been an issue.' And by the time it had become one, the stroke that had incapacitated him had left huge holes in his memory and he hadn't been able to warn her. She swallowed as an aching lump formed in her throat, but she refused to let the tears fall. To weep. 'People got married so much younger back then,' she added.

'Back then, there wasn't any alternative.'

'No...'

Her mother had been a beneficiary of the feminist movement, one of that newly liberated generation of women who'd abandoned the shackles of a patriarchal society and chosen her own path. *Motherhood without the bother of a man under her feet* was the way she'd put it in one of the many articles she'd written on the subject.

As for her, well, she'd had other priorities.

'You have to admit that it's outrageous, Freddie. Surely I can challenge it?'

'I'd have to take Counsel's opinion and even if you went to court there is a problem.'

'I think we are both agreed that I have a problem.'

He waited, but she shook her head. Snapping at Freddie wasn't going to help. 'Tell me.'

'There can be no doubt that this restriction on inheritance would have been explained to your grandfather on each of the occasions when he rewrote his will. After his marriage, the birth of your mother, the death of your grandmother. He could have taken steps then to have this restriction removed. He chose to let it stand.'

'Why? Why would he do that?'

Freddie shrugged. 'Maybe because it was part of family tradition. Maybe because his father had left it in place. I would have advised removal but my great-uncle, your grandfather came from a different age. They saw things differently.'

'Even so—'

'He had three opportunities to remove the entailment and the Crown would argue that it was clearly his wish to let it stand. Counsel would doubtless counter that if he hadn't had a stroke, had realised the situation you were in, he would have changed it,' Freddie said in an attempt to comfort her.

'If he hadn't had a stroke I would be married to Michael Linton,' she replied. *Safely married.* That was what he used to say. Not like her mother...

'I'm sorry, May. The only guarantee I can give is

that whichever way it went the costs would be heavy and, as you are aware, there's no money in the estate to cover them.'

'You're saying that I'd lose the house anyway,' she said dully. 'That whatever I do I lose.'

'The only people who ever win in a situation like this are the lawyers,' he admitted. 'Hopefully, you'll be able to realise enough from the sale of the house contents, once the inheritance tax is paid, to provide funds for a flat or even a small house.'

'They want inheritance tax *and* the house?'

'The two are entirely separate.'

She shook her head, still unable to believe this was happening. 'If it was going to some deserving charity I could live with it, but to have my home sucked into the Government coffers...' Words failed her.

'Your ancestor's will was written at the beginning of the nineteenth century. The country was at war. He was a patriot.'

'Oh, please! It was nothing but an arm twisted up the back of a philandering son. Settle down and get on with producing the next generation or I'll cut you off without a shilling.'

'Maybe. But it was added as an entailment to the estate and no one has ever challenged it. There's still just time, May. You could get married.'

'Is that an offer?'

'Unfortunately, bigamy would not satisfy the legal requirements.'

Freddie Jennings had a sense of humour? Who knew?

'You're not seeing anyone?' he asked hopefully.

She shook her head. There had only ever been one boy, man, who'd ever lit a fire in her heart, her body...

'Between nursing Grandpa and running my own business, I'm afraid there hasn't been a lot of time to "see" anyone,' she said.

'There's not even a friend who'd be prepared to go through the motions?'

'I'm all out of unattached men at the moment,' she replied. 'Well, there is Jed Atkins who does a bit for me in the garden now and then,' she said, her grip on reality beginning to slip. 'He's in his seventies, but pretty lively and I'd have to fight off the competition.'

'The competition?'

'He's very much in demand with the ladies at the Darby and Joan club, so I'm told.'

'May…' he cautioned as she began to laugh, but the situation was unreal. How could he expect her to take it seriously? 'I think I'd better take you home.'

'I don't suppose you have any clients in urgent need of a marriage of convenience so that they can stay in the country?' she asked as he ushered her from his office, clearly afraid that she was going to become hysterical.

He needn't have worried. She was a Coleridge. Mary Louise Coleridge of Coleridge House. Brought up to serve the community, behave impeccably on all occasions, do the right thing even when your heart was breaking.

She wasn't about to become hysterical just because Freddie Jennings had told her she was about to lose everything.

'But if you are considering something along those lines,' he warned as he held the car door for her, 'please make sure he signs a pre-nuptial agreement or you're going to have to pay dearly to get rid of him.'

'Make that a lose/lose/lose situation,' she said. Then,

taking a step back, 'Actually, I'd rather walk home. I need some fresh air.'

He said something but she was already walking away. She needed to be on her own. Needed to think.

Without Coleridge House, she would not only lose her home, but her livelihood. As would Harriet Robson, her grandfather's housekeeper for more than thirty years and the nearest thing to a mother she'd ever known.

She'd have to find a job. Somewhere to live. Or, of course, a husband.

She bought the early edition of the local newspaper from the stand by the park gates to look at the sits vac and property columns. What a joke. There were no jobs for a woman weeks away from her thirtieth birthday who didn't have a degree or even a typing certificate to her name. And the price of property in Maybridge was staggering. The lonely hearts column was a boom area, though, and, with a valuable house as an incentive, a husband might prove the easiest of the three to find. But, with three weeks until her birthday, even that was going to be a tough task.

ADAM WAVELL LOOKED from the sleeping infant tucked into the pink nest of her buggy to the note in his hand.

Sorry, sorry, sorry. I know I should have told you about Nancie, but you'd have shouted at me…

Shouted at her. Shouted at her! Of course he would have shouted at her, for all the good it had ever done.

'Problem?'

'You could say that.' For the first time since he'd employed Jake Edwards as his PA, he regretted not choos-

ing one of the equally qualified women who'd applied
for the job, any one of whom would by now have been
clucking and cooing over the infant. Taking charge and
leaving him to get on with running his company. 'My
sister is having a crisis.'

'I didn't know you had a sister.'

No. He'd worked hard to distance himself from his
family.

'Saffy. She lives in France,' he said.

Maybe. It had taken only one call to discover that
she'd sublet the apartment he'd leased for her months
ago. Presumably she was living off the proceeds of the
rent since she hadn't asked him for money. Yet.

Presumably she'd moved in with the baby's father,
a relationship that she hadn't chosen to share with him
and had now, presumably, hit the skids.

Her occasional phone calls could have come from
anywhere and any suggestion that he was cross-exam-
ining her about what she was doing, who she was seeing only resulted in longer gaps between them. It was
her life and while she seemed happy he didn't pry. At
twenty-nine, she was old enough to have grown out of
her wildness and settled down. Clearly, he thought as he
reread the letter, he'd been fooling himself.

I've got myself into some real trouble, Adam...

Trouble. Nothing new there, then. She'd made a career of it.

Michel's family set their bloodhounds on me.
They've found out all the trouble I was in as a
kid, the shoplifting, the drugs and they've used

it to turn him against me. He's got a court order
to stop me taking Nancie out of France and he's
going to take her away from me...

No. That wasn't right. She'd been clean for years...
Or was he still kidding himself?

A friend smuggled us out of France but I can't hide
with a baby so I'm leaving her with you...

Smuggled her out of France. Ignored a court order.
Deprived a father of access to his child. Just how many
felonies did that involve? All of which he was now an
accessory to.

Terrific.

One minute he'd been sitting in his boardroom, dis-
cussing the final touches to the biggest deal in his career, the next he was having his life sabotaged—not for
the first time—by his family.

I'm going to disappear for a while...

No surprise there. His little sister had made a career
of running away and leaving someone else to pick up the
pieces. She'd dropped out, run away, used drugs and al-
cohol in a desperate attempt to shut out all the bad stuff.
Following the example of their useless parents. Making
a bad situation worse.

He'd thought his sister had finally got herself together,
was enjoying some small success as a model. Or maybe
that was what he'd wanted to believe.

Don't, whatever you do, call a nanny agency.

They'll want all kinds of information and, once
it's on record, Nancie's daddy will be able to trace
her...

Good grief, who was the father of this child? Was
his sister in danger?

Guilt overwhelmed those first feelings of anger, frustration. He had to find her, somehow make this right,
but, as the baby stirred, whimpered, he had a more urgent problem.

Saffy had managed to get her into his office without
anyone noticing her—time for a shake-up in security—
but that would have to wait. His first priority was to get
the baby out of the building before she started screaming
and his family history became the subject of the kind of
gossip that had made his—and Saffy's—youth a misery.

'Do you want me to call an agency?' Jake asked.

'An agency?'

'For a nanny?'

'Yes... No...'

Even if Saffy's fears were nothing but unfounded neu-
rosis, he didn't have anywhere to put a nanny. He didn't
even have a separate bedroom in his apartment, only a
sleeping gallery reached by a spiral staircase.

It was no place for a baby, he thought as he stared at
the PS Saffy had scribbled at the end of the crumpled
and tear-stained note.

Ask May. She'll help.

She'd underlined the words twice.
May. May Coleridge.
He crushed the letter in his hand.

He hadn't spoken to May Coleridge since he was eighteen. She and Saffy had been in the same class at school and, while they hadn't been friends—the likes of the Wavells had not been welcome at Coleridge House, as he'd discovered to his cost—at least not in the giggly girls, shopping, clubbing sense of the word, there had been some connection between them that he'd never been able to fathom.

But then that was probably what people had thought about him and May.

But while the thought of the untouchable Miss Coleridge changing the nappy of a Wavell baby might put a shine on his day, the woman had made an art form of treating him as if he were invisible.

Even on those social occasions when they found themselves face to face, there was no eye contact. Only icy civility.

'Is there anything I can do?'

He shook his head. There was nothing anyone could do. His family was, always had been, his problem, but it was a mess he wanted out of his office. Now.

'Follow up on the points raised at the meeting, Jake.' He looked at the crumpled sheet of paper in his hand, then folded it and stuffed it in his shirt pocket. Unhooked his jacket from the back of his chair. 'Keep me posted about any problems. I'm going home.'

IT TOOK A kitten to drag May out of her dark thoughts.

Her first reaction to the news that she was about to lose her home had been to rush back to its shabby comfort—no matter how illusory that comfort might be—while she came to terms with the fact that, having lost the last surviving member of her family, she was now going to lose everything else. Her home. Her business. Her future.

Once home, however, there would be no time for such indulgence. She had little enough time to unravel the life she'd made for herself. To wind down a business she'd fallen into almost by accident and, over the last few years, built into something that had given her something of her own, something to live for.

Worst of all, she'd have to tell Robbie.

Give notice to Patsy and the other women who worked for a few hours a week helping with the cleaning, the cooking and who relied on that small amount of money to help them pay their bills.

There'd be no time to spare for the luxury of grieving for the loss of their support, friendship. Her birthday was less than a month away. *The* birthday. The one with a big fat zero on the end.

Yesterday that hadn't bothered her. She'd never understood why anyone would want to stop the clock at 'twenty-nine'.

Today, if some fairy godmother were to appear and offer her three wishes, that would be number one on the list. Well, maybe not number one…

But, while fairy godmothers were pure fantasy, her date of birth was a fact that she could not deny and, by the time she'd reached the last park bench before home, the one overlooking the lake that had once been part of the parkland surrounding Coleridge House, her legs had been shaking so much that she'd been forced to stop.

Once there, she'd been unable to find the will to move again. It was a sheltered spot, a sun trap and, despite the fact that it was the first week in November, pleasantly warm. And while she sat on this park bench she was

still Miss Mary Louise Coleridge of Coleridge House.
Someone to be respected.

Her place in the town, the invitations to sit on charitable committees were part of her life. Looked at in the cold light of day, it was obvious that it wasn't her they wanted, it was the Coleridge name to lend lustre to their endeavours. And Coleridge House.

No one would come knocking when she didn't have a grand room where they could hold their meetings, with a good lunch thrown in. An elegant, if fading house with a large garden in which to hold their 'events'.

It was the plaintive mewing of a kitten in distress that finally broke through these dark thoughts. It took her a moment to locate the scrap of orange fur clinging to the branch of a huge old beech tree set well back from the path.

'Oh, sweetie, how on earth did you get up there?'

Since the only reply was an even more desperate mew, she got to her feet and went closer.

'Come on. You can do it,' she cooed, standing beneath it, hoping to coax it back down the long sloping branch that came nearly to the ground. It edged further up the branch.

She looked around, hoping for someone tall enough to reach up and grab it but there wasn't a soul in sight. Finally, when it became clear that there wasn't anything else for it, she took off her jacket, kicked off her shoes and, skirting a muddy puddle, she caught hold of the branch, found a firm foothold and pulled herself up.

BITTERLY REGRETTING THAT he'd taken advantage of the unseasonably fine weather to walk in to the office, Adam escaped the building via his private lift to the car park.

He'd hoped to pick up a taxi at the rank on the corner but there were none waiting and he crossed the road to the park. It was a slightly longer way home, but there was less chance of being seen by anyone he knew.

Oblivious to the beauty of the autumn morning, he steered the buggy with one hand, using the other to call up anyone who might have a clue where Saffy was heading for.

His first action on finding Nancie had been to try her mother's mobile but, unsurprisingly, it was switched off. He'd left a message on her voicemail, asking her to ring him, but didn't hold out much hope of that.

Ten minutes later, the only thing he knew for certain was that he knew nothing. The new tenants of the apartment, her agent—make that ex-agent—even her old flatmate denied any knowledge of where she was, or of Michel, and he had no idea who her friends were, even supposing they'd tell him anything.

Actually, he thought, looking at the baby, it wasn't true that he knew nothing.

While the movement of the buggy had, for the moment, lulled her back to sleep, he was absolutely sure that very soon she would be demanding to be fed or changed.

Ask May. She'll help.

Ahead of him, the tall red-brick barley twist chimneys of Coleridge House stood high above the trees. For years he'd avoided this part of the park, walked double the distance rather than pass the house. Just seeing those chimneys had made him feel inadequate, worthless.

These days, he could buy and sell the Coleridges, and yet it was still there. Their superiority and the taint of who he was.

Asking her for help stuck deep in his craw, but the

one thing about May Coleridge was that she wouldn't ask questions. She knew Saffy. Knew him.

He called Enquiries for her number but it was unlisted. No surprise there, but maybe it was just as well.

It had been a very long time since he'd taken her some broken creature to be nursed back to health, but he knew she'd find it a lot harder to say no face to face. If he put Nancie into her arms.

IT IS NOT HIGH, May told herself as she set her foot firmly on the tree. All she had to do was haul herself up onto the branch and crawl along it. No problem...

Easy enough to say when she was safely on the ground.

Standing beneath the branch and looking up, it had seemed no distance at all. The important thing, she reminded herself, was not to look down but keep her eye on the goal.

'What on earth are you doing up there, Mouse?'

Sherbet dabs!

As her knee slipped, tearing her tights, she wondered how much worse this day could get. The advantage that she didn't have to look down to see who was beneath her—only one person had ever called her Mouse—was completely lost on her.

'What do you think I'm doing?' she asked through gritted teeth. 'Checking the view?'

'You should be able to see Melchester Castle from up there,' he replied, as if she'd been serious. 'You'll have to look a little further to your left, though.'

She was in enough trouble simply looking ahead. She'd never been good with heights—something she only ever seemed to remember when she was too far off the ground to change her mind.

'Why don't you come up and point it out to me?' she gasped.

'I would be happy to,' he replied, 'but that branch doesn't look as if it could support both of us.'

He was right. It was creaking ominously as she attempted to edge closer to the kitten which, despite her best efforts not to frighten it further, was backing off, a spitting, frightened orange ball of fur.

It was far too late to wish she'd stuck to looking helpless at ground level. She'd realised at a very early age that the pathetic, *Where's a big strong man to help me?* routine was never going to work for her—she wasn't blonde enough, thin enough, pretty enough—and had learned to get on and do it herself.

It was plunging in without a thought for the consequences that had earned her the mocking nickname 'Mouse', short for 'Danger Mouse', bestowed on her by Adam Wavell when she was a chubby teen and he was a mocking, nerdy, glasses-wearing sixth-former at the local high school.

Her knee slipped a second time and a gasp from below warned her that Adam wasn't the only one with a worm's eye view of her underwear. A quick blink confirmed that her antics were beginning to attract an audience of mid-morning dog-walkers, older children on their autumn break and shoppers taking the scenic route into the town centre—just too late to be of help.

Then a click, followed by several more as the idea caught on, warned her that someone had taken a photograph using their mobile phone. Terrific. She was going to be in tomorrow's edition of the *Maybridge Observer* for sure; worse, she'd be on *YouTube* by lunch time.

She had no one to blame but herself, she reminded herself, making a firm resolution that the next time she spotted an animal in distress she'd call the RSPCA and leave it to them. That wasn't going to help her now, though, and the sooner she grabbed the kitten and returned to earth the better.

'Here, puss,' she coaxed desperately, but its only response was to hiss at her and edge further along the branch. Muttering under her breath, she went after it. The kitten had the advantage. Unlike her, it weighed nothing and, as the branch thinned and began to bend noticeably beneath her, she made a desperate lunge, earning herself a cheer from the crowd as she managed to finally grab it. The kitten ungratefully sank its teeth into her thumb.

'Pass it down,' Adam said, his arms raised to take it from her.

Easier said than done. In its terror, it had dug its needle claws in, clinging to her hand as desperately as it had clung to the branch.

'You'll have to unhook me. Don't let it go!' she warned as she lowered it towards him. She was considerably higher now and she had to lean down a long way so that he could detach the little creature with the minimum of damage to her skin.

It was a mistake.

While she'd been focused on the kitten everything had been all right, but that last desperate lunge had sent everything spinning and, before she could utter so much as a *fudge balls*, she lost her balance and slithered off the branch.

Adam, standing directly beneath her, had no time to avoid a direct hit. They both went down in a heap, the fall driving the breath from her body, which was probably a good thing since there was no item in her handmade confectionery range that came even close to matching her mortification. But then embarrassment was her default reaction whenever she was within a hundred feet of the man.

'You don't change, Mouse,' he said as she struggled to catch her breath.

Not much chance of that while she was lying on top of him, his breath warm against her cheek, his heart pounding beneath her hand, his arm, flung out in an attempt to catch her—or, more likely, defend himself— tight around her. The stuff of her most private dreams, if she discounted the fact that it had been raining all week and they were sprawled in the muddy puddle she had taken such pains to avoid.

'You always did act first, think later,' he said. 'Rushing to the aid of some poor creature in distress and getting wet, muddy or both for your pains.'

'While you,' she gasped, 'always turned up too late to do anything but stand on the sidelines, laughing at me,' she replied furiously. It was untrue and unfair, but all she wanted right at that moment was to vanish into thin air.

'You have to admit you were always great entertainment value.'

'If you like clowns,' she muttered, remembering all too vividly the occasion when she'd scrambled onto the school roof in a thunderstorm to rescue a bird trapped in the guttering and in danger of drowning, concern driving her chubby arms and legs as she'd shinned up the down pipe.

Up had never been a problem.

He'd stood below her then, the water flattening his thick dark hair, rain pouring down his face, grinning even as he'd taken the bird from her. But then, realising that she was too terrified to move, he'd taken off his glasses and climbed up to rescue her.

Not that she'd thanked him.

She'd been too busy yelling at him for letting the bird go before she could wrap it up and take it home to join the rest of her rescue family.

It was only when she was back on terra firma that her breathing had gone to pot and he'd delivered her to the school nurse, convinced she was having an asthma attack. And she had been too mortified—and breathless—to deny it.

He was right. Nothing had changed. She might be less than a month away from her thirtieth birthday, a woman of substance, respected for her charity work, running her own business, but inside she was still the overweight and socially inept teen being noticed by a boy she had the most painful crush on. Brilliant but geeky with the family from hell. Another outsider.

Well, he wasn't an outsider anymore. He'd used his brains to good effect and was now the most successful man not just in Maybridge, but just about anywhere and had exchanged the hideous flat in the concrete acres of a sink estate where he'd been brought up for the luxury of a loft on the quays.

She quickly disentangled herself, clambered to her feet. He followed with far more grace.

'Are you all right?' he asked. 'No bones broken?'

'I'm fine,' she said, ignoring the pain in her elbow

where it had hit the ground. 'You?' she asked out of politeness.

She could see for herself that he was absolutely fine. More than fine. The glasses had disappeared years ago, along with the bad hair, bad clothes. He'd never be muscular, but he'd filled out as he'd matured, his shoulders had broadened and these days were clad in the finest bespoke tailoring.

He wasn't just fine, but gorgeous. Mouth-wateringly scrumptious, in fact. The chocolate nut fudge of maleness. And these days he had all the female attention he could handle if the gossip magazines were anything to judge by.

'At least you managed to hang onto the kitten,' she added, belatedly clutching the protective cloak of superiority about her.

The one thing she knew would make him keep his distance.

'I take no credit. The kitten is hanging onto me.'

'What?' She saw the blood seeping from the needle wounds in his hand and everything else flew out of the window. 'Oh, good grief, you're bleeding.'

'It's a hazard I expect whenever I'm within striking distance of you. Although on this occasion you haven't escaped unscathed, either,' he said.

She physically jumped as he took her own hand in his, turning it over so that she could see the tiny pinpricks of blood mingling with the mud. And undoing all her efforts to regain control of her breathing. He looked up.

'Where's your bag?' he asked. 'Have you got your inhaler?'

Thankfully, it had never occurred to him that his presence was the major cause of her problems with breathing.

'I'm fine,' she snapped.

For heaven's sake, she was nearly thirty. She should be so over the cringing embarrassment that nearly crippled her whenever Adam Wavell was in the same room.

'Come on,' he said, 'I'll walk you home.'

'There's no need,' she protested.

'There's every need. And this time, instead of getting punished for my good deed, I'm going to claim my reward.'

'Reward?' Her mouth dried. In fairy tales that would be a kiss... 'Superheroes never hang around for a reward,' she said scornfully as she wrapped the struggling kitten in her jacket.

'You're the superhero, Danger Mouse,' he reminded her, a teasing glint in his eyes that brought back the precious time when they'd been friends. 'I'm no more than the trusty sidekick who turns up in the nick of time to get you out of a jam.'

'Just once in a while you could try turning up in time to prevent me from getting into one,' she snapped.

'Now where would be the fun in that?' he asked, and it took all her self-control to keep her face from breaking out into a foolish smile.

'Do you really think I want to be on the front page of the *Maybridge Observer* with my knickers on show?' she enquired sharply. Then, as the teasing sparkle went out of his eyes, 'Don't worry. I'm sure I'll survive the indignity.'

'Having seen your indignity for myself, I can assure you that tomorrow's paper will be a sell-out,' he replied. She was still struggling with a response to that when he added, 'And if they can tear their eyes away from all that lace, the kitten's owners might recognise their stray.'

'One can live in hopes,' she replied stiffly.

She shook her head, then, realising that, no matter

how much she wanted to run and hide, she couldn't ignore the fact that because of her he was not only bloody
but his hand-stitched suit was covered in mud.

'I suppose you'd better come back to the house and
get cleaned up,' she said.

'If that's an offer to hose me down in the yard, I'll
pass.'

For a moment their eyes met as they both remembered
that hideous moment when he'd come to the house with
a bunch of red roses that must have cost him a fortune
and her grandfather had turned a garden hose on him,
soaking him to the skin.

'Don't be ridiculous,' she said, her insides curling up
with embarrassment, killing stone dead the little heart-
lift as he'd slipped so easily into teasing her the way he'd
done when they were friends.

She picked up her shoes, her bag, reassembling her
armour. But she wasn't able to look him in the eye as
she added distantly, 'Robbie will take care of you in
the kitchen.'

'The kitchen? Well, that will be further than I've ever
got before. But actually it was you I was coming to see.'

She balanced her belongings, then, with studied care-
lessness, as if she had only then registered what he'd
said, 'See?' she asked, doing her best to ignore the way
her heart rate had suddenly picked up. 'Why on earth
would you be coming to see me?'

He didn't answer but instead used his toe to release
the brake on a baby buggy that was standing a few feet
away on the path. The buggy that she had assumed
belonged to a woman, bundled up in a thick coat and
headscarf, who'd been holding onto the handle, croon-
ing to the baby.

CHAPTER TWO

'ADAM? WHAT ARE YOU DOING?'

'Interesting question. Mouse, meet Nancie.'

'Nancy?'

'With an i and an e. Spelling never was Saffy's strong point.'

Saffy Wavell's strong points had been so striking she'd never given a fig for spelling or anything much else. Long raven-black hair, a figure that appeared to be both ethereal and sensual, she'd been a boy magnet since she hit puberty. And in trouble ever since. But a baby...

'She's Saffy's baby? That's wonderful news.' She began to smile. 'I'm so happy for her.' The sleeping baby was nestled beneath a pink lace-bedecked comforter. 'She's beautiful.'

'Is she?'

He leaned forward for a closer look, as if it hadn't occurred to him, but May stopped, struck by what he'd just done.

'You just left her,' she said, a chill rippling through her. 'She's Saffy's precious baby and you just abandoned her on the footpath to come and gawp at me? What on earth were you thinking, Adam?'

He looked back then, frowning; he stopped too, clearly catching from her tone that a grin would be a mistake.

'I was thinking that you were in trouble and needed a hand.'

'Idiot!' For a moment there she'd been swept away by the sight of a powerful man taking care of a tiny infant. 'I'm not a child. I could have managed.'

'Well, thanks—'

'Don't go getting all offended on me, Adam Wavell,' she snapped, cutting him off. 'While you were doing your Galahad act, anyone could have walked off with her.'

'What?' Then, realising what she was saying, he let go of the handle, rubbed his hands over his face, muttered something under his breath. 'You're right. I am an idiot. I didn't think.' Then, looking at the baby, 'I'm way out of my depth here.'

'Really? So let me guess,' May said, less than amused; he was overdoing it with the 'idiot'. 'Your reason for dropping in for the first time in years wouldn't have anything to do with your sudden need for a babysitter?'

'Thanks, May. Saffy said you'd help.'

'She said that?' She looked at the baby. All pink and cute and helpless. No! She would not be manipulated! She was in no position to take on anyone else's problems right now. She had more than enough of her own. 'I was stating the obvious, not offering my services,' she said as he began to walk on as if it was a done deal. 'Where is Saffy?'

'She's away,' he said. 'Taking a break. She's left Nancie in my care.'

'Good luck with that,' she said. 'But it's no use coming to me for help. I know absolutely nothing about babies.'

'You've already proved you know more than me. Besides, you're a woman.' Clearly he wasn't taking her refusal seriously, which was some nerve considering he hadn't spoken to her unless forced to in the last ten years. 'I thought it came hard-wired with the X chromosome?'

'That is an outrageous thing to say,' she declared, ignoring the way her arms were aching to pick up the baby, hold her, tell her that she wouldn't allow anything bad to happen to her. Ever. Just as she'd once told her mother.

She already had the kitten. In all probability, that was all she'd ever have. Ten years from now, she'd be the desperate woman peering into other people's prams...

'Is it?' he asked, all innocence.

'You know it is.'

'Maybe if you thought of Nancie as one of those helpless creatures you were always taking in when you were a kid it would help?' He touched a finger to the kitten's orange head, suggesting that nothing had changed. 'They always seemed to thrive.'

'Nancie,' she said, ignoring what she assumed he thought was flattery, 'is not an injured bird, stray dog or frightened kitten.'

'The principle is the same. Keep them warm, dry and fed.'

'Well, there you are,' she said. 'You know all the moves. You don't need me.'

'On the contrary. I've got a company to run. I'm flying to South America tomorrow—'

'South America?'

'Venezuela first, then on to Brazil and finally Samindera. Unless you read the financial pages, you would have missed the story. I doubt it made the social pages,' he said.

'Samindera,' she repeated with a little jolt of concern. 'Isn't that the place where they have all the coups?'

'But grow some of the finest coffee in the world.' One

corner of his mouth lifted into a sardonic smile that, unlike the rest of him, hadn't changed one bit.

'Well, that's impressive,' she said, trying not to remember how it had felt against her own trembling lips. The heady rush as a repressed desire found an urgent response… 'But you're not the only one with a business to run.' Hers might be little more than a cottage industry, nothing like his international money generator that had turned him from zero to a Maybridge hero, but it meant a great deal to her. Not that she'd have it for much longer.

Forget Adam, his baby niece, she had to get home, tell Robbie the bad news, start making plans. Somehow build a life from nothing.

Just as Adam had done…

'I've got a world of trouble without adding a baby to the mix,' she said, not wanting to think about Adam. Then, before he could ask her what kind of trouble, 'I thought Saffy was living in Paris. Working as a model? The last I heard from her, she was doing really well.'

'She kept in touch with you?' Then, before she could answer, 'Why are you walking barefoot, May?'

She stared at him, aware that he'd said something he regretted, had deliberately changed the subject, then, as he met her gaze, challenging her to go there, she looked down at her torn tights, mud soaked skirt, dirty legs and feet.

'My feet are muddy. I've already ruined my good black suit…' the one she'd be needing for job interviews, assuming anyone was that interested in someone who hadn't been to university, had no qualifications '…I'm not about to spoil a decent pair of shoes, too.'

As she stepped on a tiny stone and winced, he took her by the arm, easing her off the path and she froze.

'The grass will be softer to walk on,' he said, immediately releasing her, but not before a betraying shiver of gooseflesh raced through her.

Assuming that she was cold, he removed his jacket, placed it around her shoulders. It swallowed her up, wrapping her in the warmth from his body.

'I'm covered in mud,' she protested, using her free hand to try and shake it off. Wincing again as a pain shot through her elbow. 'It'll get all over the lining.'

He stopped her, easing the jacket back onto her shoulder, then holding it in place around her. 'You're cold,' he said, looking down at her, 'and I don't think this suit will be going anywhere until it's been cleaned, do you?'

Avoiding his eyes, she glanced down at his expensively tailored trousers, but it wasn't the mud that made her breath catch in her throat. He'd always been tall but now the rest of him had caught up and those long legs, narrow hips were designed to make a woman swoon.

'No!' she said, making a move so that he was forced to turn away. 'You'd better send me the cleaning bill.'

'It's your time I need, May. Your help. Not your money.'

He needed her. Words which, as a teenager, she'd lived to hear. Words that, when he shouted them for all the world to hear, had broken her heart.

'It's impossible right now.'

'I heard about your grandfather,' he said, apparently assuming it was grief that made her so disobliging.

'Really?' she said.

'It said in the *Post* that the funeral was private.'

'It was.' She couldn't have borne the great and good making a show of it. And why would Adam have come to pray over the remains of a man who'd treated him like something unpleasant he'd stepped in? 'But there's going to be a memorial service. He was generous with his legacies and I imagine the charities he supported are hoping that a showy civic send-off will encourage new donors to open their wallets. I'm sure you'll get an invitation to that.' Before he could answer, she shook her head. 'I'm sorry. That was a horrible thing to say.'

But few had done more than pay duty visits after a massive stroke had left her grandpa partially paralysed, confused, with great holes in his memory. Not that he would have wanted them to see him that way.

'He hated being helpless, Adam. Not being able to remember.'

'He was a formidable man. You must miss him.'

'I lost him a long time ago.' Long before his memory had gone.

'So, what happens now?' Adam asked, after a moment of silence during which they'd both remembered the man they knew. 'Will you sell the house? It needs work, I imagine, but the location would make it ideal for company offices.'

'No!' Her response was instinctive. She knew it was too close to the town, didn't have enough land these days to attract a private buyer with that kind of money to spend, but the thought of her home being turned into some company's fancy corporate headquarters—or, more likely, government offices—was too much to bear.

'Maybe a hotel or a nursing home,' he said, apparently understanding her reaction and attempting to soften the blow. 'You'd get a good price for it.'

'No doubt, but I won't be selling.'

'No? Are you booked solid into the foreseeable future with your painters, garden designers and flower arrangers?'

She glanced at him, surprised that he knew about the one-day and residential special interest courses she ran in the converted stable block.

'Your programme flyer is on the staff noticeboard at the office.'

'Oh.' She'd walked around the town one Sunday stuffing them through letterboxes. She'd hesitated about leaving one in his letterbox, but had decided that the likelihood of the Chairman being bothered with such ephemera was nil. 'Thanks.'

'Nothing to do with me,' he said. 'That's the office manager's responsibility. But one of the receptionists was raving about a garden design course she'd been on.'

'Well, great.' There it was, that problem with her breathing again. 'It is very popular, although they're all pretty solidly booked. I've got a full house at the moment for a two-day Christmas workshop.'

Best to put off telling Robbie the bad news until after tea, when they'd all gone home, she thought. They wouldn't be able to talk until then, anyway.

'You don't sound particularly happy about that,' Adam said. 'Being booked solid.'

'No.' She shrugged. Then, aware that he was looking at her, waiting for an explanation, 'I'm going to have to spend the entire weekend on the telephone cancelling next year's programme.'

Letting down all those wonderful lecturers who ran the classes, many of whom had become close friends. Letting down the people who'd booked, many of them regulars who looked forward to a little break away from home in the company of like-minded people.

And then there were the standing orders for her own little 'Coleridge House' cottage industry. The homemade fudge and toffee. The honey.

'Cancel the courses?' Adam was frowning. 'Are you saying that your grandfather didn't leave you the house?'

The breeze was much colder coming off the lake and May really was shivering now.

'Yes. I mean, no…He left it to me, but there are conditions involved.'

Conditions her grandfather had known about but had never thought worth mentioning before the stroke had robbed him of so much of his memory.

But why would he? There had been plenty of time back then. And he'd done a major matchmaking job with Michael Linton, a little older, steady as a rock and looking for a well brought up, old-fashioned girl to run his house, provide him with an heir and a spare or two. The kind of man her mother had been supposed to marry.

'What kind of conditions?' Adam asked.

'Ones that I don't meet,' she said abruptly, as keen to change the subject as he had been a few moments earlier.

The morning had been shocking enough without sharing the humiliating entailment that Freddie Jennings had missed when he'd read her grandfather's very straightforward will after the funeral. The one Grandpa had made after her mother died which, after generous bequests to his favourite charities, bequeathed everything else he owned to his only living relative, his then infant granddaughter, Mary Louise Coleridge.

Thankfully, they'd reached the small gate that led directly from the garden of her family home into the park and May was able to avoid explanations as, hanging onto the kitten, she fumbled awkwardly in her hand-bag for her key.

But her hands were shaking as the shock of the morning swept over her and she dropped it. Without a word, Adam picked it up, unlocked the gate, then, taking her arm to steady her, he pushed the buggy up through the garden towards the rear of the house.

She stopped in the mud room and filled a saucer with milk from the fridge kept for animal food. The kitten trampled in it, lapping greedily, while she lined a cardboard box with an old fleece she used for gardening.

Only when she'd tucked it up safely in the warm was she able to focus on her own mess.

Her jacket had an ominous wet patch and her skirt was plastered with mud. It was her best black suit and maybe the dry cleaners could do something with it, although right at the moment she didn't want to see it ever again.

As she unzipped the skirt, let it drop to the floor and kicked it in the corner, Adam cleared his throat, reminding her that he was there. As if every cell in her body wasn't vibrating with the knowledge.

'Robbie will kill me if I track dirt through the house,' she said, peeling off the shredded tights and running a towel under the tap to rub the mud off her feet. Then, as he kicked off his mud spattered shoes and slipped the buckle on his belt, 'What are you doing?'

'I've been on the wrong side of Hatty Robson,' he replied. 'If she's coming at me with antiseptic, I want her in a good mood.'

May swallowed hard and, keeping her eyes firmly focused on Nancie, followed him into the warmth of the kitchen with the buggy, leaving him to hang his folded trousers over the Aga, only looking up at a burst of laughter from the garden.

It was the Christmas Workshop crossing the court-yard, heading towards the house for their mid-morning break.

'Flapjacks!'

'What?'

She turned and blinked at the sight of Adam in his shirt tails and socks. 'We're about to have company,' she said, unscrambling her brain and, grabbing the first aid box from beneath the sink, she said, 'Come on!' She didn't stop to see if he was following, but beat a hasty retreat through the inner hall and up the back stairs. 'Bring Nancie!'

Adam, who had picked up the buggy, baby, bag and all to follow, found he had to take a moment to catch his breath when he reached the top.

'Are you all right?' she asked.

'The buggy is heavier than it looks. Do you want to tell me what that was all about?'

'While the appearance of Adam Wavell, minus trousers, in my kitchen would undoubtedly have been the highlight of the week for my Christmas Workshop ladies...' and done her reputation a power of good '...I could not absolutely guarantee their discretion.'

'The highlight?' he asked, kinking up his eyebrow in a well-remembered arc.

'The most excitement I can usually offer is a new cookie recipe. While it's unlikely any of them will call the news desk at *Celebrity*, you can be sure they'd tell all their friends,' she said, 'and sooner or later someone would be bound to realise that you plus a baby makes

it a story with the potential to earn them a bob or two.'
Which wiped the suspicion of a grin from his face.

'So what do we do now?' he asked. 'Hide at the top
of the stairs until they've gone?'

'No need for that,' she said, opening a door that revealed a wide L-shaped landing. 'Come on, I'll clean up
your hand while you pray to high heaven that Nancie
doesn't wake up and cry.'

Nancie, right on cue, opened incredibly dark eyes
and, even before she gave a little whimper, was immediately the centre of attention.

May shoved the first aid box into Adam's hand.

'Shh-sh-shush, little one,' she said as she lifted her
out of the buggy, leaving Adam to follow her to the room
that had once been her nursery.

When she'd got too old for a nanny, she'd moved into
the empty nanny's suite, which had its own bathroom
and tiny kitchenette, and had turned the nursery into
what she'd been careful to describe as a sitting room
rather than a study, using a table rather than a desk for
her school projects.

Her grandfather had discouraged her from thinking
about university—going off and 'getting her head filled
with a lot of nonsense' was what he'd actually said. Not
that it had been a possibility once she'd dropped out of
school even if she'd wanted to. She hadn't been blessed
with her mother's brain and school had been bad enough.
Why would anyone voluntarily lengthen the misery?

When she'd begun to take over the running of the
house, she'd used her grandmother's elegant little desk in
her sitting room, but her business needed a proper office
and she'd since converted one of the old pantries, keep-

ing this room as a place of refuge for when the house was filled with guests. When she needed to be on her own.

'Shut the door,' she said as Adam followed her in with the buggy. 'Once they're in the conservatory talking ten to the dozen over a cup of coffee, they won't hear Nancie even if she screams her head off.'

For the moment the baby was nuzzling contently at her shoulder, although, even with her minimal experience, she suspected that wasn't a situation that would last for long.

'The bathroom's through there. Wash off the mud and I'll do the necessary with the antiseptic wipes so that you can get on your way.'

'What about you?'

'I can wait.'

'No, you can't. Heaven knows what's lurking in that mud,' he replied as, without so much as a by-your-leave, he took her free hand, led her through her bedroom and, after a glance around to gain his bearings, into the bathroom beyond. 'Are your tetanus shots up to date?' he asked, quashing any thought that his mind was on anything other than the practical.

'Yes.' She was the most organised woman in the entire world when it came to the details. It was a family trait. One more reason to believe that her grandfather hadn't simply let things slide. That he'd made a deliberate choice to keep things as they were.

Had her mother known about the will? she wondered. Been threatened with it?

'Are yours?' she asked.

'I imagine so. I pay good money for a PA to deal with stuff like that,' he said, running the taps, testing the water beneath his fingers.

'Efficient, is she?' May asked, imagining a tall, glamorous female in a designer suit and four-inch heels.

'He. Is that too hot?'

She tested it with her fingertips. 'No, it's fine,' she said, reaching for the soap. 'Is that common? A male PA?'

'I run an equal opportunities company. Jake was the best applicant for the job and yes, he is frighteningly efficient. I'm going to have to promote him to executive assistant if I want to keep him. Hold on,' he said. 'You can't do that one-handed.'

She had anticipated him taking Nancie from her, but instead he unfastened his cuffs, rolled back his sleeves and, while she was still transfixed by his powerful wrists, he took the soap from her.

'No!' she said as she realised what he was about to do. He'd already worked the soap into a lather, however, and, hampered by the baby, she could do nothing as he stood behind her with his arms around her, took her scratched hand in his and began to wash it with extreme thoroughness. Finger by finger. Working his thumb gently across her palm where she'd grazed it when she'd fallen. Over her knuckles. Circling her wrist.

'The last time anyone did this, I was no more than six years old,' she protested in an attempt to keep herself from being seduced by the sensuous touch of long fingers, silky lather. The warmth of his body as he leaned into her back, his chin against her shoulder. His cheek against hers. The sensation of being not quite in control of any part of her body whenever he was within touching distance, her heartbeat amplified so that he, and everyone within twenty yards, must surely hear.

'Six?' he repeated, apparently oblivious to her confusion. 'What happened? Did you fall off your pony?'

'My bike. I never had a pony.' She'd scraped her knee and had her face pressed against Robbie's apron. She'd been baking and the kitchen had been filled with the scent of cinnamon, apples, pastry cooking as she'd cleaned her up, comforted her.

Today, it was the cool, slightly rough touch of Adam's chin against her cheek but there was nothing safe or comforting about him. She associated him with leather, rain, her heartbeat raised with fear, excitement, a pitiful joy followed by excruciating embarrassment. Despair at the hopelessness of her dreams.

There had been no rain today, there was no leather, but the mingled scents of clean skin, warm linen, shampoo were uncompromisingly male and the intimacy of his touch was sending tiny shock waves through her body, disturbing her in ways unknown to that green and heartbroken teen.

Oblivious to the effect he was having on her, he took an antiseptic wipe from the first aid box and finished the job.

'That's better. Now let's take a look at your arm.'

'My arm?'

'There's blood on your sleeve.'

'Is there?' While she was craning to see the mingled mud and watery red mess that was never going to wash out whatever the detergent ads said, he had her shirt undone. No shaky-fingered fumbling with buttons this time. She was still trying to get her tongue, lips, teeth into line to protest when he eased it off her shoulder and down her arm with what could only be described as practised ease.

'Ouch. That looks painful.'

She was standing in nothing but her bra and pants

and he was looking at her elbow? Okay, her underwear might be lacy but it was at the practical, hold 'em up, rather than push 'em up end of the market. But, even if she wasn't wearing the black lace, scarlet woman underwear, the kind of bra that stopped traffic and would make Adam Wavell's firm jaw drop, he could at least *notice* that she was practically naked.

In her dreams… Her nightmares…

His jaw was totally under control as he gave his full attention to her elbow.

'This might sting a bit…'

It should have stung, maybe it did, but she was feeling no pain as his thick dark hair slid over his forehead, every perfectly cut strand moving in sleek formation as he bent to work. Only a heat that began low in her belly and spread like a slow fuse along her thighs, filling her breasts, her womb with an aching, painful need that brought a tiny moan to her lips.

'Does that hurt?' he asked, looking up, grey eyes creased in concern. 'Maybe you should go to Casualty, have an X-ray just to be on the safe side.'

'No,' she said quickly. 'It's fine. Really.'

It was a lie. It wasn't fine; it was humiliating, appalling to respond so mindlessly to a man who, when he saw you in public, put the maximum possible distance between you. To want him to stop looking at her scabby elbow and look at her. See her. Want her.

As if.

These days he was never short of some totally gorgeous girl to keep him warm at night. The kind who wore 'result' shoes and bad girl underwear.

She was more your wellington boots kind of woman. Good skin and teeth, reasonable if boringly brown eyes, but that was it. There was nothing about her that would catch the eye of a man who, these days, had everything.

'You're going to have a whopping bruise,' he said, looking up, catching her staring at him.

'I'll live.'

'This time. But maybe you should consider giving up climbing trees,' he said, pulling a towel down from the pile on the rack, taking her hand in his and patting it dry before working his way up her arm.

'I keep telling myself that,' she said. 'But you know how it is. There's some poor creature in trouble and you're the only one around. What can you do?'

'I'll give you my cell number...' He tore open another antiseptic wipe and took it over the graze on her elbow. Used a second one on his own hand. 'Next time,' he said, looking up with a smile that was like a blow in the solar plexus, 'call me.'

Oh, sure...

'I thought you said you were going to South America.'

'No problem. That's what I have a personal assistant for. You call me, I'll call Jake and he'll ride to your rescue.'

In exactly the same way that he was using her to take care of Nancie, she thought.

'Wouldn't it be easier to give me his number? Cut out the middle sidekick.'

'And miss out on having you shout at me?'

First the blow to the solar plexus, then a jab behind the knees and she was going down...

'That's all part of the fun,' he added.

Fun. Oh, right. She was forgetting. She was the clown...

'My legs are muddy. I really need to take a shower,'

she added before he took it upon himself to wash them, too. More specifically, she needed to get some clothes on and get a grip. 'There's a kettle in the kitchenette if you want to make yourself a drink before you go.'

She didn't give him a chance to argue, but dumped Nancie in his arms and, closing her ears to the baby's outraged complaint, shut the door on him.

She couldn't lock it. The lock had broken years ago and she hadn't bothered to get it fixed. Why would she when she shared the house with her invalid grandfather and Robbie, neither of whom were ever going to surprise her in the shower?

Nor was Adam, she told herself as, discarding what little remained of her modesty, she dumped her filthy shirt in the wash basket, peeled off her underwear and stepped under the spray.

It should have been a cold shower, something to quench the fizz of heat bubbling through her veins.

Since it was obvious that even when she was ninety Adam Wavell would have the same effect on her, with or without his trousers, she decided to forgo the pain and turned up the temperature.

CHAPTER THREE

ADAM TOOK A LONG, slow breath as the bathroom door closed behind him.

The rage hadn't dimmed with time, but neither had the desire. Maybe it was all part of the same thing. He hadn't been good enough for her then and, despite his success, she'd never missed an opportunity to make it clear that he never would be.

But she wasn't immune. And, since a broken engagement, there had never been anyone else in her life. She hadn't gone to university, never had a job, missing out on the irresponsible years when most of their contemporaries were obsessed with clothes, clubbing, falling in and out of love.

Instead, she'd stayed at home to run Coleridge House, exactly like some Edwardian miss, marking time until she was plucked off the shelf, at which point she would do pretty much the same thing for her husband. And, exactly like a good Edwardian girl, she'd abandoned a perfect-fit marriage without hesitation to take on the job of caring for her grandfather after his stroke. Old-fashioned. A century out of her time.

According to the receptionist who'd been raving about the garden design course, what May Coleridge needed was someone to take her in hand, help her lose a bit of weight and get a life before she spread into a prematurely middle-aged spinsterhood, with only her strays to keep her warm at night.

Clearly his receptionist had never seen her strip off her skirt and tights or she'd have realised that there was nothing middle-aged about her thighs, shapely calves or a pair of the prettiest ankles he'd ever had the pleasure of following up a flight of stairs.

But then he already knew all that.

Had been the first boy to ever see those lush curves, the kind that had gone out of fashion half a century ago, back before the days of Twiggy and the Swinging Sixties.

But when he'd unbuttoned her shirt—the alternative had been relieving her of Nancie and he wasn't about to do that; he'd wanted her to feel the baby clinging to her, needing her—he'd discovered that his memory had served him poorly as he was confronted with a cleavage that required no assistance from either silicon or a well engineered bra. It was the real thing. Full, firm, ripe, the genuine peaches and cream experience—the kind of peaches that would fill a man's hand, skin as smooth and white as double cream—and his only thought had been how wrong his receptionist was about May.

She didn't need to lose weight.

Not one gram.

MAY WOULD HAPPILY have stayed under the shower until the warm water had washed away the entire ghastly morning. Since that was beyond the power of mere water, she contented herself with a squirt of lemon-scented shower gel and a quick sluice down to remove all traces of mud before wrapping herself in a towel.

But while, on the surface, her skin might be warmer, she was still shivering.

Shock would do that, even without the added problem of the Adam Wavell effect.

Breathlessness. A touch of dizziness whenever she saw him. Something she should have grown out of with her puppy fat. But the puppy fat had proved as stubbornly resistant as her pathetic crush on a boy who'd been so far out of her reach that he might as well have been in outer space. To be needed by him had once been the most secret desire shared only with her diary.

Be careful what you wish for, had been one of Robbie's warnings from the time she was a little girl and she'd been right in that, as in everything.

Adam needed her now. 'But only to take care of Saffy's baby,' she muttered, ramming home the point as she towelled herself dry before wrapping herself from head to toe in a towelling robe. She'd exposed enough flesh for one day.

She needn't have worried. Adam had taken Nancie through to the sitting room and closed the door behind him. Clearly he'd seen more than enough of her flesh for one day.

Ignoring the lustrous dark autumn gold cord skirt she'd bought ages ago in a sale and never worn, she pulled on the scruffiest pair of jogging pants and sweatshirt that she owned. There was no point in trying to compete with the girls he dated these days. Lean, glossy thoroughbreds.

She had more in common with a Shetland pony. Small, overweight, a shaggy-maned clown.

What was truly pathetic was that, despite knowing all that, if circumstances had permitted, May knew she would have still succumbed to his smile. Taken care of Saffy's adorable baby, grateful to have the chance to be that close to him, if only for a week or two while her mother was doing what came naturally. Being bad by most people's standards, but actually having a life.

NANCIE BEGAN TO grizzle into his shoulder and Adam instinctively began to move, shushing her as he walked around May's private sitting room, scarcely able to believe it had been so easy to breach the citadel.

He examined the pictures on her walls. Her books. Picked up a small leather-bound volume lying on a small table, as if she liked to keep it close to hand.

Shakespeare's *Sonnets*. As he replaced it, something fluttered from between the pages. A rose petal that had been pressed between them. As he bent to pick it up, it crumbled to red dust between his fingers and for a moment he remembered a bunch of red roses that, in the middle of winter, had cost him a fortune. Every penny of which had to be earned labouring in the market before school.

He moved on to a group of silver-framed photographs. Her grandparents were there. Her mother on the day she'd graduated. He picked up one of May, five or six years old, holding a litter of kittens and, despite the nightmare morning he was having, the memories that being here had brought back into the sharpest focus, he found himself smiling.

She might have turned icy on him but she was still prepared to risk her neck for a kitten. And any pathetic creature in trouble would have got the same response, whether it was a drowning bird on the school roof— and they'd both been given the maximum punishment short of suspension for that little escapade—or a kitten up a tree.

Not that she was such an unlikely champion of the pitiful.

She'd been one of those short, overweight kids who were never going to be one of the cool group in her year at school. And the rest of them had been too afraid of being seen to be sucking up to the girl from the big house to make friends with her.

She really should have been at some expensive private school with her peers instead of being tossed into the melting pot of the local comprehensive. One of those schools where they wore expensive uniforms as if they were designer clothes. Spoke like princesses.

It wasn't as if her family couldn't afford it. But poor little May Coleridge's brilliant mother—having had the benefit of everything her birth could bestow—had turned her back on her class and become a feminist firebrand who'd publicly deplored all such elitism and died of a fever after giving birth in some desperately inadequate hospital in the Third World with no father in evidence.

If her mother had lived, he thought, May might well have launched a counter-rebellion, demanding her right to a privileged education if only to declare her own independence of spirit; but how could she rebel against someone who'd died giving her life?

Like her mother, though, she'd held on to who she was, refusing to give an inch to peer pressure to slur the perfect vowels, drop the crisp consonants, hitch up her skirt and use her school tie as a belt. To seek anonymity in the conformity of the group. Because that would have been a betrayal, too. Of who she was.

It was what had first drawn him to her. His response to being different had been to keep his head down, hoping to avoid trouble and he'd admired, envied her quiet, obstinate courage. Her act first, think later response to any situation.

Pretty much what had got them into so much trouble in the first place.

Nancie, deciding that she required something a little more tangible than a 'sh-shush' and a jiggle, opened her tiny mouth to let out an amazingly loud wail. He replaced the photograph. Called May.

The water had stopped running a while ago and, when there was no reply, he tapped on the bedroom door.

'Help!'

There was no response.

'May?' He opened the door a crack and then, since there wasn't a howl of outrage, he pushed it wide.

The room, a snowy indulgence of pure femininity, had been something of a shock. For some reason he'd imagined that the walls of her bedroom would be plastered in posters of endangered animals. But the only picture was a watercolour of Coleridge House painted when it was still surrounded by acres of parkland. A reminder of who she was?

There should have been a sense of triumph at having made it this far into her inner sanctum. But looking at that picture made him feel like a trespasser.

MAY PUSHED OPEN the door to her grandfather's room.

She still thought of it as his room even though he'd long ago moved downstairs to the room she'd converted for him, determined that he should be as comfortable as possible. Die with dignity in his own home.

'May?'

She jumped at the sound of Adam's voice.

'Sorry, I didn't mean to startle you, but Nancie is getting fractious.'

'Maybe she needs changing. Or feeding.' His only response was a helpless shrug. 'Both happen on a regular basis, I understand,' she said, turning to the wardrobe, hunting down one of her grandfather's silk dressing gowns, holding it out to him. 'You'd better put this on before you go and fetch your trousers.' Then, as he took it from her, she realised her mistake. He couldn't put it on while he was holding the baby.

Nancie came into her arms like a perfect fit. A soft, warm, gorgeous bundle of cuddle nestling against her shoulder. A slightly damp bundle of cuddle.

'Changing,' she said.

'Yes,' he said, tying the belt around his waist and looking more gorgeous than any man wearing a dressing gown that was too narrow across the shoulders, too big around the waist and too short by a country mile had any right to look.

'You knew!'

'It isn't rocket science,' he said, looking around him. 'This was your grandfather's room.'

It wasn't a question and she didn't bother to answer. She could have, probably should have, used the master bedroom to increase the numbers for the arts and crafts weekends she hosted, but hadn't been able to bring herself to do that. While he was alive, it was his room and it still looked as if he'd just left it to go for a stroll in the park before dropping in at the Crown for lunch with old friends.

The centuries-old furniture gleamed. There were

fresh sheets on the bed, his favourite Welsh quilt turned back as if ready for him. And a late rose that Robbie had placed on the dressing table glowed in the thin sunshine.

'Impressive.'

'As you said, Adam, he was an impressive man,' she said, turning abruptly and, leaving him to follow or not as he chose, returned to her room.

He followed.

'You're going to have to learn how to do this,' she warned as she fetched a clean towel from her bathroom and handed it to him.

He opened it without a word, lay it over the bed cover and May placed Nancie on it. She immediately began to whimper.

'Watch her,' she said, struggling against the instinct to pick her up again, comfort her. 'I'll get her bag.'

Ignoring his, 'Yes, ma'am,' which was on a par with the ironic 'Mouse', she unhooked Nancie's bag from the buggy, opened it, found a little pink drawstring bag that contained a supply of disposable nappies and held one out to him.

'Me?' He looked at the nappy, the baby and then at her. 'You're not kidding, are you?' She continued to hold out the nappy and he took it without further comment. 'Okay. Talk me through it.'

'What makes you think I know anything about changing a baby? And if you say that I'm a woman, you are on your own.'

Adam, on the point of saying exactly that, reconsidered. He'd thought that getting through the door would be the problem but that had been the easy part. Obviously, he was asking a lot but, considering Saffy's confidence and her own inability to resist something helpless, he was meeting a lot more resistance from May than he'd anticipated.

'You really know nothing about babies?'

'Look around you, Adam. The last baby to occupy this nursery was me.'

'This was your nursery?' he said, taking in the lace-draped bed, the pale blue carpet, the lace and velvet draped window where she'd stood and watched his humiliation at the hands of her 'impressive' grandfather.

'Actually, this was the nanny's room,' she said. 'The nursery was out there.'

'Lucky nanny.' The room, with its bathroom, was almost as big as the flat he'd grown up in.

May saw the casual contempt with which he surveyed the room but didn't bother to explain that her grandfather had had it decorated for her when she was fifteen. That it reflected the romantic teenager she'd been rather than the down-to-earth woman she'd become.

'As I was saying,' she said, doing her best to hold onto reality, ignore the fact that Adam Wavell was standing in her bedroom, 'the last baby to occupy this nursery was me and only children of only children don't have nieces and nephews to practise on.' Then, having given him a moment for the reality of her ignorance to sink in, she said, 'I believe you have to start with the poppers of her sleep suit.'

'Right,' he said, looking at the nappy, then at the infant and she could almost see the cogs in his brain turning as he decided on a change of plan. That his best move would be to demonstrate his incompetence and wait for her to take over.

He set about unfastening the poppers but Nancie, thinking it was a game, kicked and wriggled and flung her legs up in the air. Maybe she'd maligned him. Instead of getting flustered, he laughed, as if suddenly realising that she wasn't just an annoying encumbrance but a tiny person.

'Come on, Nancie,' he begged. 'I'm a man. This is new to me. Give me a break.'

Maybe it was the sound of his voice, but she lay still, watching him with her big dark eyes, her little forehead furrowed in concentration as if she was trying to work out who he was.

And, while his hands seemed far too big for the delicate task of removing the little pink sleep suit, if it had been his intention to look clumsy and incompetent, he was failing miserably.

The poppers were dealt with, the nappy removed in moments and his reward was a great big smile.

'Thanks, gorgeous,' he said softly. And then leaned down and kissed her dark curls.

The baby grabbed a handful of his hair and, as she watched the two of them looking at one another, May saw the exact moment when Adam Wavell fell in love with his baby niece. Saw how he'd be with his own child.

Swallowing down a lump the size of her fist, she said, 'I'll take that, shall I?' And, relieving him of the nappy, she used it as an excuse to retreat to the bathroom to dispose of it in the pedal bin. Taking her time over washing her hands.

'Do I need to use cream or powder or something?' he called after her.

'I've no idea,' she said, gripping the edge of the basin.

'Babies should come with a handbook. Have you got a computer up here?'

'A what?'

'I could look it up on the web.'

'Oh, for goodness' sake!' She abandoned the safety of the bathroom and joined him beside the bed. 'She's perfectly dry,' she said, after running her palm over the softest little bottom imaginable. 'Just put on the nappy and…and get yourself a nanny, Adam.'

'Easier said than done.'

'It's not difficult. I can give you the number of a reliable agency.'

'Really? And why would you have their number?'

'The Garland Agency provide domestic and nursing staff, too. I needed help. The last few months…'

'I'm sorry. I didn't think.' He turned away, opened the nappy, examined it to see how it worked. 'However, there are a couple of problems with the nanny scenario. My apartment is an open-plan loft. There's nowhere to put either a baby or a nanny.'

'What's the other problem?' He was concentrating on fastening the nappy and didn't answer. 'You said there were a couple of things.' He shook his head and, suddenly suspicious, she said, 'When was the last time you actually saw Saffy?'

'I've been busy,' he said, finally straightening. 'And she's been evasive,' he added. 'I bought a lease on a flat for her in Paris, but I've just learned that she's moved out, presumably to move in with Nancie's father. She's sublet it and has been pocketing the rent for months.'

'You're not a regular visitor, then?'

'You know what she's like, May. I didn't even know she was pregnant.'

'And the baby's father? Who is he?'

'His name is Michel. That's all I know.'

'Poor Saffy,' she said. And there was no doubt that she was pitying her her family.

'She could have come to me,' he protested. 'Picked up the phone.'

'And you'd have done what? Sent her a cheque?'

'It's what she usually wants. You don't think she ever calls to find out how I am, do you?'

'You are strong. She isn't. How was she when she left the baby with you?'

'I'd better wash my hands,' he said.

Without thinking, she put out her hand and grabbed his arm to stop him. 'What aren't you telling me, Adam?'

He didn't answer, but took a folded sheet of paper from his shirt pocket and gave it to her before retreating to the bathroom.

It looked as if it had been screwed up and tossed into a bin, then rescued as an afterthought.

She smoothed it out. Read it.

'Saffy's on the run from her baby's father?' she asked, looking up as he returned. 'Where did she leave the baby?'

'In my office. I found her there when I left a meeting to fetch some papers. Saffy had managed to slip in and out without anyone seeing her. She hasn't lost the skills she learned as a juvenile shoplifter.'

'She must have been absolutely desperate.'

'Maybe she is,' he said. 'But not nearly as desperate as I am right at this minute. I know you haven't got the time of day for me, but she said you'd help her.'

'I would,' she protested. 'Of course I would…'

'But?'

'Where's your mother?' she asked.

'She relocated to Spain after my father died.'

'Moving everyone out of town, Adam? Out of sight, out of mind?'

A tightening around his mouth suggested that her barb had found its mark. And it was unfair. He'd turned his life around, risen above the nightmare of his family. Saffy hadn't had his strength, but she still deserved better from him than a remittance life in a foreign country. All the bad things she'd done had been a cry for the attention, love she craved.

'She won't have gone far.'

'That's not the impression she gives in her note.'

'She'll want to know the baby is safe.' Then, turning on him, 'What about you?'

'Me?'

'Who else?' she demanded fiercely because Adam was too close, because her arms were aching to pick up his precious niece. She busied herself instead, fastening Nancie into her suit. 'Can't you take paternity leave or something?'

'I'm not the baby's father.'

'Time off, then. You do take holidays?'

'When I can't avoid it.' He shook his head. 'I told you. I'm leaving for South America tomorrow.'

'Can't you put it off?'

'It's not just a commercial trip, May. There are politics involved. Government agencies. I'm signing fair trade contracts with cooperatives. I've got a meeting with the President of Samindera that it's taken months to set up.'

'So the answer is no.'

'The answer is no. It's you,' he said, 'or I'm in trouble.'

'In that case you're in trouble.' She picked up the baby

and handed her to him, as clear a statement as she could make. 'I'd help Saffy in a heartbeat if I could but—'

'But you wouldn't cross the road to help me.'

'No!'

'Just cross the road to avoid speaking to me. Would I have got anywhere at all if you hadn't been stuck up a tree? Unable to escape?'

That was so unfair! He had no idea. No clue about all the things she'd done for him and it was on the tip of her tongue to say so.

'I'm sorry. You must think I've got some kind of nerve even asking you.'

'No… Of course I'd help you if I could. But I've got a few problems of my own.'

'Tell me,' he said, lifting his spare hand to wipe away the stupid tear that had leaked despite her determination not to break down, not to cry, his fingers cool against her hot cheek. 'Tell me about the world of trouble you're in.'

'I didn't think you'd heard.'

'I heard but you asked where Saffy was…' He shook his head. 'I'm sorry, May, I've been banging on about my own problems instead of listening to yours.' His hand opened to curve gently around her cheek. 'It was something about the house. Tell me. Maybe I can help.'

She shook her head, struggling with the temptation to lean into his touch, to throw herself into his arms, spill out the whole sorry story. But there was no easy comfort.

All she had left was her dignity and she tore herself away, took a step back, then turned away to look out of the window.

'Not this time, Adam,' she said, her voice as crisp as new snow. 'This isn't anything as simple as getting stuck up a tree. The workshop ladies have returned to the stables. It's safe for you to leave now.'

She'd been sure that would be enough to drive him away, but he'd followed her. She could feel the warmth of his body at her shoulder.

'I'm pretty good at complicated, too,' he said, his voice as gentle as the caress of his breath against her hair.

'From what I've read, you've had a lot of practice,' she said, digging her nails into her hands. 'I'm sure you mean well, Adam, but there's nothing you can do.'

'Try me,' he challenged.

'Okay.' She swung around to face him. 'If you've got a job going for someone who can provide food and accommodation for a dozen or so people on a regular basis, run a production line for homemade toffee, is a dab hand with hospital corners, can milk a goat, keep bees and knows how to tame a temperamental lawnmower, that would be a start,' she said in a rush.

'You need a job?' Adam replied, brows kinked up in a confident smile. As if he could make the world right for her by lunch time and still have time to add another company or two to his portfolio. 'Nothing could be simpler. I need a baby minder. I'll pay top rates if you can start right now.'

'The one job for which I have no experience, no qualifications,' she replied. 'And, more to the point, no licence.'

'Licence?'

'I'm not related to Nancie. Without a child-minding licence, it would be illegal.'

'Who would know?' he asked, without missing a beat.

'You're suggesting I don't declare the income to the taxman? Or that the presence of a baby would go unnoticed?' She shook her head. 'People are in and out of here all the time and it would be around the coffee morning circuit faster than greased lightning. Someone from Social Services would be on the doorstep before I could say "knife".' She shrugged. 'Of course, most of the old tabbies would assume Nancie was mine. "*Just* like her mother…"' she said, using the disapproving tone she'd heard a hundred times. Although, until now, not in reference to her own behaviour.

'You're right,' he said, conceding without another word. 'Obviously your reputation is far too precious a commodity to be put at risk.'

'I didn't say that,' she protested.

'Forget it, May. I should have known better.' He shrugged. 'Actually, I did know better but I thought you and Saffy had some kind of a bond. But it doesn't matter. I'll call the authorities. I have no doubt that Nancie's father has reported her missing by now and it's probably for the best to leave it to the court to—'

'You can't do that!' she protested. 'Saffy is relying on you to get her out of this mess.'

'Is she? Read her letter again, May.'

CHAPTER FOUR

THERE WAS THE longest pause while he allowed that to sink in. Then he said, 'Is there any chance of that coffee you promised me?'

May started. 'What? Oh, yes, I'm sorry. It's instant; will that do?'

'Anything.'

The tiny kitchenette was in little more than a cupboard, but she had everything to hand and in a few minutes she returned with a couple of mugs.

'I'll get a blanket and you can put Nancie on the floor.'

'Can you do that?'

She didn't answer, just fetched a blanket from the linen cupboard, pausing on the landing to listen. The silence confirmed that the workshop coffee break was over but the thought of going downstairs, facing Robbie with her unlikely visitor, was too daunting.

Back in her sitting room, she laid the folded blanket on the floor, took Nancie from Adam and put her down on it. Then she went and fetched the teddy she'd spotted in her bag. Putting off for as long as possible the moment when she would have to tell Adam the truth.

'I know you just think I'm trying to get you to take this on, dig me out of a hole,' Adam said when she finally returned. Picking up her coffee, clutching it in front of her like a shield, she sat beside him on the sofa. 'But you really are a natural.'

'I think you're just trying to avoid putting off telling me the whole truth.'

'All I know is what's in Saffy's letter.' He dragged long fingers through his dark hair, looking for once less than the assured man, but more like the boy she remembered. 'I've called some of her friends but if she's confided in them, then, aren't telling.'

'What about her agent?' she prompted.

'It seems that they parted company months ago. Her modelling career was yet another fantasy, it seems.'

May picked up the letter and read it again. 'She doesn't sound exactly rational. She could be suffering from post-natal depression. Or maybe having Nancie has triggered a bipolar episode. She always did swing between highs and lows.'

'And if she was? Would you help then?' He shook his head before she could answer. 'I'm sorry. That was unfair, but what I need right now, May, is someone I can trust. Someone who knows her. Who won't judge. Or run to the press with this.'

'The press?'

'Something like this would damage me.'

'You! Is that all you're worried about?' she demanded, absolutely furious with him. 'Yourself. Not Saffy? Not Nancie?'

Nancie, startled, threw out a hand, lost her teddy and began to cry. Glad of the chance to put some distance between them, May scrambled to her knees to rescue the toy, give it back to the baby. Stayed with her on the floor to play with her.

'The Garland Agency has a branch in Melchester,'

she said. 'I suggest you call them. They've a world class reputation and I have no doubt that discretion comes with the price tag.'

'As I said. There are a number of problems with that scenario. Apart from the fact that my apartment is completely unsuitable. You've read Saffy's letter. They'll want details. They'll want to know where her mother is. Who she is. What right I have to make childcare arrangements. Saffy is on the run, May. There's a court order in place.'

'You must have some idea where she'd go? Isn't there a friend?'

'If anyone else had asked me that I'd have said that if she was in trouble, she'd come to you.' He stared into the cup he was holding. 'I did ring her a few months ago when there was a rumour in one of the gossip mags about her health. Probably someone heard her throwing up and was quick to suggest an eating disorder. But she was bright, bubbly, rushing off to a shoot. At least that's what she said.' He shrugged. 'She was too eager to get me off the phone. And maybe I was too eager to be reassured. I should have known better.'

'She sounds almost frightened.'

'I know. I'm making discreet enquiries, but until I know who this man is I'm not going to hand over my niece. And I'm doing my best to find Saffy, too. But the last thing we need is a hue and cry.'

He put down the mug, knelt beside her.

'This time I'm the one up the drainpipe, Mouse, and it's raining a monsoon. Won't you climb up and rescue me?'

'I wish I could help—'

'There is no one else,' he said, cutting her off.

The unspoken, *And you owe me*... lay unsaid between them. But she knew that, like her, he was remembering the hideous scene when he'd come to the back door, white-faced, clutching his roses. It had remained closed to his knock but he hadn't gone away. He'd stayed there, mulishly stubborn, for so long that her grandfather had chased him away with the hose.

It had been the week before Christmas and the water was freezing but, while he'd been driven from the doorstep, he'd stayed in the garden defiantly, silently staring up at her room, visibly shivering, until it was quite dark.

She'd stood in this window and watched him, unable to do or say anything without making it much, much worse. Torn between her grandfather and the boy she loved. She would have defied her grandpa, just as her mother had defied him, but there had been Saffy. And Adam. And she'd kept the promise that had been wrung from her even though her heart was breaking.

She didn't owe him a thing. She'd paid and paid and paid...

'I can't,' she said, getting up, putting distance between them. 'I told you, I know no more than you do about looking after a baby.'

'I think we both know that your experience as a rescuer of lame ducks puts you streets ahead of me.'

'Nancie is not a duck,' she said a touch desperately. Why wouldn't he just take no an answer? There must a dozen women who'd fall over themselves to help him out. Why pick on her? 'And, even if she were,' she added, 'I still couldn't help.'

She couldn't help anyone. That was another problem she was going to have to face. Finding homes for her family of strays.

There wasn't much call for a three-legged cat or a blind duck. And then there were the chickens, Jack and Dolly, the bees. She very much doubted if the Crown would consider a donkey and a superannuated nanny goat an asset to the nation's coffers.

'Why not, May?' he insisted. He got to his feet too, but he'd kept his distance. She didn't have to turn to know that his brows would be drawn down in that slightly perplexed look that was so familiar. 'Tell me. Maybe I can help.'

'Trust me,' she said. Nancie had caught hold of her finger and she lifted the little hand to her lips, kissed it. 'You can't help me. No one can.'

Then, since it was obvious that, unless she explained the situation, Adam wasn't going to give up, she told him why.

Why she couldn't help him or Saffy.

Why he couldn't help her.

For a moment he didn't say anything and she knew he would be repeating her words over in his head, exactly as she had done this morning when Freddie had apologetically explained the situation in words of one syllable.

Adam had assumed financial worries to be the problem. Inheritance tax. Despite the downturn in the market, the house was worth a great deal of money and it was going to take a lot of cash to keep the Inland Revenue happy.

'You have to be married by the end of the month or you'll lose the house?' he repeated, just to be certain that he'd understood.

She swallowed, nodded.

She would never have told him if he hadn't been so persistent, he realised. She'd told him that she couldn't help but, instead of asking her why, something he would have done if it had been a work-related problem, he'd been so tied up with his immediate problem that he hadn't been listening.

He was listening now. And there was only one thought in his head. That fate had dropped her into his lap. That the boy who hadn't been good enough to touch Coleridge flesh, who'd shivered as he'd waited for her to defy her grandfather, prove that her hot kisses had been true, now held her future in the palm of his hand.

That he would crack the ice in May Coleridge's body between the fine linen sheets of her grandfather's four-poster bed and listen to the old man spin in his grave as did it.

'What's so important about the end of the month?' he asked. Quietly, calmly. He'd learned not to show his thoughts, or his feelings.

'My birthday. It's on the second of December.'

She'd kept her back to him while she'd told him her problems, but now she turned and looked up at him. She'd looked up at him before, her huge amber eyes making him burn, her soft lips quivering with uncertainty. The taste of them still haunted him.

He'd liked her. Really liked her. She had guts, grit and, despite the wide gulf in their lives, they had a lot in common. And he'd loved being in the quiet, ordered peace of the lovely gardens of Coleridge House, the stables where she'd kept her animals. Everything so clean and well organised.

He'd loved the fact that she had her own kettle to make coffee. That there was always homemade cake in a tin. The shared secrecy. That no one but she knew he was there. Not her grandfather, not his family. It had all been so different from the nightmare of his home life.

But taking her injured animals, helping her look after them was one thing. She wasn't the kind of girl any guy—even one with no pretensions to street cred— wanted to be seen with at the school disco.

But their meetings weren't as secret as he'd thought. His sister had got curious, followed him and blackmailed him into asking May to go as his date to the school disco.

It had been as bad as he could have imagined. While all the other girls had been wearing boob tubes and skirts that barely covered their backsides, she'd been wearing something embarrassingly sedate, scarcely any makeup. He was embarrassed to be seen with her and, ashamed of his embarrassment, had asked her to dance.

That was bad, too. She didn't have a clue and he'd caught hold of her and held her and that had been better. Up close, her hair had smelled like flowers after rain. She felt wonderful, her softness against his thin, hard body had roused him, brought to the surface all those feelings that he'd kept battened down. This was why he'd gone back time after time to the stables. Risked being caught by the gardener. Or, worse, the housekeeper.

Her skin was so beautiful that he'd wanted to touch it, touch her, kiss her. And her eyes, liquid black in the dim lights of the school gym, had told him that she wanted it too. But not there. Not where anyone could see them, hoot with derision…

They had run home through the park. She'd unlocked the gate, they'd scrambled up to the stables loft and it was hard to say which of them had been trembling the most when he'd kissed her, neither of them doubting what they wanted.

That it was her first kiss was without doubt. It was very nearly his, too. His first real kiss. The taste of her lips, the sweetness, her uncertainty as she'd opened up to him had made him feel like a giant. All powerful. Invincible. And the memory of her melting softness in the darkness jolted through him like an electric charge...

'You need a husband by the end of the month?' he said, dragging himself back from the hot, dark thoughts that were raging through him.

'There's an entailment on Coleridge House,' she said. 'The legatee has to be married by the time he or she is thirty or the house goes to the Crown.'

'He's controlling you, even from the grave,' he said.

She flushed angrily. 'No one knew,' she said.

'No one?'

'My grandfather lost great chunks of his memory when he had the stroke. And papers were lost when Jennings' offices were flooded a few years ago...'

'You're saying you had no warning?'

She shook her head. 'My mother was dead long before she was thirty, but she thought marriage was an outdated patriarchal institution...' The words caught in her throat and she turned abruptly away again so that he shouldn't see the tears turning her caramel-coloured eyes to liquid gold, just as they had that night when her grandfather had dragged her away from him, his coat thrown around her. 'She'd have told them all to go to hell rather than compromise her principles.'

He tried to drown out the crowing triumph. That this girl, this woman, who from that day to this had crossed the road rather than pass him in the street, was about to lose everything. That her grandfather, that 'impressive' man who thought he was not fit to breathe the same air as his precious granddaughter, had left her at his mercy.

'But before the stroke? He could have told you then.'

'Why would he? I was engaged to Michael, the wedding date was set.'

'Michael Linton.' He didn't need to search his memory. He'd seen the announcement and Saffy had been full of it, torn between envy and disgust.

Envy that May would be Lady Linton with some vast country estate and a house in London. Disgust that she was marrying a man nearly old enough to be her father. 'Her grandfather's arranged it all, of course,' she'd insisted. 'He's desperate to marry her off to someone safe before she turns into her mother and runs off with some nobody who gets her up the duff.' She'd been about to say more but had, for once, thought better of it.

Not that he'd had any argument with her conclusion. But then her grandfather had suffered a massive stroke and the wedding had at first been put off. Then Michael Linton had married someone else.

'What happened? Why didn't you marry him?'

'Michael insisted that Grandpa would be better off in a nursing home. I said no, but he kept bringing me brochures, dragging me off to look at places. He wouldn't listen, wouldn't hear what I was saying, so in the end I gave him his ring back.'

'And he took it?'

'He wanted a wife, a hostess, someone who would fit into his life, run his home. He didn't want to be burdened with an invalid.'

'If he'd taken any notice of your lame duck zoo, he'd have known he was on a hiding to nothing.'

She shook her head and when she looked back over

her shoulder at him her eyes were sparkling, her cheeks wet, but her lips were twisted into a smile.

'Michael didn't climb over the park gate when the gardener was looking the other way, Adam. He was a front door visitor.'

'You mean you didn't make him help you muck out the animals?' he asked and was rewarded with a blush.

'I didn't believe he'd appreciate the honour. He'd have been horrified if he'd seen me shin up a tree to save a kitten. Luckily, the situation never arose when he was around.' A tiny shuddering breath escaped her. 'You don't notice creatures in distress from the back seat of a Rolls-Royce.'

'His loss,' he said, his own throat thick as the memories of stolen hours rushed back at him.

'And mine, it would seem.'

'You'd have been utterly miserable married to him.' She shook her head.

'You aren't going to take this lying down, are you?' he asked. 'I can't believe it would stand up in a court of law and the tabloids would have a field day if the government took your home.'

'A lot of people are much worse off than me, Adam. I'm not sure that a campaign to save a fifteen-room house for one spoilt woman and her housekeeper would be a popular cause.'

She had a point. She'd been born to privilege and her plight was not going to garner mass sympathy.

'Is that what Freddie Jennings told you?' he asked. 'I assume you have taken legal advice?'

'Freddie offered to take Counsel's opinion but, since Grandpa had several opportunities to remove the Codicil but chose not to, I don't have much of a case.' She lifted her shoulders in a gesture of utter helplessness. 'It makes no difference. The truth is that there's no cash to spare for legal fees. As it is, I'm going to have to sell a load of stuff to meet the inheritance tax bill. Even if I won, the costs would be so high that I'd have to sell the house to pay them. And if I lost...'

If she lost it would mean financial ruin.

Well, that would offer a certain amount of satisfaction. But nowhere near as much as the alternative that gave him everything he wanted.

'So you're telling me that the only reason you can't take care of Nancie is because you're about to lose the house? If you were married, there would be no problem,' he said. He didn't wait for her answer—it hadn't been a question. 'And your birthday is on the second of December. Well, it's tight, but it's do-able.'

'Do-able?' she repeated, her forehead buckled in a frown. 'What are you talking about?'

'A quick trip to the Register's office, a simple "I do", you get to keep your house and I'll have somewhere safe for Nancie. As her aunt-in-law, I don't imagine there would be any objection to you taking care of her?'

And he would be able to finally scratch the itch that was May Coleridge while dancing on the grave of the man who'd shamed and humiliated him.

But if he'd imagined that she'd fling her arms around him, proclaim him her saviour, well, nothing had changed there, either.

Her eyes went from blank to blazing, like lightning out of a clear blue sky.

'That's not even remotely funny, Adam. Now, if you don't mind, I've got a house full of guests who'll be expecting lunch in a couple of hours.'

She was wearing shabby sweats but swept by him, head high, shoulders back. Despite her lack of inches, the fact that her puppy fat hadn't melted away but had instead evolved into soft curves, she was every inch the lady.

'Mouse…' he protested, shaken out of his triumph by the fact that, even in extremis, she'd turn him down flat. As if he was still a nobody from the wrong side of the tracks. 'May!'

She was at the door before she stopped, looked back at him.

'I'm serious,' he said, a touch more sharply than he'd intended.

She shook her head. 'It's impossible.'

In other words, he might wear hand stitched suits these days instead of the cheapest market jeans, live in an apartment that had cost telephone numbers, be able to buy and sell the Coleridge estate ten times over, but he could never wash off the stink of where he'd come from. That his sister had been a druggie, his mother was no better than she ought to be and his father had a record as long as his arm.

But times had changed. He wasn't that kid anymore. What he wanted, he took. And he wanted this.

'It would be a purely temporary arrangement,' he said. 'A marriage of convenience.'

'Are you saying that you wouldn't expect…?'

She swallowed, colour flooding into her cheeks, and it occurred to him that if Michael Linton's courtship had been choreographed by her grandfather it would have been a formal affair rather than a lust-fuelled romance. The thought sent the blood rushing to a very different part of his anatomy and he was grateful for the full stiff folds of the dressing gown he was wearing.

She cleared her throat. 'Are you saying that you wouldn't expect the full range of wifely duties?'

Not the full range. He wouldn't expect her to cook or clean or keep house for him.

'Just a twenty-four seven nanny,' she continued, regaining her composure, assuming his silence was assent. 'Only with more paperwork, a longer notice period and a serious crimp in your social life?'

'I don't have much time for a social life these days,' he assured her before she could gather herself. 'But there are formal business occasions where I would normally take a guest. Civic functions. But you usually attend those, anyway.'

Nancie, as if aware of the sudden tension, let out a wail and, using the distraction to escape the unexpected heat of May's eyes, he picked her up, put her against his shoulder, turned to look at her.

'Well? What do you say?'

She shook her head, clearly speechless, and the band holding her hair slipped, allowing wisps to escape.

Backlit by the sun, they shone around her face like a butterscotch halo.

'What have you got to lose?' he persisted, determined to impose his will on her. Overwrite the Coleridge name with his own.

'Marriage is a lot easier to get into than it is to get out of,' she protested. Still, despite every advantage, resisting him. 'There has to be an easier solution to baby care than marrying the first woman to cross your path.'

'Not the first,' he replied. 'I passed several women in the park and I can assure you that it never crossed my mind to marry any of them.'

'No?'

He'd managed to coax the suggestion of a smile from her.

'Divorce is easy enough if both parties are in agreement,' he assured her. 'You'll be giving up a year of your freedom in return for your ancestral home. It looks like a good deal to me.'

The smile did not materialise. 'I can see the advantage from my point of view,' she said. 'But what's in it for you? You can't really be that desperate to offload Nancie.'

'Who said anything about "offloading" Nancie?' He allowed himself to sound just a little bit offended by her suggestion that he was doing that. 'On the contrary, I'm doing my best to do what her mother asked. It's not as if I intend to leave you to manage entirely on your own. I have to go away tomorrow, but I'll pull my weight until then.'

'Oh, right. And how do you intend to do that?'

'I'll take the night watch. The master bedroom is made up. I'll pack a bag and move in there today.'

CHAPTER FIVE

'WHAT?'

The word was shocked from her.

May swallowed again, tucked a loose strand of hair behind her ear in a nervous gesture that drew attention to her neck. It was long and smooth. She had the clearest ivory skin coloured only by the fading blush...

'If we get married, people will expect us to live together,' he pointed out. 'You wouldn't want the Crown Commissioners getting the impression that it was just a piece of paper, would you? That you were cheating.'

'But—'

Before she could put her real objection into words, Nancie, bless her heart, began to grizzle.

'What do I do now?' he asked, looking at her helplessly. That, at least, wasn't an act.

'I think the fact that she's chewing your neck is the clue,' she said distractedly.

'She's hungry?'

'Feeding her, like changing her nappy, is something that has to happen at regular intervals. No doubt there's a bottle and some formula in that bag.'

She didn't wait for him to check, but went into her bedroom, fetched the bag and emptied it on the table.

'There's just one carton. I wonder what that means.'

'That we'll probably need more very soon,' he replied, picking up on her unspoken thought that it might offer a clue about how long Saffy intended to stay out of sight. Always assuming she was thinking that rationally.

'Adam!' she protested as she turned the carton over, searching for instructions.

'I'm sorry. I can plan a takeover bid to the last millisecond, but I'm out of my depth here.'

'Then get help.'

'I'm doing my best,' he replied. 'If you'd just cooperate we could both get on with our lives.'

May was struggling to keep up a calm, distant front. She'd been struggling ever since he'd stood beneath the tree in the park. Used that ridiculous name.

Inside, everything was in turmoil. Her heart, her pulse were racing.

'Please, Adam…' Her voice caught in her throat. He couldn't mean it. He was just torturing her… 'Don't…'

He lifted his hand, cradling her cheek to still her protest. His touch was gentle. A warm soothing balm that swept through her, taking the tension out of her joints so that her body swayed towards him.

'It wouldn't be that bad, would it, Mouse?'

Bad? How much worse could it get?

'It seems a little…extreme,' she said, resisting with all her will the yearning need to lean into his palm. Surrender everything, including her honour.

'Losing your home, your business, is extreme,' he insisted. 'Getting married is just a piece of paper.'

Not for her…

'A mutually beneficial contract to be cancelled at the convenience of both parties,' he added. 'Think of Robbie, May. Where will she go if you lose the house?'

'She's got a pension. A sister…'

'Your business,' he persisted.

The bank loan...

'And what about your animals? Who else will take them in? You know that most of them will have to be put down.'

'Don't!' she said, her throat so tight that the words were barely audible.

'Hey,' he said, pulling her into her arms so that the three of them were locked together. 'I'm your trusty sidekick, remember? As always, late on the scene but ready to leap into action when you need a helping hand.'

'This is a bit more than a helping hand.'

'Hand, foot and pretty much everything in between,' he agreed. 'Take your pick.'

He was doing his best to make her laugh, she realised, or maybe cry.

Either would be appropriate under the circumstances. What would her mother have done? Spit in the devil's eye? Or screw the patriarchal system, using it against itself to keep both her house and her freedom?

Stupid question. Heaven knew that she was not her mother. If she'd had her courage she'd be long gone. But all she had was her home. Robbie. The creatures that relied on her. The life she'd managed to make for herself.

As for breaking the promise to her grandfather, her punishment for that was built into the bargain of a barren marriage with a self-destruct date.

'May?' he prompted.

Decision time.

What decision...? There was only ever going to be one answer and, taking a deep breath, her heart beating ten times faster than when she'd climbed that tree, her voice not quite steady, she said, 'You're absolutely sure about this? Last chance.'

'Quite sure,' he replied, his own voice as steady as a rock. No hint of doubt, no suggestion of intestinal collywobbles on his part. 'It's a no-brainer.'

'No…' she said, wondering why, even now, she was hesitating.

'No?'

'I mean yes. You're right. It's a no-brainer.'

'Shall we aim for something a little more decisive?' he suggested. 'Just so that we know exactly where we stand?'

'You're not planning on going down on one knee?' she demanded, appalled.

'Heaven forbid. Just something to seal the bargain,' he said, taking his hand from her back and offering it to her.

'A handshake?' she said, suddenly overcome with the urgent need to laugh as she lifted her own to clasp it.

'Well, why not? Everything else appears to be shaking.'

As his hand tightened around hers, everything stilled. Even Nancie stopped nuzzling and grumbling. All she could hear was her pulse pounding through her ears. All she could see were his eyes. Not the bright silver of the boy she'd known but leaden almost unreadable. A shiver ran through her as he closed the gap between them, kissed her, but then she closed her eyes and all sense of danger evaporated in the heat of his mouth, the taste of him and the cherished bittersweet memory flooded back.

It was different. He was different.

The kiss was assured, certain and yet, beneath it all, she recognised the boy who'd lain with her in the stable loft and kissed her, undressed her, touched her. And for a moment she was no longer the woman who'd subjugated her yearning for love, for a family of her own into caring for her grandfather, creating a business, building some kind of life for herself.

As Adam's lips touched hers, she was that girl again and an aching need opened up before her, a dizzying void that tempted her to plunge headlong into danger, to throw caution to the winds and boldly kiss him back.

'Oh...'

At the sound of Robbie's shocked little exclamation, May stumbled back, heat rushing to her face.

That girl reliving the moment of guilt, embarrassment, pain when they'd been discovered...

'Robbie...'

'I thought I heard you come in earlier,' she said.

'I had a fall. In the park. Adam came to my rescue.'

'That would account for the kitten, then,' she said stiffly. 'And the trousers hanging over the Aga.'

'We both got rather muddy,' Adam said.

'I'm sure it's nothing to do with me what you were doing in the park,' Robbie said, ignoring him. 'But Jeremy is here.'

'Jeremy?' she repeated, struggling to gather her wits.

'He's brought the designs for the honey labels.'

'Has he? Oh, right...' Expanding honey production had been part of the future she'd planned and Jeremy Davidson had volunteered to design the labels for her.

'He's doing you a favour, May. You won't want to keep him waiting,' she said primly before turning to leave.

'Robbie, wait!' she began, then glanced at Adam, suddenly unsure of herself. She wanted to tell Robbie that the kiss had meant nothing. That it was no more than a handshake on a deal. Except when Robbie paused, her shoulders stiff with disapproval, the words wouldn't come.

'Go and see the man about your labels,' Adam urged, then nodded, as if to reassure her that she could go ahead with her plans. That she had a future. 'Leave this to me.'

'But Nancie…' She looked at the baby. It was easier than meeting his eyes, looking at Robbie.

'I'll bring her down in a moment.'

Adam watched as she stumbled from the room in her haste to escape her embarrassment and he could have kicked himself.

Most women in her situation would have leapt at the deal he'd offered, no questions asked, but her first response had been flat refusal, anger at his presumption, and that had caught him on the raw.

His kiss had been intended as a marker. A promise to himself that she would pay for every slight, every insult but, instead of the anticipated resistance, she had responded with a heat that had robbed him of any sense of victory. Only left him wanting more.

He did not want her.

He could have any woman he wanted. Beautiful women. The kind who turned heads in the street.

All he wanted from May Coleridge was her pride at his feet. And he would have it.

She had been his last mistake. His only weakness. Since the day he'd walked away from this house, his clothes freezing on his back, he'd never let anything, any emotion, stand in his way.

With his degree in his pocket, a mountain of debt to pay off, his mother incapable of looking after either herself or Saffy, the only job he had been able to get in his home town was in an old import company that had been chugging along happily since the days when the clipper ships brought tea from China. It wasn't what he'd dreamed of, but within five years he'd been running the company. Now he was the chairman of an international company trading commodities from across the globe.

His success didn't appear to impress May's disapproving housekeeper.

'It's been a while, Mrs Robson.'

'It has. But nothing appears to have changed, Mr Wavell,' she returned, ice-cool.

'On the contrary. I'd like you to be the first to know that May and I are going to be married.'

'Married!' And, just like that, all the starch went out of her. 'When…?'

'Before the end of the month.'

'I meant…' She shook her head. 'What's the hurry? What are you after? If you think May's been left well off—'

'I don't need her money. But May needs me. She's just been told that if she isn't married by her birthday, she's going to lose her home.'

'But that's less than four weeks…' She rallied. 'Is that what Freddie Jennings called about in such a flap this morning?'

'I imagine so. Apparently, some ancient entailment turned up when he took James Coleridge's will to probate.'

The colour left her face but she didn't back down. 'Why would you step in to help, Adam Wavell? What do you get out of it?' She didn't give him a chance to answer. 'And that little girl's mother? What will she have to say about it?'

'Nancie,' he said, discovering that a baby made a very useful prop, 'meet Hatty Robson. Mrs Robson, meet my niece.'

'She's Saffy's daughter?' She came closer, the rigid lines of her face softening and she touched the baby's curled up fist. 'She's a pretty thing.' Then, 'So where is your sister? In rehab? In jail?'

'Neither,' he said, hanging onto his temper by a thread. 'But we are having a bit of a family crisis.'

'Nothing new there, then.'

'No,' he admitted. A little humility wouldn't hurt. 'Saffy was sure that May would help.'

'Again? Hasn't she suffered enough for your family?'

Suffered?

'I met her in the park. She was up a tree,' he added. 'Rescuing a kitten.'

She rolled her eyes. An improvement.

'The only reason she told me her troubles was to explain why she couldn't look after Nancie.'

'And you leapt in with an immediate marriage proposal. Saving not one, but two women with a single bound?' Her tone, deeply ironic, suggested that, unlike May, she wasn't convinced that it was an act of selfless altruism.

'Make that three,' he replied, raising her irony and calling her. 'I imagine one of May's concerns was you, Mrs Robson. This is your home, too.'

If it hadn't been so unlikely, he would have sworn she blushed. 'Did she say that?' she demanded, instantly on the defensive. 'I don't matter.'

'You know that's not true,' he said, pushing his advantage. 'You and this house are all she has.'

And this time the blush was unmistakable. 'That's true. Poor child. Well, I'm sure that's very generous of you, Mr Wavell. Just tell me one thing. Why didn't your sister, or you, just pick up the phone and call one of those agencies which supplies temporary nannies? I understand you can afford it these days.'

He'd already explained his reasons to May and he wasn't about to go through them again. 'Just be glad for May's sake,' he replied, 'that I didn't.'

She wasn't happy, clearly didn't trust his motives, but after a moment she nodded just once. 'Very well. But bear this in mind. If you hurt her, you'll have to answer to me. And I won't stop at a hosing down.'

'Hurt her? Why would I hurt her?'

'You've done it before,' she said. 'It's in your nature. I've seen the string of women you've paraded through the pages of the gossip magazines. How many of them have been left with a bruised heart?' She didn't wait for an answer. 'May has spent the last ten years nursing her grandpa. She's grieving for him, vulnerable.'

'And without my help she'll lose her home, her business and the animals she loves,' he reminded her.

She gave him a long look, then said, 'That child is hungry. You'd better give her to me before she chews a hole in your neck. What did you say her name was?'

'Nancie, Mrs Robson. With an i and an e.'

'Well, that's a sweet old-fashioned name,' she said, taking the baby. 'Hello, Nancie.' Then, looking from the baby to him, 'I suppose you'd better call me Robbie.'

'Thank you. Is there anything I can do, Robbie?'

'Go and book a date with the Registrar?' she suggested. 'Although you might want to put your trousers on first.'

THE KITCHEN WAS EMPTY, apart from a couple of cats curled up on an old armchair and an old mongrel dog who was sharing his basket with a duck and a chicken.

None of them took any notice of him as he unhooked his trousers from the rail above the Aga and carried them through to the mud room, where the kitten had curled up in the fleece and gone to sleep. He hoped Nancie, jerked out of familiar surroundings, her routine, would settle as easily.

Having brushed off the mud as best he could and made himself fit to be seen in polite society, he hunted down May. He found her in a tiny office converted from one of the pantries, shoulder to shoulder with a tall, thin man who was, presumably, Jeremy, as they leaned over her desk examining some artwork.

'May?'

She turned, peering at him over a pair of narrow tortoiseshell spectacles that were perched on the end of her nose. They gave her a cute, kittenish look, he thought. And imagined himself reaching for them, taking them off and kissing her.

'I've talked to Robbie,' he said, catching himself. 'Put her in the picture.'

That blush coloured her cheeks again, but she was back in control of her voice, her breathing as she said, 'You've explained everything?'

'The why, the what and the when,' he assured her. 'I'll give you a call as soon as I've sorted out the details. You'll be in all afternoon?'

'You're going to do it today?' she squeaked. Not that in control...

'It's today, or it's too late.'

'Yes...' Clearly, it was taking some time for the reality of her situation to sink in. 'Will you need me? For the paperwork?'

'I'll find out what the form is and call you. I'll need

your number,' he prompted when she didn't respond. 'It's unlisted.'

Flustered, May plucked a leaflet from a shelf above her desk and handed it to him. 'My number is on there.'

For a moment they just looked at one another and he wondered what she was thinking about. The afternoons they'd spent together in the stables with him ducking out of sight whenever anyone had come near? The night when they had been too absorbed in each other to listen? Or the years that had followed...?

'What are you doing?' he asked, turning to look at the artwork laid out on the table.

'What?' He looked up and saw that she was still staring at him and her poise deserted her as, flustered, she said, 'I'm ch-choosing a label for Coleridge House honey. Do you know Jeremy Davidson? He's head of the art department at the high school.' Then, as if she felt she had to explain how she knew him, 'I'm a governor.'

'You're a school governor?' He didn't bother to suppress a grin, and yet why should he be surprised? She'd been born to sit on charitable committees, school boards. In the fullness of time she'd no doubt become a magistrate, like her grandfather. 'I hope you've done something about those overflowing gutters.'

'It was my first concern.' For a moment there was the hint of a smile, the connection of a shared memory, before she turned to Jeremy Davidson. 'Adam and I were at the high school at the same time, Jeremy. He was two years above me.'

'I'm aware that Mr Wavell is one of our more successful ex-pupils,' he said rather stiffly. 'I'm delighted to meet you.'

He was another of those old school tie types. Elegant,

educated. A front door visitor who would have met with James Coleridge's approval. His manners were impeccable, even if his smile didn't quite reach his eyes.

'I have an Emma Davidson on my staff,' he said. 'I believe her husband is an art teacher. Is that simply a coincidence or is she your wife?'

'She's my wife,' he admitted.

'I thought she must be. You're on half term break, I imagine. While she's at work catching up with Saminderan employment law, you're here, playing with honey pot labels—'

'*Was* my wife. We're separated.' His glance at May betrayed him. 'Our divorce will be finalised in January.'

'Well, that's regrettable,' he said. 'Emma is a valued member of my organisation.'

'These things happen.'

So they did. But not fast enough to save May, he thought. Were they having an affair? he wondered. Or was she saving herself for the big wedding? Or was he waiting to declare himself until he was free?

Best put him out of his misery. 'Has May told you our good news?' he asked.

'Adam...'

She knew.

'We're getting married later this month,' he continued, as if he hadn't heard her.

Jeremy's shocked expression told its own story and, before he could find the appropriate words, May swiftly intervened.

'I can't decide which design I like best, Adam. What do you think?'

He waited pointedly until Davidson moved out of his

way, then put his hand on the desk and leaned forward, blocking him out with his shoulder.

They were pretty enough floral designs with 'Coleridge House Honey' in some fancy script. About right for a stall at a bazaar.

'You produce handmade sweets too, don't you?' he asked her, looking at the shelf and picking up a fairly basic price list that, like the brochure, had obviously been printed on her computer. 'Is this all the literature that you have?'

She nodded as he laid it, with the brochure, beside the labels.

'There's no consistency in design,' he said. 'Not in the colours, or even the fonts you've used. Nothing to make it leap out from the shelf. Coleridge House is a brand, May. You should get some professional help to develop that.'

'Jeremy—'

'There's a rather good watercolour of the house in your bedroom. The country house, nostalgia thing would be a strong image and work well across the board. On labels, price lists and on the front of your workshop brochure.'

She looked up at him, a tiny frown creasing the space between her eyes.

'Just a thought.' With a touch to her shoulder, a curt nod to Davidson, he said, 'I'll call you later.'

He found Robbie in the kitchen preparing a feed for Nancie, who was beginning to sound very cross indeed. Resisting the urge to take the child from her—the whole point of the exercise was to leave Nancie in May's capable hands and not get involved in baby care, or her cottage industry, for that matter—he took a card from his wallet and placed it on the table.

'This is my mobile number should you need to get hold of me urgently.'

'Stick it on the cork board, will you?'

He found a drawing pin and stuck it amongst a load of letters, appointment cards and postcards. The kind of domestic clutter so notably absent from the slate and steel kitchen in his apartment.

'Is this bag all you have?' she asked.

'I'm afraid so. You'll be needing rather more than that, I imagine?'

'You imagine right.'

'Well, just get whatever you want. Better still, make a list and I'll have it delivered. May can give it to me when I ring her about the wedding arrangements.'

ROBBIE SAID NOTHING when May returned to the kitchen after seeing Jeremy Davidson out, just handed her the baby and the feeder and left her to get on with it, while she set about cleaning salad vegetables at the old butler's sink.

'Any hints about how to do this?' she asked, using her toe to hook out a chair so that she could sit down.

'You'll learn the way I did when your grandfather brought you home, no more than a month old,' she said abruptly.

'Robbie...'

'You'll find that if you put it to the little one's mouth she'll do the rest.' She ripped up a head of lettuce. 'Just keep the end of the bottle up so that she's not sucking air.'

May settled the baby in the crook of her arm and, as

she offered Nancie the bottle, she latched onto it, sucking greedily. She watched her for a while, then, when Robbie's silence became oppressive, she looked up and said, 'Are you angry with me, Robbie?'

'Angry with you! Why would I be angry with you?'

'You're angry with someone.'

'I'm angry with your grandfather. That foolish, pigheaded old man. Just because your mother wouldn't listen to him. Wouldn't live her life the way he wanted...'

'You're talking about the will?'

'Of course I'm talking about the will. How could he put you in such a position?'

She breathed out a sigh of relief.

She'd been anticipating a tirade about promises made and broken. About marriage being for love, not convenience. She wouldn't take a schoolgirl crush into account.

'The will wasn't about my mother, Robbie,' May said. 'It was about history. Tradition.'

'Tradition, my foot! I can't believe he'd do this to you.'

'He didn't. Not deliberately. He thought I was going to marry Michael. If he'd known...'

'Who knows anything?' she demanded. 'If I'd known my husband was going to drop dead of a heart problem when he was twenty-six I wouldn't have insisted on waiting to have a baby until we had a house, until everything was just as I wanted it...' Without warning, her eyes were full of tears. 'Life is never just as you want it, May. There are no certainties. How could he look after me and not take care of you? It's so cruel,' she said, dashing them away with the back of her hand. 'After the way

you cared for him all those years when you could have
been married, with a family of your own...'

'Hush, Robbie, it's all right. It's going to be all right,'
she repeated, wanting to go to her, comfort her but hampered by Nancie, who had snuggled into her shoulder as
if she belonged there.

'Only because Adam Wavell happened by when you
needed him.'

'He didn't just happen by. He was on his way to ask
for my help. This is a mutual aid package.'

'And if he hadn't needed you? What would you have
done then?'

'Well,' she said, 'I was going to sit down and make
a list of all the unmarried men I know. Jed Atkins was
favourite.'

'Jed!' Robbie snorted. 'Well, he'd be a safer bet than
Adam Wavell. And no baby.'

'But hundreds of relations who'd all expect to be
invited for Christmas. Would there be a turkey big
enough?'

Robbie groaned and they both laughed, but then her
smile faded and she said, 'Don't fall for him, May. It's
just a piece of paper.'

'I know.'

'Do you?' Robbie asked, her look searching, anxious. 'That kiss...'

'He kissed me to seal the bargain we'd made. It was
nothing.'

'Nothing to him.'

'And nothing to me,' she said, pressing her lips
tightly together in an attempt to stop them tingling at
the memory. Forget the desperate need that his touch
had awakened.

Trying not to read too much into his edgy reaction to Jeremy Davidson. The poor man had fallen apart when his wife left him and she'd offered him a distraction with her labels, something to keep his mind occupied. Something to make him feel needed. But the way Adam had made it so obvious that he'd been in her bedroom... If he'd been a dog, she'd have said he was marking his territory.

Which was ridiculous.

Adam only wanted her as a nanny.

'Absolutely nothing,' she said with emphasis. It was only in her head that she'd kissed him back, seduced him with her mouth and then her body...

Robbie made the 'humphing' noise she used when she was unconvinced.

'What did you expect us to do? Shake hands?' she asked, ignoring the fact that it had started out that way.

'Why not? If it's just a business arrangement.'

'We've known one another for a very long time. I see him all the time at civic functions. He's saving my home, for heaven's sake.'

'And you're saving him a world of trouble,' she replied. 'Just remember that as soon as this "family crisis" of his is resolved—'

'He'll be gone.'

'Let's just hope it isn't before he's put the ring on your finger. Signed the register.'

CHAPTER SIX

'He wouldn't...'

'Lead you on, then back out at the last minute? He has no reason to love this family. Be kind to you.'

No reason that he knew.

'He needs my help,' she said. Then, as the baby paused to draw breath, 'Do you think you can manage lunch on your own? I'll have to wash the cot down.'

'Chance would be a fine thing,' she replied, letting it go.

'Sorry?'

'You gave it to the vicar last year. For that family whose house burned down.'

'Oh, fudge! I'd forgotten.'

'Adam said to make a list of anything you need,' Robbie said, resuming her attack on the vegetables.

'Right. I'll do that,' she said, then was distracted by Nancie, who was opening her mouth like a little fish, waving her sweet, plump arms to demand her attention. May was familiar with the powerful instinct to survive in small mammals blindly seeking out their mother's milk, but this urgency in a small helpless baby went straight to her heart.

'An extra pair of hands wouldn't go amiss, either,' Robbie said. 'You've got that order for toffee to deliver by the end of the week.'

'No problem. Adam wants to help. I'll have to clear a wardrobe in Grandpa's room for him.'

'He's moving in? To your grandfather's room?'

'It's ready. And there's nowhere else until the guests have gone.' Her only response was the lift of an eyebrow. 'It's not like that, Robbie.'

She shook her head. 'Leave your grandpa's room to me. I'll see to it.'

'Thank you.' Then, as Nancie pulled away from the bottle, wrinkled up her little nose, distancing herself from it, 'Have you had enough of that, sweetheart?'

She set the bottle on the table and just looked at her. She was so beautiful. Just like her mother.

'You'll need to wind her,' Robbie said. 'Put her on your shoulder and rub her back gently.'

'Oh, right.'

She lifted her, set her against her shoulder. Nancie didn't wait for the rub but obligingly burped. Before she could congratulate herself, she realised that her shoulder was wet and something warm was trickling down her back.

'Eeugh! Has she brought it all back up?'

'Just a mouthful. A little milk goes a very long way,' Robbie said, grinning as she handed her a paper towel. 'You used to do that all the time.'

'Did I?' No one had ever talked to her about what she was like as a baby. 'What did you do?'

'Changed my clothes a lot until I had the sense to put a folded towel over my shoulder before I burped you.'

'Well, thanks so much for the warning,' she said, using the towel to mop up the worst. 'What else did I do?'

'You cried a lot. You were missing your mother.'

Right on cue, Nancie began to grizzle and May stood up, gently rubbing her back as she walked around the kitchen.

'Poor baby. Poor Saffy.'

'So what did he tell you? What is this family crisis? Where is she?'

'Adam doesn't know. She dropped the baby off at his office and ran. He showed me the note she left with the baby, but she didn't sound quite in control, to be honest. It seems that Nancie's father has found out about her problems and he's trying to get custody.'

'In other words, he's pitched you into the middle of his family's messy life.'

'Saffy told him I would help.' Then, as she saw the question forming on Robbie's lips, 'He was desperate, Robbie.'

'Clearly, if he's prepared to marry you to get a babysitter.'

'My good luck.'

'Maybe. Do you remember that young jackdaw with the broken wing that he left on the doorstep?'

He'd left all kinds of creatures until Robbie had caught him and sent him packing. After that, he'd come over the park gate, dodging the gardener, keeping clear of the house, coming to look for her in the stables. She'd made him instant coffee while he'd emptied her biscuit tin, stayed to help her clean out the cages. It had been a secret. No one at home, no one at school had known about it. Only Saffy.

'I remember,' she said. 'What about it?'

'You cried for a week when it flew away.'

She swallowed. 'Is that a warning not to get too attached to Nancie?'

'Or her uncle.' She didn't wait for denial but, tapping the tip of her knife thoughtfully against the board, said, 'There's that old wooden cradle upstairs in one of the box rooms. You could use that for now. In fact, it might be a good idea to get Nancie out of here before the Christmas lot break for lunch.'

'Can you and Patsy manage?'

'Everything's done but the salad.' She jerked her head. 'Off you go.'

Well aware that Robbie could handle lunch with one hand tied behind her back, May returned to the peace of her sitting room, fastened Nancie into her buggy and went to find the old cradle.

When it was ready, she put it at the foot of her bed. 'Here you go, sweetie,' she said, putting down Nancie, then rocking her gently, humming the tune to an old lullaby to which she'd long since forgotten the words.

'Very pretty.'

She started, looked up.

Adam was leaning, legs crossed, arms folded, against the architrave of the door between her sitting room and bedroom. He'd abandoned the muddy pinstripes for what looked like an identical suit, a fresh white shirt. Only the tie was different. It had a fine silver stripe that echoed the bright molten flecks that lifted his eyes above the ordinary grey.

'How long have you been standing there?' she demanded, hot with embarrassment.

'Long enough. Robbie directed me to the morning room to wait for the lady of the house but, since I brought my bag with me, I decided to bring it up. Put it in my bedroom. I used the back stairs.'

'Don't be so touchy. She probably thought you'd blunder in and wake Nancie.'

'She's never seen me slip over the back gate and dodge the gardener.'

'No.' She looked away. It was the first time he'd alluded to the past. The golden days before she'd lied to her grandfather, lied to Robbie and gone to the school disco with him.

'How many generations of Coleridge babies have been rocked to sleep in that cradle?' he asked, pushing himself off from the door frame, folding himself up beside her.

'Generations,' she admitted. Probably even the children of the man whose unwillingness to settle down was causing her so much grief.

'Everything in this house looks as if it's been here forever.'

'Most of it has. Unfortunately, there's one thing missing,' she said, scrambling to her feet, needing to put a little distance between them so that she could concentrate on what was important.

Kneeling shoulder to shoulder with him by the cradle she was far too conscious of the contrast between his immaculate, pressed appearance and her own.

He'd showered and smelled of fresh rain on grass, newly laundered linen. Everything clean, expensive.

She smelled of disinfectant, polish and the sicky milk that had dried on her shoulder. The band holding her hair back had collapsed so that it drooped around her face and she didn't need to check the mirror to know what that looked like. A mess.

'Nancie really should have a proper cot. Unfortunately I gave ours away. I'm going to have to run over to the baby store in the retail park after lunch and buy a few things. I can pick one up then.'

'We can do that while we're out.'

'Out?'

'That's why I'm here. I've spoken to the Registrar. He can fit us in on the twenty-ninth.'

May opened her mouth. Closed it again. Then said, 'The twenty-ninth?'

'Apparently, there have to be sixteen clear days from notice. That's the first day after that. He's free at ten o'clock. If that's convenient? It's a Monday. You haven't got anything planned for that day that you can't put off?'

She shook her head. 'We have mid-week courses and weekend courses, but Monday is always a clear day. What about you?' she asked.

'Nothing that won't keep for ten minutes,' he assured her. 'I assume you just want the basics?'

She hadn't given the ceremony any thought at all. Not since she was an infatuated teen, anyway, when she'd had it planned out to the last detail. But this wasn't an occasion for the local church scented with roses, choristers singing like angels and the pews packed with envious classmates as she swept up the aisle in a size 0 designer gown.

'The basics.' She nodded. 'Absolutely.'

'We'll need a couple of witnesses. Robbie, obviously. I thought we might ask Freddie Jennings to be the other one.'

'Good idea,' she said.

'I'm full of them today. All we need to do now is go to the office with our birth certificates and sign a few papers.'

'Now? But I can't leave Nancie.'

'Then you'll have to bring her along.'

'Yes. Of course,' she said, looking at Nancie. Looked at the buggy. Trying to imagine herself wheeling it

through town with everyone thinking it was her and
Adam's baby. 'I'd...um...better get changed.'

She grabbed the nearest things from her wardrobe.
The discarded gold cord skirt and a soft V-necked black
sweater, a fresh pair of tights from a drawer and she
backed into her bathroom. Where she splashed her face
with cold water. Got a grip.

Because she was going to arrange her wedding and
the Registrar would expect her to have made an effort,
she put on some makeup, twisted her hair up into a knot,
then stared at her reflection. Was that too much? Would
Adam think she was making an effort to impress him?

Oh, for heaven's sake. As if Adam Wavell would care
what she was wearing. And yet there was something so
unsettling about the fact that he was in her home, sitting
in her most private space, waiting for her.

It was too intimate. Too...

Nothing!

Absolutely nothing.

She wrenched open the door and he looked up, startled by the ferocity of her entrance.

Calm, Mary Louise. Calm...

'Okay?' he said.

'Fine. I just need my boots.' She took them from the
closet, pulled them on, doing her best not to think about
Adam standing at her bedroom window, Nancie against
his shoulder.

'I'll just get my birth certificate and then we can go.
I'll take Nancie if you'll bring the buggy.'

'Well, that was painless,' Adam said as they emerged
from the Registrar's Office.

May nodded, but she was very pale. And, while it

might have been painless for him, everyone who worked in the Town Hall, the Registrar's Office, had known her. They'd been eager to congratulate her and cooed over the baby, assuming it was hers.

'Why did you let everyone think Nancie was your baby?' he said.

'I thought that it would be safer.'

'Safer?' He frowned.

'For Saffy.'

He was momentarily lost for words. While everyone knew her, she was an intensely private person and inside she must have been dying of embarrassment at being the centre of attention, but she'd smiled and smiled and let everyone think whatever they wanted in order to protect his wayward sister.

'I don't know about you, but I've missed lunch...' he said. 'Let's grab a sandwich.'

'I thought we were going to the business park. Nancie will need feeding again soon.'

'You won't be any use to her if you collapse from hunger,' he said, taking her arm, steering her across the road to the thriving craft centre that had once been a big coaching inn in the centre of the town.

It was lit up for the holiday season and packed with shoppers, but the lunch time rush was over in the courtyard café and they took a table near the window where there was room for the buggy.

'A BLT for me, I think. You?'

She nodded.

He ordered, adding a pot of tea without asking. 'You've had a shocking morning—we both have. Hot, sweet tea is what the doctor orders,' he said when the waitress had gone.

'The reality is just beginning to sink in.'

'It was a terrible thing to do to you,' he said.

'What? Oh.' She shook her head. 'His memory had gone. He didn't know.'

He'd assumed that she'd been talking about the loss of her home, but it seemed that marrying him was the shocker.

Well, if she'd been looking forward to an artistic partnership with the well-bred, public school educated but presumably penniless Jeremy Davidson—divorce would strip him of a large part of his assets—she had every reason to be in shock.

But, like her ancestor before her, she was prepared to do whatever it took to hold onto the family estate. Not so much a fate worse than death as a fate worse than being a nobody, living in an ordinary little house, the wife of a man who no one had ever heard of.

'Did you sort out your honey labels?' he asked.

She stared at him, then, as their food arrived, 'Oh, the labels. I took your advice and gave Jeremy the watercolour. He's going to scan it into his computer, see what he can do with it.'

Adam discovered he wasn't anywhere near as happy about that as he should have been, considering it had been his idea, but what could he say? That he didn't want the man in her bedroom, getting hot and sweaty at the thought of her peaches and cream body nestled in all that white linen and lace.

'My advice was to use a professional.'

'How much honey do you think I produce?' she asked. 'I can't justify the kind of fees a professional designer would charge. Jeremy's doing it as a favour.'

'He's going to a lot of trouble to keep in with the

school governor,' he said, pouring the tea. Loading it with sugar before handing her a cup. 'Is there a promotion in the offing?'

'Not that I know of.' She took a sip of the tea, pulled a face.

'Not sweet enough?' he asked and was rewarded with a wry smile that tugged at something deeper than the bitter memories.

'You are so funny,' she said, taking a dummy from the baby's carrier, unwrapping it and handing it to Nancie to suck.

'May…' His phone began to ring but he ignored it. Her relationship with Davidson was more important than whatever Jake wanted. If she thought that she could carry on—

May glanced up when Adam ignored his phone. 'Aren't you going to get that? It could be Saffy.'

'What?' He took the phone from his pocket, snapped, 'Yes,' so sharply that if she'd been Saffy she'd have hung up. Clearly it wasn't because, after a moment, he said, 'Fifteen minutes.' Then, responding to her expectant look, 'My office. I'm afraid I'll have to give the business park a miss. Can I have this to go, please?' he said, holding out his plate to the waitress before turning back to her. 'Let me have a list of what you need and I'll sort something out.'

'Get Jake to sort something out, don't you mean?' she said, edgy, although she couldn't have said why. Just something about the way he'd looked at her, the way he'd said her name before his phone rang.

Was he having second thoughts?

'It's the same thing. He'll have to know where Nancie is in case Saffy turns up while I'm away next week.

And you'll need someone to call on in the event of an emergency. He'll sort out a credit card for you as well.'

'I don't need your money, Adam.'

'Maybe not, but I understand from colleagues that babies are expensive and I don't expect you to subsidise my sister. With a card you can get whatever she needs.'

'She needs love, Adam, not a piece of plastic.'

'If you give her half as much as you lavished on your broken animals then she's in good hands,' he said. 'But it's not just Nancie. You'll need a wardrobe upgrade.' Before she could respond, he said, 'The sweats are practical, and the little black dress you've been wearing to every civic reception for the last five years is a classic, but when I present you to the world as my wife I will be looking for something a little more in keeping with my status.'

Presenting her...

His status...

Which answered any question about whether he'd changed his mind. He was going to marry her, but didn't want to be seen out with her until she'd had a makeover.

'Maybe you should consider an upgrade in your wife,' she snapped. 'Get one of those skinny blondes you're so fond of to take care of Nancie,' she continued, getting up so quickly that her chair scraped against the floor, causing heads to turn.

'Now who is there in the county who could out-class Miss May Coleridge?' he enquired, catching her hand. The shock of the contact, the squeeze of his fingers around hers, warning her that she was in danger of making a scene, took the stuffing out of her knees and she fell back into her seat.

An unreadable smile briefly crossed Adam's face and

it was there again. The feeling that she'd had just before he'd kissed her. Nothing that she could pin down. Just the realisation that this Adam Wavell was not the boy who'd trembled as he kissed her. He was a man who'd been thrown the smallest lifeline and within a decade had ousted the dead wood from an old family firm, seized control and built himself an empire. That took more than hard work, brains. It required ruthlessness.

She would have felt guilty about her part in flinging him the rope secretly begging an old family friend to give him a job, but for the fact that the family had come out of it with more money that they'd ever seen in their lives before.

'I was simply suggesting, with my usual lack of finesse,' he said when she didn't respond, 'that you might want to indulge yourself in some clothes for the Christmas party season.' He was still holding her hand just firmly enough to stop her from pulling away.

He'd always had big hands, all out of proportion to his skinny wrists, but they'd been gentle with animals. Gentle with her. The kind of hands you'd want to find if you reached out, afraid, in the dark.

He'd grown into them now. But were they safe?

'I'll ask Jake to give you a call next week so that he can go through the diary with you,' he said, with just enough edge to warn her that it was not up for discussion.

'Christmas parties should be the least of your worries,' she replied, refusing to submit. 'My only concern is Nancie. And Saffy. Have you done anything about finding her?'

He released her hand, took out his wallet and exchanged a bank note for the paper bag that the waitress offered him, telling her to keep the change.

'I've called a friend who runs a security company. Even as we speak, he's doing everything he can to trace her. And he's discreetly checking out what's happening in France, too.'

Oh, damn! Of course he was looking for her... 'I'm sorry,' she said, realising that she'd allowed her pride to override common sense. 'I didn't mean to snap at you.'

His hand rested on her arm for a moment in a gesture of reassurance. 'Forget it. Neither of us are having a good day.'

'Are you going to tell Jake everything?' she asked. 'I mean that you…me…we…' She couldn't say it.

'That you…me…we are going to get married?' he asked, smiling, but not unkindly, at her inability to say the words.

She nodded.

'It's a matter of necessity, May. I'm going to have to leave him to make all the arrangements.'

'Arrangements? What arrangements are involved in a ten-minute ceremony?'

He shrugged. 'Does it have to be ten minutes? I thought we might manage something a little more exciting than the Registrar's Office.'

'Exciting? You think I need excitement?'

'Elegant, then. Somewhere where we can have lunch, or dinner afterwards so that I can introduce you to my directors and their wives.'

She opened her mouth. Closed it again.

'He'll sort out flowers, cars, photographs, press announcements. Arrange an evening reception for my staff.'

'You've given it quite a bit of thought.'

'I haven't had a baby to take care of.'

'No. It's just that I assumed... I thought...'

Adam had forgotten the way that he could read exactly what May was thinking. It had hit him with a rush when she'd lost it in the park, yelling at him for leaving Nancie, with everything she was feeling right there on her face. Nothing held back. All those years when she'd locked him out, avoided him, had disappeared in the heat of it. The truth of it.

He could read her now as she tried to come to terms not with being married to him, but everyone knowing that she was his wife. Having to act out the role in public.

'You thought that no one need know?' he prompted, calling on years of hiding what he was thinking to disguise how that made him feel.

'I... Yes...' she admitted. 'It's a paper formality, after all. I didn't expect so much fuss. Show.'

'But that's the whole point of it, May,' he said gently. 'The show.' He'd got everything he wanted after all. And so had she. But both of them were going to have to pay. In his case, it would simply be money. In hers, pride. A fair exchange... 'You wouldn't want the Crown Commissioners suspecting that you were just going through the motions to deny them Coleridge House, would you?'

'I thought asking Freddie Jennings to be a witness took care of that,' she said, her face unreadable. 'I'm sure it will make his day and once he gets home and tells his wife you needn't bother with a newspaper announcement. The news will be all around the town by nightfall.'

He didn't doubt it but the formality of an announcement in *The Times* was not something he intended to omit.

'I have to go. If you want a lift—'

'No. Thank you. I'll walk home. Introduce Nancie to the ducks.'

'Right. Well, I'll see you later. I don't know what time.'

She looked up at him, taking his breath away with an unexpected smile. 'If you're late, I'll do the wifely thing and put your dinner in the oven.'

Dinner? He'd never, in all his life, gone home to a cooked dinner. His mother's best effort was a pizza. Then it had been university and living on his own. Since his success, he was expected to be the provider of dinner in return for breakfast. At whatever restaurant was the place to be seen.

'What time do you eat?' he asked.

'It's a moveable feast. Seven?'

'I should be done by then.'

'Well, in case you're held up...' she opened the soft leather bag she carried over her shoulder, found a key fob '...you'd better have a key.' She sorted through a heavy bunch and, after hesitating over which one to give him, she unhooked a businesslike job and handed it to him. 'That's for the front door. I'll sort you out a full set before tomorrow.'

CHAPTER SEVEN

JAKE, BEING THE perfect PA, didn't raise an eyebrow when Adam informed him that he was about to get married.

He simply listened, made a few notes and an hour later returned with a list of available wedding venues for May to choose from, a guest list for lunch and the reception and a draft of the announcement to go into *The Times*.

He scanned it, nodded. 'I mean to warn you that May will be calling with a list of things she needs for Nancie.'

'I've already spoken to Miss Coleridge. I needed her full name for the announcement in *The Times* and, since you were on a conference call—'

'Yes, yes,' Adam said with an unexpected jab of irritation as he realised, looking at the draft, that he hadn't known that her name was not May but Mary. Pretty obvious now that he thought about it. It was a month name and her birthday was in December...

'Show me the list.'

'It's a bit basic,' he said. 'I suggested a few things, but she insisted that was all she needed.'

She probably had most things, he realised. Like the antique cradle. When a family lived in the same house for generations nothing got thrown away. But she would have nothing new. Bright. Modern.

He'd made a mess of the clothes thing, but she

wouldn't be able to refuse his insistence that she indulge Nancie. He wanted her to enjoy spending his money.

He wanted to make his mark on the house. Leave his imprint. Become part of the fabric of the house. Part of Coleridge history.

'Forget this, Jake,' he said. 'Call that big baby store on the business park and invite the manager to fulfil any new mother's wildest fantasies. Clothes, toys, nursery furniture. Just be sure that it's all delivered to Coleridge House before five o'clock today.'

Jake glanced at his watch. 'It's going to be tight.'

'I'm sure they'll find a way.'

'No doubt. I've ordered a credit card for May. It will be here on Monday. I'll deliver it myself.'

'A first class stamp will be quite sufficient,' he said. 'She isn't desperate.' Persuading her to use it would be the problem.

'It's no trouble. I have to pass Coleridge House on my way home and I can make sure that she's got everything she needs at the same time. I received the distinct impression, when I spoke to her, that Miss Coleridge isn't the kind of woman who would find it easy to pick up a phone to ask.'

'You're right. In fact, you might do worse than touch base with her housekeeper, Mrs Robson.'

When he'd gone, Adam sat back in his chair and turned to look out across the park to where the chimneys of Coleridge House were visible above the bare branches of the trees.

One phone call and Jake had got May's character down perfectly. She had never asked for anything. Never would. If Saffy hadn't sent him, reluctantly, in her direction today the first he—anyone—would have known about her loss would have been the 'For Sale' boards going up at the house.

Not that it would have been a totally lost opportunity. He could have bought it, moved his company in. Paved over the site of his humiliation and used it as a car park.

But that would not have been nearly as satisfying as the thought that tonight he'd sleep in James Coleridge's four-poster bed. And that in less than three weeks his granddaughter would become Mrs Mary Louise Wavell.

It took May a few moments to find her phone in the muddle of bags and boxes that had been piled up in her sitting room.

'Yes?' she snapped.

'You sound a little breathless, Mouse.'

'Adam…' She hadn't expected him to ring and if she hadn't been breathless from unpacking the cot, the sound of his voice would have been enough.

'I hope you're not overdoing it.'

'Overdoing it?' she repeated, propping the end of the cot with one hand, blowing hair out of her face. 'Of course I'm overdoing it. What on earth were you *thinking*?'

'I have no idea. Why don't you help me out?'

'I asked for a cot. One cot, a changing mat, a few extra clothes and some nappies. What I've got is an entire suite of nursery furniture. Cupboards, shelves, a changing trolley with drawers that does everything but actually change the baby for you and enough nappies, clothes, toys for an entire…' he waited while she hunted for the word '…*cuddle* of babies!'

'A cuddle?' he repeated, clearly struggling not to

laugh out loud. 'Is that really the collective noun for babies?'

'Cuddle, bawl, puke, poo. Take your pick.'

'Whoa! Too much information,' he said, not bothering to hide his amusement.

'I hate to be ungracious, Adam, but, as you can probably tell, I'm a bit busy.'

'You can leave the furniture moving until I get there.'

'Moving?' She looked around at the mess of packaging and furniture parts. 'This isn't just moving furniture, this is a construction project!'

'Are you telling me that it arrived flat-pack?'

'Apparently everything does these days.' She looked helplessly at the pile of shiny chrome bits that had come with the cot. 'And I have to tell you that I can't tell a flange bracket from a woggle nut.'

'Tricky things, woggle nuts,' he agreed.

'It's not funny,' she declared, but in her mind she saw that rare smile, the whole knee-wobbling, breath-stealing package... 'Is Jake there? He sounds a handy sort of man. Tell him if he can put this cot together I'll lavish him with Robbie's spiced beef casserole, lemon drizzle cake and throw in a slab of treacle toffee for good measure.'

'Jake is busy. I'm afraid you're going to have to manage with me.'

'You?'

'Do try to curb your enthusiasm, May.'

'No... It's just... I'm sorry, I didn't mean to sound ungrateful but I thought the whole point of this exercise was that you were *busy*. Up to your eyes in work. You couldn't even spare half an hour for lunch. Why are you calling, anyway?'

'I was going through the to-do list that Jake compiled for me and had just got to the rings.'

She lost control of the foot board of the cot, which she had been holding when the phone rang, and it fell against the arm of the sofa.

'May?' His voice was urgent in her ear.

'It's okay. Just a little flange bracket trouble.'

'Is there such a thing as a *little* flange bracket trouble?' he said, and she laughed.

Laughed!

How long was it since she'd done that?

'You've done this before,' she said.

'Once or twice,' he admitted. 'Actually, I called about the rings.'

'Rings?' The word brought her up with a jolt. 'No. I've got nuts, bolts, brackets,' she said, doing her best to turn it into a joke. Keep laughing. 'I can't see—'

'The wedding rings. I thought you'd want to choose your own.'

'No,' she said quickly.

'You're sure?'

'I meant no, you don't have to worry about it. I'll wear my grandmother's wedding ring.'

It was the ring she'd been going to wear when she married Michael Linton and took her place in society as a modern version of her grandmother. The perfect wife, hostess and, in the fullness of time, mother.

'I doubt your grandfather would be happy with the thought of me putting a ring he bought on your finger.'

'Probably not.' But it had to be better than picking out something that was supposed to be bought with love, 'forever' in your heart and pretending it was for real, she thought, the laughter leaking out of her like water from a broken pipe. 'But it's what I want.'

'Well, if you're sure.'

She was sure. Besides, if he bought her some fancy ring, she'd have to give it back but she could wear her grandmother's ring forever.

'I am. Is that it?'

'No. There's a whole list of things you have to decide on, but they can wait until I've sorted out your flange thingies from your whatnots. Give me half an hour and I'll be with you.'

'IT HAS TO GO THERE,' May declared, jabbing at the diagram with a neat unpolished nail.

They were kneeling on the floor of May's small sitting room, bickering over the diagram of a cupboard that did not in any way appear to match the pieces that had come out of the box.

He'd never noticed how small her hands were until he'd held them in his, soaping away the dirt of the park, applying antiseptic to her scratches. In the last couple of hours, as she'd held the pieces in place while he'd screwed the nursery furniture together—in between keeping Nancie happy—he'd found it increasingly difficult to concentrate on anything else.

'There is nowhere else,' she insisted.

Small, soft, pretty little hands that had been made to wear beautiful rings.

'I'd agree with you, except that you're looking at the diagram the wrong way up.'

'Am I? Oh, Lord, I do believe you're right.' She pulled off her glasses and sat back on her heels. 'That's it, then. I'm all out of ideas. Maybe it's time to admit defeat and call Jake.'

He looked up, about to declare that there wasn't anything that Jake could do that he couldn't do better, but the words died on his lips.

May had taken out her frustration on her hair and she looked as if she'd been dragged back, front and sideways through a very dense hedge. She was flushed with the effort of wrestling together the cot, then the changing trolley with its nest of drawers. None of which, despite the photographs of a smiling woman doing it single-handed on the instructions, she could ever have managed on her own.

But her butterscotch eyes were sparkling, lighting up her face and it was plain that, despite the frustration, the effort involved, she was actually enjoying herself.

And he discovered, rather to his surprise, that he was too. Which, since it couldn't possibly have anything to do with constructing flat-pack furniture, had to be all about who he was constructing it with.

'You think I'm going to allow myself to be defeated by a pile of timber?' he declared.

'What an incredibly male response,' May said with a giggle that sucked the years away.

In all the frozen years he'd never forgotten that sound. Her smile. How it could warm you, lift your heart, make everything bad go away. No other woman had ever been able to do that to him. Maybe that was why he'd never been able to forgive her, move on. As far as the world was concerned, he'd made it; inside, he was still the kid who wasn't good enough...

'Anyone would think I was questioning your masculinity.'

'Aren't you?' He'd meant it as a joke but the words came out more fiercely than he'd intended, provoking a flicker of something darker in May's eyes that sent a finger of heat driving through his body and, without thinking, he captured her head and brought his mouth down on hers in a crushing kiss. No finesse, no teasing sweetness, no seduction. It was all about possession, marking her, making her pay for all the years when he couldn't get the touch of her hands on him, her mouth, out of his head.

He wanted her now, here, on the floor.

It was only Nancie's increasingly loud cries that brought him to his senses and, as he let her go, May stumbled to her feet, picked the baby up, laid her against her shoulder, shushing her gently to soothe her, or maybe soothe herself.

'I have to feed her,' she said, not looking at him as she made her escape.

Every cell in his body was urging him to go after her, tell her how he felt, what she did to him, but if he'd learned anything it was control and he stayed where he was until he was breathing normally.

Then he turned back to the cupboard, reread the instructions. Without the distraction of her hair, her hands, her soft and very kissable mouth just inches from his own, everything suddenly became much clearer.

MAY LEANED AGAINST the landing wall, her legs too weak to carry her down the stairs, her hand pressed over her mouth. Whether to cool it or hold in the scalding heat of Adam's mouth on hers she could not have said.

It had been nothing like the kiss they'd shared that morning. That had been warm, tender, stirring up sweet desires.

This had been something else. Darker, taking not giving, and the shock of it had gone through her like lightning. She'd been unable to think, unable to move, knowing only that as his tongue had taken possession of her mouth she wanted more, wanted everything he had to give her. The roughness of his cheek, not just against her face, but against her breast. Wanted things from him that she had never even thought about doing with the man she had been engaged to.

She had been so aware of him all afternoon.

Adam had arrived, taken off his jacket and tie, rolled up his sleeves and her concentration had gone west as they'd worked together to construct the nursery furniture.

All she could think about was the way his dark hair slid across his forehead as he leaned into a screwdriver he'd had the foresight to bring with him.

The shiver of pleasure that rippled through her when his arm brushed against hers.

A ridiculous, melting softness as he'd looked up and smiled at her when something slotted together with a satisfying clunk.

When he'd grabbed her hand as she wobbled on her knees, held her until she'd regained her balance.

She'd just about managed to hold it together while they'd put together the cot. The changing trolley had been more of a challenge.

There were more pieces, drawers, and they'd had to work more closely together, touching close, hand-to-hand close. She'd had the dizzying sensation that if she turned to look at him he would kiss her, would do more than kiss her. Would make all her dreams come true.

By the time they'd got to the cupboard her concentration had gone to pieces and she was more hindrance than help. She had been looking at the plan, but her entire focus had been on Adam. His powerful forearms. His chin, darkened with a five o'clock shadow. The hollows in his neck.

She'd felt as if she was losing her mind. That if she didn't escape, she'd do something really stupid. Instead, she'd said something really stupid and her dreams had evaporated in the heat of a kiss that had nothing to do with the boy she'd loved, everything to do with the man he'd become.

ADAM WAS TIGHTENING the last screw when, Nancie fed and in need of changing, she could not put off returning to the nursery a moment longer.

'You did it!' she exclaimed brightly, forcing herself to smile. The reverse of the last years when she'd had to force herself not to smile every time she saw Adam.

'Once I'd got the woggle nuts lined up in a row,' he assured her as he tested the doors to make sure they were hanging properly, 'it was a piece of cake.'

'Would that be a hint?'

'Not for cake but something smells good,' he said, positioning a mini camera on top of the cupboard, angling it down onto the changing mat, where Nancie was wriggling like a little fish as she tried to undress her. 'This really is the business.'

'Amazing.' She leaned across to look at the monitor at the same time as Adam. Pulled away quickly as her shoulder brushed against his arm. 'She's amazing.'

They were both amazing, Adam thought.

Throughout the afternoon he'd seen a different side to the shy, clumsy girl he'd known, the dull woman she'd become. He'd struggled to see her running a business that involved opening her home to strangers, putting them at their ease, feeding them.

'You'd be better off on your own,' she'd said, and he was about to agree when he'd realised that her hand, closed tightly over a runaway nut, was shaking.

He'd wrapped his hand over hers, intending only to hold it still while he recovered the nut, but her tremor transferred itself to him, rippling through him like a tiny shock wave, throwing him off balance, and he'd said, 'Stay.'

He'd been off balance ever since.

Totally lost it with a kiss that he could still see on her bee stung lips.

'What shall I do with all this packaging?'

'There's a store room in the stables,' she said as she eased Nancie out of her pink tights. 'Look, gorgeous, you're on television.'

Then, as she realised what she'd said, she glanced up at him and he saw her throat move as she swallowed, an almost pleading look in her eyes. Pleading for what? Forgiveness? Obliteration of memory?

'It's where we hold the craft classes,' she said quickly. 'They're always desperate for cardboard.'

Nancie made a grab for her hair and May, laughing, caught her tiny hand and kissed the fingers. As Adam watched her, the memories bubbled up. He'd kissed May's fingers just that way. Kissed her lovely neck, the soft mound of her young breast.

A guttural sound escaped him and she turned, tucking the loose strand of hair behind her ear.

'Saffy is so lucky,' she said.

'Lucky?'

'To have Nancie...'

And as he looked into her eyes, he realised that the smile that came so easily to her lips was tinged with sadness.

Nearly thirty, she had no husband, no children, no life. Not his fault, he told himself. He'd come for her but she wanted this more than him. Well, he would give it to her. And she would finish what she'd started. Maybe in the hayloft…

'Is there any news of her? Saffy?' she prompted.

'Not yet,' he said abruptly, gathering a pile of flattened boxes and carrying them down into the yard, glad of the chill night air to clear his head.

It was pitch dark but the path and stable yard were well lit. There had been no horses here in a generation, no carriage for more than a century, but nothing much, on the outside, had changed.

The stable and carriage house doors shone with glossy black paint, wooden tubs containing winter heathers and pansies gave the area a rustic charm. A black-and-white cat mewed, rubbed against his legs.

There was even the smell of animals and a snort from the low range of buildings on the far side of the yard had him swinging round to where a donkey had pushed his head through the half door. A goat, standing on her hind legs, joined him.

The class had finished a while back. He'd heard cars starting up, cheerful voices shouting their goodbyes to one another as he'd finished the cupboard. But the lights were on and a girl, busy sweeping the floor, looked up as he entered and came to an abrupt halt.

'Miss Coleridge is in the house,' she said.

'I know. She asked me to bring this out here.'

'Oh, right. You want the storeroom. It's down at the bottom. The door on the left.'

He'd expected to find the interior much as it had always been, still stables but cleaned up, with just enough done to provide usable work space.

He couldn't have been more wrong.

Serious money had been spent gutting the building, leaving a large, impressively light and airy workspace.

The loft had gone, skylights installed and the wooden rafters now carried state-of-the-art spotlights that lit every corner.

A solid wooden floor had been laid, there were deep butler's sinks along one wall, with wooden drainers and stacking work tables and chairs made the space infinitely adaptable. And, at the far end, the old tack room where they'd made coffee, eaten cake and shortbread, had been converted into bathroom facilities with disabled access. Everything had been finished to the highest standard.

Fooled by those useless labels, he'd assumed this was just a cosy little business that she'd stumbled into, but it was obvious that she'd been thinking ahead. Understood that there would be a time when Coleridge House would have to support itself, support her, if she was going to keep it.

He thought he knew her, understood her. That he was in control.

Wrong, wrong, wrong…

MAY SETTLED NANCIE, not looking up when Adam returned to collect the remainder of the packaging. Then, having angled the monitor camera on to Nancie in the cot, she went downstairs and checked the kitten, who she'd introduced to the kitchen cats, a couple of old sweethearts who were well used to stray babies—rabbits, puppies, even chicks, keeping them all clean and warm.

They'd washed him, enveloped him in their warmth and, as she stroked them, they licked at her, too. As if she was just another stray.

There was a draught as the back door opened and she turned as Adam came in.

'All done? Did you manage to cram everything in?'

'No problem. That's an impressive set-up you've got out there.'

She quirked an eyebrow at him. 'Did you imagine we just flung down some hay to cover the cobbles?'

'I didn't think about it at all,' he lied, looking around the kitchen rather than meet her eyes. Looking at the animals curled up in the basket by the Aga. The cats in the armchair, licking at the kitten. 'But now I'm wondering about the other side of your business. How you cater for your guests. Make your sweets. This is a very picturesque country kitchen, but I can't see it getting through a rigorous trading standards inspection for a licence to feed the paying public.'

'Oh? And what do you know about catering standards?'

'Amongst other things, my company imports the finest coffee from across the globe. It wouldn't look good if the staff had to go to a chain to buy their morning latte.'

'I suppose not.'

May knew, on one level, that Adam was hugely successful, but it was difficult to equate the boy who'd nicknamed her Danger Mouse, who'd always been around when she'd got into trouble, who'd stood outside this house, soaked and freezing, as he'd defied her grandfather, shouting out for her to go with him, as a serious, responsible businessman with the livelihood of hundreds, maybe thousands of people in his hands.

'How do you do it?' he asked, opening the fridge.

'Well, I had two choices,' she said, dragging herself out of the past. It was now that mattered. Today. 'What are you looking for?'

'A beer.' He pulled a face. 'My mistake.'

'You'll find beer in the pantry.' And, enjoying his surprise, 'Not all our workshops are women only affairs.'

'I'll replace it.'

'There's no need.'

'I'm not a guest.' And, before she could contradict him, he said, 'Can I get you anything?'

She shook her head. 'I'm babysitting.'

'Right.' He fetched a can from the pantry, popped it open and leaned back against the sink, watching as she donned oven gloves and took the casserole out of the oven. 'Two choices?'

'I could have torn this kitchen out, replaced it with something space age in stainless steel and abolished the furred and feathered brigade to the mud room, but that would have felt like ripping the heart out of the house.'

'Not an option.'

'No,' she said and, glad that he understood, she managed a smile. 'It was actually cheaper to install a second kitchen in the butler's parlour.'

Adam choked as his beer went down the wrong way. 'The butler's parlour?'

'Don't worry. It's been a long time since Coleridge House has warranted a butler,' she said and the tension, drum tight since he'd kissed her, dissipated as the smile she'd been straining for finally broke through.

'Well, that's a relief. It must still have been a major expense. Is it justified?'

'The bank seemed to think so.'

'The bank? You borrowed from the bank?'

May heard the disbelief in his voice.

'I suppose I could have borrowed from Grandpa,' she said. She'd had an enduring power of attorney. Paid the bills. Kept the accounts. Kept the house together. No one could have, would have stopped her. On the contrary. Grandpa's accountant had warned her that big old houses like this were a money sink and she needed to think about the future. Clearly, he hadn't known about the inheritance clause, either.

'Why didn't you?'

'It was my business. My responsibility.' Hers... Then, as she saw his horrified expression, 'You don't have to worry, Adam. I don't make a fortune, but I have enough bookings to meet my obligations. You won't have to bail me out.'

'What? No... I was just realising how much trouble you would have been in if I hadn't come along this morning. If I hadn't needed you so badly that I badgered you until you were forced to explain. You would have lost the lot.'

He wasn't thinking about himself? The realisation that, as her husband, he'd be responsible for her debts.

He was just thinking about her.

'It wouldn't have been the end of the world,' she said, putting the casserole on the table, the dish of potatoes baked in their jackets. Almost, but not quite. 'Once the contents of the house were sold, I'd have been able to pay them back.'

He caught her wrist. 'Promise me one thing, May.

he said fiercely. 'That, the minute you're married, you instruct Jennings to do whatever if takes to break that entailment.'

'It's number one on my list,' she assured him.

Not that there seemed much likelihood of her ever having a child of her own to put in this position. She hadn't thought much about that particular emptiness in her life until today when Nancie had clung to her, smiled at her.

'I'll have to make a new will, anyway. Not that there's anyone to leave the house to. I'm the last of the Coleridges.'

'No cousins?'

'Only three or four times removed.'

'They're still family and there's nothing like the scent of an inheritance to bring long lost relatives out of the woodwork.'

'Not to any purpose, in this case. I'll leave it to a charity. At least that way I won't feel as if I've cheated.'

'Cheated?'

'By marrying you just to keep the house.'

'You're not cheating anyone, May. If your grandfather hadn't had a stroke you would have been married to Michael Linton.'

'Maybe.' She'd been so very young and he'd been so assured, so charming. So *safe*.

That was the one thing she could never say about Adam. Whether he was rescuing her from disaster, mucking out a rabbit cage or cleaning her wounds, as he had today, apparently oblivious to the fact that she was half naked, she had never felt safe with him.

Whenever she was near him she seemed to lose control of not just her breathing, but her ability to hold anything fragile, the carefully built protective barrier she'd erected around herself at school. One look and it crumbled.

She didn't feel safe, but she did feel fizzingly alive and, while he might not have noticed the effect he had on her, his sister hadn't missed it.

'You had doubts?' Adam asked, picking up on her lack of certainty.

'Not then.' At the time, marriage to Michael Linton had offered an escape. From her grandfather. From Maybridge. From the possibility of meeting Adam Wavell.

'And now?'

'Looking back, the whole thing seems like something out of a Jane Austen novel.'

'While your grandfather's will is more like something out of one of the more depressing novels of George Eliot.'

'Yes, well, whatever happens to the house in the future, it won't happen by default because I did nothing,' she assured him as she gestured for him to sit down. 'Actually, I'm sure the infallible Jake has it on his list but, just in case he'd missed it, you'll have to make a new will, too.'

'This is cheery.'

'But essential,' she said as she ladled meat onto a plate. 'Marriage nullifies all previous wills, which means that, should you fall under a bus—'

'Have you ever heard of someone falling under a bus?' he asked.

'Should you fall under a bus, the major part of your assets will come to me by default,' she persisted, determined to make her point. 'Not that I'd keep it,' she assured him. 'Obviously.'

'Why obviously?'

'You have a family.'

'There's always a downside,' he said, taking the plate. 'You'd get the assets, but you also get the bad debts.'

'Adam!'

'Would you entrust an international company to either my sister or my mother?' he demanded.

'Well, obviously—'

'They'd sell out to the first person who offered them hard cash, whereas you, with your highly developed sense of duty and the Coleridge imperative to hold tight to what they have, would be a worthy steward of my estate.'

She assumed he was teasing—although that remark about the Coleridges' firm grasp on their property had been barbed—but, as she offered him the dish of potatoes, his gaze was intent, his purpose serious.

'You'll get married, have children of your own,' she protested.

'I'm marrying you, Mary Louise. For better or worse.'

'That's a two-way promise,' May said, equally intent.

Adam held the look for long seconds, as if testing her sincerity, before he nodded and took the dish.

'Where's Robbie?' he asked, changing the subject. 'Isn't she eating with us?'

'It's quiz night at the pub,' she said, serving herself. Not that she had much appetite. 'She offered to give it a miss, but it's semi-final night and her team are red-hot.'

'She didn't trust me alone with you? What is she going to do? Sleep across your door?'

'Does she need to?' she asked flippantly, but as she looked up, their eyes met across the table and the air hummed once more with a tension that stretched back through the years.

All the pain, the shame she'd masked from him each time, despite every attempt to avoid one another, they'd found themselves face-to-face in public. Both of them achingly polite, while he'd looked at her as if breathing the same air hurt him.

CHAPTER EIGHT

ADAM'S HAND WAS shaking slightly as he picked up his fork. Robbie was no fool, he thought. She didn't trust him further than she could throw him and with good reason.

'Help yourself to another beer,' May prompted. 'Whatever you want.'

'I'm good, thanks,' he said, then, spearing a piece of carrot, 'I took a couple of carrots from the sack in the mud room and gave them to the donkey and his mate, by the way,' he said in a desperate attempt to bring things back to the mundane. 'I hope I didn't mess up their diet.'

'Everyone gets mugged by Jack and Dolly,' she said, clearly glad to follow his lead away from dangerous territory. 'They're a double act. Inseparable, couldn't be parted. And you're looking at the original mug. The one who took them both in.'

'I'll bet they didn't have to work anywhere near as hard as I did,' he said. 'One pitiful bleat from Dolly and I'll bet you were putty in their hooves.'

'Under normal circumstances I'd have been putty in yours,' she replied. And then she blushed. 'At least Jack keeps the paddock grazed.'

'Not Dolly?'

'She prefers bramble shoots, with a side snack of roses when no one's looking.' Maybe it was the mention of roses, but she leapt up. 'Nancie's awake,' she said, pushing back her chair, grabbing the monitor from the table. 'Help yourself,' she said, waving at the table. 'I've had enough.'

'Enough' had been little more than a mouthful, but she dashed from the room and he didn't try to stop her. Not because he believed the baby needed instant attention, but because suddenly every word seemed loaded.

He finished eating, cleared both their plates and stacked them in the dishwasher. Covered the food. Filled the coffeemaker and set it to drip. Then, when May still hadn't appeared, he went upstairs to find her.

She was sitting in the dark, watching Nancie as she slept. The light from the landing touched her cheeks, made a halo of her hair.

'May?' he said softly.

She looked up. 'Adam. I'm sorry. I'm neglecting you,' she said, getting up and, after a last look at Nancie, joining him. 'There's leftover crème brulée in the fridge...'

'What happened to the lemon drizzle cake?'

'The Christmas course ladies finished it when they had tea. I'm sorry. It was always your favourite.'

'Was it? I don't remember,' he lied. 'I'm making coffee.'

'Well, good. You must make yourself at home. Have whatever you want. You'll find the drinks cupboard in the library.'

'Library?' He managed a teasing note. 'First a butler, now a library.'

'It's not a very big library. Do you want a tour of the house? I should probably introduce you to the ancestors.'

'If you're sure they won't all turn in their graves.'

She looked up at him and for a moment he though

she was going to say something. But after a pause she turned and led the way down a fine staircase lined with portraits, naming each of them as she passed without looking. But then, near the bottom, she stopped by a fine portrait of a young woman.

'This is a Romney portrait of Jane Coleridge,' she said. 'She's the woman who Henry Coleridge had his arm twisted to marry. The cause of all the bother.'

'You have the look of her,' he said. The same colouring, the same soft curves, striking amber eyes.

'Well, that would explain it,' she said, moving on, showing him the rest of the house. The grand drawing and dining rooms, filled with the kind of furniture and paintings that would have the experts on one of those antiques television programmes drooling. There was a small sitting room, a room for a lady. And then there was the library with its vast desk, worn leather armchairs.

She crossed to the desk and opened a drawer.

'These were Grandpa's,' she said, handing a large bunch of keys to him.

'What are they all?' he asked.

She took them from him and ran through them. 'Front, back, cellar—although we don't keep it locked these days. The gate to the park.' There were half a dozen more before she said, 'This one's for the safe.'

'The safe?'

She opened a false panel in one of the bookshelves to display a very old safe.

'Family documents, my grandmother's jewellery. Not much of that. She left it to my mother, and she sold most of it to fund Third World health care.'

Which was ironic, he thought, considering how she'd died. 'Her wedding ring? Can I see it?'

She shrugged. 'Of course.' She took the keys from him, opened the safe, handed him a small velvet pouch.

He wasn't sure what he'd expected. From her insistence that she wear it, he'd imagined something special, something worthy of a Coleridge, but what he tipped into his palm was a simple old-fashioned band of gold without so much as a date or initials inscribed on the inside.

It was a ring made to take the knocks of a lifetime. In the days when this had been forged, people didn't run to the divorce courts at the first hint of trouble but stuck to the vows they'd sworn over it.

'It's not fancy,' she said, as if she felt the need to apologise.

'It's your choice, May,' he said, wishing he'd insisted on buying a ring of his own. But he'd obliterate its plainness with the flash of the ring he'd buy to lie alongside it. He kept that to himself, however, afraid she'd insist on wearing her grandmother's engagement ring, too. Always assuming her mother hadn't sold that. He didn't ask, just removed the key to the back door and the park gate and added them to his own key ring, returning the rest to the drawer. 'Can I borrow it? So that I make sure my own ring matches it.'

There was just the barest hesitation before she said, 'Of course.'

'I'll take good care of it,' he assured her. 'Shall we have that coffee now? We have to make a decision on where we're going to hold the wedding.'

'There's a fire in the morning room. I'll bring it through.'

May took a moment as she laid the tray with cups, shortbread, half a dozen of the fudge balls she'd created for the Christmas market. Anything to delay the moment when she had to join him.

While she was with Adam, she was constantly distracted by memories, tripped up by innocent words that ripped through her.

Roses…

She'd never been able to see red roses without remembering Adam standing back from the door, shouting her name up at her window, oblivious to the approaching danger.

The bunch of red roses in his fist had exploded as her grandfather had turned the hose on him, hitting him in the chest and, for a terrible moment, she had thought it was his blood.

She'd tried to scream but the sound would not come through the thick, throat-closing fear that he was dead. It was only later, much later, when it was dark and everyone was asleep, that she'd crept outside to gather up the petals by the light of her torch.

ADAM STRETCHED OUT in front of the fire. His apartment was the height of luxury, everything simple, clean, uncluttered. It had been a dream back in the days when he'd been living in a cramped flat with his mother and his sister, the complete antithesis of this room, with its furniture in what could only be described as 'country house' condition. In other words, worn by centuries of use.

But the room had a relaxed, confident air. It invited you to sit, make yourself comfortable because, after all, if you'd made it this far into the inner sanctum, you were a welcome visitor.

He leapt up as May appeared with a tray, but she shook her head and said, 'I can manage,' as she put it on the sofa table. 'Is it still black, no sugar?'

'Yes…' She remembered?

'Would you like a piece of Robbie's shortbread?' She placed the cup beside him. Offered him the plate. 'Or a piece of fudge?'

'These are the sweets you make?'

'This is a seasonal special. Christmas Snowball Surprise. White chocolate and cranberry fudge rolled in flaked coconut.'

He took one, bit into it and his mouth filled with an explosion of flavour, heat. 'You forgot to mention the rum.'

'That's the surprise,' she said, but her smile was weary and he saw, with something of a shock, that there were dark smudges beneath her eyes.

'Are you all right, May?' he asked when she didn't move, didn't pour herself a cup.

She eased her shoulder. 'I'm a bit tired. I think the fall has finally caught up with me.'

'Are you in pain?' he asked, crossing to her, running his hands lightly over her shoulder and she winced. 'You should have gone to Casualty. Had an X-ray.'

'It's just a strain,' she assured him. 'I'll be fine after a soak.' Then, before he could protest, 'I'm afraid the television is rather old, but it works well enough. And don't worry about security. Robbie will check the locks, set the alarm when she comes in.'

'Where is her room?' he asked.

That, at least, raised a smile from May. 'Don't worry. You won't run into her in her curlers. She's got her own self-contained apartment on the ground floor.' She hesitated. 'You've got everything you need?'

He nodded, touched her cheek. 'Give me the monitor. I'll take care of Nancie if she wakes.'

'No. You've got a long flight tomorrow. You'll be in enough trouble with jet lag without having a sleepless night.'

'That's why I'm here,' he said.

'Is it?' She pushed a hand distractedly through her hair, as if she'd forgotten his promise to take the night shift. 'There's no need for that. You've done your hero stint with the furniture. What time are you leaving?'

'The car will pick me up at nine.'

'I hadn't realised you were leaving so early.' She looked at the coffee on the tray in front of her. 'Another half an hour—'

'There'll be plenty of time to sort out the wedding details over breakfast. Go and soak your aches.'

ADAM COULDN'T SLEEP. He'd hung his suit in the great oak wardrobe made from trees that had been growing in the seventeenth century.

Tossed his dirty linen in the basket. Soaked a few aches of his own away in the huge roll-top Victorian bath, no doubt the latest thing when it had been installed. Having a fully grown woman fall on you left its mark and he'd found a bruise that mirrored May's aches on his own shoulder.

Then he'd stretched his naked limbs between the fine linen sheets on the four-poster bed, lay there, waiting for the sense of triumph to kick in. But, instead, all he could think about was May.

May not making a fuss, even though she'd clearly been in pain.

May trembling when he touched her. The hot, dark centre of her eyes in the moment before he'd kissed her. Wishing he was lying with his arms around her amongst the lace and frills, instead of the icy splendour of James Coleridge's bed.

THE PHONE STARTLED May out of sleep and she practically fell out of bed, grabbing for it before it woke Nancie.

'Hello?'

'May…'

'Saffy! Where are you? Are you safe?'

'I'm okay. Is Nancie all right?'

'She's fine. Gorgeous, but what about you? Where are you? Why didn't you come straight to me? You know I'd have helped you.'

'I wasn't sure. It's been a long time…'

'Come now. Adam's desperate with worry. Let me get him—'

'He's there?'

'He's staying with Nancie,' she said, keeping it simple. Explanations could wait. 'Saffy? Saffy, I've got plenty of room. You should be with Nancie,' she said quickly. But, before she'd finished, she was talking to herself.

She dialled one four seven one, to find out what number had called but the number had been withheld.

'THERE WAS NO POINT in disturbing you,' May protested in response to his fury that she hadn't bothered to come and tell him that his sister had called in the night. 'There was nothing you could do.'

In contrast to the quiet of his own apartment first thing, the kitchen was bedlam. Nancie grizzling on May's shoulder, the chicken was squawking at the cats, the dog was barking and there was some schmaltzy Christmas song on the radio. He reached out and switched it off.

'That's not the point.'

He'd spent most of the night lying awake, then when

he had fallen asleep, he'd been plagued by dreams he couldn't remember, overslept. He felt like a bear with a sore head and apparently it showed because she stuck a glass of orange juice in his hand.

'Here. Drink that.'

He swallowed it down and took a breath. The last thing he was going to tell her was that she wouldn't have been disturbing him. If she knew that he'd been lying awake, had heard the phone, she'd want to know why he hadn't come to check for himself.

He could hardly tell her that he'd lain in James Coleridge's hard bed imagining some private middle of the night exchange between her and Jeremy Davidson.

Imagining her reassuring him that her marriage would only be a paper thing. That in a year she'd be free. That if they were discreet...

Because that was what lovers did. Called one another in the small hours when they couldn't sleep.

It hadn't crossed his mind that it would be Saffy. He hadn't been thinking about her at all, he realised. Or his baby niece, crying for her mother.

May had accused him of thinking only about himself and she was right.

'Here, give her to me,' he said, taking the baby, holding her at arm's length. Shocked out of her misery, she stared back him, her cheeks flushed, her black curls in disarray, a beauty in the making. His sister's child.

There and then he made her a silent promise that, whatever happened, he would ensure that her life was very different from that of her mother. That she would always know she was cherished, loved.

She gave a little shudder.

'Don't fret, sweetheart,' he said, putting her against

his shoulder. 'We'll find your mother, but in the meantime May is doing her best so you must be good for her while I'm away.' He looked down at her. 'Do we have a deal?'

'She'll dribble on your shirt,' May warned as she clutched at him, warm and trusting.

'It'll sponge off.' Then he frowned. 'How did Saffy get your number? It's unlisted.'

'I gave it to her once. I'm sorry. If she calls again…' She stopped as she caught sight of his grip, his laptop bag. 'Maybe it's as well that you won't be here. She hung up when I said I'd get you.'

It sounded like a reproach. And, if it was, he deserved it. He'd worked so hard to distance himself from his family that now his sister was frightened to come to him.

'If she rings again, I'll do my best to persuade her to come here,' she said, then, as the doorbell rang, she glanced at the clock. 'Oh, Lord, that's your car and you haven't had any breakfast. I'm not usually this disorganised.'

'You don't usually have a baby to look after. Don't worry; I'll get something at the airport. If you need anything, you've got Jake's number. He'll know how to get in touch.' He kissed Nancie, surrendered her to May. 'We never did get around to deciding where to hold the wedding.'

'Does it matter?' she asked. Then, maybe realising that was less than gracious, 'Why don't we leave it to Jake? Let him surprise us.'

'If that's what you want.' He picked up his bags and she made to follow him, but he said, 'Don't come to the door. Stay in the warm.'

'You will be careful, Adam?'

'I'll watch out for low flying buses,' he said flippantly.

After he'd gone everything went quiet. The chicken, stupid thing, stopped tormenting the cats who, embarrassed, settled down to give each other and the kitten a thorough wash. The dog dropped his head back on his paws. Nancie sighed into her shoulder.

It was quiet, peaceful and if all the tension had gone out of the room, out of the house with Adam, he'd taken all the life with him, too.

Abandoning any thought of breakfast, she took Nancie upstairs. 'Okay, little one. This is going to be an adventure for both of us,' she said as she filled the baby bath, checked the temperature. 'Now, promise you'll be gentle with me.'

Ten minutes later, and considerably damper, she wrestled the baby into a pair of the sweetest pink velvet dungarees, then put her down in the cot and turned on the musical mobile.

She'd just finished mopping up the bathroom and changed into dry clothes when Robbie put her head around the door.

'Is the coast clear?'

'Sorry?'

'Has he gone?'

'Adam? Yes. Half an hour ago. And where were you hiding when I needed you? I've never bathed a baby in my life.'

'Then it's time you learned how. I was feeding the livestock and just look what I found sharing Jack and Dolly's bed of hay.'

She opened the door wider to reveal a shivering and

sorry looking woman, bundled up in a thick coat, head-scarf and peering at her through heavy-framed glasses.

She looked vaguely familiar... The woman in the park yesterday. She took off the glasses and pushed the scarf back to reveal glossy black hair and said, 'Hello, May.'

'Saffy!'

'I'll go and make some tea,' Robbie said, leaving them to it.

'I saw you. Yesterday.'

'I didn't mean to stay. I was going back to France, to confront Michel. I just wanted to be sure that he was bringing Nancie to you but the idiot left her on the path where anyone could have taken her...'

'That's what I said. I shouted at him.'

'Did you?' That made her smile. 'You were always shouting at him. That's how I knew you liked him,' she said. 'It's why I twisted his arm, forced him to ask you to the disco that night. You'd been so kind...' Then, 'I just wanted you to have a good time.'

'I know. Nothing that happened was your fault.' It had been hers. If she'd been braver, instead of hiding her friendship with Adam, if her grandfather had been given a chance to get to know him... 'Have you been out there all this time?'

Saffy nodded and May frowned. 'But I don't understand. If you were going to see Michel...'

'I lost my nerve. I thought I might be arrested. That the police might be watching for me at Adam's office. In the end I wandered around for a bit. Bought some food. I stayed in the library for a long time. It was late night closing. I spent as long as I could eating a burger to stay in the warm.'

'Why on earth didn't you come to me?'

'Because I'm wanted by the authorities. I didn't want to get you into trouble.'

'Oh, for goodness' sake, come here,' she said, holding out her arms and gathered her in, holding her tight.

'I tried to sleep in the park, but it was so cold and I when I tried your gate it was unlocked and I thought, maybe you wouldn't mind but when you said Adam was here... He's going to be so angry with me...'

'Not half as angry as I'm going to be with him,' she said.

Then, standing back, 'Saffy Wavell, you stink of goat. Out of those things and into the bath with you before you go anywhere near your gorgeous little girl.'

ADAM HAD JUST reached the airport when his phone rang. It was number withheld. 'Saffy?'

'Adam—'

'May...' He'd been trying to block out the scene in her kitchen. Noisy, alive, full of warmth and life, a total contrast to his own sterile existence.

He hadn't lacked for female company, but he dated women who were more interested in being seen in the gossip magazines than in anything more domestic than opening a bottle of champagne. The kind of women that his sister had always wanted to be. Tall, beautiful but, despite May's accusation, not always blonde. The colour of their hair hadn't mattered. The only unchangeable requirement was that they didn't remind him of her.

But the unexpected sound of her voice against his ear brought her so close that he felt as if she were touching him.

Just one day in her company and he was in danger of

falling under the spell she'd cast on him when he was too young to protect himself from the kind of pain that brought. Forgetting what this was about.

'Is there a problem?' he asked, keeping his voice cool.

'No. I only wanted to let you know that Saffy's here with me. That she's safe.'

Relief flooded through him. Gratitude. He held it in. 'You were right, then. She wasn't far away. Can I talk to her? Or is she determined to avoid me?'

'She's in the bath right now and then I'm going to feed her and put her to bed.'

'I'll take that as a yes.' Well, what did he expect? He'd kept her at arm's length for years. She knew he didn't want her around, reminding people who he was. Where he came from. 'I'll see what I can do about damage limitation,' he said. 'I'll get Jake to organise a family lawyer.' He could do that for her. 'Try and sort out the mess.'

'It's the weekend. Nothing is going to get done until Monday. Let me talk to her, Adam. Find out what's happened. If it can't be straightened out, I'll call Jake myself.'

'Damn it—'

'Your priority is your trip, Adam. And there's no harm in trying honey before we go for the sting.'

'You should know.' But she was undoubtedly right. In cases like this, soft words might well prove more effective than going in heavy-footed. Something that he wouldn't have had to be told if this was a business negotiation. But his family had never been exactly good when it came to relationships. 'Try it your way first, but tell Saffy she has to stay with you until I get back.'

'Oh, that will work.'

'May! I'm concerned about her. Please ask her to stay with you until I get back.'

'Better.'

'What is this, family relationship counselling?' She didn't answer. 'Tell her that I'm not angry, okay. That I'm glad she's safe.'

'Wow.'

'Sarcasm does not become you, Miss Coleridge.'

'Forget she's your sister, Adam. Think of her as some frightened creature that you've found,' she said, using his own words to her when he'd been trying to persuade her to take Nancie. 'It's in pain and you've picked it up and brought it to me.'

'Damn it!' Was she mocking him? 'Do whatever you want,' he said and hung up.

Around him, the terminal buzzed with people wheeling heavy suitcases as they searched for their check-in desks. They were harassed but excited, looking forward to going on holiday or to stay with family.

He had a sister and a mother who he kept at arm's length. Out of sight, out of mind. He had no one. No one except May. He looked at the phone in his hand, scrolled down to her number.

'Adam?'

From the way she said his name, he suspected that she hadn't moved, but had been waiting for him to call back. And he couldn't make up his mind whether the feeling that ripped through him was anger that she could read him that well or an ache for something precious that had been trampled on, destroyed and was lost forever.

'You can tell my sister,' he said, 'that, whatever happens, she can count on me. That I won't let her down. That I won't let anyone take Nancie away from her.'

'And that you won't shout at her?' she insisted, but now there was a smile in her voice.

'You're one tough negotiator, Danger Mouse. I don't suppose you'd reconsider that job offer?'

'As a nanny? I'm already redundant.'

'If you think that, you're in for a rude awakening. You now have two babies to take care of.' She didn't say a word and, after a moment, he laughed.

'Okay. I'll do my best, but you'll have to stand very close so that you can jab me with your elbow if I forget.'

'My elbow? My pleasure,' she said, but she was laughing too and he was glad he'd called.

'I have to go.'

'Yes. Please be careful, Adam.'

'May…'

'Yes?'

There was a long pause while a hundred possibilities rushed into his head.

'I'll call you in the morning. Maybe you'll have got some sense out of Saffy by then.'

CHAPTER NINE

MAY SURRENDERED HER room to Saffy so that she was next to the nursery, loaning her a nightdress since she didn't seem to have any luggage. Sorting her out some clothes.

She slept most of the day, waking only when Nancie cried to be fed, the pair of them curled up in bed together.

She and Robbie worked quietly, stripping the bedrooms, getting them ready for the next group of guests who would be arriving the following Friday for a three-day garden design course. Then she took Nancie for a walk, sticking up posters with a picture of the kitten to the lamp posts in the park on her way in to Maybridge to pick up some underwear for Saffy who, despite having given birth recently, was still at least two sizes smaller than her.

Keeping herself busy, counting off the long hours until Adam's flight landed.

By the evening, Saffy had recovered. Robbie announced she was going to the cinema with a friend, leaving them to spend the evening catching up.

'I really love Michel,' she said after she'd given chapter and verse on how they'd met. How handsome he was. How romantic. 'It's his mother. She never liked me. She is such a snob. She's done everything she can to split us up and when that didn't work she dug up all that stuff from when I was a kid. Telling Michel that I was a danger to Nancie. That I couldn't be trusted.'

'Did he ask you about it?'

'Of course and I told him everything. Not that I nearly went to jail. That you saved me. But everything else,' she said.

'You can't hide, Saffy. Michel has rights, too. And you've put yourself in the wrong. He must be frantic with worry. Not just for the baby,' she added.

'I was frightened.'

'Of course you were. Do you think it would help if I spoke to him? Explained?'

It took a while to persuade her but, an hour later, a sobbing Saffy was talking to Michel, declaring how much she loved him.

ADAM FINALLY RANG at ten the following morning.

May, in an unfamiliar bed, had scarcely slept and jumped every time a phone rang. Once it had been Jake, to let her know that Adam had arrived safely just after ten the previous evening and to ask if she needed anything.

Mostly it was Michel calling Saffy to mutter sweet nothings. Clearly the thought of losing her had brought him to his senses.

'I tried earlier, but the line was engaged.'

'It's the French lover.'

'They're talking?'

'Endlessly. I've suggested he comes to stay but, from his reluctance, I suspect he hasn't told his parents that they're reunited. *Maman* sounds like a dragon.'

'There are worse things than an overprotective mother.'

'True.'

'I'm sorry, May. At least I had one.'

'Forget it. How was the flight?'

'Long. Boring. I'd seen the film. The food was terrible. Pretty much what you'd expect.'

'Well, you've got that Presidential dinner to look forward to.'

'Not until the end of the week.' He told her his itinerary; she gave him her mobile number. 'I have to go, May. I'll call you later. Take care.'

'Take care,' she repeated softly when he'd hung up, holding the phone to her breast.

HE CALLED EVERY morning on the landline and talked, not just to her, but Saffy. Called every evening on her mobile when she was in bed. She updated him on the saga of the French lover and his mother. He told her what he'd been doing. Nothing of any importance. The words weren't important. It was hearing his voice.

MAY, UP TO her eyes preparing for the arrival of a houseful of guests as well as preparing a rush order of fudge, snatched the phone off the hook.

It was the tenth time it had rung that morning. The announcement of their forthcoming wedding had appeared in *The Times* that morning and she'd been inundated with calls. Only Adam hadn't rung.

'Yes!' she snapped as snatched up the phone.

'Whoa. Bad morning?' Adam said, making the whole hideous morning disappear with a word.

'You could say that.' But not now... 'I'm just busy. Michel and his parents are arriving this afternoon.'

'His parents?'

'It was my idea to invite them. He's finally owned up to his *maman* that the relationship is back on and he wants to marry the mother of his child.'

'Not before time.'

'His mother still thinks that Saffy is a scheming little nobody with a bad history who's not fit to clean her boy's boots, let alone raise her grandchild. I'm going to change her mind. Prove to her that the Wavells have connections. Robbie and Saffy are polishing the family silver even as we speak.'

'You're giving them the full country house experience?'

'Absolutely. The best crystal, the Royal Doulton, Patsy in a white apron waiting table. I'm even going to wear my grandmother's engagement ring. Just to emphasize that Saffy is about to become my sister-in-law.'

There was a silence, a hum on the line and for a moment she thought she'd lost the connection.

'Your mother didn't sell that?'

'It's been in the family forever. Jane Coleridge is wearing it in the Romney portrait, something I'll point out when I introduce them to the ancestors. Knock them out with centuries of tradition.'

'Just as long as they don't think that I'm too cheap to buy you one of your own.'

'Adam...'

'You've clearly got everything under control, there I'll call later and see if you've managed to cement the entente cordiale.'

He rang off. May replaced the receiver rather more

slowly. Clearly he'd been annoyed about the ring but there was no point in worrying about it.

If she was going to hit them with afternoon tea in the drawing room, install Michel's parents in state in the master bedroom and then serve the kind of traditional British food at dinner that would make a Frenchman weep with envy, she didn't have a minute to spare.

'DID I WAKE YOU?'

'No.' May had snatched up the phone at the first hint of a ring, on tenterhooks, not sure that he'd ring. 'I've just this minute fallen into bed. I wanted to lay up for breakfast in the conservatory before I turned in.'

'How did it go?'

'My face is aching from smiling,' she admitted. In truth, every muscle was throbbing, more from the tension than the effort. Catering for charity lunches, receptions, had been part of her life for as long as she could remember but so much had been riding on this. 'But in a good cause. I think Michel's *maman* is finally convinced that Saffy's youthful indiscretions were no more than high jinks.'

'If she believes that, you must have done some fast talking.'

'The fact that Grandpa was a magistrate was the final clincher, I think. And maybe the four-poster bed.'

'You put them in *my* bed?'

'In the state bedroom,' she said, chuckling. 'I dug out a signed picture that the Prince of Wales gave my great-grandfather in 1935 and put it on the dressing table.'

'Nice touch.'

'And then, of course, we wheeled out the family star.'

'Nancie?'

'Well, she played her part. But I was actually talking about you. *Maman* had no idea that Saffy's brother was the billionaire Chairman of the company whose coffee she cannot, she swears, live without.'

'Oh.'

'A double whammy. Class and cash. How could she resist? Whether you'll thank me when you've got them as in-laws is another matter. Michel and his father are both gorgeous to look at, but totally under the matriarchal thumb.'

'Why, May?'

She'd been snuggling down under the duvet, warm, sleepy and this morning's misunderstanding forgotten, loving the chance to tell him about her triumph on his behalf.

'Why what?' she asked.

'Why would you go to so much trouble for Saffy?'

'I wasn't...' She wasn't doing it for Saffy; she was doing it for him.

'Don't be coy. You've pulled out all the stops for her. What is it between you two?'

'She never told you?'

'My little sister lived for secrets. It gave her a sense of power.'

'I was being bullied. When I first went to the high school. A gang of girls was taking my lunch money every day. They cornered me, took my bag and ripped pages out of my books until I gave them everything I had.'

'Why on earth didn't you tell someone? Your year head?'

'The poor little rich girl running to teacher? That would have made me popular.'

'Your grandfather, then?'

'His response would have been to say "I told you so" and take me away. He'd always wanted to send me to some fancy boarding school.'

'Maybe you should have gone. I never got the impression you enjoyed school much.'

'I didn't. But I couldn't bear to be sent away. I didn't have a mother or a father, Adam. All I had was my home. The animals.'

Coleridge House. And a cold man who probably hated having a love-child for a granddaughter.

'What made you go to Saffy?' he asked.

'I didn't. I don't know how she found out. But one day she was at the school gate waiting for me. Didn't say a word, just hooked her arm through mine as if she was my best friend. To be honest, I was terrified. I knew they'd all gone to the same primary school.'

'It was pretty rough,' he admitted.

'Well, I thought it was some new torture, but she appointed herself my minder. Walked me in and out of school, stayed with me at lunch and break times until they got the message. I was protected. Not to be touched.'

'That's why she knew you'd take Nancie? Because you owed her.'

'No. I paid my debts in full a long time ago…' She stopped, realising that, tired, she'd let slip more than she'd intended. 'Ancient history,' she said dismissively. 'Tell me about your day, mixing with the great and good. There was something about Samindera on the news this evening, but it was a bit of a madhouse and I didn't catch it.'

'Well, obviously the fact that I had dinner with the President would make the national news,' he said.

'There's nothing wrong?' she persisted.

She'd meant to check but, by the time she'd finished, she was fit for nothing but a warm bath and bed.

'His Excellency's hand was steady enough on his glass,' he assured her.

'Oh, well, what can possibly be wrong? Tell me what you ate,' she asked, then lay back as he told her about the formal dinner, the endless speeches, apparently knowing exactly what would make her laugh.

Then, as her responses became slower, he said, 'Go to sleep, Mouse. Tell Saffy that I'll call her in the morning. And that I'll want to talk to Michel when I get home.'

'How long? Three days?' It had been nearly two weeks since she'd seen him, but it felt like a lifetime. 'Are you going to play the big brother and ask him his intentions?'

'I think he's already demonstrated his intentions beyond question. I just want to be sure that this is settled and it's not going to end in some painful tug of love scenario. Saffy might be an idiot, but she's my sister and no one is going to take her baby from her.'

'Actually, she was talking about going back with them tomorrow.'

'Show her my credit card. Ask her to go shopping with you. That should do it.'

'Too late. She's dragged me out shopping half a dozen times, although I'm not sure if it's my trousseau she's interested in or her own.'

'I hope you've been indulging yourself rather than her.'

'She's a very bad influence,' she admitted.

'That sounds promising.'

She'd been led utterly astray by his sister, and now

possessed her own sexy 'result' shoes with ridiculously high heels. And had rather lost her head in an underwear shop. Not that she anticipated a result. Adam had been very quick to make it clear that this was a marriage in name only, but at least she'd *feel* sexy. And taller.

'Just make sure she knows that I want to see her. And my mother. That I want to make things right.'

'No problem. I've invited them all to the wedding.'

There was a pause. Then he said, 'Let's elope.'

ADAM SAT ON the edge of the bed, her giggle a warm memory as he imagined her slipping into the warm white nest of her bed, already more asleep than awake.

She wouldn't have let it slip that she'd already paid her debt to his sister if she'd been fully awake. Even then, she'd done her best to cover it, move on before he pressed her to tell him what she'd done. But he hadn't needed to. He knew.

Saffy had been caught with several tabs of E in her bag when the police had raided a club a few days before his and May's big night out had been brought to an abrupt end in the hayloft.

It wasn't the first time his sister had been in trouble. She'd been caught shoplifting as a minor, drinking underage, all the classic symptoms of attention seeking. But this had been serious.

She'd sworn she'd got the tabs for friends who'd given her the money, but technically it was dealing and she was older. Culpable. But she'd shrugged when he'd found out, gone ballistic at her stupidity. Said it was sorted. And then, two weeks later, when she'd been summoned to the police station, she'd got away with no more than a formal caution. It would be on her record, but that was it.

That was what May had done. She'd talked to her grandfather, pleaded Saffy's case. And left them both wide open to the retribution of a hard old man.

What had he threatened?

What had she surrendered?

School. She'd never come back. The rumour was that she'd gone off to some posh boarding school and he'd allowed himself to believe it, hope that was what had happened, why she hadn't called him, written. Until he'd seen a photograph of her in the local newspaper, all dressed up at some charity do with her grandfather. Surrounded by Hooray Henrys in their DJs.

And him, he thought. She'd given up him to save Saffy from the minimum of three months in prison she'd have got at the Magistrates' Court. Much more if the Bench had decided the case was too serious for them and sent it up to the Crown Court. Which he didn't doubt would have happened.

No. That was wrong.

He dragged his hands through his hair. He was only seeing it from his point of view. How it had affected him.

Narrow, selfish...

May had surrendered herself. Given up every vestige of freedom for his sister. And maybe for him, too. He hadn't broken any laws, couldn't be got at that way. But he'd had an offer from Melchester University. He'd been encouraged to apply to Oxford, but he needed to be near enough to take care of his mother and sister. He had no doubt James Coleridge could have taken that from him.

Was that what May had been trying to tell him as she'd stood at her window shaking her head as he'd called her name?

Watching while the hose had been turned on him

smashing the roses he'd bought her in an explosion of red petals...

He groaned, slid from the bed to the floor as he remembered picking up the book of *Sonnets*. That was what had fallen from it. The petal from a red rose. He'd recognised it for what it was and brushed it off his fingers as if tainted...

Stupid, stupid...

If, that first time when their paths had crossed at some civic or charity reception, he'd forgotten his pride and, ignoring the frost, reached out and taken her hand, how long would she have held out?

He'd assumed that he'd caught her offside up that tree, but maybe that was all it would have taken. A smile, a, *Hello, Danger Mouse*, a touch to melt the icy mask.

But pride was all he'd had and he'd clung to it like ivy to a blasted oak.

He had to talk to her. Now. Tell her that he was sorry...

THE PHONE DRAGGED May back from the brink of sleep. She fumbled for it, picked it up. Couldn't see the number without her glasses. 'Hello?'

'May...'

'Adam? Is something wrong?'

'No... Yes...'

She heard a noise in the background. 'What was that? I heard something...'

'Thunder, lightning. Storms are ten a penny here. Are you awake?'

'Yes,' she said, pushing herself up. 'What is it? What's wrong?'

'Everything... Damn it, the lights have gone out.'

'Adam? Are you okay?'

'Yes. That happens, too. It doesn't matter…' He broke off and she could hear shouting, banging in the background.

'Adam!'

'Hold on, there's some idiot hammering on the door. Don't go away. This is important—'

Whatever else he was going to say was drowned out by the sound of an explosion. And then there was nothing.

ROBBIE FOUND HER SITTING, white-faced, frozen in front of the television, watching rolling news of the attempted coup in Samindera. Pictures of the Presidential Palace, hotels blackened by fire, shattered by shells.

Reports of unknown casualties, missing foreigners. The fierce fighting that was making communication difficult.

She fetched a quilt to wrap around her, lit the fire, made tea. Didn't bother to say anything. She knew there was nothing she could say that would mean a thing.

Jake called on his way into the office, where the directors had called a crisis meeting, promising to let her know the minute he heard anything.

The French contingent finally emerged, then, when they heard the news, they hugged both her and Saffy a lot, talking too fast for May's schoolgirl French but clearly intent on reassuring her that they were all family now.

Michel sat holding Saffy's hand, their baby on his lap, watching the news with her. And that made her feel even more alone.

She leapt up when the phone rang, but it was Freddie. He'd seen the forthcoming wedding announcement in *The Times*.

'There isn't going to be a wedding,' she said and hung up.

'May!' Saffy looked stricken. 'Don't say that. Adam's going to be all right.'

'No. He isn't.' She wrapped her arms around herself, staring at the same loop of film that was being rerun on the television screen, rocking herself the way she'd done as a child when her dog had died. 'He phoned last night. I was talking to him when…' She couldn't say it. Couldn't say the words. 'I heard an explosion. Right there, where he was. He's dead. I know he's dead and now he'll never know. I should have told him, Saffy.'

'What? But you said you were marrying him to save the house? That it was just a paper arrangement.' Then, as reality dawned, she said, 'Oh, drat. You're in love with him.'

May didn't answer, but collapsed against her and, as she opened her arms and gathered her in, shushed her, rubbing her back as if she were a baby.

WHEN ADAM REGAINED consciousness he was lying face down in the dark. His ears were ringing, the air was thick with choking dust.

As he pushed himself up, leaning back against something he couldn't see, a nearby explosion briefly lit up the wreckage of his room and the only familiar thing was the cellphone he was clutching in his hand.

He'd been talking to May. He'd had something important to tell her but someone had been hammering on the door…

He put the phone to his ear. 'May?' He began to choke

as the dust hit the back of his throat. 'May, are you still there?' No answer. He pressed the redial button with his thumb and the screen lit up, 'No signal'.

He swore. He had to find a phone that worked. He had to talk to May. Tell her that he was a fool. That he was sorry. That he loved her... Always had. Always would. And he began to crawl forward, using the light from his phone to find his way.

MAY TURNED OFF the television. Pulled the plug out of the wall. It was the same thing over and over. Regional experts, former ambassadors, political pundits all saying nothing. Filling the airways of the twenty-four hour news channels day after day with the same lack of news told a thousand different ways.

That the fighting was fierce, that communications were limited to propaganda from government and rebel spokesmen. That casualties were high and that billionaire Adam Wavell, in Samindera to negotiate a major contract, was among those unaccounted for.

'Go out, Saffy,' she said. 'Take Nancie for a walk. Better still, go back to Paris and get on with your life. There's nothing either you or Michel can do here.'

She saw Robbie and Saffy exchange a look.

'May...'

'What?' she demanded. 'It's just another day.'

Not her wedding day. There was never going to be a wedding day.

That wasn't important.

She'd have surrendered the house, her business, everything she had just to know that Adam was safe.

She jumped as the phone rang but she didn't run to pick it up. She'd stopped doing that after the first few days, when she'd still hoped against hope that she was wrong. That he had somehow survived.

Now, each time she heard it, she knew it was going to be the news that she dreaded. That they'd found his body amongst the wreckage of one of those fancy hotels in the archive footage they kept showing.

Robbie picked it up. 'Coleridge House.'

She frowned, straining to hear, and then, without a word, she put the phone into her hand.

'May…'

The line was crackling, breaking up, but it sounded like…

'May!'

'Adam…' She felt faint, dizzy and Robbie caught her, eased her back into the chair. 'Are you hurt? Where are you?'

'God knows. The hotel…rebels…city. I'm sorry… wedding…'

She could barely follow what he said, the line was so bad, but it didn't matter. Just hearing his voice was enough. He was alive!

'Forget the wedding. It doesn't matter. All that matters is that you're safe. Adam? Can you hear me? Adam?' She looked up. 'The line's gone dead,' she said. Then burst into tears.

CHAPTER TEN

ADAM CURSED THE PHONE. He'd crawled through the blasted hotel liked the Pied Piper, using his phone to light the way, gathering the dazed and wounded, leaving them in the safety of the basement while he went to find water. First aid. Anything.

All he'd found were a group of rebels, who'd taken him with them as they'd retreated. He'd had visions of being held hostage for months, years, but as the government forces had closed in they'd abandoned him and melted away into the jungle.

He returned the useless cellphone to the commander of the government forces who'd finally caught up with them that morning.

'There's no signal.'

The man shrugged.

'How long before we get back to the capital?'

Another shrug. 'Tomorrow, maybe.'

'That will be too late.'

'There's no hurry. The airport is closed. The runway was shelled. There are no planes.'

'There must be some way out of here.'

The man raised an eyebrow and Adam took off his heavy stainless steel Rolex, placed it beside him on the seat of the truck. Added his own top of the range cellphone, the battery long since flat. Then he took out his wallet to reveal dollars, sterling currency and tossed that on the pile. The man said nothing and he emptied his pockets to show that it was all he had.

'What is that?' the man asked, nodding at the tiny velvet drawstring pouch containing May's wedding ring. He opened it, took out the ring and held it up.

'If I'm not there,' he said, 'you might as well shoot me now.'

THE SILENCE AFTER hearing from Adam was almost unbearable. To know that he was alive, but have no idea where he was, whether he was hurt…

May called Jake, called the Foreign Office, called everyone she could think of but, while the government was back in control, the country was still in chaos.

'Come on. It's your birthday tomorrow. I'm going to make a chocolate cake,' Saffy declared after breakfast.

'Can you cook?' She'd seen no evidence of it in the week since she'd arrived.

'Don't be silly. You're the domestic goddess. You'll have to show me how.'

Obviously it was in the nature of a distraction, but Saffy must be climbing the wall too, she realised.

They had just put it in the oven when the back door opened and Jake, not bothering to knock, tumbled through.

'Get your passport,' he said.

'Sorry?'

'Adam called. He's been driving through the jungle for the last couple of days. He's in the back of beyond somewhere and it's going to take him at least three flights to get to the US. There's no way he can get home in time to beat the deadline, so you're going to have to go to him. I've booked you on a flight to Las Vegas—'

'Las Vegas?'

'You're getting married there, today.'

'But…' she glanced at the clock '…I can't possibly get there in time.'

'You're flying east. You'll arrive a few hours after you leave.'

'Yes!' Saffy said, jumping up and punching the air, grinning broadly.

'But…' She looked at Jake. Looked at Robbie, who was grinning broadly. 'I never bought a dress.'

'Forget the dress,' Jake said. 'You haven't got time to pack. We've barely got time to get to the airport.'

'WHAT'S THE PURPOSE of your visit to the United States, Mr Wavell?'

'I'm getting married today,' he replied.

The man looked him up and down. He'd been wearing his dinner jacket when the rebels had opened fire on his hotel. It was filthy, torn and there was blood on his shirt. It was scarcely surprising that he'd been pulled over at Immigration for a closer look.

'Good luck with that, sir,' he said, grinning as he returned his passport.

There was a driver waiting for him in the arrival hall.

'Miss Coleridge's flight is due in ten minutes, Mr Wavell,' he said, handing him an envelope containing a replacement cellphone and a long message from Jake detailing all the arrangements he'd made.

MAY PAUSED AS she entered the arrivals hall. Jake had told her she'd be met but she couldn't see her name on any

of the cards. And then, with a little heart leap, she saw
Adam and she let out a little cry of anguish. His clothes
were filthy and torn, the remains of his shirt spattered
with blood. He looked as if he hadn't slept for a week
and he'd lost weight.

And his cheek… She put out her hand to touch a
vivid bruise but he caught her hand. 'It's nothing. No
luggage?' he asked.

'I didn't have time to pack. I didn't even have time to
change,' she said, looking down at the smear of chocolate on her T-shirt. 'The wedding pictures should be interesting.' Then, keeping it light because it was all she
could do not to weep all over him, 'But you know if you
didn't want your mother to come to the wedding you
only had to say. You didn't have to go to all this trouble.'

'I called her,' he said a little gruffly. 'Called Saffy.
When I got to Dallas.' He cleared his throat. 'Dust,' he
explained. 'From the explosion.'

'Adam…'

'Let's go. Apparently we have to get a licence at the
courthouse before we go to the wedding chapel.'

'WELL, THAT WAS EASY,' May said as they walked out of
the courthouse half an hour later with their licence. 'I
hope, for your sake, that the divorce will be as simple.'

'Don't!' Then, seeing her startled look, realising that
he had been abrupt, Adam shook his head.

He might have been seized by the sudden conviction
that May was everything he'd ever wanted in a woman
but she was doing this for only one reason.

To keep her home.

Crawling through the wreckage of the hotel, it had
been the thought of May that had kept him going. The

need to talk to her, tell her how sorry he was, what a fool he'd been. The hope that maybe they might, somehow, be able to begin again.

But, as the days had passed, all that had been swept away in the need to keep his promise to her. Because words meant nothing. No amount of sorry was worth a damn unless he backed it up with action.

Then, seeing the tiny frown buckling the space between her eyes, a frown that he wanted to kiss away, 'I'm sorry. I've had the worst week of my life and I vote that today we forget about everything, everyone else and just have some fun.'

'Fun?'

That was what he'd told Jake when he'd finally got to a phone that worked. To forget all the pompous nonsense he'd planned. He had, apparently, taken his brief very seriously. Instead of a simple limo, they'd been picked up at the airport in a white vintage open-topped Rolls, the kind that had great sweeping mudguards, a wide running board, the glamour of another age.

Or maybe that *was* simple in Las Vegas.

'Any objections to that?' he asked, taking her hand as she stepped up into the car. Kept hold of it as he joined her.

'None.' May laughed out loud. 'I can't believe this. It seems unreal.'

'It is. Totally unreal,' he said, content to be sitting next to a woman wearing the biggest smile he'd ever seen. 'You've been given a magic day, stolen from the time gods by travelling east.'

'It doesn't work like that,' she said, leaning back against the soft leather, her hair unravelling, a smear of chocolate across her T-shirt. She looked exactly like the girl he'd fallen in love with, he thought, allowing himself to remember the heart-pounding edge as he'd climbed over the gate from the park. The heart lift as she'd looked up and smiled at him. He'd loved her before he knew the meaning of the word. And when he'd learned it was too late. 'I'll have to give it back when we fly home. You can't mess with time.'

'We give back the hours, but not anything that happens during them. You'll still be married. Your house will be safe. What we do, the memories we make. They are pure gain. That's why it's magic.'

She turned and looked at him. 'They should only be good memories, then.'

'They will be.'

'Seeing you in one piece is as good as it gets,' she said. 'I thought...'

May swallowed, turned away, tears clinging to her lashes. She'd promised herself she would not cry, but the shock of seeing him had been intense. She could not imagine what he'd been through while she was sitting in front of the television thinking that she was suffering.

She'd been so sure that the first thing she would do was tell him that she loved him. Worked out exactly what she was going to say on the long hours as she flew across the Atlantic, across America. But the moment she set eyes on him she knew that it was an emotional burden he didn't need. That she was doing what she'd accused him of. Thinking of herself. What she was feeling.

'Saffy was in bits,' she said when she could trust herself to speak.

'More than I deserve.'

Before she could protest, the car turned into a tropical garden and her jaw dropped as they swept up to the entrance to their hotel.

'Wow!' she said. Then, again, as they walked through the entrance lobby, 'Wow! This is utterly amazing.'

She was in Las Vegas and had expected their hotel to be large, opulent, over the top glitzy. But this was elegant. Stunningly beautiful.

'Good morning, Miss Coleridge, Mr Wavell. I hope you had a good flight?'

The duty manager smiled as he invited them to sit at the ornate Buhl desk, completely ignoring Adam's appearance. Her own.

'Just a few formalities. Miss Coleridge, you have an appointment at the beauty salon in half an hour,' he said, handing her an appointment card. 'We were warned that you would have no luggage and you'll find a selection of clothes in your size as well as your usual toiletries in your suite, as will you, Mr Wavell.'

She shook her head. 'Jake is great on the details,' she said. 'He thinks of everything.'

'You do have some messages, Mr Wavell. You can pick them up on voicemail from your room.' He looked from Adam to her and back again. 'Is there anything else I can do for you?'

'Just one thing,' Adam said. 'We're getting married this afternoon. Miss Coleridge will need something very special to wear.'

'That's not a problem. We have a number of designer boutiques within the hotel and our personal shopper is at your disposal, Miss Coleridge. I'll ask her to call you.'

And Adam looked across at her with a mesmerising smile.

'Nearly everything,' he said.

THE SUITE WAS beyond luxurious. A huge sitting room with wide curved windows that opened onto a private roof garden with a pool, a tiny waterfall, tropical flowers, a hot tub. There was an office, a bar, two bedrooms, each with its own bathroom.

There was also Julia, who introduced herself as their personal butler. While Adam picked up his messages, she had ordered a late breakfast for them, drawn them each a bath, and then unwrapped and put away their new clothes.

This is magic, May thought, sinking into the warm, scented water. She'd just closed her eyes when a phone, conveniently placed within reach so that she didn't have to move, rang once, twice. Was it for Adam? It rang again and she chided herself. This was the sort of hotel where if the phone rang in the bathroom it was for the person lying in the bath.

'Hello?'

'Good morning, Miss Coleridge. I'm Suzanne Harper, your personal shopper. I understand that you're getting married today and need something special to wear. Just a few questions and I'll get started.'

The few questions involved her colouring, style. Whether she preferred Armani, Chanel or Dior.

Dior! She couldn't afford that.

About to declare that she really didn't need anything, she thought of the way that Adam had looked at her as he'd said 'nearly everything'. He'd thought of this, arranged this. It was part of the magic and if she had to sell a picture to pay for it, it would be worth it.

'I don't have a particular preference for a designer. I'd just like something simple.'

That only left the embarrassing disclosure of her measurements.

'I'll go and see what I find,' she said thoughtfully. 'You'll be going down to the salon shortly?'

'My appointment's at twelve.'

'I'll bring a few ideas along for you to look at and we can take it from there.'

'Right.' Then, since she had the phone in her hand, she called home to let Robbie know that she'd arrived safely. Reassure Saffy that her brother was in one piece.

ADAM LOOKED UP as May appeared wrapped in a heavy towelling robe, the partner of the one he was wearing, and smelling like heaven. 'Hi.'

'Hi,' she said, perching on the side of the desk. 'Everything under control?'

'Pretty much. How about you?'

'Well, I've just been through the mind-curdling embarrassment of giving every single one of my measurements to a woman I've never met.'

'Did she faint with shock?' he asked.

'She might have. There was a very long silence.'

'She was probably struggling to hold back a sob of envy that you have the confidence not to starve yourself to skin and bones.'

'I make sweets and cakes, Adam. I have to taste them to make sure I've got them right.'

'Your sacrifice is appreciated,' he said, holding out his hand to her and, when she took it, he pulled her down onto his lap, put his arms around her, and she let her head fall against his shoulder.

She'd pinned her hair up to get into the bath but damp tendrils had escaped, curling around her face. One of them tickled his chin and he smoothed it back, kissed it where it lay against her head. Saw a tear trickling down her cheek.

'Hey... What's the matter?'

'I thought you were dead.'

'I might as well have been if I'd let you down.'

'Idiot!' she said, throwing a playful punch at his arm.

'Ouch,' he said, covering his wince with a smile. 'Is that any way to speak to a man who's offering to show you a good time?'

She opened her mouth, closed it again. 'I'm so sorry, Adam. I thought this was going to be so simple.'

'It is, sweetheart. It is. But it's time you were moving,' he said before she became aware just how simple it was. Not even the thickness of the towelling robe could for long disguise just how basic his response to holding her like this had been. 'You'll be late for your appointment.'

She gave a little yelp, rushed off to the bedroom, returning a few minutes later in linen trousers the colour of bitter chocolate, a bronze silk shirt that brought out the colour of her eyes, her thick, wayward hair curling about her shoulders. The kind of hair that could give a man ideas. If he hadn't already got them.

'I'll meet you in the lobby at half past three.'

'In the lobby? But...'

'I'll finish up here, get ready and go out for a stroll in the garden.' He needed to put some distance between himself and temptation. 'You won't want me under your feet while you're getting ready.'

'Won't I?'

Without warning, her eyes hazed, darkened, an instinctive, atavistic response to what she must see in his; the kind of hot, ungovernable desire for a woman that he hadn't felt in longer than he could remember. The kind that set his senses ablaze, threatened to overwhelm him.

'Suppose I need a hand with a zip?'

'I only know how to undo them,' he said. A warning. As much to himself as to her. May trusted him. Believed his motives to be pure.

Not that she'd blame him. Knowing May, she'd almost certainly blame herself, apologise for taking advantage of him. He wasn't sure whether the thought of that made him want to smile, or to weep for her. A little of both, perhaps, and he wanted to hold her, tell her that she was amazing, sexy, beautiful and that any man would be lucky to have her.

She didn't move. Continued to stare at him, eyes dark, lips slightly parted, her cheeks flushed.

'May!'

She started. 'I'm gone.'

MAY WASN'T SURE what had just happened.

No. She wasn't that naïve. She knew. She just didn't know *how* it had happened.

How a jokey comment fired by nervous tension had created a primitive pulse that made every cell in her body sing out to Adam, made every cell in his body respond to her so that the air shimmered like a heat haze around them. So that the rest of the room seemed to disappear, leaving him in the sharpest, clearest focus. His dark, expressive brows. The copper glints heating up his grey eyes. His mouth, lips that had kissed her to seal their bargain, kissed her again for no reason at all in a way that made her own burn just to think of them.

For a moment she leaned back against the suite door, weak to the knees with hot raw need, knowing that if he'd lifted a hand, touched her, she would have fallen apart.

And he'd known it, too.

He'd warned her. *'I only know how to undo them.'*

And, remembering just how adept he'd been with her shirt buttons, she didn't doubt it.

Even then she hadn't moved. Hadn't wanted to move.

All she'd wanted was him. To hold him in her arms. Know that he was safe. To show him with her body all the things that she couldn't say.

ADAM COULD NOT remember the last time he'd felt the need for a cold shower.

He had fudged his promise when she'd asked if he intended a paper marriage. Lied with his heart, if not his tongue, planning an ice-cold seduction, determined that she should beg for him to take her.

But he knew that she had done nothing to hurt him. She had given him her heart, her soul, would have given him her body too, if they had not been discovered before his virgin fumblings had found the mark.

It had not taken a close call with death to teach him that there was no joy in revenge, only in life. He would marry May, then, as his captive partner for a year or so, living in the same house, he would woo her. Wait for her. Propose a real marriage when the false one was at an end.

But, while he could control his own desires, if May lit up like that again he wasn't sure he could fight them both.

MAY SPENT WHAT seemed like an age in the salon. When she finally emerged, her unmanageable mess of mousy hair had been washed, trimmed and transformed. It was still mousy, but she was a very sleek, pampered mouse and her hair had gone up into a smooth twist, the only escaping tendrils those that had been teased out and twisted into well behaved curls.

The facial had toned and smoothed her skin to satin. The manicurist had taken one horrified look at her hard-working nails and transformed them with the application of acrylics. And someone she never actually got to see performed a pedicure on her feet, giving her toe-nails a French polish so exquisite that when she was ready to leave the salon, she felt guilty for putting her shoes back on.

And, all the while this had been happening, Suzanne had whisked outfits by her to gauge her reaction to style, colour and fabric.

Everyone had had an opinion and between them they'd whittled it down to four.

'That's the one,' Suzanne said when, back in their suite, she'd tried on an exquisite silk two-piece the warm, toasted colour of fine brandy. 'I knew it as soon as I saw your shirt. It's the perfect colour for you.'

'I do always feel good in it,' she admitted. 'Is it vulgar to ask the price?'

'I understood that Mr Wavell…'

'Mr Wavell is not paying for this.'

He'd already paid for a first class air fare, first class travel, the hotel, but that was all.

When Suzanne still hesitated—clearly the suit cost a small fortune—she said, 'Unless you tell me, Suzanne, you're going to have to take it back and I'll wear these trousers.'

She told her.

May did her best not to gulp, at least not noticeably. She wasn't going to have to part with some small picture by a minor artist, something she wouldn't miss. She was going to have to sell something special to pay for this. But she'd never look this good again and, whatever the sacrifice, it would be worth it, she decided, as she handed over her credit card.

'All of it, Suzanne. Shoes, bag, underwear, everything.'

'He's a lucky man.'

'I'm the lucky one,' she said, but more to herself than Suzanne and when, half an hour later, professionally made-up, dressed and ready to go, May regarded her reflection, she couldn't stop smiling.

The skirt was a little shorter than she'd normally choose and straight, a style she usually avoided like the plague but it was so beautifully cut that it skimmed her thighs in a way that made them look sexy rather than a pair of hams. But it was the jacket that had sold her.

The heavy silk had been woven into wide strips to create a fabric that reflected the light to add depth to the colour. It had exquisite stand-away revers that crossed low over her breast. And, aided and abetted by the underwear that Suzanne had chosen, the shape emphasized rather than disguised her figure.

The final touch, the shoes, dark brown suede with cutaway sides, peep toes, a saucy bow and stratospherically high heels, would have made Cinderella weep.

'You look gorgeous, May. Go break his heart.'

CHAPTER ELEVEN

ADAM CAUGHT SIGHT of himself in one of the mirrored columns and straightened the new silk tie he'd spotted in one of the boutiques.

Right now he knew exactly how a groom must feel as the minutes ticked by while he waited at the altar for a bride who wanted to give him a moment of doubt. A moment to face the possibility of life without her.

Doing his best to ignore the indulgent smiles of passing matrons who saw the spray of tiny orchids he was holding, the single matching orchid in his buttonhole and drew their own conclusions, he checked his new wristwatch.

And then, as he looked up, she was there.

Hair messed up in a band incapable of holding it, wearing baggy sweats, spectacles propped on the end of her nose, May had managed to steal his heart.

Now, as their eyes met across the vast distance of the lobby, she stole his ability to breathe, to move, his heart to beat.

May was the first to move, lifting her feet with care in her high heels, moving like a catwalk model in the unfamiliar clothes. Displaying her show-stopping ankles.

Heads turned. Men and women stopped to watch her. And then he was walking towards her, flying towards her, standing in front of her and, another first for him, he felt like a tongue-tied teenager.

'Nice flowers,' she said, looking at the spray of bronze-splashed cream orchids he was clutching. 'They really go with your tie.'

About to tell her that he'd chosen the tie, the flowers because they matched her eyes, he got a grip. 'Fortunately, they also match your suit,' he said, offering them to her.

'They're beautiful. Thank you,' she said, brushing a finger lightly over a petal, then lifting her fingers to the one in his buttonhole. 'You thought of everything.'

Nearly everything.

When he'd been clutching at straws, the last thought in his head was that he would fall in love with May Coleridge. He couldn't even say when it had happened. He'd spent the last hour wandering along the hotel's shopping mall, buying the tie, choosing flowers, looking at the yellow diamonds in Tiffany's window, trying to decide which shade would match her grandmother's engagement ring.

He took her hand, looked at it. 'I was going to buy you a ring.'

'I didn't mean...' She looked up. 'I was wearing it when Jake came for me.'

He shook his head. 'I don't think there's another ring in the world that would suit you more, so I bought this instead.' He took a small turquoise pouch from his pocket, tipped out a yellow diamond pendant. 'I think it matches.'

'Adam...' She put her hands to her cheeks as she blushed. 'I don't know what to say.'

'You don't say anything. You just turn around and let me fasten it for you.'

She might blush like a girl, he thought, as she did as

she was told and he fastened the clasp at the nape of her lovely neck. But she lived her life as a mature, thoughtful, *real* woman.

One who'd worked at making a life, a future for herself, who might need a hand down once in a while when she'd climbed above her comfort level, but never looked to anyone else to prop her up.

He felt as if he'd been sleepwalking through his life. Putting all his energy, all his heart into building up his business empire, ignoring what was real, what was important.

He was awake now, he thought as he looked at May. Wide awake and tingling with the same anticipation, excitement as any of the other men who'd been queuing up for their wedding licences this morning.

'You look amazing.' Then, because he was in danger of making a fool of himself, 'I didn't mean for you to pay for it. The suit.'

'I know, Adam. But my grandmother once told me that when a man buys a woman clothes he expects to be able to take them off her.'

That had come out so pat that he knew she must have been rehearsing it for just this moment. A reminder...

'Your grandma was a very smart woman,' he said. 'I wish she was here to see what a lovely granddaughter she has.'

'Me too.' Then, with a sudden brightening of her eyes, 'Shall we go?'

He offered her his arm and, as they walked towards the door, there was a smattering of applause. The doorman whisked the car door open for them, raised his hat and then they drove out into the soft afternoon sunshine

On the surface, May was calm, collected, knees braced, breath under control. It was the shoes that did it. Wearing heels that high required total concentration and while she was walking in them she didn't have a brain cell to spare for anything else.

The minute she slipped her hand under Adam's arm and she knew that if she tripped he'd catch her, everything just went to pot. He'd been in danger, hurt, tired, but he'd done this for her and, while the legs kept moving, everything else was just jelly.

'Are you okay?' he asked.

She nodded, not trusting herself to speak and then, just when she was absolutely sure she was going to hyperventilate, the car slowed and she saw the big sign and let out a little gasp.

'A Drive-thru Wedding?'

'You did say to let Jake surprise us,' Adam reminded her. Then he groaned. 'You hate it. I'm so sorry, May. This is all wrong. You look so elegant, so beautiful. Maybe it's not too late—'

'You deserve something more than this, May. Something special. The hotel has a wedding chapel. Maybe they can fit us in—'

'No!' He looked so desolate that she took his hand in hers, all the shakes forgotten in her determination to convince him. 'This is absolutely perfect,' she assured him. 'I love it.'

And it was true; she did. It was sweet. It was also as far from anything she could ever have imagined as possible. A wedding to make her laugh rather than cry. Nothing solemn about it. Nothing to break her heart.

'I love it,' she repeated.

I love you...

The minister, dressed in a white suit, was waiting at the window. 'Miss Coleridge? Mr Wavell?'

'Er, yes…'

'Welcome to the Drive Thru Wedding Chapel. Do you have your licence?' he asked.

Adam took it from his jacket pocket, handed it over for him to check it.

'Are you both ready to take the solemn vows of matrimony?'

He looked at her.

'Absolutely,' she said quickly.

He turned to Adam, who said, 'Positively.'

They said their vows without a hitch. Adam slipped her grandmother's ring onto her finger. Opened his palm for her to take the second plain gold band, exactly like hers, only much larger.

It was as if the whole world was holding its breath as she reached for it, picked it up, slipped it onto his finger.

'I now pronounce you man and wife. You may kiss the bride.'

'May I kiss the bride, Mrs Wavell?' he asked.

She managed to make some kind of sound that he took for yes and, taking her in his arms, he touched his lips to hers in what began as a barely-there kiss but deepened into something that melted her insides and might have lasted forever but for the command from the photographer to 'hold that for one more.'

They collected the pictures, along with the souvenir certificate of their wedding vows at the next window.

'Photographic evidence,' he said, glancing through them, offering her a picture of them kissing with the Drive Thru Wedding sign behind them. 'Maybe we should send it to *Celebrity*?'

'Set a new trend in must-have weddings, you think?'

'Maybe not. But it should keep Freddie happy until Jake has organised all the legal registrations.'

She nodded, then said, 'There's just one more thing.' He waited. 'Where are the burger and fries?'

'I'm sorry?'

'A drive thru wedding should have a drive thru wedding breakfast.'

'You're hungry?' he asked.

'Hollow.'

She'd been so wrapped up in taking care of her grandfather, the house, keeping her mind occupied with the workshops. Never giving herself a moment to think. She was, she'd discovered, starving, but not for food.

The emptiness went far deeper than that.

She was hungry for Adam to look at her as he had in their suite. To touch her. To touch him. To kiss him, be his lover as well as his friend. Yearned for his child to hold. To be, if only for a magic afternoon, his wife in every sense of the word.

'I don't know whether it's lunch time, dinner time or breakfast time,' she said a touch light-headedly, 'but I haven't eaten since I left the plane and you should know that I'm not a woman who's accustomed to subsisting on a lettuce leaf.' She turned as they passed a familiar logo. 'There! We could drive in there and pick up a cheeseburger and some fries.'

He grinned. 'You are such a cheap date, May.'

'Hardly. You've already paid for a first class air fare, a hotel suite fit for a prince and a diamond pendant.' He touched the diamond where it lay in the hollow of her throat. 'It's clear that you need a wife to curb your extravagance. But I will want a strawberry milkshake.'

THEY WERE LAUGHING over their impromptu picnic as they arrived back in their suite.

Julia, undoubtedly warned of their return by the front desk, was waiting for them with champagne on ice, a tray of exotic canapés, chocolates, a cake. And a basket of red roses so large that it seemed to dominate the huge room.

May went white when she saw them.

'Could you take those away, Julia?' she managed. 'I'm allergic to roses.'

'Of course, Mrs Wavell. Congratulations to you both.'

'Thank you.'

That was Adam. She couldn't speak. Couldn't look at him. Didn't move until she felt his hand on her shoulder.

'It's okay, May. I know.'

'Know?' She looked up at him. 'What do you know?'

'About the rose petals.'

She stared at him, scarcely daring to breathe.

'What do you know?' she whispered.

'I know that you gathered them up and pressed them between the pages of a poetry book.'

Gathered them up. That made it sound like something pretty. But it hadn't been pretty, any of it. She'd crawled around on her hands and knees in the dark, slipping where the water had frozen, refusing to give up until she had them all. She couldn't pick them up in gloves and her hands had been so cold that she hadn't felt the scrapes, the knocks.

'How? No one knew...'

'I picked it up when I was waiting for you in your sitting room. A petal fell out. I didn't realise the significance until later, when I understood what you'd done for Saffy. That was why I called you the second time

You saved my life. If I'd been in bed instead of sitting on the floor talking to you…'

'He gave me a choice,' May said quickly, not wanting to hear how close she'd come to losing him. Not when he was here, safe. 'Swear that I would never speak to you, contact you, ever again. Or Saffy would go to jail.'

'But once she'd been cautioned…'

'I gave my word. He kept his.' She lifted her hands to his face, cupping it gently. Kissed the bruise that darkened his cheekbone. 'Forget it, Adam. It's over.'

'How can it ever be over?' he said. 'It was your face that kept me going when I was crawling through that hotel. The thought of you…'

She stopped his words with a kiss, then slowly began to unfasten her jacket.

'What are you doing?'

'Making up for lost time,' she said, letting it drop. 'Taking back what was stolen from us.' She unhooked her skirt, hesitated, looked up and her eyes, liquid bronze beneath long dark lashes, sent a charge of heat through him that wiped everything from his brain. 'Any chance of some help with the zip?'

Never taking his eyes from her face, he lowered the zip and then, as the skirt slithered to the floor, he left his hand on the warm curve of her hip as he lowered his lips to hers.

It was as if they were eighteen again. Teenagers, touching each other, awed by the importance of it, realising that this was a once and forever moment that would change them both.

This was how she'd been then. Lit up. Telegraphing what she wanted with eyes like lamps. She'd been both shy and eager. Naïve and bold. Innocent as a baby and yet knowing more than he did. Knowing what she wanted. What he wanted. Slowing everything down, making him wait, making him feel like a god...

She was doing it now. Unfastening the buttons of his shirt as she backed him towards the bedroom, pushing it off his shoulders. Kissing each bruise she uncovered with a little groan until he bent and caught her behind the knees.

Lost in the heat of her kisses, the pleasure of her touch he felt reborn, made over until, her tiny cries obliterating everything but one final need, he was poised above her to make her, finally, his.

'Please, Adam,' she begged as he made her wait. 'Please...'

And in those three words his world shattered.

He rolled away from her, practically throwing himself from the bed in his shame, his desperation to escape what he'd so nearly done.

It took May a moment to gather herself, but then, concerned that after his ordeal he was sick, hurt, she grabbed a robe, found him slumped in a chair, his head in his hands.

'What is it? Darling, please.' She knelt at his feet 'Are you hurt? Sick?'

'No.'

She sat back on her heels. 'Tell me.'

'I was going to make you beg.'

She frowned, took his hand, but he pulled it away.

'I was going to make you beg. Take you in you grandfather's bed.' He looked up. 'When you told m you were going to lose your house, do you think I wa touched with concern? I was cheering. I had you. I wa going to wipe out the Coleridge name with my own. Pa rade you as Mrs Adam Wavell, the wife of the kid from the sink estate. Take you in your grandfather's bed and make you beg.'

'So, what are you saying? That I didn't beg hard enough?' she asked. 'Or do you want to wait until we get home? Do it there?'

His head came up.

'No! No...' He shook his head. 'I was wrong. I don't deserve you, but I thought if I waited, wooed you, showed you that I was worthy of you, maybe, at the end of the year, when you could be free if you wanted to be, I could ask you then to marry me properly.'

'A year?'

'As long as it takes. I love you, May. I've never wanted another woman the way I wanted you. Want you.'

'No.' She shook her head. Stood up. Took a step back.

'I spent a week of agony thinking you were dead. Regretting that I hadn't told you how much I love you when I had the chance. And then, idiot that I was, I decided not to burden you with my emotional needs. Well, here it is. I understand why you felt the way you did, but I've waited more than ten years for you to finish what you started, Adam Wavell.' She untied the belt of the robe she'd thrown about her. Let it drop to the ground. 'I'm not prepared to waste another year. How about you?'

She held out her hand, held her breath for what seemed like forever before he reached out, took it, then pulled her to him.

THE BELL-RINGERS WERE waiting to give it everything they had. The choir was packed with angel-voiced trebles and, behind May, the church was crowded with everyone she knew. And lots of people she didn't but planned to in the future. Freddie was there. Adam's mother. Saffy with Michel and his parents, Nancie decked out in pink frills as an honorary bridesmaid. Robbie, standing as her matron of honour.

It was exactly as she'd imagined it all those years ago. Every pew end decorated with a knot of roses, myrtle and ivy. The bouquet of bronze David Austin roses she was carrying, one taken for Adam's buttonhole.

Nearly as she'd imagined. Not even the celebrated local designer, Geena Wagner, could squeeze her into a dress her usual size. The truth was that one of her seamstresses had been working on her gown as late as last night—letting it out half an inch around the waist to accommodate the new life she and Adam had created on their impromptu honeymoon.

Exactly as she'd imagined and totally different. What she hadn't known as a teenager was how she would feel.

That dream had been the yearning for triumph of an unhappy girl. Make-believe. Window-dressing.

Today it was real and as she and Adam stood before the altar and the vicar began to speak… 'Dearly beloved, we are gathered here today to bless the marriage of May and Adam Wavell…' the overwhelming emotion was that of joy, celebration of a blessed union, of love given and received.

* * * * *

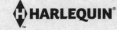

COMING NEXT MONTH FROM

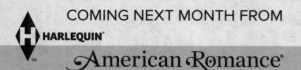

HARLEQUIN

American Romance

Available February 3, 2015

#1533 THE TWINS' RODEO RIDER
Bridesmaids Creek • by Tina Leonard

Cisco Grant's heart belongs to Suz Hawthorne, but the people of Bridesmaids Creek have determined he is meant for another! Can he win the woman of his dreams—and still save the town's matchmaking reputation?

#1534 LONE STAR VALENTINE
McCabe Multiples • by Cathy Gillen Thacker

Lily McCabe is forced to ask her unrequited love, former law school classmate Gannon Montgomery, for emergency help when her four-year-old son's biological father sues her for custody. Can Lily and her old flame keep things just professional?

#1535 THE COWBOY'S VALENTINE
Crooked Valley Ranch • by Donna Alward

It's only temporary. That's what Quinn Solomon keeps tellin' himself about staying at Lacey Duggan's ranch. The woman drives him crazy! But then things really heat up between them at the Valentine's Day dance...

#1536 KISSED BY A COWBOY
by Pamela Britton

Jillian Thacker and Wes Landon should be a match made in heaven...except Jillian is terrified of commitment, and Wes needs her to love him—and his baby daughter, too. Is that two hearts too many?

YOU CAN FIND MORE INFORMATION ON UPCOMING HARLEQUIN® TITL
FREE EXCERPTS AND MORE AT WWW.HARLEQUIN.COM.

HARCN

SPECIAL EXCERPT FROM

HARLEQUIN

American Romance

Read on for a sneak peek at
THE TWINS' RODEO RIDER
by USA TODAY *bestselling author Tina Leonard,*
part of the **BRIDESMAIDS CREEK** *miniseries.*

"Kiss me." He leaned close to the window to give her prime access.

"Why would I want to do that?" Suz's blue eyes widened.

"Because I have nice lips. Or so I've been told. Pucker up, dollface."

"I don't pucker for anyone who calls me 'dollface,' unless you want me to look like I bit into a grapefruit. Now *that* kind of pucker may be available to you."

He laughed. "So much sass, so little honesty."

She sniffed. "I'm trying to *save* you, cowboy, not romance you. Don't confuse this."

He sighed. "No kiss? I really feel like I need to know you're the woman of my dreams, if you're determined win me. And a kiss tells all."

"Oh, wow." Suz looked incredulous. "You really let at line out of your mouth?"

"Slid out easily. Come on, cupcake." He closed some stance between her face and his in case she changed her nd. *Strike while the branding iron was hot* was a very orthwhile strategy. It was in fact his favorite strategy.

"If I kiss you, I probably won't like it. And then what motivation do I have to win the race? I'd just toss you back into the pond for Daisy."

He drew back, startled. "That wouldn't be good."

Suz nodded. "It could be horrible. You could be a wet kisser. Eww."

"I really don't think I am." His ego took a small dent.

"You could be a licky-kisser."

"Pretty sure I'm just right, like Goldilock's bed," he said, his ego somewhere down around his boots and flailing like a leaf on the ground in the breeze.

"I don't know," Suz said thoughtfully. "Friends don't let friends kiss friends."

"I'm not that good of a friend."

"You really want a kiss, don't you?"

He perked up at these heartening words that seemed to portend a softening in her stance. "I sure do."

"Hope you get someone to kiss you one day, then. See you around, Cisco. And don't forget, one week until the swim!"

Don't miss
THE TWINS' RODEO RIDER
by USA TODAY *bestselling author Tina Leonard!*

Available February 2015,
wherever Harlequin® American Romance® books
and ebooks are sold.

www.Harlequin.com